THE
BETTER
OF
MᶜSWEENEY'S

sum up: Timothy McSweeney was the name of a man who wrote letters to this journal's editor, when he was a child and teenager, living outside of Chicago. The letters were also directed to his mother, whose maiden name was McSweeney. So these letters would come periodically, and would be written in a strange and beautiful hand, and would insist that their author, Timothy McSweeney, was related to this Chicago family. Does this all make sense so far? Well, these letters were usually written on the backs of and inside various mailing vehicles—pamphlets, brochures, etc.—all featuring pre-paid postage of one kind or another. In many of these envelopes we would find train schedules recopied, plane reservations, the names of hospitals and doctors, plans and demands. The writer seemed intent on coming to visit and establish new roots. ¶ Now, around the recipients' household, there was general agreement that the letters were written by an eccentric or prankster, and they were either discarded or kept in a drawer. But still, in the mind of the younger of the letters' two recipients, they held strong allure. First, they were very pretty, very much a kind of mail-art. The letters also offered, however remote, the possibility of a long-obscured and probably very dark secret. What if his mother really *had* another brother, named Timothy, who had for whatever reason been ostracized, or sent away, when young? This theory was supported, eerily enough, by the postmark on all letters sent: Boston—a city very, very close to Milton, Mass., the hometown of the McSweeneys. ¶ But these letters ceased coming sometime around 1987. And then, more than ten years later, this journal came about, named for this Timothy for reasons easily enough inferred. We never expected to discover anything further about Timothy, though during the life of the journal we have met many McSweeneys. First, we heard from a few dozen, from all over the land, who bought or subscribed to the journal for its name only. One such reader, whose name is, we think, Rob, actually showed up at the former 9th Street, Brooklyn, home office of McSweeney's just to say hello. He was in the Navy, was stationed in California and was out East visiting someone or other. He had a crewcut and he and his fiancée were both very nice. They were given a nice T-shirt for their trouble. ¶ There were also, of course, the Massachusetts McSweeneys, they of www.mcsweeneys.com. We long had an involuntary association with them, having our home at www.mcsweeneys.net, and thus having confused many would-be visitors to either site. Eventually these McSweeneys—no relation to anyone relevant here—became our friends and we shared, for some time, responsibility for one combined Web address, called the Mega-McSweeney's Site. It did not work out perfectly, but we parted as friends. ¶ Recently, as one might have expected to happen at some point, we took on, as an intern, a bona fide McSweeney. His name was Ross McSweeney and he attended Columbia University, a college in New York City with a very good reputation. He started helping us, when time permitted, in the late summer of 2000. Sometime in mid-December, though, he, as the poet sings, "dropped a bomb on us." ¶ It was at an impromptu gathering at a New York nightspot, a gathering where people who were helping McSweeney's in different capacities could meet each other and drink free drinks. This was the first time I—(I just ditched the third-person device again)—met Ross, who, through some quirks of scheduling, I had missed a few times previously. Ross was a man of maybe twenty, who looks like he sang or should be singing in a choir. Or maybe a barber shop quartet. We do not know if he indeed sings, but he is clean-cut and kind. We sat on low soft stools and had this conversation: ¶ "So you're Ross McSweeney." ¶ "Yes." ¶ "Where are you from?" ¶ "Boston." ¶ "Ha! Maybe we're related." (With small chuckle and dribble of beer on shirt.) ¶ "Actually, we're not, I don't think, but I should tell you something. I think I'm related to Timothy." ¶ It was that quick. Good god. ¶ Then he related his story. You must trust that this is true: ¶ One day, about a year and a half ago, Ross's sister—then a student at the Iowa Writer's Project and now a noted poet— encountered a copy of McSweeney's, this journal, at Iowa City's local independent bookstore, which is called Prairie Lights. She brought it home to Boston to show her family, amused by the journal's title. Her father looked it over with interest. ¶ Ross's father is named David McSweeney. David McSweeney grew up with two older brothers and a younger sister, Kathleen. They were raised in the Dorchester section of Boston, which is close to Lower Mills, on the border of Milton, Mass. David McSweeney, Ross's dad, had two older brothers. Closest in age was Denis. The eldest was named Timothy. ¶ Ross was telling me all of this in a bar, surrounded by people. Somewhere behind us, Kevin, our then-web-editor, was spilling his drink on someone. But what was at first unclear in Ross's telling was just how Timothy singled out my McSweeneys, given that there were surely hundreds if not thousands in the greater Boston area. ¶ "Well," said Ross, "the thing started, we think, with your grandfather. He was an obstetrician, right?" ¶ I told him yes, he was. My grandfather was an obstetrician in Boston. He delivered some ridiculous number of babies over many decades, and was well-loved—our house was and is full of heavy laquered plaques bearing his name. He even co-invented a precursor to the contemporary home-pregnancy test. His name was Daniel J. McSweeney. One more fact: for a very long time, Daniel McSweeney held the world-record for the number of cesareans performed on the same woman. He perfomed twelve cesareans on the same woman, for twelve successive babies. This is true. ¶ "Well," said Ross, "we're pretty sure he delivered Timothy." ¶ Oh Lord. ¶ "And then my grandparents, my dad's parents, adopted him." ¶ "So Timothy wasn't a McSweeney by birth?" ¶ "No." ¶ "Oh god. Wow." The story continues, but I'll sum up: Timothy was a talented young man who attended art school and even got an MFA, spending some time after that teaching art. But thereafter his life was troubled, and eventually was hospitalized. It was while in treatment centers that he wrote letters to us and to others, seeking perhaps to answer questions about his life and provenance. ¶ It's very strange to know, now, that there is a real person behind this journal's name, and it is unsettling to know that what we presumed to be a stranger's prankish eccentricity had a far less cavalier source. We respectfully dedicate this and all issues to the real Timothy, and nod our heads in restless kinship with him, and wish him comfort and joy. He is fortunate to have supporting him a family of such strength and compassion. ¶ THERE ENDS THE STORY OF TIMOTHY MCSWEENEY. And here is an odd and inconsequential story regarding ISSUE FOUR: I wanted to have the stories bound separately. I had been told a dozen or so stories about book-writing authors having very unpleasant experiences with the conception and execution of their jacket covers, so, being the very annoying sort of crusader-with-misdirected-energy that I was at the time, Issue Four became, in part, a call to arms with regard to authors' control over their own covers. I wrote a mostly-silly screed/Bill of Rights about the subject, and I made sure to allow each author included the right to art-direct their own cover. This was fine, and worked out well—most authors relished the opportunity, and many got their own friends involved—but the covers were not the problem. The box was the problem. By this point in the life of McSweeney's, Sean Wilsey was a part of the very small group that had a hand in putting the magazine out. Sean was working elsewhere at the time, so he contributed stories, contacts with writers, and various editing help. This was his first trip to Reykjavik, and it was January, I believe. Iceland in January is not awesome. It's monochromatic and slushy and cold (though not as cold as you might fear). With the boxes, Oddi, which had done such an extraordinary job with the first three issues of McSweeney's, was at a loss. They had never made a box before. They had no idea how to make a box. So they brought in more Icelanders. They brought in the most knowledgeable maker of boxes on their island nation of 260,000. The man was from a company called Boxmaker. This is true. Sean and I, and the man from Boxmaker, and Bjossi—our main contact at Oddi, and as sweet a man as you will meet on that island or any other—sat around a conference table for many hours trying to figure out what kind of box would be possible, might be affordable and could be made from the sort of pulp they have and keep in Iceland. Let me tell you, there were some ugly and funny options presented. [Related fact: the Icelanders are not great users of cardboard. They use very little, and manufacture almost none. Thus, it was very much like asking the people of Guam to help build a ski slope.] They really puzzled over it, and Sean and I did, and after a few days we arrived at the box that you might have seen — it is very pretty, but hopelessly delicate. There are perhaps six or seven undamaged, un-ruined Issue 4 boxes extant. It is not a strong box, but the boxmakers at Boxmaker did their best. ¶ WHILE WE WERE IN ICELAND, THOUGH: we saw many things, had very good Italian food, and walked around in the slush. It was during this trip that we came upon the idea of publishing a book about electrical engineering on boats. Sean and I were in an antiquarian bookstore on a small street in the less-busy part of Reykjavik, and there we bought many books we could not understand. One of those books was about electrical engineering on boats, and contained many beautiful diagrams. I brought this book home to the US, and decided that McSweeney's needed to revive the popularity—I assumed the volume I bought, dated 1924, had caused stampedes of books about electrical engineering on boats. So we put a notice on the McSweeney's website, asking for proposals from people who wanted to write a book about this sort of thing. We received about a hundred such proposals and we were frightened. The falcon could not hear the falconer. The winning proposal, by the very wonderful writer named Amy Fusselman, concerned her father, who had recently passed away. He was not an electrical engineer, but he had spent time on a boat, in the navy, and this was, we thought, close enough. The book turned out beautifully, was loved by all who read it, and taught us something. This episode was an example, and there are many more, where the story overwhelmed the form. We've always been interested in form here, and we try to help or at least allow writers to explore, expand, break and remake what it means to write a story. At the same time, early on in our publishing history, we were intoxicated with the idea that books could be brought into the world if we willed them to be. That is, we had done some math, and we had discovered that we could print a few thousand copies of a book about electrical engineering on boats, and it was likely that we could find a few thousand buyers for that book. It was a strange thing, a strange world that would allow such a possibility. And so we asked for proposals for these kinds of books, and Amy's proposal won, and instead of being an odd, diagram-filled sort of exercise in book art, it was an extremely moving, elegiac love letter to the author's deceased father, and a study of a woman on the verge of motherhood. ¶ And thus that episode, and this book, demonstrates that both the random, the experimental, and the straightforward-and-gut-twisting can coexist, can inform each other, can cross-pollinate even, and we are all the better for it. Too often, the world of books goes through hand-wringing and then extermination, when the powers-that-be decide either that a) All books should be form-busting and structurally brave; or else the opposite, that all books that attempt in any way whatsoever to move the medium of fiction in any new direction are practicing "gimmacry" or even "gimcrackery." It is exhausting and [continued on page 362]

[*Below find some of the best letters, commissioned and otherwise, that ran in the first bunch of issues of the journal.*]

DEAR MCSWEENEY'S,

I am currently at an amusement park convention—that is, a convention for those in the amusement park business. Almost immediately upon entering the convention, I found myself in front of a booth full of stuffed animals, the kind you can win as prizes.

"So," I said to the proprietor, "how much do all these cost?"

"Between fifty cents and $2.50," he said.

There was a long pause.

"Where do they come from?" I asked.

"China," he said. "We buy them from factory close-outs."

Another long pause.

"I always wondered where they came from," I said.

"China," he said.

TIM CARVELL
NEW YORK, NEW YORK
1999

DEAR EDITOR,

Why do you play that dog-turd music? says legendary rock critic Lester Bangs. It's New Year's Day 1981, less than a month after John Lennon's murder, and the Mekons are at a media punk rock party somewhere on frozen Manhattan. The whole city seems to be nursing a giant twitchy hangover.

Er... Don't really know but that's a pretty accurate description, we reply.

What! snarls Lester, you're meant to defend yourselves!

Why? It is dog turd music.

Lester ponders this for a moment. He is a big bear of a man in a black winter coat and beret with dark rings under his eyes. I've read his stuff in the *NME*; the manic older American who took punk rock to heart.

That's a totally revolutionary concept, a band that doesn't even like itself! He seems genuinely impressed.

It turns out that he'd been at the Gang of Four/Mekons/Au Pairs gig at Hurrah's the night before and actually likes our band. The dog-turd jibe is a Bangsian ice-breaker and we don't give a shit because while this is our first US gig ever, it's probably our last anywhere. We're at a fairly terminal stage of disintegration (sacked by Virgin Records, bass player run off to join the Venezuelan Symphony, sick of playing last year's flavour to the dwindling gaggles of violent morons who'd annexed the British punk scene, sick of each other, skint, gone back to art school etc.) and if New York seems a long way to come to expire, shit! It worked for Sid!

Come round tomorrow, says Lester, and gives us his address (above a Chinese restaurant in the West Village, no doorbell, just yell Lester). Duty-free vodka and forty-eight hours of constant local hospitality see Tom and Kevin jump the next Laker back to Gatwick but Chalkie, Corrigan and me stick around for the whole week.

The next afternoon perturbed Manhattan diners gawk as two under-wrapped punk rockers huddle together on the sidewalk screaming Lester! Lester! up at the sky. Blimey, they're a long way from Filbert Street. After a few minutes a window opens and a pair of stereo speakers are lowered purposefully down towards the street blaring the indelicate one chord thrash of "32 Weeks," our first single. This is more than a little disconcerting and things get worse when Lester sticks his huge head out and starts shouting along.

Hey! listen! this is you! He is swinging the speakers back and forwards on their wires several feet above our heads as snow spirals down between the buildings in big fluffy clumps. By the time he lets us in our ears are numb, brittle and blue.

Up in his apartment the entire floor is covered in LPs and 45s all out of their sleeves, some cracked and trodden into the carpet, others decorated with little spatters of vomit. We've brought beer but Lester doesn't want any, he wants one of us to go back outside and get him a Vick sinex inhaler from the drugstore. I volunteer but get the squirty-squeezy-liquid kind and not the sniffy-shove-up-your-nose kind that he wanted. He is visibly upset so Chalkie rushes out into the blizzard to find the correct product. On his return he is greeted at the door by an eager Lester armed with a tiny toffee hammer. Deep in concentration, he picks his spot and swings with expert precision, smashing the inhaler's cylindrical plastic casing to reveal the chemically infused gauze swab within. Placing it in his mouth like a communion wafer he swallows hard, eyes rolling up into his skull, and slumps heavily back into an armchair, beaming. Lester has been up for quite a few days.

Over the next week Lester Bangs is our guide through New York; drinking and yelling at the Mudd Club, wandering round the Village, introducing us to Robert Quine of the Voidoids, taking us to Bleeker Bob's record store, telling me what to buy (Otis Rush, *Groaning The Blues: Original Cobra Recordings 1956-58*; and

Mars, *The Mars EP*) and talking up the Mekons to anyone who'll listen. We meet Joey Ramone's mum walking down the street arm in arm with Lester's shrink, an elegant couple in matching fur hats: Hi, Lester, are you going to see the boys tonight? —Uh, where they playin'? Hey did you meet Jon? He's in the Mekons, they're the most revolutionary band in the history of rock and roll... Lester is hilarious, a permanently outraged and outrageous conversationalist. He bemoans the current state of the West Village: This is where the Velvet Underground used to live, now the only person you ever run into is Wendy O'-fuckin'-Williams... Why do I have to see Tom Verlaine washing his socks every time I go to the laundromat? He does his best to be offensive and he's pretty good at it. On Patti Smith: She looks like a dead dog on the side of the road (which he credited to the Runaways), or She is one unappealing piece of flounder (which I'm sure was one of his own). He rounds off a particularly disgusting tale about Lou Reed, a hooker and an alleged glass coffee table with Why are all our heroes perverts? Out of the blue he offers to write the sleeve notes for our next record. We hadn't planned to make one but why not?... He sits crosslegged on the floor and types furiously for an hour...

What's an English beer?

Er... Tetleys.

Thanks.

When we finally released *The Mekons Story* LP in late 1982 we had to do some pretty savage editing to fit it all on the sleeve. Lester has a go at the *NME*, Eno's Music For Pizzerias, Patti Smith, Troy Donahue, Virgin Records and John Lydon, who wails, I must give it up and knocks over his bottle of Tetley's on hearing our new record. Here's my favorite bit: They are better than the Beatles. They are even better than Budgie and REO Speedwagon combined... They gave me fifteen hundred dollars for writing these notes. All their daddies are rich which is why they get to keep putting out this swill. I have never heard this album, I never will... He never did.

At some point we're in his apartment and he pulls out an acoustic guitar and a tape machine and starts recording some of his songs so I can have a cassette to take back to Leeds. I still have it: five strange sad songs, sung virtually a capella, which reveal the idealism and vulnerability that tempered the decibel-mouth wisecracking and poison pen. There's a song about Andy Warhol, the melody ripped off Bob Dylan's "115th Dream": I don't mean to seem bitter, no, you've made your contribution to the popular notion that no heart is the solution. On "There's A Man In There" he's the reluctant witness to some public burning hosted by Manhattan socialites. Lester saw himself as a resistance leader battling a (currently in progress) spontaneous and unplanned mass movement on the part of human beings in the West to jettison as many emotions as possible, the deification of numbness and/or the stultifyingly bland...

The last night I'm in New York the phone rings at 4 a.m. and it's Lester in the middle of writing a play about the death of John Lennon. You gotta come over, now. But I'm too tired and it's time to go home.

JON LANGFORD
CHICAGO, ILLINOIS
1999

DEAR EDITOR,
Did you know that Jerry Lewis turned down the role of the killer in *Cruising*, the lead in *Being There*, and the title role in *Charly*? What's more, he turned down the Robert Shaw part in *Jaws*, and the role of Salieri in *Amadeus*. Also Peter Ustinov's part in *Logan's Run*. Can you imagine him as Humbert Humbert? Apparently he couldn't. And we will never have the privilege of knowing how he would have handled *Portnoy's Complaint*—he turned down a chance to star in and direct that film. He was also screen-tested for the Sterling Hayden role in *The Godfather* and the John Hurt role in *Alien*, though it is unclear whether he was actually offered these parts or not. How different might be the history of American film in the '70s had he actually taken the roles of the wiretapper in *The Conversation,* Popeye Doyle in *The French Connection,* or Lex Luthor in *Superman*—though I suppose we can be grateful to him, in a sense, for the opportunities given Gene Hackman, who certainly did not disappoint in these parts. Nor is it likely he could have improved on Jason Robards' portrayal of Ben Bradlee in *All the President's Men,* or on Rip Torn's performance in *The Man Who Fell to Earth.* Perhaps most frustrating for the film buff is the knowledge that Alfred Hitchcock, the Master of Suspense, died before realizing his hope of casting Lewis in a thriller. Lewis had previously turned down the Martin Balsam part in *Psycho* and the Sean Connery part in *Marnie*. Equally tantalizing is the large Lewis role trimmed out of *Nashville* during last-minute edits—in interviews Lewis claims it as his masterwork. Robert Altman attempted to make it up to him, but

an embittered Lewis turned down parts in Altman's next seven films. He also turned down the parts that went to Walter Matthau in both *Charley Varrick* and *King Creole,* thus missing his chance to work with veteran director Don Siegel (as well as to appear opposite Elvis Presley). He also turned down the John Lithgow part in *Blow Out* and the part that was reworked for Richard Pryor in *Blue Collar.* He refused the part Jack Lemmon played in *The China Syndrome,* though it was later pointed out that the role was developed for Lemmon and Lewis was never offered it. He also refused the role of the off-screen voice of Charlie in the hit television series "Charlie's Angels," a role taken by John Forsyth, later of "Dynasty." Unquestionably, *Excalibur* would have been a different film completely had Lewis not dropped out during the first week of shooting to be replaced by Nicol Williamson as Merlin. He also turned down the role of the arsonist in *Body Heat.*

Strangely, Jerry Lewis was never considered for any part by Michael Cimino.

JONATHAN LETHEM
BROOKLYN, NEW YORK
1999

DEAR EDITOR,

It was one of those moments on television you remember—a watermark, a revelation. One of those segments you turn over and over in your mind and linger over and get haunted by and... changes you. Like Jack Ruby or white Bronco or Challenger. Like Before—and After. I'm speaking of the day Rosie O'Donnell confessed on the air that she had cleaned her niece's fish tank with a sponge and the antibacterial agents in said sponge had killed the fish. Dead! And it was like—boom!—sponges are that good? The squishy pink wipes with which I clean the many splendored surfaces of mon appartement are so technological, so advanced, that they could off not just an organism, but an animal? An actual flushable creature with gills and mass and a name even? I thought, this is why this continent was settled, however cruelly. This is true pilgrim's progress. Cleanliness. Godliness. America. Not that I've confirmed that the interior sponge weapons are an American innovation (that would require a phone call) but I just know in my heart that such a darling and deadly advancement is domestic to these shores. And anyway, I was looking, per usual, for an enemy. My mistake was staring me in the face right there in the verb: looking. Only the slacker hate-mongers go for the seeable opponents, silly antagonisms based on race or architectural abberations like purple house paint in a neighborhood planned in beige. No, your major enemies have always been unseen and kind of ill-defined: the Devil, communism, the ozone thing. And even though my silly critic job offers loads of antiopportunities ("Downwithphotorealism LizPhair-GratefulDeadTheSteelers!") there are times when there is nothing more lovable than the hate implicit in the magic word *antibacterial*. I have little or no control over practically anything: street crime, the opposite sex, my liquor bills, CNN. And yet, thanks to the thoughtful folks at Lysol, Softsoap, Dawn, and Dow, my whole house is anti-! My hands are anti-, my dishes are anti-, my counters are anti-, even (and this is a recent product development) my toilet is anti-. This may be a silent protest; there are no loud-mouthed Abbie

Hoffmans running around yelling at the germs. Think unspoken power. Think Alan Greenspan. Each antibacterial squirt, every antibacterial spray, is a cold war wrapped inside a stealth attack tied up with the bow of annihilation. Call me paranoid. Call me girly. Call me what you what you will. But before you go on about marketing ruses and it's-only-a-name and that according to the so-called experts these expensive products don't fare any better than plain old soap and water, I refer you to Rosie O'Donnell's niece's fish. Ask them. Ask them if you can.

Best,
SARAH VOWELL
CHICAGO, ILLINOIS
1998

DEAR EDITOR,
I've been looking for material that your readers might find interesting, and I think I have something. Following are the world's worst cities to visit if they are named after local landmarks:

1. Liverpool (England)
2. Braintree (Massachusetts)
3. Peabody (Massachusetts)
4. Medicine Hat (Alberta)
5 Worms (Germany)
6. Urine (Illinois)
7. Colostomy (Tunisia)
8. Scrotum (Connecticut)
9. King of Prussia (Pennsylvania)
10. Smyrna (Georgia)

All the best,
DON STEINBERG
CENTRAL PENNSYLVANIA
1998

DEAR MCSWEENEY'S,
Everybody in this whole town drinks. They don't drink your typical store-bought liquors, however. They drink moonshine whiskey and it is served up in glass jars. Moonshine is a clear liquid which looks like water, but has a much stronger kick, like about 150 proof. It is produced in stills located up in the "hollers" where lawmen cannot find them. Old folks here claim that the "white lightin'" has "medicinal qualities," which may very well be true because there are many people here who are over one hundred years old, and they drink moonshine every day.

Sometimes, if moonshine whiskey is made a little too strong it will cause the drinker to go blind after just a few sips. There are a number of folks around here who walk around blind as bats due to the effects of poorly made moonshine. They don't get better; they just stay blind.

This guy who lives near me has that disease called narcolepsy, which means he will fall asleep at any given moment. He fell asleep while he was mowing his lawn and the lawn mower got away from him and rolled into a penned-up area where his daughter kept baby rabbits. Most of them survived, but a few didn't, and he had a lot of explaining to do when his daughter walked outside and saw what happened.

I've never even eaten rabbit stew, but I have eaten squirrel and it tastes a lot like a rabbit would probably taste. One time I was fishing with my cousin and we caught what was probably the ugliest looking fish you've ever seen in your life. It had warts and spines all over it and tentacles, too. Neither one of us wanted to touch it so we just cut the line and let it sink back down to the bottom.

On a recent trip to New York City I met this girl who was over six feet tall and claimed to have played on the Junior Olympic volleyball team. She had blonde hair and also said, "I enjoy surfing naked."

"I'd like to see that," I said.

"Oh, I bet you would," she said.

Later on that same night I met a guy who'd been punched in the face moments after withdrawing money from an automatic teller machine. His nose was all swollen and bloody. "They took $60 from me," he said. "The bills were all straight and crisp."

Then I spent $60 in a peep show booth where you could give a woman $20 and she would dance around naked behind the clear plastic. This woman was Hispanic and had a little mustache. She smiled as she danced and I liked her so much I paid her three times.

Back in Virginny, I went to a country music concert and the singer was taking swigs of some kind of stiff drink between each verse of his songs. Moonshine! By the end of the show he was shitfaced and seemed not to know where he was. After that experience I myself went to a party where moonshine was being served. I had a few drinks and was almost too tipsy to drive home. Luckily, I was riding a bicycle instead of driving a car, because upon leaving the party I managed to ride the bike straight into a hedge. I got up and was soon after arrested by some policemen who were out on night patrol. I spent the night in the clinker with a few other men, one of whom's name was James. He was impotent. He told me a sad story about how he had been staying at this woman's house for a few weeks, but he couldn't satisfy her, not at all. James had those little red veins you often see in the face of a hard drinker.

Listen, do you think that, as Americans, we eat too much fast food? It's not even that fast, when you think about it. I've spent like fifteen minutes waiting in line at McDonald's and the food isn't even that good. Often, you will hear young kids extol the virtues of McDonald's food, especially here in rural Virginia, but I definitely think they are wrong.

That guy James, the one who I had met in the jail cell, had $20 in his pocket and the first thing he did when he got out was go find a liquor store and buy himself a bottle of Kentucky Deluxe Whiskey.

I thought of James a few weeks later when I had an extra jar of "white lightnin'" corn liquor, and I knew I wouldn't, or shouldn't, drink it. I found old James at an outdoor rock-n-roll show which was being put on for free by the town council. He was wasted and couldn't even talk right. He sounded like an entirely different person, like he had a chicken in his throat or something. I almost wanted to reach down in there and see. I gave him the jar of bootleg whiskey and he spilled it all over his shirt. He was so wet, he looked like he'd been thrown in a lake. I'm sure those hundred-year-old folks who live near me now would shake their heads and say, "what a waste of moonshine," when they heard about that.

Love,

ARTHUR BRADFORD
RURAL VIRGINIA
1999

DEAR EDITOR,

Back at the amusement park convention, I inadvertently offended a representative of the Ripley's Believe It or Not! museums by insinuating that a shrunken head on display was fake. It was, he assured me, real. "We have probably the largest collection of shrunken heads in the world," he said proudly, "outside of some tribe in the Amazon, of course."

TIM CARVELL
NEW YORK, NEW YORK
1999

DEAR EDITOR,
Oliver Teller (born Telkmariam) and I have lost touch. I know you sometimes facilitate this kind of thing and would appreciate your printing this letter.
Sincerely,
LYNNE TILLMAN
NEW YORK, NEW YORK

DEAR OLLIE,
It's been a long time. I think of you sometimes, and I know you think of me. I take a perverse satisfaction in that, even in the jaded ways you disguise me in your so-called fictions. I really don't care. But I just read your "manifesto against the past." No one "votes for guilt." I also have "funny mental pictures" of that mansion we lived in on the Hudson. It wasn't "haunted," except by an unghostly Timothy Leary. Everyone said he dropped acid there. Everyone said they used to have wild parties. Even back then the term *wild parties* bothered me. No one ever gave details.

You and I were the only non-psych students living in the mansion. You and they were older, graduate students, but they were all research psychologists and thought everyone else was crazy, so they devised experiments to prove it. There was that one sullen guy who worked with rats. He had a big room near mine. I used to look in as I passed it. He kept his shoes under the chair of his desk in a certain way, everything in his room had a specific order, and if his shoes were moved even a quarter inch, he went crazy.

Remember when he drove his car into a wall? Then he disappeared. Remember it's my past, too, you want to "throw into the garbage, to be carted away by muscular men and sent floating on a barge to North Carolina."

One night, you brought a friend home from Juilliard, a fellow student. If you recall, our dining room had dark walls and no electricity. We ate by candlelight—there were many candles in different states of meltdown on the long table. I can't remember exactly how many people were around the table that night. About ten, I think.

Before dinner, one of the research psychologists suggested it'd be fun to put blue vegetable dye in the mashed potatoes. Your friend wouldn't know. We'd act as if the potatoes weren't blue, just the usual white, and even though your friend might protest and insist that they were blue, we'd keep insisting they were white. None of us would relent. We'd just pretend he was crazy for thinking they were blue. We cooked this up in the kitchen. When you came in with him, someone took you aside and told you. You went along with it. Everyone has a streak of sadism, one of the psych guys said.

I can't remember who brought in the potatoes, we all participated, though, and then we all sat down around the big wooden table. The blue mashed potatoes were served in a glass bowl. Even by candlelight, they were bright blue.

We passed the food. When the bowl of blue potatoes reached your friend, he reacted with delight. Blue mashed potatoes, he said. Someone said, They're not blue. Your friend said, They're not? They look blue. Someone else said, No, they're not. You were sitting next to him.

The potatoes kept going around. Your friend said, again, They really look blue. Everyone acted as if nothing was happening. Your friend kept looking at the bowl. He became visibly agitated. He said, They look blue. Someone said, Maybe it's the candlelight. The flames have a bluish tinge. Your friend kept looking, squinting his eyes. Then he insisted, They look blue to me. Someone said, with annoyance, Would you stop it? They're not blue. Your friend turned quiet. He kept looking, though, and we all kept eating.

The coup de grace, I guess you'd call it, was dessert. In the kitchen, someone decided to dye the milk blue. The cake, coffee, and blue milk were brought to the table. We served the blue milk in a glass pitcher. No one said much as the pitcher went around the table. Your friend watched silently. When it came to him, he stared at the pitcher and poured the blue milk into his coffee. This time, he said nothing. Nothing. At that point, I ran into the kitchen. I couldn't control myself.

Later, you told him. After dinner, when you were alone with him, you told him. But I'm wondering, after all these years, did he ever forgive you? What happened to him? Does he still play the trombone?

You were good, Ollie. But somehow, in "regurgitating the past and moving on," I'm "the reckless prankster" whose "promiscuous heart" you broke. The only thing in that house you ever broke was your musician friend and crazy Roger's green plates.

Whatever,
LYNNE TILLMAN
NEW YORK, NEW YORK
2002

DEAR MCSWEENEY'S,
Melvin Toff told me he used to hate the sport of boxing for its pretensions to valor, grace, art, its "history" of "pageantry." Then he confirmed what a glorious sewer, what an unapologetically sick practice, it had become in recent times, and called it cool. By the time we'd met, Melvin had taught himself all the most famous tragedies of the ring, not just the date and place but the purse involved, the amount each boxer was supposed to've made. He held that "the value of each man is determined by the amount he would accept to receive a public beating." He recounted vivid descriptions of brain-deadening blows which made millions: Jerry Quarry's subdural hematomas, nerve damage to the brainstem of Frank "The Animal" Fletcher, gliding contusions inside "Sugar" Ray Leonard's brain. Through Melvin's eyes, boxing's noble past was just a fast-forward collapse of noses, heads, spirits.

May, 1995, Melvin and I pulled into Las Vegas; he intent on watching grown men slug one another, me intent on gambling most of our money away. At the 21 table, my cocktail waitress had a ponytail and acne; I worked to turn her into an old love —someone I'd lost—without success. She was just another in the long line of somebodies I'd never get to know. She sized up my sad situation, inquired, "Is there anything more I can do for you?"—she drew a slow breath, re-emphasized—"Anything at all?" I could conceive requesting only that she become someone else; instead I shook my head, "Of course not."

The highlight of our visit was to be the battering of L.A.'s gorgeous "Golden Boy" De La Hoya as he went after the belt that belonged to brawling

Rafael Ruelas. But first, on the under-card, Gabriel Ruelas, Rafael's elder brother, defending his title against some tiny long-haired Colombian who wouldn't fall down. The Colombian's name: Jimmy Garcia. Though completely out-punched from second one, Garcia stood and stood, shaking off referees and physicians that he might accept more blows to the face and ribs. The flags, pennants, the streamers dripped red, the colorful floor slogans grew ruined from Garcia's blood. After eleven rounds they called it. Garcia went over to his corner where, finally, he sat. I was relieved. He appeared disappointed. A moment passed, and Garcia lost consciousness. Melvin was thrilled. EMTs loaded Garcia onto a waiting ambulance. The next fight promptly began. For the next two weeks, Gabriel Ruelas prayed at Jimmy Garcia's hospital bedside, but it achieved little. He succumbed to his brain injuries on the anniversary of my divorce—May 19.

It was our second murder together, the first being Peter Tosh. Tosh always seemed a friend, keeping in close touch (via car stereo) until the bad-luck day Melvin and me dashed through a motel in Gallup for a bucket of ice and afterward, just like that, found his murder awaiting us at the top of the news hour. Our fault? Melvin Toff's tenderness boiled away, never to return. His solution was to joke: someone had, like, exploded Peter Tosh's consciousness, man, literally blown his mind, had reshaped his head laterally, he'd got hisself kilt, a bepistoled individual had done to him what Listerine does to bad breath and now Tosh's career was down the drain, he was all over, as in—ha ha—all over the drapes and carpets, &c. None of his jokes were effective, of course. I immediately flipped my Tosh tapes over, scanning their other sides; where, for example, on the back of my copy of "Bush Doctor," I found Melvin had home-taped me some Warren Zevon.

I know it seems like a big deal leaping Tosh to Zevon in nothing flat, but I stink oh-so-bad at grieving. And I admit, devouring them in this order, with Tosh first as the palate cleanser, it took forever before I tasted "the thing" about Zevon; namely, that he oozed disloyalty, a Bel Air whistleblower who took enigmatic pride in running down the old order (himself right along with it), a self-loathing traitor to his Linda Ronstadt class. His characters, initially sympathetic, unveiled their true ugliness in a wink, gave themselves away with an inopportune sigh. So his sessions were in truth subversive (although they sounded SoCal bland, miked and mixed so that you could almost hear the coke-nosed engineers as they blithely unwrapped still more reels of overpriced Ampex two-inch).

Melvin always challenged me as to why there had been no musical yet about boxing, imagining librettos recounting Oliver McCall's inner turmoil during the Lennox Lewis title bout or the aria potential of Golota's castrato-inducing Bowe low-blows. He loved to point out how boxing and music are two such similar sports: the potential for ugliness, the stand-alone arrogance of each. Where else are your bare privates made so public, except (perhaps) when performing live sex acts for money?

The truth is, sensitive singer/songwriter types no longer lose sleep over what transpires in the boxing ring. The last such tune, the one that killed pugilistic anthems rather as *The Searchers* killed Westerns, was probably Warren Zevon's "Boom Boom Mancini," one of Melvin Toff's favorites, in which Zevon's infamous chilliness hits a fate-obsessed apex. At the outdoor arena of Caesar's Palace (where thirteen years later we cheered the death of Jimmy Garcia), Ray "Boom Boom" Mancini had hammered blood clots loose in the head of Duk Koo Kim. It was the most vile thing any Mancini had performed, Melvin liked to hiss, since no-relation Henry directed the Pink Panther Philharmonic at the Hollywood Bowl.

The sinister Cochise-on-the-warpath tribal blues of Zevon's "Boom Boom Mancini," said Melvin Toff, is the unresolvable drama of darkness eternally in our midst. Mancini is a hero troubled by nothing, least of all a conscience. "Hurry home early," dryly encourages the singer, perhaps quoting a boxing advertisement, "Hurry on home. 'Boom Boom' Mancini is fighting Bobby Chacon." To back up this advice, Zevon spends two verses applauding Mancini's ferocity. Then, out of nowhere, at the bridge, Mancini meets Death, in the form of the deceased former champion Kim. Mancini shrugs. We suddenly understand that this is where such courage always lands us; the true glory of boxing is callousness.

Bobby Chacon was our local favorite, former champion featherweight, former champion junior lightweight, the bad-ass from Oroville. People I knew drove more than two hours into Reno that January night, 1984, to watch the ring fill with ghosts. The match would, it was widely believed, be well-attended by the spirit world. Not only was the expectation that Mancini would be distracted by a

vision of his murder victim but Chacon was to be visited by his first wife, who'd killed herself two years prior rather than watch the man she loved continue to box. (Common lore had it she appeared still to enjoy popping up at such events now and again.) And there was the small matter of the soul of Chacon's unborn child which sat ringside in the belly of his second wife.

They near-rioted, chucked magazines and shoes, ice cubes, and beer cans, they, the near-capacity crowd of 11,104, when referee Richard Steele stepped in, a minute-seventeen into round three, before Chacon could even drop, before any of the planned-for ghosts showed up at all. Even the heavyweight champion, Larry Holmes, rarely a great enthusiast for things supernatural, complained it was too soon. "I had to almost kill Leon Spinks before Steele would stop it."

But Chacon was so grateful he thanked the referee for intervening. "You said you were my friend but if you were my friend," Chacon challenged Mancini afterward, "why'd you have to beat me up so bad?" Chacon seemed to forget momentarily that this was "Boom Boom" Mancini, after all, and he could stagger anybody, friends or enemies, with successive jabs, whack their chins and cut their eyes, drop them with unseen left hooks which connected like thrown concrete, because he was Boom Boom Mancini... just as Holmes also hadn't remembered the terrifically bad manners of bragging about nearly killing a man in the ring within earshot of a boxer who actually had. Warren Zevon remembered for both of them—but his "'Boom Boom' Mancini" is about something else, not the boxer or the sport but the futility of forgiveness. This singer won't grant absolution, which is fine by "Boom Boom" Mancini; he knows better than to seek it. The value of a life has become exactly what Melvin Toff calculated; the price one accepts to be beaten in public.

Or maybe that's not Zevon's point at all. Maybe the point is the abruptness of the song's shift—that a paean to a brave athlete can become, within a measure or two of music, a horror story. Every moment of life presents some opportunity to wreck—you miscalculate a shift in traffic or forget to pull out before coming. Somehow we find ourselves outside relationships, without love. Sometimes it's not even a choice, just an unfair confluence, bad luck. Let's say you uncharacteristically lose your temper—but it's when the paparazzi's around; perhaps a lethal shot discharges from the pistol you were promised was unloaded. This was Mancini's fate—in executing his job's responsibilities he merely traveled one punch too far and spattered blood all over his formerly playful nickname. Now he's hailed on the street as "the guy who killed that Korean." Now Melvin Toff never tells me what he's feeling. Zevon's lumbering voice in "'Boom Boom' Mancini" says it all, his affect flattening as the batteries in his heart audibly peter out. Hearing this, I cannot help but admit how, given a second chance, we'd kill Jimmy Garcia all over again without even hesitating.

CAMDEN JOY
SOMERVILLE, MASSACHUSETTS
1999

DEAR McSWEENEY'S,
Please assure me that I qualify as the very first subscriber in Bethel (50+ air-miles west of Anchorage, population 5,000+, and approximately the same latitude as the unspellable-by-memory capital of Iceland. Not found in the tourist propaganda, i.e., no glaciers, no mountains, no eagles, no totem poles, no igloos, a city government that can't decide what to do about tourism [and not without the occasional tawdry sex scandal] but rather, miles of tundra, a big river, dust, mud, mosquitoes, salmon, and migrating birds by summer; and all that is cold by winter, during which time the dogs leave post-intestinal packets of springtime aesthetic delight. Throughout it all, the airplanes keep the villages supplied with diapers, sodapop and similac [and the rest of the mail... that's my job], the ravens feast at the dumpsters, people drop cigarette butts, spit tobacco juice and hock scrofulous phlegm. The Korean and Albanian taxi drivers have an occasional disagreement, Yup'ik adolescent males walk around with baggy pants and Chicago Bulls jackets... As the Chamber of Commerce likes to boast, "Bethel is Special." Though, to be honest, it's not such a bad place... as long as I have my ten days off every month and the travel perquisites accorded to an airline pilot, i.e., an "exit strategy," to use the mil-speak parlance of the government and corporate media), Alaska (population 500,000, half of which is in Anchorage) to your ever-so-peculiar periodical publication.

Let me know. I enjoy feeling special. Enclosed is my check for $28.00.
With Sincerity & Expectation,
DEAN F. CULLY
BETHEL, ALASKA
1999

Dear Editor,

Five years ago, I played an angry gay teenager in a small coming-of-age film. The angry gay teenager ends up finding true love with a shy girl from the high school. The other characters were my character's mom; a young guy from my class (initially the crush-object of the shy girl) who has a heavy-duty affair with the mom; and the young guy's sister, a fashion model who becomes an ice-skating showgirl in Las Vegas.

The movie's dialogue was idiosyncratic and, it must be said, not very much like the way young people talk, but there were some genuinely poignant scenes. The mother-daughter competition and the young characters' sexual discoveries were treated with disarming frankness.

I needed a job. But I was also really fond of my character. She was the closest character to myself I'd ever played. Also, though nobody would guess from watching the movie, the action was ostensibly set in Minnesota, where I grew up.

Toward the end of the shoot, we worked on a scene set "four years later." My character and her girlfriend were at the showgirl's house in Las Vegas. Visually, the scene was an homage to the charming scene in that old movie *That Touch of Mink,* where the two leading ladies chat while lying in single beds set at an L-shaped angle. Light streamed in from the windows of the showgirl's guest room, which was really in suburban Long Island. The beds were decked out in frilly white eyelet. A desolate Western magic-hour light streamed into the room, golden and sad, thanks to lavender filters, gigantic beige Japanese paper lanterns, and big silver bounce cards. In the scene, my girlfriend and I engaged in distracted small talk until I suddenly broke down and asked if she would list me as a beneficiary in her will. I quickly explained that my own mother had not listed me in her will, a fact I discovered in high school, when I had run an errand to this safety deposit box, only to discover the hurtful and bitter truth. The scene ultimately turns into this big profession of commitment and, by the end, winds up being touching, in spite of how arcane it sounds.

I was having a hard time connecting to the whole safety deposit box thing. I could understand the hurt/left-out aspect, but I had a hard time getting to the extreme vulnerability that the character seemed to need. I just couldn't get past the safety deposit box part of it. It seemed so clinical.

As actors, my girlfriend and I were friendly enough, but we weren't what anyone would call soulmates. So in order to do the scene I had to do some emotional substitution. I found this thing, rather randomly, that had come up in my mind a few times.

I thought about this time when I was around eleven. My two sisters and I were with my Dad at a cabin in Wisconsin that my folks had rented for the summer. It was early October, and we had returned to bring home the last of our stuff, shut off the water, and close it up for the winter. It was Saturday morning, overcast, beyond brisk but just shy of cold. We were talking about what to eat for lunch. There were a couple of cans of Spaghetti-O's, which we wanted. My dad was concerned that there would either be too much or not enough— I can't remember which. My sister

Ingrid and I got into a combative argument about which one of us could eat a whole can of Spaghetti-O's:

Ingrid: I can eat a whole can. I will.

Me: No you can't.

Ingrid: Yuh-huh, I CAN. I'm gonna.

Me: You never ate a whole can. No way.

Ingrid: I have so.

Me: WHEN?

My dad got up from where he was sitting, screamed, "God!" and lurched past us, letting the screen door slam behind him. Ingrid and I watched as he walked a few feet and stopped in front of the fence. He faced the fence and clenched his fists, his barrel chest heaving. He exhaled through his mouth, hissing, and shook his head. We glanced at each other, still mad, but mesmerized by Dad. He generally had a demeanor of gruff good-heartedness, but he was not to be messed with. He taught at a vo-tech school and had a lot of tough students—ex-cons, addicts, lost souls. His usual method of controlling other people's bad behavior was to wind his arm up like a pitcher and then pound his fist on the nearest available flat surface. He was intense and quick to anger, but this was the closest we'd ever seen him come to losing it.

After a few seconds I followed him out to the fence and stood behind him. He wouldn't acknowledge me. I kept saying, over and over, "Daddy, please, I'm sorry, I'm so sorry, I didn't mean it." And then, "Daddy, I didn't mean to make you mad, I'm sorry." But he wouldn't even look at me. He didn't wave me away or say a word. He just kept drawing in and expelling huge breaths. I freaked out. I was scared to go any closer to him, and began to cry. All I remember after that is somehow ending up in the tiny bathroom, sitting on the toilet seat, blankly staring at the crimp of the thin metal baseboard where it met the carpet. So I relived all of that while I did the big scene. It worked, but it was exhausting.

The coming-of-age film was screened for exactly one week at the Quad Cinema, a tiny art-house place on 13th Street, and was reviewed kindly by Steven Holden of the *New York Times*. I saw the movie once, at its small premiere in Los Angeles, with my then-manager, who hated it because he thought I looked fat in the love scenes. The movie was never sold for distribution or released on video. I don't even have a copy of it. All I have is a ten-minute sample I got during editing—just a rough-cut of the big scene and a couple of others. My then-manager refused to let me use the big scene in my reel because it was too sad, and also because in it, my nose is red from crying.

COLLEEN WERTHMANN
NEW YORK, NEW YORK
2002

DEAR MCSWEENEY'S,
There can be no more soul-searching experience than reading another writer's complete works in a systematic fashion. I recently accepted an assignment to contribute to a guidebook to contemporary fiction. I was in charge of four authors. Thus I spent nine straight action-drunk days last August devouring the entire oeuvre of a writer of legal thrillers; five frequent-flying weeks in which I read everything by a California science fictioner only in the air (which complemented his dreamy style by the by); a half week with the

novels of an acclaimed essayist/less-acclaimed novelist; and a lovely Thanksgiving weekend re-reading a quartet of small town tragicomedies by one of America's quiet geniuses. What made my heart sink was each author's inadvertent repetition, their crutches, and odd little obsessions. The legal thriller author was guiltiest of all, not only because he resorted to the same trite phrases in book after book, but because of the insidious nature of his hackery. For instance, unable or unwilling to spend a couple of minutes thinking up another way to describe a beautiful woman, there is a hottie in almost every one of his books who isn't wearing makeup, but who "needed none." But mostly, the repetitions spoke to the way writers are both driven by their obsessions and/or trapped by the circumstances of biography. In my assigned authors this was either distracting or endearing. Like, I got the feeling that the thriller writer might be a secret alcoholic because of the overabundance of male characters with a love for "the taste of beer." That's how he puts it: "the taste of beer." The essayist/novelist, a native of California, always manages to plant a "jacaranda tree" into her narratives. I, a dual native of dogwood and douglas fir country, had never heard of such flora. I looked it up: "Any of several trees of the genus Jacaranda, native to tropical America, having compound leaves and clusters of pale-purple flowers." The jacaranda's appearance (in four books) became a little madeleine of irritation, a jolt out of narrative action which is even more annoying when you're getting paid crap and thus fiscally rewarded for speed, speed, speed. The quiet genius, bless him, has a lovely habit of giving birth to a male character with a

feeling for books; there's the boy from a broken home who finds solace in a corner of the public library, or the sexagenarian laborer whose disability sends him to community college where he secretly enjoys his first and last philosophy class.

I leave out those authors' names not to protect the innocent, but rather to appease my own incompetence. I mean, they're novelists, a job which thankfully limits their output. I read them as a journalist, horrified that anyone reading everything I ever wrote (dozens if not hundreds of pieces) all in a weekend would know me for the bumbler I am. And since I work mostly as a critic, a job with the inherent pitfall of coming up with fresh new ways to say "good" or "bad," I tremble at the thought that a Nexis search in my name would unearth something like 394 repetitions of the word "crummy" alone. Or that I have mentioned the cancelled television drama "My So-Called Life" at least eighteen times in the last two years, in everything from a review of the new album by Slayer to last week's meditation on the legacy of World War II. And it wasn't even my favorite show! Or the Elvis obsession: Said one academic after we appeared together on a public radio talk show devoted to the admittedly lame topic "defining cool," "You have some good ideas." (Thanks!) "But you have got to get over Elvis." The truth is, I live in a cozy little world of pop music and TV shows and my writing will reflect this. Still, it could be worse. I switched to words after a teen fling with composing orchestral music. One reason I quit the symphonic life was the claustrophobia of being locked into the chromatic scale—twelve measly notes. I didn't want to spend the next fifty years beating the perfect fifth to death. Not that English is the most choice-happy language to get stuck with. (Though ending sentences in prepositions certainly expands one's options.) I'm reminded of the multilingual space aliens in Jonathan Lethem's novel *Girl in Landscape*—a book I actually paid cash money for. [note: symmetry unplanned, but appreciated—Ed.] The Archbuilders, as they're called, come from a planet with around fifteen thousand native languages. Each Archbuilder speaks hundreds of tongues. They are said to be fascinated with English, however, because "Archbuilders describe English as a language of enchanting limitations… English words seem, to an Archbuilder, garishly overloaded with meaning." How generous! I feel better, don't you? Think I'll celebrate with the taste of beer. In the Archbuilder scenario, then, falling back on my old friend "crummy" might not be the failing of a lazybones on deadline, but rather a jacaranda in bloom, bursting with the pale-purple flowers of significance.

SARAH VOWELL
CHICAGO, ILLINOIS
1999

P.S. I am not wearing makeup, because I need none.

DEAR EDITOR,

I'm still at the convention. Characters Unlimited makes cute animatronic dummies—life-sized plastic Santa Clauses and wizards that talk and move. Steve Jenkins, the company's sales rep, told me that the company's target market isn't so much amusement parks as shops and arcades, and that they make their characters to order—they cost a few thousand dollars apiece.

I asked Jenkins about the oddest request the company's ever filled.

He didn't have to think; he pulled out a photo album and began to flip through it. "A guy in Wisconsin," he said. "His mother died, and he missed her. He wanted to put his head on her lap like he used to. So he sent us everything—photos of her, her false teeth, her underwear. And we made a replica of her."

He arrived at the page of photos devoted to this man, who looked to be in his mid-40s, cuddling up to his prosthetic mother. "He put her in a rocking chair in the living room," Jenkins said.

TIM CARVELL
NEW YORK, NEW YORK
1999

DEAR MCSWEENEY'S,

No, I'm afraid I still don't have anything to submit to your upcoming issue. So instead of submitting a complete work, because I don't see that happening anytime soon, I thought I might submit a working list of stories which I have recently or not so recently quit, abandoned, or forsaken, complete with short summaries of each failed effort, in order to give you some idea why they've been sent down. Besides, I like listing. It cheers me up. Though, of course, this list will serve only as a sample of what I might've submitted, had I finished any of these particular stories, and is no way intended to reflect the vast killing fields of my hard drive.

Most recently, as of this past month or two, or last July—July, 1999, to be exact—I quit working on a story that's currently untitled. There are two reasons why this story doesn't have a working title, and why it's not officially untitled, like, say, Untitled #1, either: the first reason being that I rejected this story's first working title, "Animals Are Our Friends," and the second working title, though much improved, "The Second Coming of Ethel Merman," was, likewise, rejected. In any case, that story begins:

> My daughter bats headless chickens out of the trees with an old broom.

Of course, there's more to it than that sentence, like eight or nine pages more, but due to nagging syntactical doubts with the first sentence, I've put that story on the back burner for the time being. (Long ago, I bought into that idea that no one will read beyond a first sentence; it's make or break, you know; so I put a lot of pressure on the perfect first sentence.) I really don't know why I should start worrying about syntax now, I never have before, but still. And I wouldn't say I've abandoned this story just yet, I'd prefer to say its fate is undecided.

Besides which, I'm extremely, extremely superstitious, when it comes to my writing. I honestly believe that I'm really asking for trouble, talking about a story, even mentioning a story before it's finished; so as a rule, I never talk about my stories with anyone; and the closer the acquaintance, the more liable I am to failure. But anyone at all, really. Like when I meet people, and they politely ask what I do, and I try to spit out something about writing, and if they should then ask about my writing, I just tell them, I'm sorry, I can't really talk about it, and we both seemed relieved. Anyway, that's the second reason why I can't talk about this story or call it by a proper title, really, as I'm not ready to give up on it

yet. Because every time I have ever discussed a story before it's finished, I've abandoned the story. So forget I mentioned it.

Coincidentally, the next story on my list also has a chicken theme, and it, too, falls into the category of unfinished-but-not-yet-completely-abandoned stories, a work in progress, a piece of non-fiction that I've simply called "Pinkie," for the lack of a proper title, and hoping to dodge the jinx, and so as not to confuse it with any other, for the past year or two. And, as of today, the story of Pinkie still begins:

> Honestly, there was no Pinkie, and Pinkie was certainly not my grandfather, though there was a doll called "Pinky," and a man called "Winky," and the true story of Joe "Winky" Edmunds is this: as a child, no more than five or six, Joe Edmunds and his older brother were playing in the yard during the time of slaughter, when the boys noticed the ax left cleft in the tree stump. So the elder brother dared the younger brother to a game of chicken, to place his left hand on the butchering block, and the younger brother accepted the dare. Not to be bested by his younger brother, the elder dared the younger to spread his fingers wide apart, and the younger accepted the dare. All right, then, I'm going to give you to the count of three, and then I'm going to swing, the elder said, focusing his aim. He thought, of course, the younger would flinch as soon as he moved the ax, so the elder brother, said, One...? The younger didn't move his finger. Then he said, Two...?

But still the younger didn't move a muscle. Finally, the elder brother said, This is your last warning, Are you going to move your hand or not? And his little brother just looked him in the eye. All right, then, Three…? he called, before he swung the ax, severing his little brother's last digit to the palm. As for Winky, Joe got the nickname by winking his maimed hand hello and goodbye. No, though I once claimed Winky, or rather, Pinky, to be my grandfather, he was not; Winky was my grandfather's lifelong best friend, and close to blood, but not really.

I haven't really got a handle or even an angle, for that matter, on this story; as is, it trails off, shortly thereafter. What's more, what I've just shared happens to be the truth, so part of the problem is that there isn't exactly any fiction to the story, just yet. I really have no idea where it might lead, once I begin to twist into some form of fiction, but I think it's pretty flexible, and it could go in any direction.

Case in point, and this isn't a story, per se, it's just a related anecdote of sorts… A year or two ago, I told this anecdote to a new acquaintance, who then, a few nights later—the very next night, in fact—accused me of threatening to castrate him. Before I could even tell him the truth, that Winky was not my grandfather, nor was Pinky, though Pinky was a Madame Alexander doll I named in honor of Winky Edmunds, because she was suitably dressed in a pink chiffon gown with a pale pink bonnet and her precious little fingers were curled, such that the last fingers couldn't be seen… Well, before I could explain myself or the truth, my acquaintance accused me of threatening to castrate him. I was shocked; I didn't know where to begin. When did I threaten to castrate you? I asked, assuming he must be joking. Pinky: the story of Pinky was obviously a threat to castrate me, he claimed, in utter seriousness, taking another bite of his cone.

Here's what I want to know: Why in the world would said man ask me out for a drink (and later, ice cream) if he honestly—honestly believed I was threatening to castrate him? Really, what would possess him? Something definitely doesn't sound right. And I'm not asking you to believe me, and I know I can be pretty roundabout, but still, if I were going to threaten to castrate a man, why wouldn't I just come out and say so? I tried to figure it out, I mean, from his point of view, maybe he was thinking that I was insinuating that I was like the older brother, and he was the younger brother? But even if that was the case, how did we get from his thumb to his balls? I don't see it. But still, part of the reason I backed off from writing about Pinky or Winky or trying to write anything related was the fear of how many male readers might also misunderstand and incorrectly assume I was threatening to castrate them as well. Still, I swear, if I were even going to try and fictionalize my threat, I'd just put my cards on the table, like, off the top of my head, oh:

> Much to my surprise, John invited me out for a drink the day after I threatened to castrate him.

For the record, John is not the man's real name. And of course I still deny threatening him, so. The only question that remains is, Could there be a story in what I see to be the obvious answer to this guy's conclusion? I mean, that could be a pretty interesting story, some guy who invites a woman out for beer and Haagen Dazs after she's threatened to castrate him, don't you think? And I'd especially enjoy reading the story if someone else would write it for me. Really, comedy or horror, Southern Gothic, Western, or on the road, it could just be so fucked up and excellent, I think. If someone wants to borrow the idea, by all means, please be my guest. If they want, they can even borrow the first working title I rejected, which I was also considering rejecting as the first sentence of the story, before I abandoned the idea:

> "Do you think it's because they don't get enough light, over there, the English?"

Mm, but you know what, I'm not in favor of opening with dialogue. I don't know where this bias came from. Well, actually, I know perfectly well—no idea why I fibbed about that either—it's no great secret that this dialogue bias came from some interview I read during an especially nonproductive period; a writer who said he hates stories that begin with dialogue, and I guess I thought, Oh, God, I better not begin with dialogue, or there will be another person in the world who'll hate my story just as much as I do, from the very start. It was one of the Harrys, who said that, either Harry Mathews or Harry Crews, and I used to confuse the two, but now I simply don't remember which. But to this day, I still don't open with dialogue and I still get hung up on first

sentences. Of course I realize I place far too much importance on writing a great first sentence, but as often as I write them, wouldn't you think the odds would be in my favor?

As for the other non-fiction possibility, that non-fiction piece that we once discussed, just before I guess you forgot to write me back or lost my email again, the tentatively working titled, "Red Hot Variations." So titled because our school colors were red and white, and "Red Hot," the cheer, itself, was always a big crowd pleasing cheer, and there were no less than four variations on this particular number, including, "Red hot! Red HOT! R-e-d-h-o-t, once it stars, it never stops...," indeed, and a far simpler title, at least less of a mouthful, than its competitor, "The (Domo Arigato) 'Mr. Roboto' Debacle"—don't ask. It was an essay which began, or rather, which would prove a painfully honest essay on the subject of cheerleading:

> Of course, there are some things that I choose to forget. In particular: cheerleading. Because I could never truly forget that I was once a cheerleader, I simply chose to forget the fact. And in less than five years after the fact, I remembered having been a cheerleader so infrequently, it was as though I had completely forgotten; and less than ten years later, it was as though I'd forgotten cheerleading for so long that it had simply never happened to me. (In fact, I forgot so successfully that only I just remembered that I was not once a cheerleader, but twice, actually: seventh and eighth grade; wrestling and basketball, respectively.) Regardless, for the past

several years, I could hear or read mention of cheerleading, literally or figuratively, without any recollection; and without any personal recollection of having once been a cheerleader, myself, I could even watch professional, collegiate, and high school cheerleaders, live or televised, with interest, curiosity, and bemusement.

For example, a few months ago (a year ago, now), when an article in *Women Outside* about the Collegiate Cheerleading Championship happened to catch my eye, I began to read the article, genuinely interested to know what compelled these young women to cheer. Coincidentally, my boyfriend Daniel was friends with the writer, and as he walked by, he noticed the article, and remembered having heard mention of the assignment. How is it? he asked, glancing over my shoulder, seeming equally interested and enthusiastic. Well, I think Marshall's perfectly intelligent, and frankly, I expected more of him, I said, shrugging, then reading aloud:

Daytona Beach is a killing field—so smiles, people, smiles! Christie Neal, a University of Louisville co-captain, looks over at one of the hulking guys on her squad. She knows instinctively that he needs a word of support, for she has the experience. At twenty-two, she has been on two championship teams already, as many as any cheerleader ever. She is blond and ninety-six pounds. Her waist, from the looks of it, is seven epidermal layers thicker

than a spinal column. She locks eyes with the boy, gauging the type of motivation he requires at this instant. A flurry of ideas and emotions races through her mind until a well-earned wisdom settles across her features. She leans forward; her shoulders recoil and the corners of her mouth begin to burst apart. "Get jiggy with it!" she shrieks instructively. "Get jiiigggyyy with iiiiiittttt!"

For she has the experience, I enunciated, nodding my head: a flurry of ideas and emotions races through her mind until a well-earned wisdom settles... Get jiggy with it. Huh... Is—is that... sarcasm? I mocked, tapping my index finger against my lips, before losing all interest, and tossing the publication across the table. You know, I don't think there's anything wrong with a little insight, once in a while, I concluded, sitting down beside Daniel on the couch, as he looked at me curiously for a moment, and then gave my shoulder a supportive squeeze. No further comment; the article was immediately forgotten. And to this day, my boyfriend still doesn't know the truth about my past. (Now he does; I had to tell him.) But now that I remember, and in all fairness to the writer, I should also admit that I've been asked, hypothetically, were I to have a daughter, one day, what would be the most frightening, the most horrific image of a daughter I could possibly imagine? To which I have answered, without hesitation: a cheerleader—that would be my worst nightmare, hands down.

Part of the problem with writing this cheerleading essay thing was that I knew, as soon as I wrote even this much, I knew that it was really about cowboys; cheerleading was just the natural segue, because naturally, I can't talk about one without discussing the other—just forget that one, too, the cowboy idea. See what I mean, though —I hexed myself with an actual title and discussion. Even though I didn't write enough to get to this part, the long and short of it is that last I heard, Kip Kilstrom, the one who used to hang his girlfriends from their Wrangler jeans' pant loops from the top ledge of our school lockers, he was still in prison for wife battery, out West, and that's why he was not able to attend the class ten-year high school reunion (I didn't attend, either, but it was the reunion that reminded me of cowboys and thereby, cheerleading, and then, several months later, that article). But I just remembered her name, the name of the eighth grade cheerleader who he and several of his friends held down in the back of the bus and tore off her red cheerleading bloomers: her name was Andrea. I haven't remembered her in years.

Well. Next on the list is "Naked." What's most unusual about this particular story is that I finished it—yes!— although, taking a second look, I didn't like it, and I soon grew to loathe the story, so I sent it down. It's pretty self-explanatory, but still, the story line is basically this: a woman answers her front door naked, and the postman doesn't take any notice, and she feels such a loss that she hits the streets; walks straight out her front door. Now this story

came out of a three-month dry spell. Months passed without a single sentence on my computer screen, and the related depression.

Friends tried to help, first by offering encouragement, then empathy, then sympathy, then condolences, seeing that I was inconsolable and I simply would not be convinced out of my thoroughly morbid funk, and finally, one night, talking on the phone, a friend suggested an exercise in spontaneity, to which I agreed because I was so incredibly despondent and desperate, I would've agreed to anything, even that, even though it sounded hokey and kind of humiliating, like that's how bad it was, you know, that's how low I'd sunk, and so the idea was that he threw me a sentence, or even just an opening, or a few words, max, and I just had to respond; finish the sentence. He suggested, A woman crossed the room... What next? Your turn, he said. So, A woman crossed a room, became, The woman crossed the room, naked... Well, actually, before that edit occurred, I asked him if he couldn't give me a better sentence, start things off on the right foot? He had to give me something better to work with, I said, and then I argued that I didn't like that sentence and I wouldn't write that sentence, to begin; it didn't sound at all like the sort of thing I'd say... He managed to persist, that time, even though I said The woman crossed sounded better than A woman crossed. And as to why the woman has to be crossing some nondescript room for no apparent reason, naked, write it off to yet another failure of my imagination. Against all odds, I finished that story, though.

I just looked, a minute ago, but I can't seem to find that file or the print out, I must've thrown them both away. I seem to remember it went something to the effect:

> The woman crossed the room, naked, but the postman took no notice, handing her a pink slip...

It went something like that. But like I said, I sent this story down not only because I didn't like it, but also because it had no plot and not much action and nothing really happened. In short, it just didn't hold my attention from the very beginning, you know. Before I rejected it, though, I submitted it to a reputable publication, but of course it was rejected, and then I simply agreed with that assessment. For a while, after the publication's rejection, I was thinking that maybe I'd rewrite the story; change the woman to a man, see what happened. But in truth, now I think that would interest me even less.

Maybe it was the naked story that led to "August" (absolutely no recollection why I titled it that, but I'm fairly predictable, so maybe I began the story in the month of August?), which was loosely based on these upstairs neighbors I used to have, a NYU girl and her boyfriend who were involved in the classic screaming sex/screaming argument cycle, waking me in the middle of the night, breaking windows and leaving a trail of broken glass in my old courtyard. Cliché, I know, but honestly, these two were so loud that I once heard their passion from the mailroom—in another building. Three hundred square feet studios separated by eight-foot ceilings, your neighbors are literally on top of you. And because I, for one, have never heard such a talker in my life— she really had a script, this one, you know, Oh god! Oh, there! There, there! Do it to me! Stick your big hot cock...

I always lost it with that "hot cock" part, I couldn't help but laugh, so I'd cover my mouth, you know, and then I'd think, Why am I covering my mouth? Besides, how could they hear me if I couldn't even hear myself laughing over them?

Well, the humor of the situation wore thin after a few weeks. I'd just be minding my own business, trying to drink my coffee, it just got to be too much... So the first time I heard them from the mail room, I thought it was a joke, you know, a bad porn imitation, with all the heat and the sticking, and never simply, pussy, always with the my wet pussy—had to be a joke, I thought. But no. After a few months of that, those two were openly discussed amongst my other neighbors, returning from work, all of us checking our mail, trying not to laugh; a line up of shaking shoulders at the mail boxes, as we sifted bills. To be honest, one night, a few of us got into a karaoke contest during their act. Actually, it got to the point that I could call friends and hold out the phone, with my arm raised, the phone reached within a foot or two of their window, which was always open (I had mentioned it so many times that friends insisted I call them, so I did). If my friends were on another line at their respective jobs, I had ample time to call their personal answering machines. As for my neighbors, last I heard, they'd become engaged, apparently, because the girl wrote "The Future Mrs. So-and-So," across her name in the mailroom: gag.

Well, back to the story, so far, it's proven to be a very short story, with the protagonist ending up on her fire escape, where a crowd's gathered to listen, and the crowd mistaking the protagonist for the source of the disturbance. I know that doesn't sound very interesting, and maybe I'm not describing it well, but at least there is an ending to speak of. I'm willing to give the ending the benefit of the doubt, because, having finished a complete draft, I showed this story to a friend, and he said, "The ending's great, but the beginning's not strange enough." And I had to agree with him, there was a problem with the beginning, but then I couldn't think of anything particularly strange. Nevertheless, this story remains on my list, that is, accessible, in case a really strange introduction should ever occur.

And as far as my questionable behavior, I do realize that I probably should've called the management company, but I didn't know how to state my complaint to Robert Gordon (he was kind of sleazy anyway, one of those skinny guys who lives in New York and wears tight jeans with cowboy boots and plaid hunting jackets, nice enough but definitely on the sleazy side; the occupancy of our building was like 90 per cent female, and I'd have to say, by and large, very attractive women). I guess it called for a level of maturity I lacked, so then I considered calling when Robert Gordon wasn't there, after five, so I wouldn't have to feel awkward or embarrassed or like the sex police or something, which led me to thinking I should just leave him a message, or, assuming he wouldn't be able to fully appreciate the severity of the situation, because it had to be heard to be believed, maybe I'd let him hear just how bad it really was, because those two kept all hours, five, six, seven, I could call anytime, but then he wouldn't know who left the message, either, because I couldn't talk over them. Maybe that's where the story should begin, with Robert Gordon receiving an obscene voice mail at the office, but by now,

I'm at peace with its abandonment.

Next on the list, "Sleep." It's been a while, and now that I look at it, I have no idea what this story is about. Sleep? Absolutely no idea what the hell I was talking about. I don't know, maybe I wasn't even referring to a story idea…? Never mind. Oh—right! I remember. "Sleep"—of course, sleep—sleep, how could I forget the sleeping beauties story?

See, I once had an acquaintance who put herself through school stripping. I know it's pretty cliché, so far, but here's the catch: my acquaintance once told me that the worst thing that ever happened to her on the job was the day she fell asleep on the stage, because she'd been out all night, and no one was there, in the club, when she got out on the stage, so she lay down for a moment and then she dozed off, and when she finally woke, there were a dozen men, masturbating, simply watching her sleep, fully clothed in her Catholic school uniform or her cheerleading skirt or whatever it was. (Of course I was concerned for her well-being, but by the time she told me, she'd moved on, and it's an awful thing, I know, but I've always regretted not asking her to describe the scene for me.) For her, though, that was an incredible violation of her privacy. And considering the way things ebb and flow, I've always been fascinated with the idea of a sleeping fad overtaking the strip club scene. Like if the industries were plagued with Ambien addiction, I don't know. Then again, I guess enough time has passed since she first told me that story, with so few details to work with and my own inability to translate her experience, or even my own experience of what she told me, that I'm not longer intrigued by the idea at all.

I'm currently at work on the last

story on the list, and I'm playing with fire, here, but I'll tell you a little about that story, anyway. Several years ago, I read this interview with a porn star that specialized in gangbanging. The article included a photo of her at an event in which she had sex with about three hundred men at one time, and there she was, on her back, smiling at the camera (a brunette, actually). I've never gotten that smile out of my head, it was so genuine: she wasn't porn pouting or anything; you could even see her gums. And sometimes, when I see something in the papers, like that former Wall Street investor who's being investigated for leaking information to a XXX porn queen, if that wasn't a match made in heaven, or whatever, I'll think of her smile. My only question—well, I have many, many questions, actually, but still—my question is this: Where does one go from there? You know what I mean? So that's where I thought I'd begin. Right now, the unofficial working title is, "The Former World Record Holder Settles Down," and it's nothing fancy, but I have a first sentence, as well:

I don't bowl for fun.

It's not going to win any awards, that sentence, but I think it's all right, for now. Well, anyway, I have a good start on this story, and I'm extremely hopeful. I'll let you know.
COURTNEY ELDRIDGE
New York, New York
2000

DEAR MCSWEENEY'S,
Hello, it is me, Morgan Phillips. I was working on something for your publication/s, but then I stopped. The piece described a situation I was very

angry about, but then I stopped being angry about it, and instead became sort of sad. That's when I stopped working on the piece.

Also, the a capella group has been taking up much of my time. Complicated harmonies, and boisterous camaraderie. You know.

A "pal" of mine died recently, and I wrote a eulogy. It occurred to me that you might want to put it in your publication/s. Perhaps on the cover. Out of respect.

If you are not able to use it, please write me a brief, irreverent note of rejection. At the end, type the following: :)

That way I'll know.
MORGAN PHILLIPS
New York City
1999

EULOGY FOR CARLOS
by MORGAN PHILLIPS

CARLOS SMELLED like peanut butter. He did his business once a day, at about six in the morning. He didn't need to eat much, maybe half a sandwich and one of those box juices.

Usually people toss a dirty son of a gun a quarter and they feel Christian for the rest of the month. Not with Carlos. One look at him and they'd dig deep. Twenties, sometimes. He'd just sit there, clinking his change, wheezing through the harmonica. The harmonica was my idea.

After Carlos died I had a dream about him. He said that he missed me, and I started crying. He was floating in the air, like a little baby angel. That was the most beautiful dream I'll ever have.

I'm not going to say where I buried him. It didn't take long at all, him being so compact. One day a scientist is going to dig up his bones and get really excited.

THE CEILING

by KEVIN BROCKMEIER

THERE WAS A SKY that day, sun-rich and open and blue. A raft of silver clouds was floating along the horizon, and robins and sparrows were calling from the trees. It was my son Joshua's seventh birthday and we were celebrating in our back yard. He and the children were playing on the swing set, and Melissa and I were sitting on the deck with the parents. Earlier that afternoon, a balloon and gondola had risen from the field at the end of our block, sailing past us with an exhalation of fire. Joshua told his friends that he knew the pilot. "His name is Mister Clifton," he said, as they tilted their heads back and slowly revolved in place. "I met him at the park last year. He took me into the air with him and let me drop a soccer ball into a swimming pool. We almost hit a helicopter. He told me he'd come by on my birthday." Joshua shielded his eyes against the sun. "Did you see him wave?" he asked. "He just waved at me."

This was a story.

The balloon drifted lazily away, turning to expose each delta and crease of its fabric, and we listened to the children resuming their play. Mitch Nauman slipped his sunglasses into his shirt pocket. "Ever notice how kids their age will handle a toy?" he said. Mitch was our next-door neighbor. He was the single father of Bobby Nauman, Joshua's strange best friend. His other best friend, Chris Boschetti, came from a family of cosmetics executives. My wife had taken to calling them "Rich and Strange."

Mitch pinched the front of his shirt between his fingers and fanned himself with it. "The actual function of the toy is like some sort of obstacle," he said. "They'll dream up a new use for everything in the world."

I looked across the yard at the swing set: Joshua was trying to shinny up one of the A-poles; Taylor Tugwell and Sam Yoo were standing on the teeter swing; Adam Smithee was tossing fistfuls of pebbles onto the slide and watching them rattle to the ground.

My wife tipped one of her sandals onto the grass with the ball of her foot. "Playing as you should isn't Fun," she said: "it's Design." She parted her toes around the front leg of Mitch's lawn chair. He leaned back into the sunlight, and her calf muscles tautened.

My son was something of a disciple of flying things. On his bedroom wall were posters of fighter planes and wild birds. A model of a helicopter was chandeliered to his ceiling. His birthday cake, which sat before me on the picnic table, was decorated with a picture of a rocket ship—a silver white missile with discharging thrusters. I had been hoping that the baker would place a few stars in the frosting as well (the cake in the catalog was dotted with yellow candy sequins), but when I opened the box I found that they were missing. So this is what I did: as Joshua stood beneath the swing set, fishing for something in his pocket, I planted his birthday candles deep in the cake. I pushed them in until each wick was surrounded by only a shallow bracelet of wax. Then I called the children over from the swing set. They came tearing up divots in the grass.

We sang happy birthday as I held a match to the candles.

Joshua closed his eyes.

"Blow out the stars," I said, and his cheeks rounded with air.

That night, after the last of the children had gone home, my wife and I sat outside drinking, each of us wrapped in a separate silence. The city lights were burning, and Joshua was sleeping in his room. A nightjar gave one long trill after another from somewhere above us.

Melissa added an ice cube to her glass, shaking it against the others until it whistled and cracked. I watched a strand of cloud break apart in the sky. The moon that night was bright and full, but after a while it began to seem damaged to me, marked by some small inaccuracy. It took me a moment to realize why this was: against its blank white surface was a square of perfect darkness. The square was without blemish or flaw, no larger than a child's tooth, and I could not tell whether it rested on the moon itself or hovered above it like a cloud. It looked as if a window had been opened clean through the floor of the rock, presenting to view a stretch of empty space. I had never seen such a thing before.

"What is that?" I said.

Melissa made a sudden noise, a deep, defeated little oh.

"My life is a mess," she said.

Within a week, the object in the night sky had grown perceptibly larger. It would appear at sunset, when the air was dimming to purple, as a faint granular blur, a certain filminess at the high point of the sky, and would remain there through the night. It blotted out the light of passing stars and seemed to travel across the face of the moon, but it did not move. The people of my town were uncertain as to whether the object was spreading or approaching—we could see only that it was getting bigger—and this matter gave rise to much speculation. Gleason the butcher insisted that it wasn't there at all, that it was only an illusion. "It all has to do with the satellites," he said. "They're bending the light from that place like a lens. It just looks like something's there." But though his manner was relaxed and he spoke with conviction, he would not look up from his cutting board.

The object was not yet visible during the day, but we could feel it above us as we woke to the sunlight each morning: there was a tension and strain to the air, a shift in its customary balance. When we stepped from our houses to go to work, it was as if we were walking through a new sort of gravity, harder and stronger, not so yielding.

As for Melissa, she spent several weeks pacing the house from room to room. I watched her fall into a deep abstraction. She had cried into her pillow the night of Joshua's birthday, shrinking away from me beneath the blankets. "I just need to sleep," she said, as I sat above her and rested my hand on her side. "Please. Lie down. Stop hovering." I soaked a washcloth for her in the cold water of the bathroom sink, folding it into quarters and leaving it on her night stand in a porcelain bowl.

The next morning, when I found her in the kitchen, she was gathering a coffee filter into a little wet sachet. "Are you feeling better?" I asked.

"I'm fine." She pressed the foot lever of the trash can, and its lid popped open with a rustle of plastic.

"Is it Joshua?"

Melissa stopped short, holding the pouch of coffee in her outstretched hand. "What's wrong with Joshua?" she said. There was a note of concern in her voice.

"He's seven now," I told her. When she didn't respond, I continued with,

"You don't look a day older than when we met, honey. You know that, don't you?"

She gave a puff of air through her nose—this was a laugh, but I couldn't tell what she meant to express by it, bitterness or judgment or some kind of easy cheer. "It's not Joshua," she said, and dumped the coffee into the trash can. "But thanks all the same."

It was the beginning of July before she began to ease back into the life of our family. By this time, the object in the sky was large enough to eclipse the full moon. Our friends insisted that they had never been able to see any change in my wife at all, that she had the same style of speaking, the same habits and twists and eccentricities as ever. This was, in a certain sense, true. I noticed the difference chiefly when we were alone together. After we had put Joshua to bed, we would sit with one another in the living room, and when I asked her a question, or when the telephone rang, there was always a certain brittleness to her, a hesitancy of manner that suggested she was hearing the world from across a divide. It was clear to me at such times that she had taken herself else-where, that she had constructed a shelter from the wood and clay and stone of her most intimate thoughts and stepped inside, shutting the door. The only question was whether the person I saw tinkering at the window was opening the latches or sealing the cracks.

One Saturday morning, Joshua asked me to take him to the library for a story reading. It was almost noon, and the sun was just beginning to darken at its zenith. Each day, the shadows of our bodies would shrink toward us from the west, vanish briefly in the midday soot, and stretch away into the east, falling off the edge of the world. I wondered sometimes if I would ever see my reflection pooled at my feet again. "Can Bobby come, too?" Joshua asked as I tightened my shoes.

I nodded, pulling the laces up in a series of butterfly loops. "Why don't you run over and get him," I said, and he sprinted off down the hallway.

Melissa was sitting on the front porch steps, and I knelt down beside her as I left. "I'm taking the boys into town," I said. I kissed her cheek and rubbed the base of her neck, felt the cirrus curls of hair there moving back and forth through my fingers.

"Shh." She held a hand out to silence me. "Listen."

The insects had begun to sing, the birds to fall quiet. The air gradually became filled with a peaceful chirring noise.

"What are we listening for?" I whispered.

Melissa bowed her head for a moment, as if she were trying to keep count of something. Then she looked up at me. In answer, and with a sort of weariness about her, she spread her arms open to the world.

Before I stood to leave, she asked me a question: "We're not all that much alike, are we?" she said.

The plaza outside the library was paved with red brick. Dogwood trees were planted in hollows along the perimeter, and benches of distressed metal stood here and there on concrete pads. A member of a local guerrilla theater troupe was delivering a recitation from beneath a streetlamp; she sat behind a wooden desk, her hands folded one atop the other, and spoke as if into a camera. "Where did this object come from?" she said. "What is it, and when will it stop its descent? How did we find ourselves in this place? Where do we go from here? Scientists are baffled. In an interview with this station, Dr. Stephen Mandruzzato, head of the prestigious Horton Institute of Astronomical Studies, had this to say: 'We don't know. We don't know. We just don't know.'" I led Joshua and Bobby Nauman through the heavy dark glass doors of the library, and we took our seats in the Children's Reading Room. The tables were set low to the ground so that my legs pressed flat against the underside, and the air carried that peculiar, sweetened-milk smell of public libraries and elementary schools. Bobby Nauman began to play the Where Am I? game with Joshua. "Where am I?" he would ask, and then he'd warm-and-cold Joshua around the room until Joshua had found him. First he was in a potted plant, then on my shirt collar, then beneath the baffles of an air vent.

After a time, the man who was to read to us moved into place. He said hello to the children, coughed his throat clear, and opened his book to the title page: "Chicken Little," he began.

As he read, the sky grew bright with afternoon. The sun came through the windows in a sheet of fire.

Joshua started the second grade in September. His new teacher mailed us a list of necessary school supplies, which we purchased the week before classes began—pencils and a utility box, glue and facial tissues, a ruler and a notebook and a tray of watercolor paints. On his first day, Melissa shot a photograph of Joshua waving to her from the front door, his backpack wreathed over his shoulder and a lunch sack in his right hand. He stood in the flash of hard white light, then kissed her good-bye and joined Rich and Strange in the car pool.

Autumn passed in its slow, sheltering way, and toward the end of November, Joshua's teacher asked the class to write a short essay describing a community of local animals. The paragraph Joshua wrote was captioned "What Happened to the Birds." We fastened it to the refrigerator with magnets.

There were many birds here before, but now there gone. Nobody knows where they went. I used to see them in the trees. I fed one at the zoo when I was litle. It was big. The birds went away when no one was looking. The trees are quiet now. They do not move.

All of this was true. As the object in the sky became visible during the daylight—and as, in the tide of several months, it descended over our town—the birds and migrating insects disappeared. I did not notice they were gone, though, nor the muteness with which the sun rose in the morning, nor the stillness of the grass and trees, until I read Joshua's essay.

The world at this time was full of confusion and misgiving and unforeseen changes of heart. One incident that I recall clearly took place in the Main Street Barber Shop on a cold winter Tuesday. I was sitting in a pneumatic chair while Wesson the barber trimmed my hair. A nylon gown was draped over my body to catch the cuttings, and I could smell the peppermint of Wesson's chewing gum. "So how 'bout this weather?" he chuckled, working away at my crown.

Weather gags had been circulating through our offices and barrooms ever since the object—which was as smooth and reflective as obsidian glass, and which the newspapers had designated "the ceiling"—had descended to the level of the cloud base. I gave my usual response, "A little overcast today, wouldn't you say?" and Wesson barked an appreciative laugh.

Wesson was one of those men who had passed his days waiting for the rest of his life to come about. He busied himself with his work, never marrying, and doted on the children of his customers. "Something's bound to happen soon," he would often say at the end of a conversation, and there was a quickness to his eyes that demonstrated his implicit faith in the proposition. When his mother died, this faith seemed to abandon him. He went home each evening to the small house that they had shared, shuffling cards or paging through a magazine until he fell asleep. Though he never failed to laugh when a customer was at hand, the eyes he wore became empty and white, as if some essential fire in them had been spent. His enthusiasm began to seem like desperation. It was only a matter of time.

"How's the pretty lady?" he asked me.

I was watching him in the mirror, which was both parallel to and coextensive with a mirror on the opposite wall. "She hasn't been feeling too well," I said. "But I think she's coming out of it."

"Glad to hear it. Glad to hear it," he said. "And business at the hardware store?"

I told him that business was fine. I was on my lunch break.

The bell on the door handle gave a tink, and a current of cold air sent a little eddy of cuttings across the floor. A man we had never seen before leaned into the room. "Have you seen my umbrella?" he said. "I can't find my umbrella, have you seen it?" His voice was too loud—high and sharp, fluttery with worry—and his hands shook with a distinct tremor.

"Can't say that I have," said Wesson. He smiled emptily, showing his teeth, and his fingers tensed around the back of my chair.

There was a sudden feeling of weightlessness to the room.

"You wouldn't tell me anyway, would you?" said the man. "Jesus," he said. "You people."

Then he took up the ashtray stand and slammed it against the window.

A cloud of gray cinders shot out around him, but the window merely shuddered in its frame. He let the stand fall to the floor and it rolled into a magazine rack. Ash drizzled to the ground. The man brushed a cigarette butt from his jacket. "You people," he said again, and he left through the open glass door.

As I walked home later that afternoon, the scent of barbershop talcum blew from my skin in the winter wind. The plane of the ceiling was stretched across the firmament, covering my town from end to end, and I could see the lights of a thousand streetlamps caught like constellations in its smooth black polish. It occurred to me that if nothing were to change, if the ceiling were simply to hover where it was forever, we might come to forget that it was even there, charting for ourselves a new map of the night sky.

Mitch Nauman was leaving my house when I arrived. We passed on the lawn, and he held up Bobby's knapsack. "He leaves this thing everywhere," he said. "Buses. Your house. The schoolroom. Sometimes I think I should tie it to his belt." Then he cleared his throat. "New haircut? I like it."

"Yeah, it was getting a bit shaggy."

He nodded and made a clicking noise with his tongue. "See you next time," he said, and he vanished through his front door, calling to Bobby to climb down from something.

By the time the object had fallen as low as the tree spires, we had noticed the acceleration in the wind. In the thin strip of space between the ceiling and the pavement, it narrowed and kindled and collected speed. We could hear it buffeting the walls of our houses at night, and it produced a constant low sigh in the darkness of movie halls. People emerging from their doorways could be seen to brace themselves against the charge and pressure of it. It was as if our entire town were an alley between tall buildings.

I decided one Sunday morning to visit my parents' gravesite: the cemetery in which they were buried would spread with knotgrass every spring, and it was necessary to tend their plot before the weeds grew too thick. The house was still peaceful as I showered and dressed, and I stepped as quietly as I could across the bath mat and the tile floor. I watched the water in the toilet bowl rise and fall as gusts of wind channeled their way through the pipes. Joshua and Melissa were asleep, and the morning sun flashed at the horizon and disappeared.

At the graveyard, a small boy was tossing a tennis ball into the air as his mother swept the dirt from a memorial tablet. He was trying to touch the ceiling with it, and with each successive throw he drew a bit closer, until, at the height of its climb, the ball jarred to one side before it dropped. The cemetery was otherwise empty, its monuments and trees the only material presence.

My parents' graves were clean and spare. With such scarce sunlight, the knotgrass had failed to blossom, and there was little tending for me to do. I combed the plot for leaves and stones and pulled the rose stems from the flower wells. I knelt at the headstone they shared and unfastened a zipper of moss from it. Sitting there, I imagined for a moment that my parents were living together atop the ceiling: they were walking through a field of high yellow grass, beneath the sun and the sky and the tousled white clouds, and she was bending in her dress to examine a flower, and he was bending beside her, his hand on her waist, and they were unaware that the world beneath them was settling to the ground.

When I got home, Joshua was watching television on the living room sofa, eating a plump yellow doughnut from a paper towel. A dollop of jelly had fallen onto the back of his hand. "Mom left to run an errand," he said.

The television picture fluttered and curved for a moment, sending spits of rain across the screen, then it recrystallized. An aerial transmission tower had collapsed earlier that week—the first of many such fallings in our town—and the quality of our reception had been diminishing ever since.

"I had a dream last night," Joshua said. "I dreamed that I dropped my bear through one of the grates on the sidewalk." He owned a worn-down cotton teddy bear, its seams looped with clear plastic stitches, that he had been given as a toddler. "I tried to catch him, but I missed. Then I lay down on the ground and stretched out my arm for him. I was reaching through the grate, and when I looked beneath the sidewalk, I could see another part of the city. There were people moving around down there. There were cars and streets and bushes and lights. The sidewalk was some sort of bridge, and in my dream I thought, 'Oh yeah. Now why didn't I remember that?' Then I tried to climb through to get my bear, but I couldn't lift the grate up."

The morning weather forecaster was weeping on the television.

"Do you remember where this place was?" I asked.

"Yeah."

"Maybe down by the bakery?" I had noticed Melissa's car parked there a few times, and I remembered a kid tossing pebbles into the grate.

"That's probably it."

"Want to see if we can find it?"

Joshua pulled at the lobe of his ear for a second, staring into the middle distance. Then he shrugged his shoulders. "Okay," he decided.

I don't know what we expected to discover there. Perhaps I was simply seized by a whim—the desire to be spoken to, the wish to be instructed by a dream. When I was Joshua's age, I dreamed one night that I found a new door in my house, one that opened from my cellar onto the bright, aseptic aisles of a drugstore: I walked through it, and saw a flash of light, and found myself sitting up in bed. For several days after, I felt a quickening of possibility, like the touch of some other geography, whenever I passed by the cellar door. It was as if I'd opened my eyes to the true inward map of the world, projected according to our own beliefs and understandings.

On our way through the town center, Joshua and I waded past a cluster of people squinting into the horizon. There was a place between the post office and the library where the view to the west was occluded by neither hills nor buildings, and crowds often gathered there to watch the distant blue belt of the sky. We shouldered our way through and continued into town.

Joshua stopped outside the Kornblum Bakery, beside a trash basket and a newspaper carrel, where the light from two streetlamps lensed together on the ground. "This is it," he said, and made a gesture indicating the iron grate at our feet. Beneath it we could see the shallow basin of a drainage culvert. It was even and dry, and a few brittle leaves rested inside it.

"Well," I said. There was nothing there. "That's disappointing."

"Life's disappointing," said Joshua.

He was borrowing a phrase of his mother's, one that she had taken to using these last few months. Then, as if on cue, he glanced up and a light came into his eyes. "Hey," he said. "There's Mom."

Melissa was sitting behind the plate glass window of a restaurant on the opposite side of the street. I could see Mitch Nauman talking to her from across the table, his face soft and casual. Their hands were cupped together beside the pepper crib, and his shoes stood empty on the carpet. He was stroking her left leg with his right foot, its pad and arch curved around her calf. The image was as clear and exact as a melody.

I took Joshua by the shoulders. "What I want you to do," I said, "is knock on Mom's window. When she looks up, I want you to wave."

And he did exactly that—trotting across the asphalt, tapping a few times on the glass, and waving when Melissa started in her chair. Mitch Nauman let his foot fall to the carpet. Melissa found Joshua through the window. She crooked her head and gave him a tentative little flutter of her fingers. Then she met my eyes. Her hand stilled in the air. Her face seemed to fill suddenly with movement, then just as suddenly to empty—it reminded me of nothing so much as a flock of birds scattering from a lawn. I felt a kick of pain in my chest and called to Joshua from across the street. "Come on, sport," I said. "Let's go home."

It was not long after—early the next morning, before we awoke—that the town water tower collapsed, blasting a river of fresh water down our empty streets. Hankins the grocer, who had witnessed the event, gathered an audience that day to his lunch booth in the coffee shop: "I was driving past the tower when it happened," he said. "Heading in early to work. First I heard a creaking noise, and then I saw the leg posts buckling. Wham!"—he smacked the table with his palms—"So much water! It surged into the side of my car, and I lost control of the wheel. The stream carried me right down the road. I felt like a tiny paper boat." He smiled and held up a finger, then pressed it to the side of a half-empty soda can, tipping it gingerly onto its side. Coca-Cola washed across the table with a hiss of carbonation. We hopped from our seats to avoid the spill.

The rest of the town seemed to follow in a matter of days, falling to the ground beneath the weight of the ceiling. Billboards and streetlamps, chimneys and statues. Church steeples, derricks, and telephone poles. Klaxon rods and restaurant signs. Apartment buildings and energy pylons. Trees released a steady sprinkle of leaves and pine cones, then came timbering to the earth—those that were broad and healthy cleaving straight down the heartwood, those that were thin and pliant bending until they cracked. Maintenance workers installed panels of light along the sidewalk, routing the electricity through underground cables. The ceiling itself proved unassailable. It bruised fists and knuckles. It stripped the teeth from power saws. It broke drill bits. It extinguished flames. One afternoon the television antenna tumbled from my rooftop, landing on the hedges in a zigzag of wire. A chunk of plaster fell across the kitchen table as I was eating dinner that night. I heard a board split in the living room wall the next morning, and then another in the hallway, and then another in the bedroom. It sounded like gunshots detonating in a closed room. Melissa and Joshua were already waiting on the front lawn when I got there. A boy was standing on a heap of rubble across the street playing Atlas, his upraked shoulders supporting the world. A man on a stepladder was pasting a sign to the ceiling: SHOP AT CARSON'S. Melissa pulled her jacket tighter. Joshua took my sleeve. A trough spread open beneath the shingles of our roof, and we watched our house collapse into a mass of brick and mortar.

I was lying on the ground, a tree root pressing into the small of my back, and I shifted slightly to the side. Melissa was lying beside me, and Mitch Nauman beside her. Joshua and Bobby, who had spent much of the day crawling aimlessly about the yard, were asleep now at our feet. The ceiling was no higher than a coffee table, and I could see each pore of my skin reflected in its surface. Above the keening of the wind there was a tiny edge of sound—the hum of the sidewalk lights, steady, electric, and warm.

"Do you ever get the feeling that you're supposed to be someplace else?" said Melissa. She paused for a moment, perfectly still. "It's a kind of sudden dread," she said.

Her voice seemed to hover in the air for a moment.

I had been observing my breath for the last few hours on the polished undersurface of the ceiling: every time I exhaled, a mushroom-shaped fog would cover my reflection, and I found that I could control the size of this fog by adjusting the force and the speed of my breathing. When Melissa asked her question, the first I had heard from her in many days, I gave a sudden puff of air through my nose and two icicle-shaped blossoms appeared. Mitch Nauman whispered something into her ear, but his voice was no more than a murmur, and I could not make out the words. In a surge of emotion that I barely recognized, some strange combination of rivalry and adoration, I took her hand in my own and squeezed it. When nothing happened, I squeezed it again. I brought it to my chest, and I brought it to my mouth, and I kissed it and kneaded it and held it tight.

I was waiting to feel her return my touch, and I felt at that moment, felt with all my heart, that I could wait the whole life of the world for such a thing, until the earth and the sky met and locked and the distance between them closed forever.

SAINT CHOLA

by K. KVASHAY-BOYLE

SKATER. HESHER. TAGGER. Lesbo-Slut. Wanna-be. Dweeb. Fag. Prep. What-up. Bad-ass. Gangster. Dork. Nerd. Trendy. Freaky. In a few weeks it'll be solid like cement, but right now nobody knows yet. You might be anything. And here's an example: meet Mohammadee Sawy. Hypercolor T-shirt, oversized overalls with just one hook fastened, the other tossed carefree over the shoulder like it's no big thing. In walks Mohammadee, short and plump and brown, done up for the first day with long fluffy hair and a new mood ring, but guess what, it's not *Mohammadee* anymore. Nope, because dad's not signing you up today, you're all by yourself and when you get the form where it says Name, Grade, Homeroom, you look around and take the pen Ms. Yoshida hands you and you write it in big and permanent: Shala M. Sawy. And from now on that's who you are. Cool.

It's tough to do right but at least you learn what to want. You walk the halls and you see what's there. I want her jeans, I want her triple-pierce hoops, I want her strut, I want those boobs, I want that crowd, I want shoes like those, I want a wallet chain, I want a baby-doll dress, I want safety pins on my backpack, I want a necklace that says my name. Lipstick. I want lipstick. Jelly bracelets. Trainer bras from Target. It could be me. I could be anyone. KISS FM, POWER 106, Douche-bag, Horn-ball. Fanny packs! Biker shorts! And suddenly, wow, Shala realizes that she has a surge of power inside that she never knew was there. Shala realizes that she's walking around and she's thinking Yup, cool, or No way! Lame!

Shala? That sounds good. And that's just the way tiny Mrs. Furukawa says it in homeroom when she calls roll. She says *Shala.* And Shala Mohammadee Sawy? She smiles. (But not so much as to be uncool because she's totally cool.) And she checks out the scene. There's a powerhouse pack of scary Cholas conspiring in the back row, there's aisle after aisle of knobby, scrawny white-boy knees sprouting like weeds from marshmallow sneakers, and there are clumps of unlikely allies haphazardly united for the first time by the pride of patriotism: Serrania Avenue, row three, Walnut Elementary, row five, or MUS, first row. Forty faces. Shala knows some of them. Ido, Farah, Laura Leaper, Eden, Mori Leshum, oh great, and him: Taylor Bryans. Barf. But the rest? They're all new.

In Our World, fourth period, Shala learns current events. It's social studies. The book's heavy. But then there's a war. And then Shala's embarrassed to say Niger River out loud, and she learns to recognize Kuwait and a kid named Josh gets a part in a movie with Tom Hanks, but that's nothing she tells Lucy because she used to roller-skate at Skateland with the kid from *Terminator II.* And he's cuter. Way cuter.

It's L.A. Unified where there's every different kind of thing, but it's just junior high so you're just barely starting to get an idea of what it means to be some different kind of thing. There are piercings. There are cigarettes. Even drug dealers. And with all that, there's the aura of danger all around, and you realize, for the first time, that you could get your ass kicked. You could get pounded after school, you could get jumped in the bathroom, you could get jacked-up, beat-up, messed-up, it's true, and the omnipresent possibility swells every exchange.

Mrs. Furukawa's new husband is in the Army. She says so. She wears the highest heels you've ever seen a person wear. Her class reads *The Diary of Anne Frank* but you know you're set, you already read it. Plus *A Wrinkle in Time*, and you read that one too. At home your mom says Get out the flag, we want them to know what side we're on.

On television every night Bush says Sad-dum instead of Suhdom and your dad says it's a slap in the face. Your dad, the Mohammad Sawy from which your Mohammadee came, says it's on purpose, just to drive that bastard nuts. You practice saying the name both ways, the real way and the slap-his-face way.

Gym class is the worst because you have to get naked and that is the worst. Gym is what your friends feared most in fifth grade when you thought about junior high and you tried so hard to imagine what it would be like to be with other people and take your clothes off (Take your clothes off? In front of people? Strangers-people? Oh yeah right. Get real. No way.) and you started trying to think up the lie you'd have to tell your parents because they just wouldn't get it. A big important thing is Modesty. You know that. It's your cultural heritage, and naked is certainly not Modesty. On the first day just to be sure, you raise your hand and ask If you were a non-strip every day would you fail? And Ms. DeLuca says Yes.

Some kids ditch but it's been three months. It's too late now. You're stuck with who you are by now and even though you're finally Shala you're still a goody-good brainy dweeb. And dweebs just don't ditch. Not like you want to anyway. Except in Gym. That's when you do want to. You sit on the black asphalt during roll call with your gym shirt stretched over your knees so that it's still all bagged out twenty minutes later when the volleyball crashes bang into your unprotected head for the fifteenth time like it's been launched from some mystery rocket launcher and it's got a homing device aimed straight for you.

At twelve, no one knows anything yet, so what kind of name is Shala? Who can tell? And, plus, who'd even consider the question if parents didn't ask it? Sometimes kids slip up to you in the crush of the lunch line and speak quick Spanish and expect you to answer. Sometimes kids crack jokes in Farsi and then shoot you a sly glance just before the punch line. Sometimes you laugh for them anyway. Sometimes you'll try and answer *Sí*, and disguise that Anglo accent the best you can. *Sí, claro.* But the best is when a sleep-over sucks and you want to go home and you call up your mom and mumble Urdu into the telephone and no one knows when you tell your mom I hate these girls and I want to leave.

On Tuesday a kid wears a T-shirt to school and it says "Nuke Em" and when Mrs. Furukawa sees it she's pissed and she makes him go to the office and when he comes back he's wearing it inside out. If you already saw it you can still kind of tell though. mE ekuN.

After school that day your cousin asks if you want to try Girl Scouts with her. Then she gets sick and makes you go alone. When you get there it's totally weird for two reasons. First, your cousin's older by one year and she already wears a hijab and when you went over to get her she dressed you up. So now you're wearing a hijab and lipstick and your cousin's shirt, which says "Chill Out." Uncool. But what could you say? She's all sick and she kept cracking up whenever you put something else of hers on and she's so bossy all the time and then before you knew it the carpool's honking outside and your aunt shouts that you have to go right now. So you do. Then, second of all, you don't know anybody here. They're all seventh graders. It sucks.

They're baking banana nut bread and the girl who gave you a ride says that you smell funny. What's worse than smelling funny? The first thing you do is you go to the bathroom and wash your hands. Then you rinse out your mouth. You try to keep the lipstick from smearing all over the place. You sniff your armpits. As far as you can tell, it seems normal. In the mirror you look so much older with Aslana's hijab pinned underneath your chin like that.

When you walk out of the bathroom you bump into the Girl Scout mom and almost immediately she starts to yell at you like you spilled something on the carpet.

Um, excuse me but this is a feminist household and hello? Honey, that's degrading, she says.

She must be confused. At first you wonder, is she really talking to me, and like in a television sitcom, you turn around to check if there's someone else standing behind you.

Don't you know this is America, sweetheart? I mean have you heard of this thing feminism?

Yeah I'm one too, you say, because you learned about it in school and it means equality between the sexes and that's a good idea.

That's sweet. She looks at you. But get that thing off your head first, she says. You know you don't have to wear it. Not here. No one's gonna arrest you. I didn't call the police or anything, honey—what's your name?

The Girl Scout mom shakes her Girl Scout head and she's wearing a giant Girl Scout outfit that fits her. She looks weird. Like an enormous kid, super-sized like French fries. You can just be yourself at our house, honey, she assures you. You can. What, your mom wears that? She's forced to? Right? Oh, Jesus Christ. Look at you. Well you don't have to, you hear me? Here, you want to take it off? Here, com'ere, honey.

And when you do she helps you and then after you're ashamed that you let her touch it. Then you mix the banana nut dough and you think it looks like throw-up and that same girl says that you still smell like a restaurant she doesn't like. You really, really want to leave. Maybe if you stand still, you think, no one will notice you. On the wall there's a picture of dogs playing cards. Your cousin's hijab is in your backpack and you hold your whole self still and imagine time flowing away like milk down your throat until it's gone and you can leave.

*   *   *

There are Scud missiles, yeah, but in sixth grade at LAUSD, there are more important things. Like French kisses. There's this girl who claims she did one. You just have to think What would that be? because no one would ever kiss you. At least until you're married. Lucy Chang says it's slutty anyway. Lucy Chang is your best friend. You tell her about Girl Scouts and she says Girl Scouts is lame.

On the way home from school you get knocked down by a car. With a group of kids. It's not that bad, kind of just a scary bump, from the guy doing a California-stop which means rolling through the stop sign. At first he says sorry and you say it's okay. But when you suck up all your might and ask to write down his license plate number he says no. Your dad must be a lawyer, he says, is that it? What, look, you're not even hurt, okay? Just go home.

You have some friends with you. You guys were talking about how you could totally be models for a United Benetton ad if someone just took a picture of you guys right now. You're on your way to Tommy's Snack Shack for curly fries and an Orange Julius. Uhh, I think we should probably just go, alright, Noel says, It's not that bad so we should just go.

Yeah, go, the man says. Don't be a brat, he says, Just go.

Okay fine, you say, Fine I'll go, but FIRST I'm gonna write it down.

He's tall and he looks toward the ground to look at you. Just mind your own business, kid, she doesn't want you to. No one wants you to, he says.

Well I'm gonna, you say.

Look, you're not hurt, nobody's hurt, what do you need to for?

Just in case, you say. If it scares him you're happy. You're in junior high. You know what to do. Stand your ground. Make your face impassive. You are made of stone. You repeat it more slowly just to see if it freaks him out. *Just. In. Case*, you say and you're twelve and if you're a brat then wear it like a badge.

At mosque there's a broken window. It's a disgrace, your father says, Shala, I tell you it's a damn disgrace. The hole in the window looks jagged like a fragile star sprouting sharp new points. It lets all the outside noise in when everybody's trying to pray and cars rush past grinding their brakes.

There's a report in Language Skills, due Monday, and you have to have a thesis so on the way home from mosque your mom helps you think of one. Yours is that if you were living in Nazi times you would have saved Anne Frank. Your mom says that's not a thesis. Hers is that empathy and tolerance are essential teachings in every religion. You settle for a compromise: Because of Anne Frank's tolerance she should be a saint.

At home while your mom makes dinner she stands over the stove as you peel the mutant-looking ginger root and there are lots of phone calls from lots of relatives. What are we going to do, your mom keeps demanding each time she talks into the phone, What? Tell me. What are we going to do?

Saddam does something. You know it because there are television reports. Everyone's worried for your older brother. He's studying in Pakistan with some friends and if he leaves now then he'll be out one whole semester because his final tests aren't for two more months. He's big news at the mosque. Also people are talking about the price of gas and how much it costs just to drive downtown.

Then Bush does something back, and the phone cord stretches as your mom marches over and snaps the TV off like she's smashed a spider.

The ginger and the asafetida and the mustard seed sauté for a long time until they boil down and then it is the usual moment for adding in the spinach and the potato and the butter but instead the moment comes and goes and the saag aloo burns for the first time that you can remember and the delicate smell of scorched spice swirls up through the room as you watch your mom demand her quite angry Urdu into the receiver and you realize that she doesn't even notice.

You know why she's upset. It's because everyone can tell Ahmad's American and he can't disguise it. He smells American, he smiles American, and his T-shirts say "Just Do It" like a dare. And lots of people hate America. Plus, in that country, in general in that country, it's much more dangerous. Even just every time you visit, you swallow giant pills and still your weak sterile body gets every cold and all the diarrhea and all the fevers that India has to offer. It's because of the antiseptic lifestyle, your mother insists. Too clean.

In Science, fifth period, you learn that everything is made out of stardust from billions of years ago. Instead of it being as romantic as Mr. Kane seems to think it is, you think that pervasive dust feels sinister. You know what happened to

Anne Frank, and you can't believe that when she died she turned back into people dust, all mixed up with every other kind of dust. Just piles and piles of dust. And all of it new.

There are plenty of other Muslim kids. Tons of them at school. Everyone's a little freaked out. In the hall, after science, you see an eighth grader get tripped on purpose and the kid who did it shouts, Send Saddam after me, MoFo, I'll kick his ass too!

After school that day at Mori Leshum's house everyone plays a game called Girl Talk, which is like Risk, except it takes place at the mall. It gets old fast. Next: crank calls! 1-800-SURVIVAL is 1, 8, 0, 0, 7, 8, 7, 8, 4, 8, 2, 5. Uh hi, I just got in a car accident and YOU SUCK A DICK! You laugh and laugh but when it comes time for your turn to squeal breathy oinks into the phone the way you've heard in movies, you chicken out and everyone concludes that oh my god you're such a prude. Well at least I'm not a total perv, you say. Oi, oi, oh! Wooo! Ahh! moans Jackie and when Mori's shriveled grandma comes in the room to get you guys pizza, you all shut up fast for one quick second and then burst into hilarity. The grandma laughs right back at you and she has a dusty tattoo on her arm and it's not until years later that you realize what it is. Oh that, says Mori, It's just her boyfriend's phone number. She says she put it there so she won't get it lost.

Some things that you see you can't forget. On your dad's desk in his office where you're not supposed to touch anything, you see a book called *Vietnam,* and it's as thick as a dictionary and it has a glossy green cover. At random you open it up and flip. In the middle of a sentence is something about sex so you start to read quick. And then you wish you didn't. You slam it shut. You creep out of the office. You close your eyes and imagine anything else, and for a second the shattered starshape of your mosque window flashes to the rescue and you cling tight and you wish on it and you wish that you hadn't read anything at all. *Please,* you think, and you try to push the devastation shoved out through the sharp hole the same way you try to push out the sound of horns and shouts when you say prayer. *Please,* you think, but it doesn't work and nothing swoops in to rescue you.

* * *

Sex Ed is only one quarter so that for kids like you, whose parents won't sign the release form, you don't miss much. Instead of switching mid-semester, you take the biology unit twice and you become a bit of an expert on seed germination. Lucy tells you everything anyway. Boys get wet dreams and girls get cramps, what's that all about? she says. You look at her handouts of enormous outlined fallopian tubes and it just sort of looks like the snout of a cow's face and you don't see what the big deal is. You do ask, though, Is there a way to make your boobs grow? And Lucy says that Jackie already asked and No, there isn't. Too bad. Then Lucy says, I must, I must, I must increase my bust! And then you call her a Horndog and she calls you a Major Skank and then you both bust up laughing.

When it happens it happens in the stall at McDonald's. Paula Abdul is tinny on the loudspeaker. Lucy's mom asks what kind of hamburger you want and you say you don't eat meat, it has to be Fish Filet, please. With sweet-and-sour sauce, please. Then Lucy says Grody! and then you and Lucy go off to the bathroom together and while she's talking to you about the kinds of jeans that Bongo makes, and every different color that there is, and how if you got scrunchies to match, wouldn't that be cool? you're in the stall and you realize it like a loose tooth. Lucy, oh my god Lucy, check this out, wow! It happened!

Are you serious, she says, Are you serious? Oh my god, are you sure?

I'm sure, you say, and you breathe in big chalky breaths that stink of bathroom hand-soap, powdered pink. When you guys come back to the table and you eat your meal it seems like a whole different thing being in the world. And it is.

That night you ask your mom if you can stay home from school on account of the occasion. She doesn't let you. She does ask you if you want to try her hijab on, though, and you don't tell her about Aslana's. Shala, she says, Shala, I don't know about right now. This just may not be the time. But it has to be your choice. You don't have to if you don't want to, but you do have to ask yourself how do you represent yourself now as a Muslim Woman in this country where they think that Muslims are not like you, Shala, and when you choose this, Shala, you are showing them that they know you and that you are nice and that you are no crazy, no religious nut. You are only you, and that is a very brave thing to show the world.

Now when you guys walk home, you're way more careful about not trusting any cars to do anything you expect them to. When you get to the 7-11, you try different ways of scamming a five-finger discount on the Slurpees. The woman behind the counter hates kids. Timing is everything. Here's how it goes: one person buys and you mix every color all together and try to pass from mouth to mouth and suck it gone before it melts. It's hard because of brain freeze. You try to re-fill and pass off, which the woman says counts as stealing and is not allowed, but that's only when she catches you. Trick is, you have to look like you're alone when you buy the cup or she'll be on to you and then she'll turn around and watch the machine. So everyone else has to stand outside with the bum named Larry and then go in one by one and sit on the floor reading trashy magazines about eyeshadow while the buyer waits in line. Today that's you. You wait in line. You've got the collective seventy-nine cents in your hand. You freeze your face still into a mask of passivity and innocence.

As the trapped hotdogs roll over sweating on their metal coils, you hear the two men in front of you discussing politics and waiting with their own single flavor Slurpees already filled to the brim and ready to be paid for in full.

Same goddamn ground war we had in 'Nam, and hell knows nobody wants to see their baby come home in a body bag. Hey.

The way I see it is, you got two choices, right? Nuke the towel-heads, use your small bombs, ask your questions later, or what you do is convert.

With you on the first one, buddy.

No, no listen: *convert.* Hell yeah, whole country. To Islam. To mighty Allah.

Shit, man, you and the rag-heads?

But I got a point, right? Right? 'Cause what'd you think these fuckers want? Right? Oh yeah, hey uh, pack of Lucky Strikes, huh? And how 'bout Superlotto? Yeah, one of those, thanks.

Next: you. You try to gauge how much this straggly woman sees. Can she tell? Muslim? Mexican? Does she know that your clothes are Trendy, that your grades are Dweeby, that your heart is Goodygoodie? Your face: unreadable, innocent, frozen. One Slurpee. Please.

You walk around the counter and toward the magazines and when your friends see you, you try to look triumphant and cool and with it. But you feel like a cheat. Like maybe if it is stealing, you might not be such a good Muslim, you might be letting your kind of people look bad.

Not *stealing,* says Lucy. Sharing. It's just sharing.

So you share. You slurp cherry-cola-blueberry-cherry layers until your forehead aches. Then Jackie opens up her mouth and throws her head back and gets down on her knees and another girl pulls the knob and you all stop to watch the Slurpee slurped straight from the machine. Gross, someone says, but you're all impressed with the inventiveness and Jackie's daredevil status is elevated in everyone's eyes.

Oh, for Christssake! Give me a break! You goddamn good-for-nothing kids, get out of here! Get! Never again! You're banned, you hear me? Banned! Out! Get out!

Scatter giggling and shrieking across the parking lot, and the very next day dare each other to go back like nothing happened and you know you can because you know she can't tell the difference between any of you anyway. You could be anyone for all she knows.

The day you try it out as a test, someone yanks hard from behind and when it gets ripped off your head, a lot of hair does too. You think about how when hard-ass what-up girls fight they both stop first and take out all their earrings. It hurts enough to make you cry but you try hard not to. *Please don't let me cry, please, please don't let me cry.* First period, and Taylor Bryans sees your chubby lower lip tremble and he remembers the time you corrected his wrong answer in front of the whole class (Not pods! *Seeds!* Duh!) and he starts up a tough game of Shala-Snot-Germs and the cooties spread from hand to hand all around the room as your face gets hotter and hotter and your eyeballs sting and your nose drips in sorrow. Your dignity gathers and mounts as you readjust the scarf and re-pin the pin. You can't see anyone pass Germs, you can't hear anyone say your name. You are stone. You are cool. You will not cry. Those are not tears. The bell rings.

Then the bell rings six more times at the end of six periods and when you get home that day you have had the hijab yanked on seven occasions, four times in first period, and you've had your feet stomped twice by Taylor Bryans in the lunch line, and after school a group of eighth graders, all of them past puberty and huge with breasts in bras, surrounded you to gawk and tug in unison. And you've made up your mind about the hijab. It stays. No matter what. The fury coils in your veins like rattlesnake lava, the chin pushes out to be held high, the face is composed and impervious and a new dignity is born outraged where there used to be just Shala's self-doubt. It stays, you think, No matter what.

Still, at home you cry into your mom's sari and you shout at her like she's one of the merciless, I'm just regular, you wail. I'm the same as I ever was!

Oh baby, come on, shhh, it's going to be okay, she says. And then your mom suggests that maybe right now might not be the right time to start wearing this. She assures you that you are okay either way, that you can just take it off and forget about it. She says all this, sure, but she wears hers knotted firmly underneath her own chin as she strokes your back with reassurance.

That night, before you get into bed, you think about your brother and what it must be like for him. You look in the bathroom mirror and you slip the hijab on over your young hair and you watch like magic as you're transformed into a woman right before your very eyes. You watch like magic as all of the responsibilities and roles shift and focus.

You get it both ways. In your own country you have to worry, you have to get you hair pulled. And in India there you are: the open target, so obvious with your smooth American feet and your mini Nike backpack, the most hated. With anger and envy and danger all around you. The most hated. The most spoiled. An easy mark. A tiny girl. With everything in the world, and all of it at your disposal.

You think about your brother and you wonder if he's scared.

As you get dressed for bed you check things out with a hand mirror. You poke at the new places you hadn't looked at before. You look at the shape in the hand mirror and you think *Hello me*. It's embarrassing even though it's only you. You feel a whole new feeling. You think about how much you hate Taylor Bryans. Indignation rises up like steam. You stand there in the bathroom with blood on your hands and you know it. *I am Muslim,* you think, *I am Muslim, hear me roar.*

In third-period PE the waves of hot Valley sun bake off the blacktop asphalt and from a distance you see squiggly lines of air bent into mirage and your head is cooking underneath the scarf and your ears feel like they're burning in the places where they touch the cloth and your hair is plastered to the back of your neck with sticky salty sweat and when you group up for teams, someone yanks hard. You topple right over. You scrape your knees and through the blood they're smudged sooty black. Everyone turns around to look, and a bunch of girls laugh quietly behind hands. The hijab is torn from where the pin broke loose and your dad is right, it's way better that it isn't a knot or you might choke. Your neck is wet with a hair-strand of blood from where the popped-open pin tip slipped along skin. And you figure, That's it. Forget it. I quit. I'm ditching. I hate you.

Someone says, Aw shit, girl, you okay?

You scramble up and walk tall and leave the girls in their bagged-out PE uniforms and you go back into the cool dank locker room where you can get naked all by yourself for once. As you wash the gravel out of your hands you stare at yourself in the mirror. You think *Bloody Mary* and squeeze your eyes shut tight, but when you open them it's still just your face all alone with rows and rows of lockers. No demon to slice you down.

Now when you walk in late you're not Nobody anymore, you're not Anyone At All. Instead, now, when you walk in you have to brace yourself in advance, and you have to summon up a courage and a dignity that grows strong when your eyes go dull and you stare into unfocused space inches away while Taylor Bryans and Fernando Cruz snicker and snicker until no one's looking and then they run up and shout in your face: Arab! Lardass! Damn, you so ugly you ooogly!

Your inner reserves fill to full when Fernando stomps on your feet and your white Reeboks get all smeared up and your face doesn't even move no matter how much it hurts.

The bell rings. Lunch. You push and shove your way into the cluster of the Girls' Room, and there's no privacy and you try to peer into the tagged-up piece of dull-shine metal that's bolted to the wall where everyone wants a mirror, but there are girls applying mascara and girls with lip-liner and the only air is a fine wet mist of aerosol AquaNet and it's too hard to breathe and you can't see if it's still pinned straight, because that last snatch was like an afterthought and it didn't even tug all the way off. But you can't make your way up to the reflection and you can't see for sure. So here it comes, and then you're standing there in the ebb and flow of shoulders and sneakers and all of a sudden here it comes and you're sobbing like you can't stop.

Hey girl, why you crying? You want me to kick some motherfucker's ass for you, girl? 'Cause I'll do it, bitch, I'm crazy like that. You just show me who, right, I'll do it, homegirl.

And through your tears you want to throw your arms around the giant mountainous chola and her big-hearted kindness and you want to kiss her Adidas and you want to say Taylor Bryans' name and you want to point him out and you want his ass kicked hard, but you stop yourself. You picture the outcome, you picture the humiliation he'd feel, a skinny sixth grader, a scrub,

the black eye, the devastation of public boy-tears, the horror of having someone who means it hit you like an avalanche. You look over your back and past
all the girl-heads, the stiff blonds and permed browns and braided weaves, the
dye jobs, the split ends, all of them elbowing and pushing in to catch a dull
distorted glimpse in graffitied monochrome, and you smooth over the folds of
your safe solid black hijab and you snuffle up teary dripping snot and you picture what it would be.

You picture her rush him: Hey BITCH, yeah I'm talking to you, *pendejo*,
that's right you better run outta my way whiteboy, cuz I'm going to whup
your ass, punkass motherfucker! You picture her and she's like a truck. Taylor
Bryans stops cold and then he startles and turns to flee but she's already overcome him like a landslide, and she pounds him like muddy debris crushing
someone's million-dollar home. You picture the defeat, the crowd of jeering
kids, Fight! Fight! Fight! The tight circle of locked arms, elbow in elbow so
the teachers can't break it up, the squawk of adult walkie-talkies and then the
security guards, the assistant principal, and all the teachers on yard duty, all of
them as one, all charging over to haul kids out of the fray and into detention,
and all the while you can picture him like he's a photograph in your hand: the
tears, the scrapes, the bruises, the giant shame in his guilty nasty eyes and you
know that it wouldn't solve a thing and you suspect that it probably wouldn't
even stop him from pulling your hair out and stomping on your feet and you
picture it and you open up your heart and you forgive him.

Then you gather up all that new dignity, and then you look up at her, stick
your covered head out of the girls' bathroom, and point.

*On August 5, 2000, twenty letters were sent by Daniel O'Mara to the chief executive
officers of twenty Fortune 500 companies. This is one; four more follow.*

Hugh L. McColl, Jr.
CEO, Bank of America Corp.
100 N. Tryon Street
Charlotte, NC
28255

Dear Mr. McColl,

I realize that you are a busy man so I will get to the point. I have recently been writing
some passages from the point of view of a dog named Steven, and I would like you to
see an example. Here is one:

> I am Steven and I was born in a box of glass, on newsprint cut to ribbons. I am
> here now, five years later, and my paws, once white like paper, are now white
> like ivory. I have walked streets! And over fields! Have seen things! The hands
> of children I've bitten! They look delectable and taste so fine!
>
> I have to move. I have to move. I can jump a mile. I'm that kind of dog — I can
> jump a goddamn mile. I'm a great dog. I see colors like you hear jetplanes.
>
> I'm going to find a hole. I'm going to find a tiny tiny tiny hole and walk
> through like goddamn Gandhi.

That is all for now.

D.

Daniel O'Mara
5811 Mesa Drive
Austin, TX
78731

THE TEARS OF SQUONK, AND WHAT HAPPENED THEREAFTER

by GLEN DAVID GOLD

IN LATE MARCH, 1916, a week before the Nash Family Circus came to Tennessee, their spotty poster advertisements clung to the sides of buildings throughout the railroad town of Olson. Olson was best described as sleepy, save for the constant rattle of the railroad yards; it was not at all a place for murder. And the Nash Family and their hired performers seemed anything but evil.

The posters, stock images dated and fading already, promised tame acts. A horseback rider here, a clown there, a roaring lion, and finally a pair of juggling clowns pasted next to each other to lend some small company. Taken together, they looked as forlorn as the orphans who sometimes stood outside the tent and imagined far greater attractions than those that ever actually wheezed through their paces under the single, patched canvas big top.

The talents of the Nash family clowns were generally tepid. Some of the horses had been remarkable in their youth, true, but they were tired—granted, only half as tired as the acrobats, who mostly daydreamed of returning to Germany when the war was over. No, what the Nash Family Circus had to offer was the moral backbone of its patriarch, Ridley Nash.

Nash had been in the circus business since 1893, when the traveling carnival had been born. A cook in Chicago, and a splendid mimic of the world's cuisines, he had made the daily meals at the international pavilions at the Colombian Exposition. He had been so impressed by the clean family entertainment, he purchased his first wagon then and there, on credit, from a dealer in the dry goods pavilion.

By 1916, he was referred to as "Colonel" Nash, which dismayed him privately, as he had never served in the army, and he felt the term disrespected those who had. Still, it was the custom among traveling circuses to have a faux colonel at the helm, and so he bore it manfully.

Among the Nash Family Circus posters was a broadside of printed text which Nash had set himself. He insisted that every word be true, beginning with "A Moral Entertainment," and ending with "23 Years of Dealing Squarely with the American Public." In between were other promises, such as "8 funny clowns," and if the eighth clown was under the bottle that night, to keep the count honest, Colonel Nash donned the red nose and let himself be hit with the slapstick.

At the center of the broadsheet was a woodcut of an elephant, Mary, billed as the third-largest elephant in captivity. She was seen in a headdress and cape, with an indication by her side that she stood twelve feet at the shoulder.

The elephant was indeed the third-largest in captivity, and she stood exactly as high as the Colonel claimed, and one morning had been measured three inches taller, but the Colonel kept the smaller number, as he could count on it being verified.

The posters he'd designed to showcase the elephant were for many years treasured, not for their moral authority, but simply for how Mary was shown both head-on and from the side. Nash felt this presented her headdress and cape *squarely*, to use his preferred term, but more than one spectactor to her final performance commented—before spiriting away a copy of the broadsheet—how prescient the Colonel had been in showing her as if she were posed for a police blotter's mug book.

The morning of Mary's last day, roustabouts swung sledgehammers along the stake line, and ring-makers were leveling the field exactly forty-two feet in all directions from the center pole, which was erected by a line of ten men chanting as they had since the days of Dan Rice, "Easy, easy, easy, PULL."

The sky was iron gray with clouds, and the humidity brought an odd smell, something rusted and cruel, from the train yards, which surrounded and dwarfed the town. Tiny Olson sat in the shadow of Wildwood Hill, the top of which was a graveyard for freight cars. In the town, the parade band attempted in vain to tune their ratty instruments, and beyond and above them was the hulking, distant silhouette of Ol' 1400, the McKennon Railway's one-hundred-ton train derrick, which was used to snatch trains off the track and then drop them, helpless as baby turtles, onto the scrapheap.

The parade was a chance to show the town just a little for free, to build anticipation for that evening's show. At 11 a.m., the brass band was fully engaged and marching: the scruffy and heartbroken Nash children, plus two pony boys and a mule skinner who had some legitimate use for the slide trombone. Next were the three acrobats who normally did handsprings in the street, but because of the mud, they rode on the back of a flatbed cart pulled by goats, and made a human pyramid at one end, tumbled down, then reassembled at the other end. Next came the eight funny clowns, most of whom seemed, at 11 a.m., not so much funny as wrestling with philosophical discontents.

The sole clown of merit was Squonk. When he and Mary had joined the Nash Family early in the season, the Colonel billed Squonk in the programs as "Joseph Bales, portraying Squonk the Clown," in the spirit of full disclosure, but Bales, a trained artist who had studied in Europe, was furious. "Nash," he said, folding his arms, "I'm a trained artist. And when I studied in Europe, we didn't give away our names, not for the world." Bales argued that pantomime, makeup, false nose, and floppy Bibleback shoes were all poetics, in the Aristotelian sense, intended to preserve mystery. Grudgingly, mostly to keep the temperamental Bales at ease, Nash—who wasn't quite sure about the Aristotelian reference, though it sounded impressive—billed him from then on, in entirety, as "Squonk."

That morning, Squonk—in his dunce's cap and bloated single-piece checked suit with three yellow pom-poms down the front—seemed to be everywhere at once, miming the trombonist's slide and puffed-out cheeks, then threatening to topple the human pyramid. In what warmed the crowd as a rib-tickling lampoon (though it lacked the same effect on his peers, who glared daggers at him), Squonk became stern with the other clowns, tutting their performances. He showed them the proper way to toss a child into the sky, lofting and catching a small girl and handing her a daisy all in one motion as smooth and delicate and transparent as glass.

But this was just the warm-up for the big finish. At the head of the parade, two front door men began to wave their arms, standing as if to block the side streets. They cried out, "Hold your horses! Here comes the elephant!"

The crowd fell to a respectful hush, as there was something glorious and humbling about seeing, once a year at most, such an impossible beast. Some regarded the bizarre mix of parts—trunk, tusks, huge ears—as evidence of the existence of a bounteous and clever God. Nash, who was swayed by the God argument, also spent stray moments here and there staring Mary in the eye, sensing within her a wonderful intelligence. Squonk wrote out a quotation for him to use during his pitch: "Comte Georges Leclerc de Buffon, famed naturalist from France, tells us the elephant 'by his intelligence makes as near an approach to man, as matter can approach spirit.'"

Hence the warning about horses. Elephants would tolerate being chained to a freight car and stuck with a hooked pole and forced to stand on their hind legs and trumpet. But they would not tolerate horses. The mere fact of horses drove them into an atavistic frenzy. The eye clouded over, almost as if *musth*, the elephant madness, had invaded the brain.

When the street was thought to be secure, Squonk loped forward, dropping all of his humorous antics. His years of European training rushed to the forefront. His rigid posture, his head tilted upward, arms flourishing gracefully, indicated that behind him stood a magnificent work of art known as an elephant. The crowd produced a kind of applause that was at once awed and hesitant.

Mary walked slowly, trunk held forth in a question mark that tilted left and right as she marched through the muck. She wore a sequined headdress, and a long cape with a Shakespearean ruff. There was a kind of knife-scarring on her ear, an M, made to indicate her name (elephant theft was rare, but costly). The more educated patrons of the circus, upon seeing the outfit, and the M, understood at once how fitting her name was. They would murmur, *Queen Mary*, as the ground trembled with each step.

Bales had trained Mary in a unique manner—she was never humiliated into squirting water at the crowd, or balancing a ball with her trunk. He was more demanding, more of a martinet than that. Mary performed ballet.

Thus the Nash broadside included mention of Mary's dynamic performances for the crowned heads of Europe (citing, as per Bales's resume, Carlos II of Spain and Sophia of Greece, since Nash was aware that "crowned heads" was an unacceptably vague term that invited suspicion). The crowd at the parade was there to see ballet, and, had the show at Olson gone as had every other performance that season, Mary would have indulged them with one simple motion, a curtsy, that would have guaranteed a full house that night. It was such an indescribable gesture that most members of every previous crowd were driven to sputter to friends, "You have to see it—you just have to see it."

Alas, at 11:15, as the town clock was striking the quarter-hour, Mr. Timothy Phelps, senior director of the McKennon Railway, arrived at the parade via the narrow alley between the Second National Bank and

Tannenbaum's hardware store. He appeared mounted, with exquisite form, on his English saddle-backed horse, Jasper.

What happened next was so terrible, so simple, so unbelievable, that townspeople's memories could never have been trusted to relay it accurately. In fact, the story would surely have been demoted to the realm of folklore were it not for a single motion picture camera.

The Pathé Prevost Camera, the camera of choice for professionals, had but one drawback: if the camera fell over and struck a hard object, the film stock tended to explode into flames. An amateur filmmaker named Alexander Victor was experimenting that morning with acetate "safety" film. He'd ridden the rails of the American South, tinkering with improvements in the optical range finder, and shooting endless locomotives in transit, train-crew razorbacks waving at the camera. Today, he had alighted on the circus parade, which was ideal to him for its interesting motion.

He hand-cranked his camera on the sidewalk, directly across from the alley-way. And so local memories, hazy in other details, are precise in this regard, all of them, no matter where they were that day, recalling it from the same vantage point. Their memories took on the scratched negative, the variable speed and mysterious lighting of amateur film. Mary broke from the parade route, trotting left with an almost magnetic attraction to Jasper and his rider, scattering to the four winds the townspeople between her and her quarry. Standing next to the brick wall of the bank, Phelps and his horse—rather a grayish smear in the frame-by-frame dissection of the scene—nervously paced back and forth, but couldn't make up their collective mind, and then Mary, headdress and cape buffeting with each step, was upon them. It was as if she needed to scratch an itch against the rough bricks, one quick flex of her shoulder, forward, then one slower, luxurious kind of return back, and horse and rider were no more.

This was horror enough. But next, camera still rolling, citizens of Olson sepia blurs crossing the foreground, Mary lowered one front foot to Phelps's back, as if holding the corpse steady, and then she wrapped her trunk around his neck. The next motion was fluid, like drawing a reluctant cork out of a champagne bottle.

There was pandemonium in the streets, people unsure of exactly which direction constituted proper fleeing, and Alexander Victor's film ends with a man in bowler hat running his way, his vest and watch fob suddenly filling up the screen, and then, blackness.

Nash, rooted in the mud, hadn't seen exactly what happened, but tried to calm the situation, his clear showman's bellow ineffective. He saw the village blacksmith run forward and withdraw a pistol from his apron, which he proceded to empty at Mary's flank. The bullets made small pockmarks in Mary's hide, and she flapped her ears in concern, but she continued walking and there was no further outcome.

Squonk stood paralyzed, his jaw wavering, in the middle of the street. He removed his pointed, conical hat, and lowered his head. He put his palm over his eyes as Mary, his friend and companion, approached him and gingerly reached out her trunk for the apple she always received at the end of every parade.

The rumor that the show must go on was one started by patrons and furthered by newspaper men who liked how it sounded. Many a circus folds without a second thought, and Nash knew, at noon, and at one o'clock and at two o'clock, that there would be no performance that night. He had returned Mary to her freight car, and put most of his men around it to guard her. When a group of townspeople approached, excited as boys invited to their first dance, and armed with rifles, pistols, and sticks of dynamite, Nash stopped them himself. Nash had expected them, and had been girding himself all afternoon to tell a lie. It was the first lie he knowingly told the public.

"You can't kill an elephant that way," he announced.

His tone was so authoritative, so dismissive, he wondered where his voice was coming from. He sounded as if he were reciting Leviticus. "A gun, even a stick of dynamite, that will in no way pierce this beast's hide."

The men of Olson exchanged glances. There was a problem at hand, but some of them were known to be clever, and it was only a matter of time until someone yelled, "Electricity!"

Nash shook his head. "Edison himself attempted that once and failed. It just made the elephant angry." His second lie.

This caused murmurs, and Nash knew where this would go, a building kind of frustration and impatience. As soon as one man was telling the rest he could call his cousin in Frazer, who had a cannon from the War Between the States that might still work, Nash stopped them. He found himself saying, more of a circus man than he'd ever been, "We will settle it tonight, gentlemen. We will not leave this town without settling it, publicly, fully, and demonstrably." He wasn't sure why he added that last word, but it seemed to hold promise to the men, who, upon being assured that Mary would die somehow, turned, and walked away, holding their pistols or their rifles forlornly.

So the Colonel sat in his wagon, which was parked atop its brass brake shoes in a swampy depression nearest Mary's freight car. He was unsure of what to do. His elephant had killed someone—apparently done so with vigor, though he hadn't seen it, and continued to have his doubts. There was a very reasonable demand for vengeance. The idea of having a murderous animal in his charge made him feel ill. But what made him feel worse was the deeper source of his lie to the townspeople: if Mary were killed, he could never pay off his loan.

The finances of a circus were as arcane and toxic as the combinations of Ural Mountain herbs the property men used to jazz up the Sterno squeezings they swilled on long winter evenings. There were loan-outs, buy-backs, reverse repurchase agreements for contracts based on projected earnings. In short, Nash only owned Squonk and Mary's contract because he had guaranteed a bank in Chicago $8,000, payable in installments through the end of the summer season. He had paid off $1,500 so far. There was no way he could now make up the balance, and for him, financial responsibility was the basis of modern civilization. He had never pitted that belief against his belief in animals' basic nobility, and when the two forces rubbed together like this, the friction upset him.

At three o'clock he called Joseph Bales into his wagon to see how best to proceed. Bales entered with his head hung low, and when Nash began to speak—he began with an overall statement of how he still believed in the intelligence of the elephant, and was about to discuss whether female elephants perhaps fell under the sway of *musth*—Bales interrupted him. "Hanging," he said.

"Pardon?"

It was a conversation Nash would recall, helplessly, without conscious effort, many times for the rest of his life. The specifics were worn away, but the general feeling of dread was quite solid.

"Mary committed a crime," Bales said. "She should pay. By hanging. It would be poetic."

Usually Bales spoke in sentences forged from many dependent clauses welded together by sarcasm. Tonight he sounded like a different person. Determined, a man who has made the right choice quickly, begging for no time to reconsider it. He leaned forward and pointed with one articulated, bony finger, out the window. And there, on the hilltop, was the one-hundred-ton railroad derrick, looming just like a gallows.

Nash shook his head, but said nothing. Bales stood, put his hand on the door handle, and as a way of departing, jammed his hat down upon his head. His back was shaking, shoulders quivering. Then, determined, he whispered, "And it would be more poetic, still, in the deepest sense—poetic justice— when we charge admission."

When the door closed, Nash stared after it, his own eyes welling up. A terrible taste came into his mouth, a vile copper flavor, exactly like that of a penny.

That night, the whole town of Olson turned out on Wildwood Hill. Also present were the whole towns of Softon, Burroughs, Myers, and Carmel, over two thousand people, each of whom had paid the exorbitant sum of two dollars for the privilege of standing among the train wreckage to see an elephant hanged.

Nash himself elected not to attend. That an animal would be done such violence broke his heart. Just before dusk, he returned to Mary, who stood chained in her freight car, and looked her one last time in the eye. He saw within the same intelligence and kindness he had always seen. The longer he stood, the less he could forgive himself for taking the financially responsible way out of this. He retreated to his bed for the rest of the sleepless night.

Alexander Victor set up his camera, to no great effect. Even by the kerosene-fueled pan lights, with their reflectors and occasional flashes, there was not enough light, through the silt and smoke drifting over the excited crowd, to see anything more than vague shapes, suggestions of some tribal ritual.

Wildwood Hill was a gentle slope of about two hundred feet, with spiraling rails and a footpath, terminating in the antediluvian detritus of trains gone extinct. There were men and women and children walking gaily up the path, finding good vantage points surrounding the final length of railway track. The derrick's wheelhouse, belching diesel smoke, sat atop a powerplant the size of a locomotive. And extending from the wheelhouse, at the midpoint of its iron belly, was a kind of mechanical trunk: a muscular crane with a superstructure of steel girders, and at the end of it, a dull steel hook.

At seven o'clock, the doors to Mary's freight car were thrown open and she was led by torchlight along the pathway to the hill. The crowd, upon seeing her at a great distance, cheered for a while, but as her stride was stiff and slow, and the circular pathway uphill quite long, they soon lost their appetite for cheers, and fell instead into muted conversations.

When she finally appeared, it looked at first as if Mary would pass toward the derrick without trouble, but when she came upon the crowd, she froze solid. Some swore that she seemed to eye the steel hook, but perhaps her psychology was more simple than that. She was usually led to perform at this time of night, and yes, she was wearing her headdress and cape, and yes, there was a cheering crowd. But no tent. And the tenor of the crowd, for a creature that lived on emotion over reason, must have frightened her.

She shied away from the path, and it took several quick pokes of the elephant stick to keep her from retreating. Still, no power in the world could get her to go forward to her fate. Long minutes passed this way, with the crowd yelling out its disappointments, until resolution came from an unlikely source. A figure fought his way through the shoulder-to-shoulder overalls. It was Joseph Bales, out of his uniform. No makeup. Woolen jacket, beaten work trousers, a derby. From his occasional missteps and slurred speech, it was apparent he had ladled out applejack for himself from the canned heat wagon. If you looked closely, you could see a fine tapestry of broken capillaries around his eyes, which he wiped at with the back of his sleeve.

Mary immediately reached out her trunk for her friend, who patted her gently. "This way," he said, and walked several steps toward the derrick. She followed, but then stopped, and nothing, not all the pats and praise and reassurances in the world, could get her closer to the hook.

Bales tried to smile at her, but failed. Just as the crowd began again to grow unruly, he held out his hands to his sides, palms out, as if trying to stop a fight. He put his head down, and let out a sigh of awful resignation.

When he next raised his head—plainface or not—it was Squonk the Clown who looked up, light and limber as a dishrag. He did a mild leap, from foot to foot, and then back again, then once forward, once back, and then he pointed back at Mary. Understanding passed through her, and she, too, put her feet outward, then back. Then she stepped to the left, then the right, then turned around in a full circle. The audience let out a lusty cheer—Mary was doing her ballet!

The pas de deux was based on Plastikoff's La Chauvre-Souris Dorée, a rare work in that it celebrated not courtship, but daily love, the often-pale and unnoticed emotions that pass between a man and wife. When Squonk performed a saut de l'ange, Mary, who could not of course jump with all four feet in the air, nevertheless responded by extending one leg behind her, and her opposite forward leg straight ahead, in a perfect arabesque.

She did not notice that, far overhead, the crane was swinging into position.

Finally, Squonk performed a series of assembles sur la point, jumping with his legs together, turning in midair, going up on his toes, springing again, with a kind of grace that would seem unrepeatable until Mary followed him, shuffling in a circle like a trolly on a turntable. For her big finish, she did exactly what she'd done a thousand times before—rear legs slightly crossed, lowering herself until she was almost belly to the ground, and dropping her head as if in supplication: a perfect curtsey.

And that was when Squonk stepped forward and slipped the hook into the chain around her neck.

She startled backward, but it was too late. Gears far away, deep in the power plant, began to grind. Mary stood up herself, shaking her head like a dog shedding water. And then her forelegs were lifted off the dusty ground. She walked on her two legs, balancing, and the turbine whined awfully as something seemed to slip, and she started to return to the earth—briefly, though—as the crane applied inexorable force, she was pulled upward again, and her rear legs were removed from the earth, too.

All around, on the tops of dead scrap, of passenger cars stripped bare, of tankers gone to rust, the men and women and children lost their ability to cheer. An elephant is not meant to leave the ground, and the sight is sickening, a kind of rebuke to the natural order—fossils found in a churchyard, a rainfall of salt cod in the desert. There was a hush under the smoldering pan lights. Mary's stubby legs kicked in the air, and then, just once, after long moments, the eye startled wide in recognition of what was happening. The trunk sprung straight, a quick and disappointed half-strangling trumpet, and then she went limp.

No one knows for certain how long the elephant hung over Wildwood Hill. A man schooled in night photography offered to let people pose with the corpse, but there were no takers. There was a general call toward Squonk, and then confusion, then realization: he was gone. He had probably turned away the moment the crane began its work. He was never seen again.

A year passed. Then another. The Nash Family soldiered on, barely, sending in cash to cover a good portion of Mary and Squonk's contract, and then making small monthly payments. There was no longer a big finish to the Colonel's circus. Instead, Nash added a trained chimpanzee who, dressed in a toga, rode in a chariot pulled by two basset hounds. He also added a castaway from the Sparks circus, Captain Tiebor, who had a team of sea lions he claimed were college graduates. Nash dutifully wrote that into his new broadsides, and if that absurdity troubled him, he said nothing about it. He still claimed to offer a moral entertainment, though there was no longer a chronological measure of his dealing squarely with the American public.

In winter, 1918, the family went off the road for a season. Nash went alone to a rented ranch-style hacienda in an unincorporated valley not far from Los Angeles, California. His idea, expressed vaguely to the family he left behind, was to find new talent associated with the motion picture industry—perhaps some tumblers or wild animal acts were dissatisfied with the life behind the camera, and perhaps they truly wanted to see the world.

But the words seemed hollow to him, and in their letters, no one asked him how the quest was going. Since Mary's hanging, Nash had been direction-less. He knew no one in Los Angeles or its environs, which he found lonely and strange—acres of olive groves and citrus trees somehow mysteriously kept alive in the desert climate. He half-heartedly visited Famous Players once, but was turned away at the secretarial pool when he couldn't remember the name of the man he was supposed to meet. He spent the rest of the afternoon riding the trolley cars home.

When he cared to think about it in culinary terms, a habit he retained from his previous career, Nash believed there were two types of circus attrac-tions: the sweet and the sour. The sweet consisted of wholesome entertain-ments that were exactly as presented: the trapeze, the animals, the clowns. The sour were those that relied on fooling people. The India rubber pickled punks in jars, talked up as two-headed babies. The pink lemonade they sold that was actually water the clowns had washed their tights in. They had seemed too easy to keep apart, those worlds, but at some point Nash had crossed a line, and gone sour himself.

One February afternoon, Nash was interrupted in his morning ritual of shaving by a knock at his door. He peered out the keyhole, worried that it might be an associate come to take him back early to the circus; but no, the man on the other side of the door was no one he knew. Wiping away the foam, Nash let him in.

The stranger's face was broken and scorched, with patches of red skin among wrinkles, the expression a perpetual wince, as if he'd spent every moment of his life in hostile weather. His age was impossible to guess. He wore the familiar black cape and hat of a railway detective, which was the main reason Nash had so readily let him in.

Unaccustomed to company, Nash fumbled to offer him coffee, which the stranger accepted, announcing at the same time his name, "Leonard Pelkin." Pelkin had once been a railway detective, he continued, but he had retired and was now working privately.

They sat on either side of a galley that had been built into Nash's small kitchen, cramped but breezy, with a good view of the valley over Nash's shoulder. Pelkin took the opportunity to admire it while digging a portfolio out of his knapsack.

"Might I ask you some questions?"

"Certainly."

Pelkin carefully removed a stack of four-by-five photographs. As if dealing a hand of poker, he placed them face down in a field of five. "It's about a murder," Pelkin said. He cleared his throat, as if he had more to say. Nash nodded, to indicate he was being helpful. Pelkin nodded back, and then took a sip of coffee. He gestured with the coffee cup, toward the photographs. "Suspects," he continued.

Then he turned over the photographs, each making a confident snap as they went face up.

For a moment, Nash was silent.

"These are murder suspects?" he finally asked.

Pelkin nodded. "Do you recognize any of them?"

"They're elephants," Nash said.

"Look again."

Nash didn't need to look. He was upset, as he felt this was a problem that had been handled long ago, destroying a good part of himself in the bargain.

"I'm sure they're elephants. If you're here, talking to me, then you know why I'd know that."

Pelkin put up a finger. "One elephant," he said. "Just one."

The five photographs had been taken years apart, the earliest ones streaked and bubbling with emulsion. Each of them showed an elephant in the midst of carnivals or circuses—Nash recognized a wagon from the Sells organization, and a Ringling banner, and, finally, his own sagging big top, whose patches were as identifiable as surgical scars. It was like the sun breaking over a mountaintop.

"Mary," he said.

"Can you indicate where you see her?" Pelkin asked.

"Are you serious? She's the elephant standing before my tent."

"Is that her in the other photographs?"

It was hard to tell. In one, she wore a kind of tiara, in the rest, she was unadorned. "It could be."

"Did she have any identifying marks?"

"Well. Well. She was exactly twelve-foot tall. Is that what you mean?"

Pelkin's eyes narrowed. "Twelve foot? Or twelve-foot, three-inches?"

"No, exactly twelve-foot, as per the broadsides." He blew out his cheeks. "Of course, that one morning in Denver, she seemed to be twelve-foot-three."

Pelkin brought his hand down on the table hard enough to make the spoons jump.

"Yes!"

He leaned forward, and said, as if trying to be calm, "Is it possible she was, all those other times you measured her, slouching?"

"I don't understand."

Pelkin eased away. He looked over Nash's shoulder, at the elm trees beyond the window. "Any other marks you remember?" he asked, faintly.

"She had an M on her ear."

"Like this?" Pelkin thumbed through some photographs until he found what he was looking for, and snap, it went down on the table: It was a close-up of an elephant's ear.

Nash nodded. "Yes, except Mary had an M and this elephant has an N."

Weighing that statement with a frown, Pelkin brought out a fountain pen, shook it, then added a single down-stroke. "An M like this, is what Mary had?"

"I'm sorry, how many elephants have letters on their ears? Perhaps all of them. I've only examined one up close."

And at once there came forth the bitterness Nash had been trying so hard not to taste. The glimpses he'd had into Mary's eye, the raw mind he'd seen there, how she had been betrayed.

"One elephant, I'm thinking," Pelkin said. "There was an elephant named Nommi, with Ringling, and four years ago she killed a man. I think they just hustled her out the back way in the middle of the night, changed her name, and sold her to you."

"That's impossible," Nash said, but as he did, he brought up the photographs one by one and stared at them. "These are Nommi?"

"One of them is. One is of a Sells elephant, name of Veronica. She was a killer too, six years ago. And the name, see, if you—" Pelkin awkwardly put up two fingers to make a V, and then joined with them a finger from the other hand, which made a backward N. He moved his fingers around, trying to get it right, and then gave up. "Before that, Ionia. That's the one with the tiara."

Nash wanted to tell Pelkin that he was insane, but could somehow not move his mouth to form the words. He had a sickly feeling, one tinged with guilt, as if he himself were being accused.

"The man Mary trampled in Olson, he was on a horse," he said, meaning by this to begin a conversation that would end with Mary being, if not blameless or excusable, than at least understandable: an animal pushed beyond her natural limit.

"Mary didn't exactly trample Phelps, did she?" Pelkin said.

"Well..."

Pelkin started packing up his photographs, and Nash hoped this meant it was over. But instead, there was a new photograph to study. It was about eight inches tall, and of such length that it came in a roll which Pelkin unwrapped. He smoothed it out, then weighted it down at either end with coffee cups.

It was a safari shot. Five men at the center, in white pith helmets, Springfields cracked open across their laps. Native bearers of a tribe Nash did not recognize were to the left and to the right. Some of them covered their faces before the camera, but left the rest of themselves exposed, including the women, a detail Nash dwelt on for a shameful amount of time before realizing what, exactly, he was being shown.

The five hunters were all posing with their trophies: one man atop them, two on either side, two kneeling before them—a half-dozen dead African elephants.

"Oh, my lord," Nash cried.

There were pencil marks around the men's faces, which were half-crinkled in the photograph, hardly recognizable to begin with. Pelkin tapped on the image of one man to the right, whose rifle was jauntily slung over his shoulder. "Timothy Phelps," he said, "when he was a much younger man. The Southern Crescent Railroad, in 1889, took its senior-most managers on safari to the dark continent. Five of them are now dead. Killed by elephants." He picked up his coffee cup; the photo rolled shut. "An elephant."

Nash smoothed out the photo, holding it open himself. He stared until full understanding settled in on him. He felt buoyed by it; he could make sense of this. Almost giddily, he whispered, "Mary's family, then?"

"What?"

"The elephants who were killed here on the hunt. They're Mary's family, aren't they? She's been having her revenge."

There was a rotten silence in the room as Pelkin sized him up, astonished. Not in a pleasant way. At once, the sourness of the circus returned to Nash. Pelkin's look was the kind reserved for the lowest hick, the kind who buys the Fiji Mermaid, the he/she dancer blow-off, the pickled punks, and the lemonade, all of it, hook, line, and lead-heavy sinker.

"You think..." Pelkin grinned. "You think Mary, an elephant, is the mastermind, or something?"

"Well."

"Look." Pointing again into the group of hunters. Toward the left, isolated from his comrades, arms folded, wearing no gun himself, was Joseph Bales.

"Oh! How? How?" Nash paused, helplessly.

"You know him as Bales, right? That's not his name. His name is Bowles. The clever ones, when they change their names, make them similar enough they'll answer to them in their sleep. Bowles was supposed to be promoted, and he wasn't. I hear he was a terrible safari member, made a big fuss about everything, spent hours telling his fellow men around the campfire how uneducated they were. After the safari, he was fired. He went bitter, Nash. How bitter, no one knew. Some bitter guys, they scheme but they don't have any follow-through. They fade. Not Bowles. He went out and became a circus clown, the way some of the really bitter ones do. For the last dozen years, he has been luring these men to their deaths. The day before your circus arrived in Olson, Phelps received a telegram telling him to ride his horse to the parade, as a wonderful surprise was waiting." Pelkin shook his head. "Wasn't so wonderful, in my opinion."

For a great deal of time, Nash said nothing. He felt he should say something, but the specifics eluded him. Pieces of this macabre plot surfaced: Bowles scheming revenge, Bowles becoming a circus clown, alighting on the poetic justice of death-by-elephant. Finally, he said, "Aristotle."

"What?"

"He liked Aristotle," he said, blushing a bit.

Pelkin shrugged, and then wrote Aristotle on the back of one of the photographs. "Any ideas where Bowles might have gone?"

"Why did he kill her?"

"Pardon?"

With no difficulty, Nash was back in the circus wagon, with Bales opposite him, Bales holding back tears—or was he actually crying them?—and determined to have Mary hanged. "He said killing her would serve justice."

"Oh. Yeah, the justice expert. Sure. He was done, Nash. He'd managed to get her out of trouble four times before that. Slipped away in the dead of night four times, changing her name, changing his name. This time, he didn't need her anymore. He'd killed everyone he wanted to, and this way he wasn't going to leave any evidence behind."

"Hmmph." Nash nodded. "So he betrayed her."

"Sure," Pelkin said. Like most railway detectives, he was terse, but when revealing secrets he took a shameless delight in relaying the horrors behind them. "They were partners. She didn't know the game was rigged until the blow-off."

"I see."

He now wanted Pelkin to depart, as he was beginning to feel a strange and restless feeling, as if impatient for a loved one returning from a long trip. He wanted to throw open the door, look down the drive, and see, bags in hand, himself. He hardly listened as Pelkin snapped out another pair of photographs.

"These men, though, it seems Mary—or whatever her name was at first— she killed them in 1902. That was two years, as far as I can tell, before she met Bowles. It was a pretty fair partnership, I'd say. A good match."

"Yes, yes, I see," Nash said, impatiently. He was beginning to listen not to Pelkin but to a story unfolding in his brain. Mary, an animal, whose impulses were harnessed by a bad man. The tragedy of her life, coupled with the sheer evil of Bowles, made him hurry through the remainder of the interview with Pelkin. He was unsure of all things in the world, save one: he needed to be alone.

The conversation continued for less than five minutes. Pelkin had confirmed the trail was cold here. Abruptly, he shook Nash's hand, and he left.

When Nash was quite alone, he dug out a wax pencil and a sheet of butcher paper, and began to write down all he remembered about Mary, trying to balance the good (her intelligence and, generally speaking, kindness) with the bad—her having murdered people, for instance. He remembered then the salty tracks on Squonk's cheeks—if they had been there at all—and as he thought of them glistening, they enraged him. False, awful, sour, heedless crocodile tears, the worst kind of carny, the lowest of men, working Nash like a sucker.

He wrote long into the afternoon, had a snack, and then began to rewrite everything into a short and morally instructive playlet, which could be performed by a small circus. It was about a wicked clown and the elephant he tricked. When he was done, Nash realized he was about to shop for another elephant, and he made a note to send out wires to Sarasota, where the circus exchange kept track of such requests.

From 1919 to 1924, the Nash Family presented their circus as ever, sometimes lucky enough to adhere to a strict schedule when times were good, other times blowing the route and wildcatting it until business caught on again. The lynchpin of their show was Nash's playlet, a melodrama that featured the impish and terrible antics of Moxie, a clown, and Regina, a luckless and sad elephant suffering fits during which she accidentally murdered people. Finally, she was taken outside, and, as seen in a silhouette projected against the raw canvas tent, hanged until dead.

In his broadsides, and his talking before the performance, Nash explained that every word was the truth, including the hanging, though he had changed the names. It was said that the finale was done in shadow because of its graphic and disturbing nature, which was true, but actually secondary to its function as a special effect. Nash would never really harm the elephant, whom he loved: a second love, the cautious kind. This one was named Emily, and she had credentials so spotless her owner liked to say she could run for the Senate.

The crowds were entertained and disturbed by the spectacle, which was never quite the success Nash hoped. When the flaps to the tent opened after each performance, the crowds were hesitant to leave, and some audience member stayed behind to talk to Nash. There had been rumors, promulgated in whispers by other Nash Family performers, that Mary had killed even before she'd met Squonk. He was an awful man, to be sure, but wasn't Mary herself also guilty? Wasn't the execution, even if facilitated by Squonk, somewhat just? And Bales, did he escape, just like that? Did he kill again? Why wasn't he brought to justice in the end? And though Nash tried to answer the questions, he always grew flustered, as if the audience were missing the point, and he would retire to his wagon for the night.

There is no record of the last performance; it was never truly historical or important. It was unusual, a sort of passion play on a pachydermic scale, but though generous in spirit, it was too small a venue—melodrama—to incorporate a serious truth: just as there are intelligent, wicked men, there are intelligent, wicked elephants. A thing of pure nature is not by necessity a good thing.

Just before the turn of the new century, the story of Mary was determined to be folklore, a confused truncation of the truth, something contradicted by old-time Olsonites, rerouted by oral historians: all a lie, it was now said. There were rumors of an amateur film (long-since disintegrated "safety" film that was no more stable than nitrate in the end)—exactly the kind of red herring "evidence" that indicated an urban legend at play. There had indeed been posters featuring an elephant named Mary, and several years later an odd play about hanging an elephant. But this was a play put on nowhere better than a circus, and it was apparent people had confused this with the truth. An elephant hanged? Papers were composed in the anthropology department of the University of Tennessee about the conflation of lynching narratives with that of an elephant. It was explained that the story evolved from a need to dehumanize the victims, or, in a contradictory interpretation, to enrage the very people who would never lift a finger to protect a fellow human being.

When facing the past, and attempting to do so squarely, it's difficult to understand what is marvelous, what is real, what is terrible, and what points overlap.

But there has been a recent development: Wildwood Hill, long ago surrounded by the blue fencing and tarpaulins of a Superfund site, has been purchased by the petrochemical combine that inherited the land in a deal with the vanished McKennon Railroad. There is a move to cap the area in advance of a toxic waste cleanup, and the first gesture is to dig wells into the hill's core, to test the soil for penetration of leeching chemicals.

Ten yards from the end of the tracks, under debris from six generations of abandoned railroad technology, is an excavation site twenty feet wide and twenty feet deep, scratched out of the clay almost a hundred years ago, and filled in again almost immediately. At the center, among the roots and weeds, the tiny stones and shards of broken glass and metal, lie elephant bones.

Caked with dirt, dark with dried tissues, they also gleam with a necklace of stainless steel chain, and there is a shroud, once probably red, once likely ruffled and imperial, now as decayed and colorless as the dirt.

Note: This story could only have been written with the aid of
The Day They Hung the Elephant *by Charles Edwin Price.*

DO NOT DISTURB

by A.M. HOMES

MY WIFE, THE DOCTOR, is not well. In the end she could be dead. It started suddenly, on a country weekend, a movie with friends, a pizza, and then pain.

"I liked the part where he lunged at the woman with a knife," Eric says.

"She deserved it," Enid says.

"Excuse me," my wife says, getting up from the table.

A few minutes later I find her doubled over on the sidewalk. "Something is ripping me from the inside out."

"Should I get the check?" She looks at me like I am an idiot.

"My wife is not well," I announce, returning to the table. "We have to go."

"What do you mean—is she all right?"

Eric and Enid hurry out while I wait for the check. They drive us home. As I open the front door, my wife pushes past me and goes running for the bathroom. Eric, Enid, and I stand in the living room, waiting.

"Are you all right in there?" I call out.

"No," she says.

"Maybe she should go to the hospital," Enid says.

"Doctors don't go to the hospital," I say.

She is a specialist in emergency medicine. All day she is at the hospital putting the pieces back together and then she comes home to me. I am not the one who takes care. I am the one who is always on the verge.

Austrian Officer's Gilt Cross

"Call us if you need us," Eric and Enid say, leaving.

She lies on the bathroom floor, her cheek against the white tile. "I keep thinking it will pass."

I tuck the bath mat under her head and sneak away. From the kitchen I call a doctor friend. I stand in the dark, whispering, "She's just lying there on the floor, what do I do?"

"Don't do anything," the doctor says, half-insulted by the thought that there is something to do. "Observe her. Either it will go away, or something more will happen. You watch and you wait."

Watch and wait. I'm thinking about our relationship. We haven't been getting along. The situation has become oxygenless and addictive, a suffocating annihilation, each staying to see how far it will go.

I sit on the edge of the tub, looking at her. "I'm worried."

"Don't worry," she says. "And don't just sit there staring."

Earlier in the afternoon we were fighting, I don't remember about what. I only know—I called her a bitch.

"I was a bitch before I met you and I'll be a bitch long after you're gone. Surprise me," she said, "tell me something new."

I wanted to say I'm leaving. I wanted to say, I know you think I never will and that's why you treat me like you do. But I'm going. I wanted to get in the car, drive off and call it a day.

The fight ended with the clock. She glanced at it. "It's six thirty, we're meeting Eric and Enid at seven; put on a clean shirt."

She is lying on the bathroom floor, the print of the bathmat making an impression on her cheek. "Are you comfortable?" I ask.

She looks surprised, as though she's just realized she's on the floor.

"Help me," she says, struggling to get up.

Her lips are white and thin.

"Bring me a trash can, a plastic bag, a thermometer, some Tylenol, and a glass of water."

"Are you going to throw up?"

"I want to be prepared," she says.

We are always prepared. The ongoing potential for things to go wrong is our bond, a fascination with crisis, with control. We have flare guns and fire extinguishers, walkie talkies, a rubber raft, a small generator, a hundred batteries in assorted shapes and sizes, a thousand bucks in dollar bills, enough toilet paper and bottled water to get us through six months. When we travel we have smoke hoods in our carry-on bags, protein bars, water purification tablets, and a king-sized bag of M&M's.

She slips the digital thermometer under her tongue; the numbers move up the scale—each beep is a tenth of a degree.

"A hundred and one point four," I announce.

"I have a fever?" she says in disbelief.

"I wish things between us weren't so bad."

"It not as bad as you think," she says. "Expect less and you won't be disappointed."

We try to sleep; she is hot, she is cold, she is mumbling something about having "a surgical belly," something about "guarding and rebound." I don't know if she's talking about herself or the NBA.

"This is incredible," she sits bolt upright and folds over again, writhing. "Something is struggling inside me. It's like one of those alien movies, like I'm going to burst open and something is going to spew out, like I'm erupting."

She pauses, takes a breath. "And then it stops. Who would ever have thought this would happen to me—and on a Saturday night?"

"Is it your appendix?"

"That's the one thought I have, but I'm not sure. I don't have the classic symptoms. I don't have anorexia or diarrhea. When I was eating that pizza, I was hungry."

"Is it an ovary? Women have lots of ovaries."

"Women have two ovaries," she says. "It did occur to me that could be Mittelschmertz."

"Mittelschmertz?"

"The launching of the egg, the middle of the cycle."

At five in the morning her temperature is one hundred and three. She is alternately sweating and shivering.

"Should I drive you back to the city or to the hospital out here?"

"I don't want to be the doctor who goes to the ER with gas."

"Fine."

I'm dressing myself, packing, thinking of what I'll need: cell phone, note book, pen, something to read, something to eat, wallet, insurance card.

We are in the car, hurrying. There's an urgency to the situation, the unmistakable sense that something bad is happening. I am driving seventy miles an hour.

"I think I'm dying," she says.

I pull up to the emergency entrance and half-carry her in, leaving the car doors open, the engine running; I have the impulse to drop her off and walk away.

The emergency room is empty. There is a bell on the check-in desk. I ring it twice.

A woman appears. "Can I help you?"

"My wife is not well," I say. "She's a doctor."

The woman sits at her computer. She takes my wife's name and number. She takes her insurance card and then her temperature and blood pressure. "Are you in a lot of pain?"

"Yes," my wife says.

Within minutes a doctor is there, pressing on my wife. "It's got to come out," he says.

"What?" I ask.

"Appendix. Do you want some Demerol?"

She shakes her head. "I'm working tomorrow and I'm on call."

"What kind of doctor are you?"

"Emergency medicine."

In the cubicle next to her, someone vomits.

The nurse comes to take blood. "They called Barry Manilow, he's a very good surgeon." She ties off my wife's arm. "We call him Barry Manilow because he looks like Barry Manilow."

"I want to do right by you," Barry Manilow says, as he's feeling my wife's belly. "I'm not sure it's your appendix, not sure it's your gall bladder either. I'm going to call the radiologist and let him scan it. How's that sound?"

She nods.

I take the surgeon aside. "Should she be staying here? Is this the place to do this?"

"It's not a kidney transplant," he says.

The nurse brings me a cold drink. She offers me a chair. I sit close to the gurney where my wife lies. "Do you want me to get you out of here? I could hire a car and have us driven to the city. I could have you med-evaced home."

"I don't want to go anywhere," she says.

Back in the cubicle, Barry Manilow is talking to her. "It's not your appendix. It's your ovary. It's a hemorrhagic cyst; you're bleeding and your hematocrit is falling. We have to operate. I've called a gynecologist and the anesthesiologist—I'm just waiting for them to arrive. We're going to take you upstairs very soon."

"Just do it," she says.

I stop Barry Manilow in the hall. "Can you try and save the ovary? She very much wants to have children. It's just something she hasn't gotten around to yet—first she had her career, then me, and now this."

"We'll do everything we can," he says, disappearing through the door marked Authorized Personnel Only.

I am the only one in the surgical waiting room, flipping through copies of Field and Stream, Highlights for Children, a pamphlet on colon cancer. Less than an hour later, Barry Manilow comes to find me. "We saved the ovary. We took out something the size of a lemon."

"The size of a lemon?"

He makes a fist and holds it up. "A lemon," he says. "It looked a little funny. We sent it to Pathology." He shrugs.

A lemon, a bleeding lemon, like a blood orange, a lemon souring in her. Why is fruit used as the universal medical measurement?

"She should be upstairs in about an hour."

When I get to her room she is asleep. A tube poking out from under the covers drains urine into a bag. She is hooked up to oxygen and an IV.

I put my hand on her forehead. Her eyes open.

"A little fresh air," she says, pulling at the oxygen tube. "I always wondered what all this felt like."

She has a morphine drip, the kind she can control herself. She keeps the clicker in hand. She never pushes the button.

I feed her ice chips and climb into the bed next to her. In the middle of the night I go home. In the morning she calls, waking me up.

"Flowers have been arriving like crazy," she says, "from the hospital, from the ER, from the clinic."

Doctors are like firemen; when one of their own is down they go crazy.

"They took the catheter out, I'm sitting up in a chair. I already had some juice and took myself to the bathroom," she says, proudly. "They couldn't be nicer. But of course, I'm a very good patient."

I interrupt her. "Do you want anything from the house?"

"Clean socks, a pair of sweat pants, my hair brush, some toothpaste, my face soap, a radio, maybe a can of Diet Coke."

"You're only going to be there a couple of days."

"You asked if I needed anything. Don't forget to feed the dog."

Five minutes later she calls back—crying. "Guess what, I have ovarian cancer."

I run out the door. When I get there the room is empty. I'm expecting a big romantic crying scene, expecting her to cling to me, to tell me how much she loves me, how she's sorry we've been having such a hard time, how much she needs me, wants me, now more than ever. The bed is empty. For a moment I think she's died, jumped out the window, escaped.

In the bathroom, the toilet flushes. "I want to go home," she says, stepping out, fully dressed.

"Do you want to take the flowers?"

"They're mine, aren't they? Do you think all the nurses know I have can-cer? I don't want anyone to know."

The nurse comes with a wheelchair; she takes us down to the lobby. "Good luck," she says, loading the flowers into the car.

"She knows," my wife says.

We're on the Long Island Expressway. I am dialing and driving. I call my wife's doctor in New York.

"She has to see Kibbowitz immediately," the doctor says.

"Do you think I'll lose my ovary?"

She will lose everything. Instinctively I know that.

We are home. She is on the bed with the dog on her lap. She peaks beneath the gauze; her incision is crooked, the lack of precision an incredible insult. "Do you think they can fix it?" she asks.

In the morning we go to Kibbowitz. She is again on a table, her feet in the stirrups, in launch position, waiting. Before the doctor arrives she is interviewed and examined by seven medical students. I hate them. I hate them for talking to her, for touching her, for wasting her time. I hate Kibbowitz for keeping her on the table for more than an hour, waiting.

She is angry with me for being annoyed. "They're just doing their job."

Kibbowitz arrives. He is enormous, like a hockey player, a brute and a bully. I can tell immediately that she likes him. She will do anything he says.

"Scootch down a little closer to me," he says settling himself on a stool between her legs. She lifts her ass and slides down. He examines her. He peeks under the gauze. "Crooked," he says. "Get dressed and meet me in my office."

"I want a number," she says. "A survival rate."

"I don't deal in numbers," he says.

"I need a number."

He shrugs. "How's seventy percent."

"Seventy percent what?"

"Seventy percent live five years."

"And then what?" I ask.

"And then some don't," he says.

"What has to come out?" she asks.

"What do you want to keep? "

"I wanted to have a child."

This is a delicate negotiation; they talk parts. "I could take just the one ovary," he says. "And then after the chemo you could try and get pregnant and then after you had a child we could go in and get the rest."

"Can you really get pregnant after chemo?" I ask.

The doctor shrugs. "Miracles happen all the time," he says. "The problem is you can't raise a child if you're dead. You don't have to decide now, let me know in a day or two. Meanwhile I'm going to book the operating room for Friday morning. "Nice meeting you," he says, shaking my hand.

"I want to have a baby," she says.

"I want to have you," I say.

Beyond that I say nothing. Whatever I say she will do the opposite. We are at that point—spite, blame, and fault. I don't want to be held responsible.

She opens the door of the consulting room. "Doctor," she shouts, hurrying down the hall after him, clutching her belly, her incision, her wound. "Take it," she screams. "Take it all the hell out."

He is standing outside another examining room, chart in hand.

He nods. "We'll take it though your vagina. We'll take the ovaries, the uterus, cervix, omentum, and your appendix if they didn't already get it in Southampton. And then we'll put a port in your neck and sign you up for chemotherapy, eight rounds should do it."

She nods.

"See you Friday."

We leave. I'm holding her hand, holding her pocketbook on my shoulder trying to be as good as anyone can be. She is growling and scratching; it's like taking a cat to the vet.

"Why don't they just say eviscerate? Why don't they just come out and say on Friday at nine we're going to eviscerate you—be ready."

"Do you want a little lunch?" I ask as we are walking down the street. "Some soup? There's a lovely restaurant near here."

She looks flushed. I put my hand to her forehead. She's burning up. "You have a fever. Did you mention that to the doctor?"

"It's not relevant."

Later when we are home, I ask, "Do you remember our third date? Do you remember asking me—how would you kill yourself if you had to do it with bare hands? I said I would break my nose and shove it up into my brain and you said you would reach up with your bare hands and rip your uterus out through your vagina and throw it across the room."

"What's your point?"

"No point, I just suddenly remembered it. Isn't Kibbowitz taking your uterus out through your vagina?"

"I doubt he's going to throw it across the room," she says. There is a pause. "You don't have to stay with me now that I have cancer. I don't need you. I don't need anyone. I don't need anything."

"If I left, I wouldn't be leaving because you have cancer. But I would look like an ass, everyone would think I couldn't take it."

"I would make sure they knew it was me, that I was a monster, a cold steely monster, that I drove you away."

"They wouldn't believe you."

She suddenly farts and runs embarrassed into the bathroom—as though this is the first time she's farted in her life. "My life is ruined," she yells, slamming the door.

"Farting is the least of it," I say.

When she comes out she is calmer. She crawls into bed next to me, wrung out, shivering.

I hold her. "Do you want to make love?"

"You mean one last time before I'm not a woman, before I'm a dried old husk?"

Instead of fucking we fight. It's the same sort of thing, dramatic, draining. When we're done, I roll over and sleep in a tight knot on my side of the bed.

"Surgical menopause," she says. "That sounds so final."

I turn toward her. She runs her hand over her pubic hair. "Do you think they'll shave me?"

I'm not going to be able to leave the woman with cancer. I'm not the kind of person who leaves the woman with cancer, but I don't know what you do when the woman with cancer is a bitch. Do you hope that the cancer prompts the woman to reevaluate herself, to take it as an opportunity, a signal for change? As far as she's concerned there is no such thing as the mind/body connection, there is science and there is law. There is fact and everything else is bullshit.

Friday morning, while she's in the hospital registration area waiting for her number to be called, she makes another list out loud: "My will is in the top left drawer of the dresser. If anything goes wrong pull the plug. No heroic measures. I want to be cremated. Donate my organs. Give it away, all of it, every last drop." She stops. "I guess no one will want me now that I'm contaminated." She says the word contaminated, filled with disgust, disappointment, as though she has soiled herself.

It is nearly eight p.m. when Kibbowitz comes out to tell me he's done. "Everything was stuck together like macaroni and cheese. It took longer than I expected. I found some in the fallopian tube and some on the wall of her abdomen. We cleaned everything out."

She is wheeled back to her room, sad, agitated, angry.

"Why didn't you come and see me?" she asks, accusitorily.

"I was right there the whole time, on the other side of the door waiting for word."

She acts as though she doesn't believe me, as though I went off and screwed a secretary from the patient services office while she was on the table.

"How're you feeling?"

"As though I've taken a trip to another country and my suitcases are lost."

She is writhing. I adjust her pillow, the position of the bed.

"What hurts?"

"What doesn't hurt? Everything hurts. Breathing hurts."

Because she is a doctor, because she did her residency at this hospital, they give me a small folding cot to set up in the corner of the room. Bending to unfold it, something happens in my back, a hot searing pain spreads across and down. I lower myself to the floor, grabbing the blanket as I go.

Luckily, she is sleeping.

The nurse coming in to check her vital signs sees me. "Are you in trouble?" she asks.

"It's happened before," I say. "I'll just lie here and see what happens."

She brings me a pillow and covers me with the blanket.

Eric and Enid arrive. My wife is asleep and I am still on the floor. Eric stands over me.

"We're sorry," Eric whispers. "We didn't get your message until today. We were at Enid's parents—upstate."

"It's shocking, it's sudden, it's so out of the blue." Enid moves to look at my wife. "She looks like she's in a really bad mood, her brow is furrowed. Is she in pain?"

"I assume so."

"If there's anything we can do, let us know," Eric says.

"Actually, could you walk the dog?" I pull the keys out of my pocket and hold them in the air. "He's been home alone all day and all night."

"Walk the dog, I think we can do that," Eric says, looking at Enid for confirmation.

"We'll check on you in the morning," Enid says.

"Before you go; there's a bottle of Percocet in her purse—give me two."

During the night she wakes up. "Where are you?" she asks.

"I'm right here."

She is sufficiently drugged that she doesn't ask for details. At around six she opens her eyes and sees me on the floor.

"Your back?"

"Yep."

"Cancer beats back," she says and falls back to sleep.

When the cleaning man comes with the damp mop, I pry myself off the floor. I'm fine as long as I'm standing.

"You're walking like you have a rod up your ass," my wife says.

"Is there anything I can do for you?" I ask, trying to be solicitous.

"Can you have cancer for me?"

The pain management team arrives to check on my wife's level of comfort.

"On a scale of one to ten how do you feel?" the pain fellow asks.

"Five," my wife says.

"She lies," I say.

"Are you lying?"

"How can you tell?"

The specialist arrives, "I know you," he says, seeing my wife in the bed. "We went to school together."

My wife tries to smile.

"You were the smartest one in the class and now look," he reads my wife's chart. "Ovarian cancer and you, that's horrible."

My wife is sitting up high in her hospital bed, puking her guts into a metal bucket, like a poisoned pet monkey. She is throwing up bright green like an alien, like nothing anyone has seen before. Ted, her boss, stares at her, mesmerized.

The room is filled with people—people I don't know, medical people, people she went to school with, people she did her residency with, a man whose fingers she sewed back on, relatives I've not met. I don't understand why they don't excuse themselves, why they don't step out of the room. They're all watching her like they've never seen anyone throw up before—riveted.

She is not sleeping. She is not eating. She is not getting up and walking around. She is afraid to leave her bed, afraid to leave her bucket.

I make a sign for the door. I borrow a black magic marker from the charge nurse and print in large black letters: Do Not Disturb.

They push the door open. They come bearing gifts, flowers, food, books. "I saw the sign, I assumed it was for someone else."

I am wiping green spittle from her lips.

"Do you want me to get rid of everyone?" I ask.

I want to get rid of everyone. The idea that these people have some claim to her, some right to entertain, distract, bother her more than me, drives me up the wall. "Should I tell them to go?"

She shakes her head. "Just the flowers, the flowers nauseate me."

An hour later, I empty the bucket again. The room remains overcrowded. I am on my knees by the side of her hospital bed, whispering "I'm leaving."

"Are you coming back?" she whispers.

"No."

She looks at me strangely. "Where are you going?"

"Away."

"Bring me a Diet Coke."

She has missed the point.

It is heartbreaking seeing her in a stained gown, in the middle of a bed, unable to tell everyone to go home, unable to turn it off. Her pager is clipped to her hospital gown, several times it goes off. She returns the calls. She always returns the calls. I imagine her saying, "What the hell are you bothering me for—I'm busy, I'm having cancer."

Later, I'm on the edge of the bed, looking at her. She is increasingly beautiful, more vulnerable, female.

"Honey?"

"What?" Her intonation is like a pissy caged bird—cawww. "What? What are you looking at? What do you want?" Cawww.

"Nothing."

I am washing her with a cool washcloth.

"You're tickling me," she complains.

"Make sure you tell her you still find her attractive," a man in the hall tells me. "Husbands of women who have mastectomies need to keep reminding their wives that they are beautiful."

"She had a hysterectomy," I say.

"Same thing."

Two days later, they remove the packing. I am in the room when the resident comes with long tweezers like tongs and pulls yards of material from her vagina, wads of cotton, gauze, stained battlefield red. It's like a magic trick gone awry, one those jokes about how many people you can fit in a telephone booth; more and more keeps coming out.

"Is there anything left in there?" she asks.

The resident shakes his head "Your vagina now just comes to a stop, it's a stump, an unconnected sleeve. Don't be surprised if you bleed, if you pop a stitch of two." He checks her chart and signs her out. "Kibbowitz has you on pelvic rest for six weeks."

"Pelvic rest?" I ask.

"No fucking," she says.

Not a problem.

Home. She watches forty-eight hours of Holocaust films on cable TV. Although she claims to compartmentalize everything, suddenly she identifies with the bald, starving prisoners of war. She sees herself as a victim. She points to the naked corpse of a woman, "That's me," she says. "That's exactly how I feel."

"She's dead," I say.

"Exactly."

Her notorious vigilance is gone. As I'm fluffing her pillows, her billy club rolls out from under the bed. "Put it in the closet," she says.

"Why?" I ask, rolling it back under the bed.

"Why sleep with a billy club under the bed? Why do anything when you have cancer?"

During a break between *Schindler's List*, *Shoah*, and *The Sorrow and the Pity* she taps me, "I'm missing my parts," she says. "Maybe one of those lost eggs was someone special, someone who would have cured something, someone who would have invented something wonderful. You never know who was in there. They're my lost children."

"I'm sorry."

"For what?" she looks at me accusingly.

"Everything."

"Thirty-eight-year-olds don't get cancer, they get Lyme disease, maybe they have appendicitis, on rare occasions in some other parts of the world they have Siamese twins, but that's it."

In the middle of the night she wakes up, throws the covers off, "I can't breathe, I'm burning up. Open the window, I'm hot, I'm so hot."

"Do you know what's happening to you?"

"What are you talking about?"

"You're having hot flashes."

"I am not," she says as though I've insulted her. "They don't start so soon." They do.

"Get away from me, get away," she yells. "Just being near you makes me uncomfortable, it makes my temperature unstable."

On Monday she starts chemotherapy.

"Will I go bald?" she asks the nurse.

"Most women buy a wig before it happens," the nurse says, plugging her into the magic potion.

I am afraid that when she's bald I won't love her anymore. I can not imagine my wife bald.

One of the other women, her head wrapped in a red turban, leans over and whispers, "My husband says I look like a porno star." She winks. She has no eyebrows, no eye lashes, nothing.

We shop for a wig. She tries on every style, every shape and color. She looks like a man in drag, like it's all a horrible joke.

"Maybe my hair won't fall out?" she says.

"It's okay," the woman in the wig shop says. "Insurance covers it. Ask your doctor to write a prescription for a cranial prosthesis."

"I'm a doctor," my wife says.

The wig woman looks confused. "It's okay," she says, putting another wig on my wife's head.

She buys a wig. I never see it. She brings it home and immediately puts it in the closet. "It looks like Linda Evans, like someone on *Dynasty*. I just can't do it," she says.

Her scalp begins to tingle. Her hair hurts. "It's like someone grabbed my hair and is pulling as hard as they can."

"It's getting ready to go. It's like a time bomb. It ticks and then it blows."

"What are you, a doctor? Suddenly you know everything about cancer, about menopause, about everything?"

In the morning her hair is falling out. It's all over the pillow, all over the shower floor.

"Your hair's not really falling out," Enid says when we meet them for dinner. Enid reaches and touches her hair, sweeps her hand through it, as if to be comforting. She ends up with a hand full of hair; she has pulled my wife's hair out. She tries to put it back, she furiously pats it back in place.

"Forget that I was worried about them shaving my pubic hair, how 'bout it all just went down the drain."

She looks like a rat, like something that's been chewed on and spit out, like something that someone tried to electrocute and failed. In four days she is eighty percent bald.

She stands before me naked. "Document me."

I take pictures. I take the film to one of those special stores that has a sign in the window—we don't censor.

I give her a baseball cap to wear to work. Every day she goes to work; she will not miss a day, no matter what.

I, on the other hand, can't work. Since this happened, my work has been non-existent. I spend my day as the holder of the feelings, the keeper of sensation.

"It's not my fault," she says. "What the hell do you do all day while I'm at the hospital?"

Recuperate.

She wears the baseball cap for a week and then takes a razor, shaves the few scraggly hairs that remain and goes to work bald, without a hat, without a wig—starkers.

There's something aggressive about her baldness.

"How do you feel?" I ask at night when she comes home from the hospital.

"I feel nothing."

"How can you feel nothing? What are you made of?"

"I am made of steel and wood," she says, happily.

As we're falling asleep she tells me a story, "It's true, it happened as I was walking into the hospital. I accidentally bumped into someone on the side-walk. 'Excuse me,' I said and continued on. He ran after me, 'Excuse me, Excuse me. You knocked my comb out of my hand and I want you to go back and pick it up.' 'What? We bumped into each other, I said excuse me, that will have to suffice.' 'You knocked it out of my hand on purpose. You're just a bald bitch. A fucking bald bitch.' I wheeled around and chased him. 'You fucking crazy ass,' I screamed. 'You fucking crazy ass,' I screamed it about four times. He's lucky I didn't fucking kill him," she says.

I am thinking she's lost her mind. I'm thinking she's lucky he didn't kill her.

She gets up and stands on the bed—naked. She strikes a pose like a body builder. "Cancer Man," she says, flexing her muscles, creating a new super hero. "Cancer Man!"

Luckily she has good insurance. The bill for the surgery comes—it's item-ized. They charge per part removed. Ovary $7,000, appendix $5,000, the total is $72,000 dollars. "It's all in a day's work," she says.

We are lying in bed. I am lying next to her, reading the paper.

"I want to go to a desert island, alone. I don't want to come back until this is finished," she says and then looks at me. "It will never be finished—do you know that? I'm not going to have children and I'm going to die."

"Do you really think you're going to die?"

"Yes."

I reach for her.

"Don't," she says. "Don't go looking for trouble."

"I wasn't. I was trying to be loving."

"I don't feel loving," she says. "I don't feel physically bonded to anyone right now, including myself."

"Will we ever again?"

"I don't know."

"You're pushing me away."

"I'm recovering," she says.

"It's been eighteen weeks."

Her blood counts are low. Every night for five nights, I inject her with Nupagen to increase the white blood cells. She teaches me how to prepare the injection, how to push the needle into the muscle of her leg. Every time I inject her, I apologize.

"For what?" she asks.

"Hurting you."

"Forget it," she says, disposing of the needle.

She rolls far away from me in her sleep. She dreams of strange things.

"I dreamed I was with my former boyfriend and he turned into a black woman slave and she was on top of me, between my legs, a lesbian slave fantasy."

"Could I have a hug?" I ask.

She glares at me. "Why do you persist? Why do you keep asking me for things I can't do, things I can't give?"

"A hug?"

"I can't give you one."

"Anyone can give a hug. I can get a hug from the doorman."

"Then do," she says. "I need to be married to someone who is like a potted plant, someone who needs nothing."

"Water?"

"Very little, someone who's like a cactus or an orchid."

"It's like you're refusing to be human," I tell her.

"I have no interest in being human."

This is information I should be paying attention to. She is telling me something and I'm not listening. I don't believe what she is saying.

I go to dinner with Eric and Enid alone.

"It's strange," they say. "You'd think the cancer would soften her, make her more appreciative. You'd think it would make her stop and think about what she wants to do with the rest of her life. When you ask her what does she say?" Eric and Enid want to know.

"Nothing. She says she wants nothing, she has no needs or desires. She says she has nothing to give."

Eric and Enid shake their heads. "What are you going to do?"

I shrug. None of this is new, none of this is just because she has cancer—that's important to keep in mind, this is exactly the way she always was, only more so.

A few days later a woman calls; she and her husband are people we see occasionally.

"Hi, how are you, how's Tom?" I ask.

"He's a fucking asshole," she says. "Haven't you heard? He left me."

"When?"

"About two weeks ago. I thought you would have known."

"I'm a little out of it."

"Anyway, I'm calling to see if you'd like to have lunch."

"Lunch, sure. Lunch would be good."

At lunch she is a little flirty, which is fine, it's nice actually, it's been a long time since someone flirted with me. In the end, when we're having coffee, she spills the beans, "So I guess, you're wondering why I called you?"

"I guess," I say, although I'm perfectly pleased to be having lunch, to be listening to someone else's troubles.

"I heard your wife was sick, I figured you're not getting a lot of sex and I thought we could have an affair."

I don't know which part is worse, the complete lack of seduction, the fact that she mentions my wife not being well, the idea that my wife's illness would make me want to sleep with her, her stun-gun bluntness—it's all too much.

"What do you think? Am I repulsive? Thoroughly disgusting? Is it the craziest thing you ever heard?"

"I'm very busy," I say, not knowing what to say, not wanting to be offensive, or seem to have taken offense. "I'm just very busy."

My wife comes home from work. "Someone came in today—he reminded me of you."

"What was his problem?"

"He jumped out the window."

"Dead?"

"Yes," she says, washing her hands in the kitchen sink.

"Was he dead when he got to you?" There's something in her tone that makes me wonder, did she kill him?

"Pretty much."

"What part reminded you of me?"

"He was having an argument with his wife."

"Oh?"

"Imagine her standing in the living room, in the middle of a sentence and out the window he goes. Imagine her not having a chance to finish her thought?"

"Yes, imagine, not being able to have the last word?"

"Did she try and stop him?" I ask.

"I don't know, " my wife says. "I didn't get to read the police report. I just thought you'd find it interesting."

"What do you want for dinner?"

"Nothing," she says. "I'm not hungry."

"You have to eat something."

"Why? I have cancer. I can do whatever I want."

Something has to happen.

I buy tickets to Paris, "We have to go." I invoke the magic word, "It's an emergency."

"It's not like I get a day off. It's not like I come home at the end of the day and I don't have cancer. It goes everywhere with me. It doesn't matter where I am, it's still me—it's me with cancer. In Paris I'll have cancer."

I dig out the maps, the guide books, everything we did on our last trip is marked with fluorescent highlighter. I am acting as though I believe that if we retrace our steps, if we return to a place where things were good, there will be an automatic correction, an psychic chiropractic event, which will put everything into alignment.

I gather provisions for the plane: smoke hoods, fresh water, fruit, M&M's, magazines.

"What's the point," she says, throwing a few things into a suitcase. "You can do everything and think you're prepared, but you don't know what's going to happen. You don't see what's coming until it hits you in the face."

She points at someone outside. "See that idiot crossing the street in front of the truck, why doesn't he have cancer? He deserves to die."

She lifts her suitcase—too heavy. She takes things out. She leaves her smoke hood on the bed. "If the plane fills with smoke, I'm going to be so happy," she says. "I'm going to breathe deeply, I'm going to be the first to die."

I stuff the smoke hood into my suitcase, along with her rain coat, her extra shoes, ace bandages for her bad ankle, reusable ice packs just in case, vitamin C drops. I lift the suitcases, feeling like a pack animal, a sherpa.

In France, the customs people are not used to seeing bald women. They call her "Sir."

"Sir, you're next, Sir. Sir, please step over here, Sir."

My wife is my husband. She loves it. She smiles. She catches my eye and strikes a subdued version of the super hero/body builder pose, flexing. "Cancer Man," she says.

"And what is the purpose of your visit to France?" the inspector asks. "Business or pleasure?"

"Reconciliation," I say, watching her—Cancer Man.

"Business or pleasure?"

"Pleasure."

Paris is my fantasy, my last-ditch effort to reclaim my marriage, myself, my wife.

As we're checking in to the hotel, I remind her of our previous visit—the chef cut himself, his hand was severed, she saved it and they were able to reattach it. "You made medical history. Remember the beautiful dinner they threw in your honor."

"It was supposed to be a vacation," she says.

The bell man takes us to our room—there's a big basket of fruit, bottles of Champagne and Evian with a note from the concierge welcoming us.

"It's not as nice as it used to be," she says, already disappointed. She opens the Evian and drinks. Her lips curl. "Even the water tastes bad."

"Maybe it's you. Maybe the water is fine. Is it possible you're wrong?"

"We see things differently," she says, meaning she's right, I'm wrong.

"Are you in an especially bad mood, or is it just the cancer?" I ask.

"Maybe it's you?" she says.

We go for a walk, across the river and down by the Louvre. There could be nothing better, nothing more perfect and yet I am suddenly hating Paris, hating it more than anything, the beauty, the fineness of it is dwarfed by her foul humor. I realize there is no saving it, no moment of reconciliation, redemption. Everything sucks. It is irredeemably awful and getting worse.

"If you're so unhappy, why don't you leave?" I ask her.

"I keep thinking you'll change."

"If I changed anymore I can't imagine who I'd be."

"Well if I'm such a bitch, why do you stay?"

"It's my job, it's my calling to stay with you, to soften you."

"I absolutely do not want to be softer, I don't want to give another inch."

"Well, I am not a leaver, I worked hard to get here, to be able to stay."

She trips on a cobble stone, I reach for her elbow, to steady her and instead unbalance myself. She fails to catch me. I fall and recover quickly.

"Imagine how I feel," she says. "I'm a doctor and I can't fix it. I can't fix me, I can't fix you—what a lousy doctor."

"I'm losing you," I say.

"I've lost myself. Look at me—do I look like me?"

"You act like yourself."

"I act like myself because I have to, because people are counting on me."

"I'm counting on you."

"Stop counting."

All along the Touileries there are Ferris wheels, the world's largest Ferris wheel is set up in the middle.

"Let's go," I say, taking her hand, pulling her toward them.

"I don't like rides."

"It's not much of a ride. It's like a carousel, only vertical. Live a little."

She gets on. There are no seat belts, no safety bars. I say nothing. I am hoping she won't notice.

"How is it going to end?" I ask while we're waiting for the wheel to spin.

"I die in the end."

The ride takes off, climbing, pulling us up and over. We are flying, soaring; the city unfolds. It is breathtaking and higher than I thought. And faster. There is always a moment on any ride where you think it is too fast, too high, too far, too wide, and that you will not survive.

"I have never been so unhappy in my life," my wife says when we're near the top. "It's not just the cancer, I was unhappy before the cancer. We were having a very hard time. We don't get along, we're a bad match. Do you believe me?"

"Yes," I say, "We're a really bad match. We're such a good bad match it seems impossible to let it go."

"We're stuck," she says.

"You bet," I say.

"No. I mean the ride, the ride isn't moving."

"It's not stuck, it's just stopped. It stops along the way."

She begins to cry. "It's all your fault. I hate you. And I still have to deal with you. Every day I have to look at you."

"No, you don't. You don't have to deal with me if you don't want to."

She stops crying and looks at me. "What are you going to do, jump?"

"The rest of your life, or my life, however long or short, should not be miserable. It can't go on this way."

"We could both kill ourselves," she says.

"How about we separate?"

I am being more grown up than I am capable of being. I am terrified of being without her but either way, it's death. The ride lurches forward.

I came to Paris wanting to pull things together and suddenly I am desperate to be away from her, to never have this conversation again. She will be dying and we will still be fighting. I begin to panic, to feel I can't breathe. I have to get away.

"Where does it end?"

"How about we say goodbye."

"And then what? We have opera tickets."

I can't tell her I'm going. I have to sneak away, to tip toe out backward. I have to make my own arrangements.

We stop talking. We're hanging in mid-air, suspended. We have run out of things to say. When the ride circles down, the silence becomes more definitive.

I begin to make my plan. In truth, I have no idea what I am doing. All afternoon, everywhere we go, I cash travelers checks, I get cash advances, I have about five thousand dollars worth of francs stuffed in my pocket. I want to be able to leave without a trace, I want to be able to buy myself out of whatever trouble I get into. I am hysterical and giddy all at once.

We are having an early dinner on our way to the opera.

I time my break for just after the coffee comes. "Oops," I say, feeling my pockets, "I forgot my opera glasses."

"Really?" she says, "I thought you had them when we went out."

"They must be at the hotel. You go on ahead, I'll run back. You know I hate not being able to see."

She takes her ticket. "Hurry," she says. "I hate it when you're late."

This is the bravest thing I have ever done. I go back to the hotel and pack my bag. I'm going to get out. I'm going to fly away. I may never come back. I will begin again, as someone else, someone who wants to live, I will be unrecognizable.

I move to lift the bag off the bed, I pull it up and my knee goes out. I start to fall but catch myself. I pull at the bag and take a step—too heavy. I'll have to go without it. I'll have to leave everything behind. I drop the bag, but still I am falling, folding, collapsing. There is pain, spreading, pouring, hot and cold, like water down my back, down my legs.

I am lying on the floor, thinking that if I stay calm, if I can just find my breath, and follow my breath, it will pass. I lie there waiting for the paralysis to recede.

I am afraid of it being over and yet she has given me no choice, she has systematically withdrawn life support: sex and conversation. The problem is that despite this, she is the one I want.

There is a knock at the door. I know it is not her, it is too soon for it to be her.

"Entrée," I call out.

The maid opens the door, she holds the Do Not Disturb sign in her hand.

"Oooff," she says, seeing me on the floor. "Do you need the doctor?"

I am not sure if she means my wife or a doctor, a doctor other than my wife.

"No."

She takes a towel from her cart and props it under my head, she takes a spare blanket from the closet and covers me with it. She opens the Champagne and pours me a glass, tilting my head up so I can sip. She goes to her cart and gets a stack of night chocolates and sits beside me, feeding me Champagne and chocolate, stroking my forehead.

The phone in the room rings; we ignore it. She refills my glass. She takes my socks off and rubs my feet. She unbuttons my shirt and rubs my chest. I am getting a little drunk. I am just beginning to relax and then there is another knock, a knock my body recognizes before I am fully awake. Everything tightens. My back pulls tighter still, any sensation below my knees drops off.

"I thought something horrible happened to you. I've been calling and calling the room, why haven't you answered? I thought you'd killed yourself."

The maid excuses herself. She goes into the bathroom and refreshes my cool washcloth.

"What are you doing?" my wife asks.

There is nothing I can say.

"Knock off the mummy routine. What exactly are you doing? Were you trying to run away and then you chickened out? Say something."

To talk would be to continue; for the moment I am silenced. I am a potted plant and still that is not good enough for her.

"He is paralyzed," the maid says.

"He is not paralyzed, I am his wife, I am a doctor. I would know if there was something really wrong."

THE MAN FROM OUT OF TOWN

by SHEILA HETI

SINCE HIS FIRST day in town the man had been looking for a nice girl to spend good times with, but none of the girls would have him. He wasn't sure why but suspected it had to do with his status. The waitress who served him corroborated this when she called him a bum, even though he was not living on the street and he had two suits.

Not until his roommate found out the cause of his sorrowful mood did he call up a girl he had known from the park and invite her over for a dinner of pork and mashed potatoes with nutmeg.

It was her high ass that mysteriously lifted itself up to her waist that caused the man to see what a nice girl she was, and how pleasant she could be to spend good times with. She also had a sweet smile and some pretty funny things to say, and whenever she laughed the sun would stream a last dying ray in through the window. Noticing all this the roommate kept playing good tunes, and by the end of the night the man and the girl were dancing together and she was laughing into his shoulder; a good sign.

In the morning she sat on his couch in a denim shirt and yesterday's underwear, and her voice seemed deep when she said, "I'm going to be late for work."

"It's Sunday though."

"Still," and she looked out the window and the grayness of the day convinced her. Wandering into his room she found her suit and zipped it up, and left his apartment with a goodbye shrug. Following her with his eyes as she walked to the bus stop, the man knew that this was not the girl who would be agreeable to spending good times with him. It was not easy to explain.

In the afternoon he walked down the boardwalk, drinking warm soda from a red-and-white cup that was waxy on the outside and was gradually melting, when a man with a dog caught up to him and threw his arm around his shoulder and asked in a jaunty voice what the matter was.

The man who was new in town was startled because he did not expect city people to care about each other, but he answered saying, "It's that the woman who came over last night seemed to really like me but she left this morning without making plans to see me again."

"I know what it's like. I thought it must be women that were troubling you because of that troubling look on your face. You ought to come to where I work tonight, because there are plenty of pretty ladies where I work."

"Where do you work?"

"A dance club."

"Oh no," said the man who was from a small town. "I don't mean that I want to pay a woman to take off her clothes."

That night as he sat in a booth by the wall, a tall voluptuous woman with red hair came and sat across from him. When she spoke her voice was tiny and girlish, and when he spoke back her eyes lit up, knowing a good man when she saw one. If he found her interest in him any consolation he did not show it, and continued to order drinks which cost seven dollars.

"Let me put that next one on my tab," she said, and adjusted her body in such a way that her breasts raised themselves parallel to the table. The man did not fail to notice this.

"Would you like to come home with me tonight?" he asked.

Growing suspicious, she said, "I thought you were a different sort of man, that's what Henry told me, and now you ask me the question everyone asks."

"I'm so ashamed," he responded sincerely. "I didn't mean it that way, but I don't like being alone, and you seem like a kind woman who would be a pleasure to spend good times with, even just talking."

She found this genuine enough, and was touched that there was nothing of the brute in him; perhaps Henry was right. Even her so-called sisters, whom she hastily consulted in the back room, gave approving nods when they saw his modest eyes looking mainly at the fixtures.

The apartment was sticky because of the heat, and it wasn't long before they were lying in their underwear on his bed, and he was telling how he had become a widower so young, which was a lie for he had never been married, or even in a real relationship twice. Since she had noticed him not noticing the dancers when she returned to the back room to get her regular clothes, she believed what he was saying; every word of it. There were simple ways some ladies had of telling a good guy from a bad, and her way was as stupid as any.

Quite soon she found herself giving him head, and was trying her hardest because he seemed so patently not to be enjoying it. When he laid her he did so with great care and the air of a depressive, which made her trust him all the more.

It wasn't three weeks before they decided to live in a new apartment together, which caused tension between the man and his roommate until a replacement was found.

Their life together was a gentle life of great delicacy and consideration, as they both felt sorry for the man, and he was also harbouring a great confusion at his sorrowful mood not being alleviated by the presence of this woman with the red hair.

Since in their hearts they both expected her to become pregnant, when she eventually did it was no great surprise. He merely stroked her arm as she lay at the base of the bed and cried about money. "I must go live with my sister," she told him. There was no part of her that was enthusiastic about living the life of a dancer with a young child. "Do you want to come with me?" she asked.

He grew anxious at this request and took a long stroll. Her sister lived in a small town with a husband and three children, and the man who was from out of town had deliberately moved out of his town and had barely been in the city a year. When he thought about it now, the woman with the red hair hadn't been so difficult a catch; not so terribly hard to find a girl to spend good times with in a metropolis; he didn't know why he hadn't thought of it sooner. He declined and she ran away with her bags and her tears.

But it wasn't so easy the second time around to get a nice girl, and the man soon grew lonely. After two months he was forced to take in a roommate, but the only one he could find was smelly and young with a belly that hung out without discretion. This situation made the man even more lonesome than before, and one day at one o'clock in the afternoon he decided to visit the woman with the red hair. Walking past a fountain on his way to the train station, he passed a girl of late teenage years who was blond and who he supposed would like the companionship of a man like him. Dragging her into the park he tore out two-thirds of her hair.

FAT LADIES FLOATED IN
THE SKY LIKE BALLOONS

by AMANDA DAVIS

FAT LADIES FLOATED in the sky like balloons.

That was the year we forgot our dreams and woke, bewildered, muttering. It was spring when I noticed them turning in the sky, this way and that, drifting gently on a breeze. They looked lovely from a distance but somehow I knew it was a bad sign. It could mean only one thing: my ex-boyfriend was back in town.

Sure enough, I ran into Fred Luck later that day. I was walking home from grooming the dogs when there he was on a bench by the town square watching the fat women twist against the cloudless sky. You! he yelled and leapt up. He was a man of surprises.

It's been a long time, I replied. I couldn't quite look him in the eyes. I kept thinking don't do it don't do it but somehow I sensed it was only a matter of time. He had eyes like licorice: shining and bitter.

Eloise! Fred called again, though he was only inches away. I've been waiting for you to walk by!

You can't just march back in to someone's life, I tried to say, but it came out: Oh, Yes, Well.

We stood for a moment studying each other, each with our motives hidden in our sleeves. Actually mine weren't very well-hidden. Fred, when he could take the time to focus on me, had been an incredible lover and I was feeling a little bit lonely.

Fred, I started.

It's Jack now, he said, I changed my name.

Jack Luck, I asked? I was thinking with noodles. I was thinking with duck sauce and white rice.

He nodded. I think I look more like a Jack than a Fred, he told me and shoved his hands deep into his pockets.

It was true. He did the name Jack justice.

You were bringing up the property value of Fred though, I blushed. Redeeming it, kind of.

Thanks, he said and smiled.

That part was simple. I brought him home when I knew my house would be empty and made dinner. On the way there he told me how wrong he'd been to leave, how much he'd missed me. I knew his words were empty, the empty husks of beetles long wandered off, the shell game I always lost. Still I let him touch me. Gentle now, I said.

He had his problems. Disappearance wasn't the worst of it, nor was the plight of the innocent fat ladies. Fred couldn't control himself. He was what Florence, my godmother, called bad news.

He's a natural disaster and you're trailer city, Florence rasped, then took another drag of her cigarette. He's an itchy rash, a pimple under the skin. He's a toothache and you're just numbing the gum, girlie. You need to pull his mean self out and toss it away.

But I love him, I said in the smallest voice those words could afford.

Oh girlie, Florence said, That's the worst of it.

When we first met I was more trusting. I had just begun to groom dogs and I thought it sweet when Fred showed up at the shop to meet me. I was so swept along by his sexy ways that I didn't complain when he launched the Apeson's poodle into the highest branches of the sycamore in front of the library or some-how elevated the Henderson's Affenpinscher and left it running circles in the air above the kennel roof. I thought to myself, He's an unusual guy, soul of an artist, I'll have to smooth some edges is all. Then he impaled the Lorsinski's cat on a lamppost and dropped a city bus on the Lawson's Dalmatian.

How the hell did he learn those tricks? Florence had asked me, sucking on a cigarette, curled in smoke.

I don't know, I told her, twirling my hair.

Well, why can't he stop it?

I don't think he knows what he's doing until it's too late, I answered. I was looking out the window of her house at the Meyerson's puppy, romping around in their yard. I don't think he means to, I said, but I wasn't entirely sure about that.

I'm leaving something out. See, the other thing was my laugh. I have a terrible laugh, all my life a wretched, horrible laugh. When I laugh, sounds come out of my throat that violate the rest of the world. My laugh causes injury: it makes people nauseous or crazy. Stop that awful sound, they scream, running from my vicinity with their hands clamped over their ears. It's so bad that the movie theater wouldn't allow me in to see films. That's a violation of my rights, I told them, until they set up private screenings. The projectionist would leave the building and sit on the sidewalk. I went and got him when each reel ran out.

So you can imagine what it meant to meet a man who didn't mind. The first time I laughed around him—we were sitting on my porch when a nervous frantic giggle escaped and I tried to snatch it back with my hand, to stuff it back down my throat—he just tucked a curl behind my ear and whispered, You are so beautiful.

And like that I was putty. It didn't even bother me that the potted plants that had been resting so quietly beside us on the porch were floating near our heads. It didn't even bother me when they smashed to bits during our first kiss. All that mattered was Fred and the way he held me. All that mattered was the idea of watching a movie with someone else.

Now by the time Fred became Jack, I had married a guy named Steve. So of course I brought Jack home to meet him. Steve wasn't his real name—his real name sounded like a kind of sausage—but he'd paid me a lot of money to become his wife and felt Steve made him sound like a naturalized citizen. Though he didn't like my laugh, he'd hired me to be his wife so he wouldn't be deported to the gray, depressive country that spawned him. When Steve learned of Jack it seemed to upset him, though his inner life wasn't always clear to me. We had trouble communicating.

You and me are bloodletting, he said while Jack was in the bathroom.

You and me are bouillabaisse, he tried again. Bakers.

No, I said, flipping the pages of a shiny magazine. I didn't even look up.

Borrowing, he said. Burrowing.

Blowing? I offered. I enjoyed frustrating him.

No! You are not understanding. You and me like tree, he tried.

Bush? I flipped a page.

No!

(Flip, flip) Brain!

Jack is borrowing wife, he began again, his desperate hands flailing about. Husband forgets husband is forgotten.

I threw down the magazine and rose from the armchair as Jack reentered. Back later, I said.

See, love was not part of the bargain. I know love never is, etc., etc., but I expected more respect. I'll be your wife, I had told him. Professionally. Like a job, I'd said. You hire me and that's my job: wife. Nothing else.

Right, he'd said, beaming. Wife.

It wasn't until later that I realized how little he understood.

So he didn't like Fred. But everyone liked Fred. It was part of the way of the universe: people met and liked Fred. That was how the world was formed. But not Sausage Steve. The first thing he said when he met Fred was: He is not the good man. He is not the husband for you.

Right, I told him, you hired me. He disappeared. He's just my obscenely perfect ex-boyfriend who has a strange effect on people.

Steve didn't get it. He is the no good, he muttered and glared at Fred.

Jack né Fred was many things, I must agree, but not really a bad person, exactly. I mean he acted irresponsibly, sure, but generally because of a helpful impulse, I thought, not a malicious sensibility.

Still, I felt things in the back of my head, forgotten dreams maybe, fleeting thoughts, the sense that I had a running list of things I was losing, things left behind. When we walked out of the house, I looked at Fred but he had his hands in his pockets staring at the night sky, the fat ladies blocking the stars like black holes, like gasps of breath, like forgotten clouds. I shook my head at the way that I felt, yearning for his touch, the anger I'd been storing hidden somewhere distant. He waited for me to catch up, then he put his arm around my shoulders, kissed my forehead and I followed him home.

In the morning we had breakfast at a diner near the park. I sipped coffee and Fred gnawed a banana muffin. The staff watched us, frightened—they had seen the damage Fred could do. This probably isn't such a great idea, I began in my head, but what I said was, Nice day.

On the radio there was much debate over how to get the fat ladies down from the sky. They waved happily in the daylight but I imagined they must be hungry by now.

But I thought maybe this was the evolution of things, the way the world spun. Maybe this was true for the fat ladies too—that one minute something was an orange and the next it was a peach. And maybe they would drop quietly as they lost weight until they landed here like the rest of us, drawn, haggard, and dreamless, all their glorious roundness gone.

EULOGY FOR
SAUL STEINBERG

by IAN FRAZIER

IN THE MONTHS since Saul died, the people who knew him and loved him have talked about him a lot. We call each other up, we get together, and sometimes we find ourselves talking about him for hours. We do this for the obvious reasons; but we also talk about him, I think, because he was a marvel. And knowing him was like encountering a marvel in nature—as if you were walking through the woods and you saw a bear, you saw a mountain lion. When that happens you talk about it, you can't help yourself. You try and recapture the experience, you try to describe it, over and over you try and convey it to other people, and you don't succeed, usually. Your words are unequal to it; your words are "clumsy," to use a favorite adjective of Saul's.

I talked about Saul one afternoon recently—I spent all afternoon downtown with Saul's friend, the man who worked for him, Anton van Dalen, and we talked as we sat on Anton's roof. Anton keeps pigeons, and pigeons were flying, white pigeons in the sky. And we just talked about Saul, about things we remembered of him. In his studio Anton showed me a postcard that Saul had made, and it was a landscape with figures in it. And then on the back, there was the message, and then Anton's address. Saul had written Anton's name and address, and then instead of putting a postage stamp on it, he had painted a postage stamp, and had drawn the cancellation mark, and in the center of the mark, instead of point of origin it just said "Steinberg." And he had dropped it in a postbox, and it had been delivered by the post office without comment or objection.

This reminded me of Saul's affinity for the mail, which was supernatural. I lived far from him—much of the time that we were friends I lived far away, and we communicated a lot through the mail. And the delight of seeing his handwriting on an envelope in a bunch of mail elevated the mail to such a degree—every time I went to get the mail there was a possibility that with the throwaways from Publisher's Clearing House and whatnot there would be this amazing missive from Saul. And I remembered him telling me that when he was a boy in Bucharest his father would sometimes take him when he went to mail a letter. And when they got to the postbox, his father would lift him up, and after they dropped the letter in, Saul would yell the destination of the letter into the slot, just to be doubly sure. The city that they often mailed letters to I can't quite pronounce, but it was "Buzau." And Saul would shout "BUZAU!" into the mailbox slot. I think of that often when I mail letters—of Saul yelling into the slot. I've tried it myself, and it's quite satisfying.

Saul's friend Prudence Crowther told me of Saul's collection of experiments he made with the mail, many of you know them I'm sure. He mailed blocks of wood that he would draw to look like letters, he mailed a seagrape leaf—if you've ever been to Key West, those are the big oval leaves that are all over the sidewalks at certain time of the year there. He said they're kind of like phonograph records—they just last forever—and he wrote an address on a seagrape leaf and put a stamp on it and mailed it, and it was delivered. He mailed a dollar bill, Prudence said. He wrote an address on a dollar bill and put a stamp on it, and the post office delivered it carefully wrapped in clear plastic.

Hedda Sterne, Saul's wife, recently told me, "Reality accommodated Saul." And it was absolutely true; reality sometimes would just line up perfectly with Saul's vision of what it should be. The example she gave me was that when Saul was in the army, once for some kind of demolition practice he had to blow up a tree. So he went and put an explosive charge right at the base of the tree, and uncoiled the wire and got away and pushed the plunger, and when the dust cleared, the tree was exactly where it had been before. And he went up and looked at it, and what had happened was that the charge had blown the tree straight up in the air, and the tree had fallen straight down and landed exactly in the hole where the charge had been, and was just as it had been before—as if the laws of physics didn't apply around Saul, but only some sort of higher cartoon law.

I went to dinner with him one night, and instead of ordering two desserts, he said, "Well we don't need two desserts, let's just order one dessert, and we'll split it." And so when the waiter came, he said, "We'll have one dessert, and a blank plate." Anybody else would have said "an extra plate." "A blank plate." And when the plate came, it was a thing of beauty. It was just a plate, with a red border, a blue border—I forget—but it was a blank plate, and now I wish that I had just asked if I could have the plate, and had taken it home and put it on my wall.

The power that Saul had over ordinary reality was almost magical sometimes. I went with him once to Atlantic City to gamble. We took the bus, and Saul said, "It's good to ride on a bus, because on a bus you are at a noble height—you're at the height of a man on horseback." And that has made me like buses a lot more, just that one idea that I'm at a noble height when I'm on a bus. We got to Atlantic City, and we went to the casino that he had picked out. He went right to the roulette table. He said, "Now we will divide." He said he didn't want me breathing down his neck, but I had to see what he was going to do. He was wearing a light-colored blazer, light slacks, a white fedora, and he began to put the chips on the big board with the roulette numbers, those old-styled numbers, like Victorian-type numbers— you don't see them much anymore outside of casinos. They're numbers that he really had a feeling for, and the way he put the chips down on them, it was like he was making a drawing. And each time the wheel spun, Saul's number would come up, and the chips began to accumulate in front of him in a pile. And the pile got bigger and bigger. Well, the croupier apparently was skilled in dealing with magic, and he guessed that Saul didn't particularly like to have a fuss made over him, so the croupier was doing so, like, "Well look at this!"—making a big production about Saul's success. Soon, there was a big crowd around Saul. The pile of chips was mounting up to the top of his shirt- front, and he was still placing these inspired bets, and he tried to cash the chips in for larger denomination chips, because they would create a less imposing pile that would attract fewer onlookers. But the croupier would not let him do that, and eventually Saul became annoyed with all the attention, and he scooped his pile of chips into his white fedora, and he went to the window and cashed them in. He always did well at roulette.

I think about him often just in little things, and about off-the-cuff remarks he made that changed my view of a thing forever. Some years ago I was trying to learn Russian, and I was wrestling with the Cyrillic alphabet, and I said to Saul, "This alphabet—it's got a lot of letters, and some of them are really strange." Saul said, "Those aren't letters, those are sneezes." And now certain Cyrillic letters will always be sneezes to me.

I was glad to hear the Rossini piece with the meows that was played, because I want to end by talking about Saul's cat. He had the most amazing cat. It was a black Siamese; Saul called him Papoose. I think originally Papoose was the cat of his friend Sigrid Spaeth, and I know the cat lived with Sigrid in her apartment, and then also lived in Saul's house on Long Island. And this cat was completely aware of Saul at all times. He was a very tactful and very smart cat. He used to ride on Saul's shoulders, around his neck like a kind of boa or something, and put his chin on Saul's shoulder while Saul drove, and with his head next to Saul's he looked out the windshield. Papoose was a very sensitive and nice cat around the house, and then he would just disappear. And he'd be gone in the woods—he'd be gone for hours or days. My wife and I went to visit Saul in Amagansett, and he had told us about Papoose, and he said, "Papoose isn't here right now, but he'll be back at the end of the day—I'm sure he'll be back at the end of the day." And at the end of the day, Saul said, "Ah! Papoose." And he looked all the way at the other end of the lawn, a long expanse of lawn, and there was Papoose just coming out of the brush. And Saul slid open the door, and stood on the stoop, and Papoose saw him, and Papoose ran, and he ran absolutely full-speed gallop— there was nothing tentative about it, he crossed the lawn in a second. It was the kind of run you would never see a cat do. It was a dog type of run, it was that kind of heedless, headlong run, and he got right up to Saul's shins and then brushed against him, and Saul smiled and laughed and said, "Well, here's Papoose."

If you loved Saul you were like Papoose. You just went to him. Heedlessness was the key, a tempered sort of heedlessness. You gave your heart, and you didn't worry too much about the details. Saul was complicated, of course, and things that he liked he sometimes also disliked, and this included himself, and sometimes it included his friends. And this uncertainty kept me off balance—I would think that I had to be a particular way in order to merit his attention, that I had to be interesting or I had to be funny. After a while I stopped worrying about that; I just trusted Saul's affection. I knew that my affection was there, and I knew that Saul's was, too, under everything that he did. It was under his work, it was under his relationships with his friends, it informed the way he saw the world. Hedda said to me recently, "Saul had a great tenderness for the world." And sometimes this affection would appear suddenly—it would just surface, and it was dazzling. Anton reminded me of a gesture Saul had which I hadn't thought of for a long time. Unexpectedly sometimes he would turn to you and put one arm out and say, "Embrace me"—and you would embrace him.

Saul, we embrace you, our love follows you. We will miss you. God bless you.

THE OBSERVERS

by PAUL LA FARGE

To observe is to destroy. —*Paul Poissel*

I.

LET ME BEGIN by saying that when I built the observatory I had no intention of looking into the past. The truth is that I didn't intend to build the observatory at all; it grew out of a web of circumstance, the way mushrooms grow out of dimness and rain. First there was one of those March storms which strike you as a planned and personal affront, like a stalker who goes away for three weeks and then calls you in the middle of the night to let you know that you will have no lasting reprieve, now or ever. The sky turned green, then black. It spat hailstones which struck birds dead off the trees and left dents in the tin roofs of buildings downtown. The hail turned to ice when it touched the ground; snowplows plowed into parked cars and no one was allowed to drive anywhere. My girl-friend went outside to mail some letters, slipped, and broke her wrist; medics with specially ridged shoes had to rescue her from the sidewalk. The papers called it the storm of the fin-de-siècle, and the Weather Bureau, where I worked, hadn't seen it coming. As soon as the roads cleared, I was instructed to come up with a slogan for the Bureau's face-saving campaign. "The message here is that no one's perfect," said the Creative Director. "We've got to tell them that on every life a little rain must fall." I worked at it all day, trying to come up with

Bronze Star for Ashanti, 1896

something philosophical and optimistic. All I could think of were smashed cars, shattered roofs, the tiny carcasses of swallows frozen to the ground. When the Creative Director came around for my input, I shook my head.

"What have you got for us?"

I showed him the piece of paper with the only slogan I had been able to think of: *These are the omens of the rites that failed.*

"What is this? Is this a fucking joke?" The Director tore the page into quarters, and let them fall.

The next day the buses were blazoned with the slogan APRIL SHOWERS MAY BRING FLOWERS, and I was out of work. I told my girlfriend what had happened. "You really fucked up," she said. I tried to explain that something was actually wrong, that the storm was a sign of something being actually wrong. What I said was: "We shouldn't pretend that we can see the future, and when we do, the future laughs at us."

"Maybe so." She cradled her splinted wrist. "But what are you going to do now?"

I told her that I'd think of something. But I spent my days watching historical television and wishing that I could have been a saint, a gangster, a cowboy, or an astronaut, some profession in which my actions would have been writ large but very far away. My girlfriend, a medical transcriptionist, nursed her wrist and carried on her numerous intimate friendships by telephone, late at night. She told me that I couldn't go on like this forever, spending my savings on take-out food and televised boxing. I didn't look up. "Did you know that the Roman Emperor Nero was only one of a series of emperors with the same name?"

On June 1 she left me for a voice at the other end of the telephone line, in an area code that had recently been created to contain the excess population of Cleveland. Without her I couldn't afford the rent on our apartment, so I packed everything up and drove north to Commonstock, where my father still lived in our old house. It was too big for him now, but he didn't want to give up the lawn, the elms, the view of Lake Commonstock, and the fish that washed up on its shores every morning, victims of the acid rain. I moved back into the room where I'd grown up. Nothing about it had changed except that, the summer after my freshman year of college, I'd taken down the poster for *The Wind in the Willows* from over my bed, and put up a photograph of a veiled woman smoking a Gauloise. When I was in college I thought she looked mysterious; now she seemed, at most, cold and a little vapid, the kind of woman who said *evidently* when she meant *yes*. I took her down and put Frog and Toad in their old, iconic position, pulled my college books from the shelves and put my childhood books back in their places. For a week I lived among the glories of the last unequivocally happy period of my life, the years between twelve and fifteen, when childhood had done its worst and I, already a survivor, felt newly hatched and capable of anything. Then I found my journal from that time. On January 25th, the day I turned fifteen, I'd written: *We waste our time feeling sorry for animals, whereas in fact the animals should feel sorry for us.* That night I took Frog and Toad down and moved my children's books back into the attic.

In college I studied philosophy, because I still believed that you could understand the world by thinking about it. When that turned out not to be true I forgot most of what I'd read, but one thing stays with me, one moment: that part at the end of the *Symposium* where Socrates says, "Starting from individual beauties, the quest for the universal beauty must find you ever mounting the heavenly ladder, stepping from rung to rung—that is, from one to two, and from two to every lovely body, from bodily beauty to the beauty of institutions," and so on. The heavenly ladder. What a beautiful idea that was: that, just by thinking about it, you could climb away from everything familiar, from the earth to the sky and up and up and up.

My father looked around my empty room and asked me what I was going to do next.

"Why," I said, "I'm going to build an observatory." I hadn't thought of doing anything like that before. In fact I'd never been much interested in the stars. I knew from camping trips and the like that you were supposed to be able to see figures in among them. I'd owned one of those illustrated books that gives you the pictures of animals and hunters and so on, and the other pictures, so dissimilar, of disjoint stars with lines between them. The analogy between the two sets of illustrations was hard enough to grasp when it was confined to the book; when it blossomed to fill the entire vastness of the night sky it became entirely unmanageable. I could never make out anything smaller than the Milky Way, the moon, and its reflection in Lake Commonstock. It was the idea of the observatory that appealed to me. I would build myself a structure, small, sealed, windowless except for the telescope-slit in the roof, and entirely my own.

"Ah," my father said.

"I want to do something with my hands. I've never built anything before."

"Didn't you used to build model airplanes?"

He should have known. The airplanes were his idea, to engage me when, as a little boy, I seemed already to have grown tired of what life had to offer in the way of scheduled activities. "Those were toys. This is going to be for real. A real working observatory." I thought about what it would look like. "It's going to have a roof that turns. So that I can see stars in different parts of the sky."

"Why do you want to see the stars?"

"What's wrong with the stars?"

"Let me see if I understand. You want something that will challenge you."

"There are comets and nebulas."

"But not challenge you too much."

"Black holes, and pulsars and quasars."

"Why don't we go camping?" This had been another of my father's enthusiasms when I was a child. "We'll go to Mount Head, spend a few days tooling around. The two of us. Plenty of stars up there. Hm?"

"Just the other day I read that scientists have discovered a new planet. Unlike the others, this one doesn't move."

My father left the room, his head bowed in defeat.

Of course he had to have a hand in planning it. Together we trudged up and down the property with an old sextant which had been sitting, unused, on our mantel ever since we moved to Commonstock. My father said that it belonged to the sea captain who had lived in the house before us, but as the previous tenant was an insurance broker, I had always suspected that it was a decorator's touch, imported from a Mystic junk shop to fulfill someone's vision of a settled life in New England. My father made a show of holding one end of it to his eye and tilting the other until, from his perspective, it was level with the tops of the trees; after which he showed me the instrument and recorded its reading in degrees. Whether this is the approved use of the sextant I do not know; but in any event there was only one place on the property where the observatory could go: a sort of knoll halfway between the house and the water, from which you had an unobstructed view of the lake, the neighbors' houses, and the gentle rise of Mount Head in the background. The knoll stood at the center of our view from the house; an observatory built there would block the line of sight from the house to the water. Nonetheless my father, excited by his newfound competence with the sextant, gave me permission to build there and even required, based on his table of measurements, that I do so.

That night when the sky turned the color of blue ink I went to sit on the knoll. The moon hadn't risen and the air was still; there must have been thousands of stars visible overhead. I knew none of them by name. The stars were named by Arabs, in their desert long ago, separating with their naked eyes the numberless unnamed stars from the handful they had made their own. The stars were a pale jumble to me, but I could see the Arabs clearly enough. They sat up very straight on the sand dunes and drank cups of Arabian coffee while their horses waited patiently under the trees. The Arabs traded gold rings and drank coffee and then, almost as an afterthought, they named the stars.

The Commonstock public library had a large collection of back issues of the relevant periodicals: *Sky*, *Telescope Making*, *Zenith*, and *Azimuth*. With their help I began my initiation into the world of semianonymous individuals who share a personal relation to the sky. I read about their telescopes, their Newtonians and refractors and Cassegrains, and saw, as if with their eyes, the heavens in blurry magnification, almost without color but painfully evocative in their detail, as though each celestial object were a tremendously important word uttered just out of earshot. I read about their observatories and their marital problems, the two equally complex and durably tied together. I had never suspected that so many people took refuge from the world in small rooms, alone, all night. Their letters—"7th July. Magnificent Saturn at 2317 hours. Tried to get my wife to come out and see it"—comforted me, and I smiled angelically at the other inhabitants of the Commonstock Library's reading room. Not all the news in the magazines was good: it turned out that, given the cost of materials and my inexperience at building large structures, the domed observatory that I'd first imagined was impracticable. Leafing through plans for various home-grown structures, I came across a model called the "Rolling Ridge Observatory," invented by Robert E. Reisenweber of Erie, PA. It looked like an outsized sentry box with a roof that rolled away onto an adjacent scaffold to expose the telescope to the stars. No specialized parts were necessary for its construction, and from start to finish it would cost less than a thousand dollars. I pinned a photograph of the Rolling Ridge Observatory to my wall, and for a long time it was the only decoration in my room.

* * *

"Have you ever worked with lumber?" asked the building-supply man. His posture implied habitual skepticism. Commonstock is a town of summer houses; he must have been tired of weekend visitors coming to him with their ever-unrealized plans for decks, gazebos, extra rooms.

"I have plenty of time," I said. "My father lives here."

The building-supply man grunted. "What kind of foundation have you got?"

"Nothing yet."

"Well, what are you going to use?"

It hadn't occurred to me that I would need a foundation. Looking at the plans again, I saw that Robert E. Reisenweber had built his observatory on a preexisting concrete slab, presumably a relic left in his backyard by the last civilization to inhabit Erie, PA.

"I guess concrete."

"You'll need someone to pour it, then." The building-supply man wrote "George" and a number on the back of a business card. "Where are you from?"

"New York."

"You like it there?"

"Too many streetlights," I said. "You can't see a damn thing, at night."

"Ah." The building supply man shrugged, his suspicions about New Yorkers confirmed. "Well, call George if you want that concrete."

I had thought ten feet by eight for the foundation but George said it would have to be bigger. "Wouldn't be room to swing a cat in there, otherwise." I tried to tell him that my plans for the observatory didn't involve swinging cats. "I'm not coming over for anything less than twelve by twelve," he said, and so it was decided. The day before he came my father and I went out with shovels to dig the pit, like archaeologists unearthing an ancient burial mound. It felt good to be working at something again. The sun was bright and simple overhead, and the air smelled of fresh water. My father and I grunted at each other happily. George hadn't told us how deep to dig the foundation, so we outdid ourselves. It was waist-deep by the time we dropped our shovels, exhausted, and sat facing each other in the fresh earth.

"You were never a difficult child," my father said. "Only you were always solitary."

My foot touched something hard. "Is that a skull?"

My father rubbed at it. "It's a rock," he said. "You kept to yourself so much we wondered if you were all right."

"What kind of rock?"

"Just a rock. Then it seemed like you turned out all right." He looked at me sadly. "Did you hear Julie Eisenman got married again?"

"She was married before?"

"To a veterinary surgeon."

"Ah."

"Didn't you used to like her?"

"Did I?" It was possible. I had certainly liked people, even as a child. Or it might have been another of the things my father concocted for me. Dostoyevsky, in *The Brothers Karamazov*, says that the devil exists to give our lives events. But no, we have parents for that. "When was the wedding?" My father wasn't listening to me. He had pulled a muscle in his back, and I practically had to carry him out of the excavation.

George, who on the telephone had sounded large and mirthful, turned out to be a scrawny man with a long neck, pigeon toes, and the face of a hawk. He laughed when he saw our pit.

"Is it too deep?"

"Depends whether you're building an observatory or a bunker."

He walked off, laughing, and returned at the wheel of a cement truck with the words POULIADIS CONSTRUCTION written on the side in fading red paint. The truck left deep and muddy furrows in the grass. My father watched from a lawn chair as we poured bags and bags of cement into the pit. It soon became clear that we would not fill it; when we ran out of cement, the foundation—which would double as the floor of the observatory—was about three feet below the level of the ground. It meant installing a flight of steps down into the observatory, which was not at all in the plans. I had no instructions for building stairs; I turned to my father with a helpless look that must have been familiar to him from my model-building days. He waved at me from the lawn chair. "Good work!" he shouted. "Just a few feet to go!" George pointed out that the stars were already so far away that a few feet of altitude wouldn't make any difference. Which was true, but didn't make me feel any better. I had always thought of observatories as high places, but mine would be reached by stepping down. It didn't feel right.

"Beer?" George asked.

I thought he had them in the truck, but when I came over he said, "Climb up. That's the spirit."

He drove us to a bar in town, where I drank beer while George told me about the semicriminal activities by which he lived. "You hear those birds?" he asked.

"Sure."

"Those are *my* birds." Apparently the paper mill paid George to drive upstate, to the places where the air was still clean, to net birds and bring them back to Commonstock, where most of them died from the mill's yellowish exhaust. He had also, at various times, stocked the lake with fish, hauled toxic sludge down to the naval laboratory at New London, and even, he claimed, spray-painted leaves yellow and red for a busload of Japanese tourists who came to see the New England fall early in a year when the fall came late. It was as though he had been given the job of making sure that Nature still looked as though it worked the way it used to. We drank beer, smoked cigarettes, and flicked the butts into the lake. The sun was warm on my shoulders and the backs of my hands. It was ridiculous for me to worry about the observatory. A few feet up or down wouldn't make any difference, or, if they did, I could fix it. I slumped in my chair, and listened to the song they were playing inside the bar, about how birds were free but two dollars wouldn't buy you a drink any more. Which wasn't true, I thought, happily, at least not about the birds.

As the summer thickened I felt myself growing more solid, as though I was absorbing some of the durability of my construction. I went back to the building-supply man, bought wood and nails and flanged pieces of metal, screw mounts and bolts and threaded rods and wheels, casters and switches and sockets and a red-sheathed bulb to illuminate the interior. I bought glue strong enough to hold a pickup truck up in midair, an electric drill, screwdriver and screw extractor, a portable power saw, a utility belt, an apron with pockets for things I couldn't name. I stored the tools in the garage at night, but by day I carried them all with me to the building site and laid them out on the ground, in the hope that some stranger, passing by, would see their metal parts shining in the sunlight and think, What a lot of tools this family has! How practical these people are! George Pouliadis came by several times to see how I was doing, and each time his truck creaked into our driveway I felt a sense of camaraderie, as though he and I were each, in our own ways, restoring the world to a happier state.

Like anyone who invests in power tools for the first time, I thought about the end of civilization and how to prepare for it. I went to the grocery store and bought some dried fruit, instant cocoa, a camping stove, Band-Aids, and a bottle of iodine. I told my father that I was preparing for minor accidents and cold nights, but in fact the darkest contingencies occupied my imagination: civil unrest, war, new plagues that would turn the bones of men to jelly and their hearts to ice. Only I would remain, safe in my observatory, with my cocoa and iodine, taking notes dispassionately on the emergence and transit of the stars. I drove in to Mystic to pick up my telescope, an eight-inch Newtonian that promised optimal magnification at a reasonable price. It had been years since I visited the old seaport, which has been restored to look as it did in the days when ships went out full of spears and came home with cargoes of blubber and ambergris, whalebone and whaleskin and stories. The three-masted ships, the wooden sidewalks, the storefronts offering salt-water taffy, chandlery, and provisions, and sailcloth, impressed me with their optimism. It's not too late to turn back, said the signs for Ropes Unlimited, the Sky Shoppe, the Bit-o-Ivory, and the Cape Horn Café. I walked to the car, whistling, carrying the telescope on my shoulder in a vaguely military fashion.

II.

George Pouliadis was right: the observatory, when I'd finished nailing the siding to its exterior, and despite everything promised by the good Mr. Reisenweber, looked like a sort of low fortress established to defend our house from lake-borne invaders. I was delighted and couldn't wait until nightfall to try a few preliminary sightings. I screwed the base of the telescope to the metal pillar anchored in the floor, tightened everything, and then, with a sweep of the arm, like a conductor bringing his orchestra to life, I rolled back the roof and let light fall for the first time on the telescope's uncovered lens. My first discoveries, as I angled the scope low across the lake, were as follows: one, that it was nearly impossible to focus on anything, and, two, that everything I saw through the telescope was upside-down. Trees waved beneath the lake; below them the mountains sank into a bottomless blue distance. I studied the mountains first because they were the farthest away. There was Mount David, and there Mount Redthorn, and between them the rocky crown of Mount Head. Swinging downward, that is, upward, the telescope brought me flying over the autumnal forest. Then a white blur. I tightened the adjusting screws and, by touching the knobs very gently, managed to bring the image into focus. It was a house on the other side of the lake, where a girl was standing on the porch. She pulled her long brown hair back and tied it in a bun, so that I could see her face, which was perfectly detailed, like the tiny cities in the background of Northern Renaissance paintings. I didn't recognize the house, although it looked like it belonged in Commonstock: white clapboard with green trim and shutters, the porch probably put on by summer people, object of the building-supply man's contempt. The girl stretched her arms downward to the sky. The light had a way of finding the hollows of her body which made her seem more solid, more three-dimensional, than any of the women I had held, touched, known. She turned, and for a moment I saw, or thought I could see, the shadows on either side of her spine. Then she left the telescope's field of vision, which was not large; and by the time I had loosened the tripod's screws and adjusted the instrument, she had vanished entirely. The porch was empty and the house, from this distance, was still. I looked up from the telescope, but my mind did not return to the observatory for a long time, and when it did the place seemed strange, overlarge, and too quiet. I climbed the steps to the lawn and stood blinking in the sunlight.

That night she was in her bedroom with the curtains drawn back and the window partly open. She was playing cards by herself. From the way she moved her head, I guessed that the radio was on. Every two or three minutes she looked up at the door, as though she were waiting for someone to come in. Then she dealt her cards again, played, stopped, looked again at the door. I was afraid that I was abusing the power of the telescope, so I released the screws and let the instrument find its way among the stars. There was nothing but darkness up there. Now and then a bright object would wobble across, and I tried to fix it in my sights. Even with the telescope, though, the stars were dimensionless, colorless, less realistic even than the signs that represented them on maps. I switched on the radio, looked for music that would make what I saw more poignant. But there was no music on the air, only people talking, in pleasant voices, disturbances on the other side of the planet, and the need to be vigilant at home.

The next morning was overcast, threatening, as though the sky were looking for the words to break a difficult piece of news. I drove around the lake, past the Bendetsens', the Hoffmanns', the Rothsteins', past the deserted house of Donald Patriss, the famous animal trainer (he summers in Commonstock), the houses of various neighbors, acquaintances, friends, and strangers. I couldn't find the white house with green trim. Of course I was still an amateur with the telescope. Although I might see something quite distinctly, I had no idea what it was looking at, or where in the unmagnified world it was to be found.

When I came back, George was showing the observatory to half a dozen children in wool sweaters and sturdy shoes.

"Not the worst piece of work I've seen around here," he said, rubbing his chin.

"Thanks."

"Hope you don't mind."

The children ignored the telescope and the cleverly weighted roof, and went straight for the cocoa.

"Don't touch that stuff," George growled at them, but I'm sure half my packets of Swiss Miss ended up in their pockets all the same.

"Sorry," George said. "They're German." He explained that he'd been hired to take the children on a weekend hike in Highwash State Park. "We're looking for fossils," he confided.

"I didn't know there were any up there."

"Wie viele Asteroide kennen Sie?" a child asked. "Ich, dreißig."

"I don't speak German, sorry."

"It's a regular trilobite graveyard." George winked.

I thought of him seeding the hills with prehistoric fish and ferns, purchased probably at a museum souvenir shop. The children wouldn't be disappointed. "Bring one back for me," I said.

"Raus, Kinder," he hollered. "Alle Kinder raus!"

Not long after he left for the park, it started to snow. I went to the supermarket to replace the cocoa stolen by the German children. Julie Eisenman, the veterinary surgeon's wife, was there, pushing a shopping cart of strangely forlorn produce: root vegetables and paper towels and carpet-cleaning supplies, nothing festive or indulgent or even brightly colored.

"I wondered when you'd turn up," Julie said. "Your father said you were back in town."

"He tells me you're married."

"That's right."

"How is it?"

Julie shrugged. "You should come over for dinner some time. Carl loves to entertain."

She reached up to get a bottle of Windex. In that moment, her arm upstretched, her head tilted back, and the collar of her blouse falling away from her throat, she looked just like the girl I'd seen through the telescope. Julie's eyes were deeper set, and she wore her hair up, but otherwise they were as alike as two frames of film, separated only by time.

"Julie," I said, tenderly. "You look wonderful."

"So call me."

"No," I said. "*Really* wonderful."

She took my arm and pulled me to the deserted aisle where they keep the pens and paper. "Your father is worried about you," she murmured.

"I don't know why."

"He thinks you should talk to someone. It might make you feel better."

"He can think what he likes."

"That's just what someone who was having problems would say."

"I'm not having problems."

"I heard about your girlfriend. I'm sorry."

A child came up and asked if we knew where they kept the secret notebooks.

"This is all there is, sweetie," Julie said. Then to me: "Although I hear she wasn't much of a loss."

The child was looking at us.

"Why don't you come tonight?" Julie asked.

"All right."

She gave me her address: on the other side of the lake.

I drifted out of the supermarket, into a suddenly opaque world. The snow stuck in the trees, on the cars, on my eyebrows. I walked down the street, my eyes half-closed and my mouth open. I tried to taste the difference between the snowflakes, to understand each one separately, and to know what all of them together added up to.

When we were fourteen, Julie Eisenman and I searched Lake Commonstock together for buried treasure. We dove down as far as we could go and extended our hands into the ropy seaweed. We pulled up shells, shoes, beer bottles older children had tossed into the water. Once, when we were coming out of the water, I gave her a white stone I'd found. She kissed me on the mouth and hugged me so that I could feel her stomach bare against my stomach. "Do you want to come over?" she asked. "Maybe later," I said, afraid that she wanted something bright and terrible from me. "Come tonight." She waved to me from the porch and I could see her ribs move in and out with her breathing. I walked home on the side of the road, trying to make my feet hurt by pressing them against the sharp sides of stones. I didn't go that night, because I was afraid to sneak out of my house, afraid to walk the lake's edge in darkness, afraid of what would happen if I went to her.

The radio called the whiteness outside a winter storm. Schools were dismissed early, and travelers were cautioned. I made tea for my father, and told him I'd run into Julie Eisenman in town. I tried to tell him about my discovery. "With the telescope I can see things that happened years and years ago," I said. "It's like everything that ever happened is happening now, somewhere very far away. Or not now, really, because everything we see in the sky is very old." I showed him an article from *Azimuth*, the most literary of the magazines for sky enthusiasts. "The Telescope: Window into a Lost World?" it was called. The author of the article explained how, if a large enough lens could be erected in space at a great enough distance from the earth, hypothetical beings would be able, even now, to see our planet as it was in the past. "Through their telescopes they could watch Plato and Socrates, Michelangelo and Van Gogh, and perhaps learn more about them than we know today."

"Why would aliens want to see Plato, though?"

"That's not the point. The point is that telescopes are always looking at the past."

My father gave me a look which I remembered from the summers of my childhood. He used to go away for a few weeks every August to a special camp for teachers, from which he'd return, sunburnt and bug-bitten, with the distant stare of a man who has climbed a real mountain to see past an imaginary horizon. While he was away, my fifteenth summer, my mother moved to Ohio. After that his stare got closer and closer, until you felt sure that it would have to take you in, but it didn't. It was as though the world of faraway things had closed in around him, displacing everything which had, until then, been close up.

"It must be something about gravity waves. Gravity waves bending light back to the earth."

"When you were little you had everything you needed," my father said. "We loved you very much."

"You don't believe me? Come and see for yourself."

"We loved you so very much," he said, looking past me, out the window, at the observatory. Covered in snow, it looked like an igloo. He stared at it as though he couldn't understand how this igloo, this bunker, this hermetic thing had come to be on his lawn, squarely between him and the beloved lake which he couldn't see in any case on account of the snow.

Julie and her husband lived in an old farmhouse, which had been remodeled inside to look like a gallery where domestic life in New England was on display. Track lighting picked out a quilt, a ceramic tureen, the kitchen island where Carl stood chopping vegetables. Small and brightly scrubbed, he struck me as one of those superficially cheerful people who crush small objects in their hands when you're not watching. Julie on the other hand emitted beauty and calm. She'd let her hair down and put on a flowered summer dress despite the weather. We had a drink in the den and talked about the blizzard, as the radio called it now. Apparently it hadn't snowed this much this early in the year since 1915.

"Mythical weather," Carl joked. "It means we're near the end."

"The end of what?"

"It's nothing compared to the storm we had this spring in New York."

"Just my point. The giants are breaking out of Jotunheim," Carl said.

"Jotunheim?"

"Carl, you're so obscure."

"The storm we had in New York was bad, too."

"Isn't your water boiling?"

Carl got up to check the pot. I moved closer to Julie on the sofa, and let my hand touch the side of her hand. "I've missed you," I said. She looked at me fondly for a moment, then moved to the other side of the sofa, and stayed there until we went in to dinner.

Carl wanted to know if the observatory had been difficult to build.

"Not really," I said. "All you need is some basic know-how."

"I'll bet you need more than that."

"I had a little help with the foundation. But I did all the rest myself."

"And it's holding up?" Julie asked.

"Why wouldn't it hold up?"

"No one's doubting you," Julie said. Carl assured me that he could never have done anything like it, himself.

"What do you mean, you wouldn't have done it? You don't think the observatory was a good idea?"

"Carl just means that you must have spent a lot of time on it."

"Lots of people build their own observatories. Ordinary people, who live in Pennsylvania and states like that."

"Sure, of course they do."

"Are you saying something's wrong with all of us?"

"Relax, no one's saying anything."

I asked Carl some questions about veterinary surgery. He looked puzzled and answered that he didn't know, really; his business was naming new varieties of plants which came out of a laboratory in Missouri.

I don't remember how the conversation went after that.

After dinner, when Carl went into the kitchen to do the dishes, Julie pinched my arm. "Bastard," she said, "how could you?" I didn't see that I'd given any offense. In my opinion, healing sick animals is one of the noblest professions imaginable, nobler even than healing sick people, because from animals there is little hope even of gratitude.

"The veterinary surgeon," Julie said, "was my old husband."

"What was his name?"

"Anselm."

"What was wrong with him?"

"He couldn't stop talking about animals."

"Julie," I said, "do you ever think about me romantically?"

"No."

"You don't ever wish that I'd kissed you again?"

"We never kissed."

"Yes, we did." I told her about the stone and the lake, and how she invited me to come over. "You played cards that night while you waited for me. But I never came."

"You're drunk," she said.

"That's not the point." I explained that I was the owner of a telescope, purchased at the Sky Shoppe, in Mystic, Conn., which could see into the past. I explained to her about the age of the stars, and the giant lens in space, and told her how, by means of its manifold mirrors, its lenses and tubes and motorized mount, my telescope was capable of receiving light that had left the earth years and years ago. "I can see you in your room when you were fourteen," I said. "I can see everything as if it were happening now."

"You're completely drunk," said Julie.

"You were beautiful," I said.

"Carl, take him home. He can't drive."

I don't remember the ride back around the lake. Apparently I told Carl to stop so that I could get out and vomit. Apparently—it's Carl who says so—I knelt there a long time, retching sometimes and sometimes just looking into the water.

III.

After that the blinds in Julie's window were closed. I made a new discovery, though: there was a fire burning on Mount Head. Little shapes moved around it, some quickly and others quite slow. At first I couldn't make anything of them, but as I watched the shapes resolved themselves into figures, and the figures into children. They were waving and jumping up and down as they ran around the fire. What were they doing that for? I wondered if their parents knew they were up there, or if they'd snuck away and were engaged in something illicit. Probably they were drinking beer and when they'd finished dancing, they would go off into the bushes and fondle one another. I was elated. This, I thought, is how an astronomer must feel when a new comet appears in his well-mapped field of night: what an incredible glory to have, if only for a moment, sole possession, so to speak, of a celestial object. I felt the same way about the children. Because I was the only one observing them, they were mine, even more mine than they would have been if they came at that very moment into my observatory—their real proximity, in fact, would only have made a mess of all my tenderness for them, which was, in that moment, so strong that I had to wipe my eyes to keep from moistening the eyepiece.

Happy children, I thought, and closed the roof of the observatory. I made cocoa on my spirit stove, and thought about Julie young and old, and how age burns people down, so that instead of dancing around fires they go shopping and marry cinders of men with names like Carl and Anselm. Of course the same thing might be true of stars. If you could see a star as it is now, not as it was thousands of years ago, it might be a great disappointment: a great black hulk turning in the void, a lump which you would not know at all.

The next night the children were up there again, dancing with even more energy than the night before, although their fire seemed a little smaller. Were they lost? Perhaps what I mistook for dancing was actually them signaling for help, waving their arms and shouting for a grownup to come and rescue them from their unaccustomed height. But what could I do? They were lost not only in time but in space; what I saw through the telescope had taken place years before, perhaps in an altogether different place. Now one of them appeared to be waving a flag. I remembered a story I had read long ago about children who play a game on an island in the middle of a lake. It ended badly, I think. But these children seemed to be enjoying themselves. It was impossible, I know, but in the quiet of the observatory I thought I could hear their festive howling.

It snowed again on Thanksgiving, so I went to the movies in Commonstock. One of those millennial pictures was playing, about a prehistoric plague unleashed on Los Angeles when a mysterious being, possibly extraterrestrial, is exhumed from the tar pits. In the end the sexy, no-nonsense biologist and the wisecracking ex-priest save the earth by contacting friendly aliens, who arrive with the antidote and a thousand years of mysteries bundled on their tiny, reddish shoulders.

I ran into George Pouliadis on the way back to my car. He looked as though he'd aged ten years; his face was scratched and he wore the beginnings of a beard which didn't suit him.

"Have you got fifty dollars?" he asked me.

"What for?"

"I'll pay you back the next time I see you."

"Sure." It was the least I could do, after all the times he'd helped me. "How was the hike? Did you see many fossils?"

"Ssh!"

"What? I thought you liked nature."

"Nature," George said, "will kick our ass every time. Every time." He climbed into his truck and drove off, and, as far as anyone knows, he was never seen in Commonstock again.

My father came to see me in the observatory. He studied the pictures of the children I'd taken with my telescope's photographic attachment. In one picture you can see the children clearly, leaping up against the background of the fire. In another they seem to be holding hands, although it's possible that two of them, upright, are carrying a third, supine, between them.

"What are these?"

"Just things in the sky."

"Are those galaxies?" He pointed to the separate tongues of the fire.

"I believe it's a nebula," I said.

"God, a nebula. What about this?" He pointed to a child's torso.

"Dark matter."

He whistled. "We should show these to the astronomers. I bet they don't see pictures like this every day."

"I'll bet they don't."

"They're really some pictures."

"Yes, they are."

"By the way, have you seen George lately?"

"No. Why?"

He shook his head. "I knew he was no good, ever since he dug that foundation too deep."

I pointed out that the foundation was our work, not George's.

"Hm," he said. "These are really some pictures."

"Yes, they are."

"You're all right, aren't you?"

"Never better."

After the Thanksgiving storm, the children were gone from the mountaintop. I looked for them night after night, on Mount Head and the neighboring hills, but their fire was burned out, their dance over. It was hard for me to get used to their absence. I spent the days on the sofa, reading magazines; after dark, sometimes, I walked a little way along the edge of the lake. One night, entirely by accident, I saw what I think was a planet, hanging over a jagged field of trees. The planet was dim, stippled, unmoving, and more or less without interest, compared to the other things I'd seen, but at least it reminded me not to give up looking. We run around as if it were the end of the world, and everything were lost, when all the while, without knowing it, we have been populating heaven with our mistakes.

In January I left Commonstock and drove back to New York, where I found work at an ad agency, researching the market for a new kind of storm drain. I rented an apartment in Ozone Park, high above the scattered streetlights, and set up my telescope in a portable mount that I built myself. I don't use it often now, but some nights I sit up late, looking northeast through the eyepiece. I wonder what became of my children, and how they came down from the mountain, and when, and when, they will come to me.

MOLLUSKS

by ARTHUR BRADFORD

MY FRIEND KENNETH and I were looking through some old automobiles we had found out in a field. We thought maybe there was something valuable in them. One time Kenneth found an old radar gun in a similar situation, the kind cops use to check a car's speed. It didn't work, but he kept it for parts.

These cars out in the field seemed like they had once been on fire. The paint was all bubbly and peeled. There were plants and other vegetation growing up practically through the floorboards. Under the seat of an old Ford I found myself a silver cup. Solid silver, imagine that.

Kenneth crawled inside a green Pontiac which was set apart from the rest of them. He'd been in there not even a minute when I heard him yelling for me to come over. I took my time and he kept yelling, "Hurry up! Hurry up, you gotta see this…"

So I made my way around to the passenger side door where I could see Kenneth gazing at something he'd found in the glove compartment. I peered inside too and what a sight it was. Right there in that glove box sat a quivering yellow slug about the size of a large loaf of bread.

Kenneth and I watched it for a while, just to see it move. Its skin was all glistening, covered with slime.

"Jesus Christ," said Kenneth.

So we decided to take the giant slug home with us. Actually, it was

Kenneth's idea. He said, "I know what we're gonna do. We're taking this puppy home."

Now I wouldn't necessarily have thought of it that way but then it's Kenneth who has the business sense. He is several years older than me and used to make his living doing this sort of thing. We found ourselves a big plastic bag, the kind they give you at the supermarket, and I held it open while Kenneth rolled the slug over. It just fell in there, plop. That slug was heavy, like a big ham, a little softer maybe.

Here's what we had scavenged in just about fifteen minutes at that place: a silver cup (solid silver, mine), an old Zippo lighter (broken, Kenneth's), and a giant slug (maybe ten pounds, Kenneth's, mostly).

I held the slug on my lap on the drive back. Kenneth wanted me to be very careful with it. "Don't break its skin," he kept saying. "Don't let any salt get on it." Right, where was I going to find salt?

We went straight to Kenneth's house. He lives in a nice place but it's all trashed since he and his crazy wife Teresa never throw anything away. I heard Kenneth say this once, he said, "It costs ten dollars a month to have them fuckers come over here and haul away the garbage. Why should I pay that? Give me one good reason?"

Kenneth was particularly excited at the prospect of showing the slug to his wife Teresa. He was so excited that he screeched into the driveway and knocked over some plastic milk crates full of trash. "Whoops," he said, and then he hopped out of the car.

"Teresa baby, you got to COME QUICK! You got to come out here and see this! You got to see what we found today!" he yelled.

Out comes Teresa and her eyes are all wide like she can't wait to see what we have in store for her. Teresa is very small, childsize almost. She and Kenneth make a funny couple, what with him being so uncommonly stout. I don't know what Teresa thought we had in that plastic bag, but it sure wasn't a big yellow slug.

She screamed and then went over to Kenneth and kicked him in the shin. She said, "What the fuck did you bring that here for?"

Kenneth was busy holding his aching shin so I piped up, "We figure someone will pay us for it."

"Yeah, right," said Teresa. She put her little hands on her hips. "That thing is disgusting."

I began to feel embarrassed. "Oh God," I thought, "Just look at me. What a fool." After all, I was the one holding the bag. I must have looked like some sort of creep.

But Kenneth stuck to his guns. He said, "Disgusting does not mean undesirable."

Teresa didn't buy that and she whirled around and stomped back into the house. What a firebrand. See, I knew she was Kenneth's wife, but even so I liked her quite a lot. THOU SHALT NOT COVET THY NEIGHBOR'S WIFE, right? Well fuck that, I thought, look at Kenneth. He's no Casanova. He collects slugs. Where does he get off marrying a woman like Teresa?

We put the giant slug in one of Kenneth's old fish tanks. Actually, the tank still had fish in it, but Kenneth dumped them out to make room for the slug. He dumped them right on the floor of his garage where they flipped about on the cement.

"I'll show her," he kept saying, "I'll make a mint off this slug and then you and me will go off on a trip without her."

"Yeah right," I said. But what I was really thinking was, "This is my chance." I know, it was crass of me, but remember, Kenneth had just dumped a bunch of helpless fish onto the ground. Where was the compassion in that?

So, while Kenneth was tending to the slug, I went inside and found Teresa. She was at her loom, weaving. She had an enormous loom in the house. It took up a whole room and there was string and yarn everywhere. She made rugs with it.

I said to Teresa, "Hey, I've got a surprise for you."

She said, "It better not be another fucking mollusk."

"No," I said, "it's a cup, solid silver."

I held out the cup I had found and Teresa stopped working. She had this way of raising just one eyebrow. It was a very sexy thing to do. She said, "Are you sure you want to give that to me?"

I wasn't making much money then and she was right, I needed everything I got. So I said, "Oh, maybe I SHOULD hold onto it," and she nodded knowingly. What a vixen.

Then Kenneth walked in saying, "I've got some phone calls to make."

It turned into night. Outside it grew dark and for hours and hours Kenneth kept at it on the phone.

"Yeah, Leroy," he would say, "I've got something very unusual here. I think you're gonna like this... Yeah, right...We found it this afternoon... It's a giant slug... Over ten pounds, easy... What?... Oh come on, Leroy... Leroy?... Fuck." And then he'd try somewhere else.

Meanwhile, I was doing my best with Teresa.

"That's a nice rug you're making," I said.

"Thank you," she said. Her childlike hands scampered up and down the vertical strings. The rug was made of many colors, bright yellows and blazing reds. The truth is it was very ugly. I would have gotten sick having something like that on my floor.

Kenneth: "Hi, Mr. Logan... Yes, Bob Willis referred me to you... Right, he said your organization might be interested in a scientific find I've come across..."

"I'm sorry about the slug," I said to Teresa.

She said, "Oh, that's okay. I'm used to Ken's bullshit by now."

Bullshit! I thought to myself, she's dissatisfied!

Kenneth yelled over the phone, "Oh Jesus! That's awful! You people ought to be gassed!" He slammed down the receiver and came running over to us.

"Those Satanists wanted to *burn* the slug!" he said, "They've got some kind of voodoo ritual involving mollusks! Isn't that fucked?" Kenneth looked tired. He'd been pulling his greasy hair this way and that.

"I think you're getting too attached to that thing, honey," said Teresa.

"Yeah," I said. "How much were they going to pay you?"

Kenneth looked shocked. He spun around and stormed off in a huff. "You Nazis!" he called out. "Fucking sellouts!"

Teresa turned to me and she said, "Can you and me go and talk somewhere private?"

I said, "Sure." All I could think was, "Now's my chance, now's my chance."

There was no where to move in that trash-filled house so we ended up in the garage. There was that giant slug, sitting in the fish tank, all lit up and glowing yellow. What a monster! It was too big for the tank. Part of its slimy tail slapped up against the glass.

"I sure hope that thing doesn't escape," I said.

Teresa looked up at me with solemn eyes and she said, "I haven't told Kenneth about this yet. I haven't told anybody. I'm with child."

"Oh, hey," I said, "a baby."

Teresa began to cry and I took her into my arms. I put my hand on her stomach. "Where's the kid?" I asked her. I couldn't feel it.

"It's not big enough yet," she said.

"Okay," I said.

We stood there holding each other in that strange aquarium light. I took my hand off of Teresa's stomach and motioned toward the quivering slug. "Maybe your baby will come out like that," I said. I'd intended it as some sort of joke, but Teresa didn't take it like that.

"Oh God," she said.

I moved a little closer and under my foot I felt the body of one of those dead fishes go squish. It wasn't very romantic, but I leaned down and kissed her all the same.

Teresa didn't push me away, but she didn't seem very turned on either. Her lips were cold, as a matter of fact. So I stopped kissing her. I hugged her tight and pulled her little body close to mine. I whispered in her ear, "I can take you away from all this Teresa. I can take care of you."

Of course, I couldn't. I had always looked up to Kenneth. I don't know why I decided at that moment that I was a better man for Teresa. But it didn't matter. Kenneth walked into the garage as we were hugging like that and he stood there shocked. He looked first at Teresa, and then at me, and then at Teresa again.

Then he looked at the slug. "Dammit," he said.

He went over to the garage door and heaved it open. The night air rushed in. Kenneth walked back to the tank and reached his hands inside. With a loud grunt he hoisted the beast up and over his head. He stood there holding it high, like a first-place trophy, or a prize fish, and he looked down upon Teresa and me.

"I'll be damned," he said, "if I'm gonna let this slug come between us."

Kenneth dashed out the garage door, slug in hands, and heaved it with all his strength into the night. It landed with a dull thud out on the lawn.

"I don't care how much they were going to pay me," he said, almost tearful.

Of course, I let go of Teresa at that point and she rushed over to Kenneth and wrapped her arms around him. Kenneth wiped his hands on his pants, to get rid of the slime, and then he hugged her too. I stood there feeling like a true heel at this point, but I had to admit that things looked better this way.

The slug made its escape that night, leaving a thick trail of ooze which disappeared into the woods. Perhaps it found some other abandoned glove compartment to call home. I found out later that some collector had offered Kenneth five hundred dollars for that slug, so it wasn't an empty gesture, tossing the animal away like that. I was sad at first to hear about that money lost. I thought Kenneth was a fool. But then I thought, Who are we to decide the fate of the earth's creatures? It was the Mollusks, after all, who first inhab- ited this earth. They roamed the land for millions and millions of years before any of us were even born.

Robert G. Miller
Chief Executive Officer
Rite Aid
30 Hunter Lane
Camp Hill, PA
17011

Dear Mr. Miller,

You do not know me and this matter does not directly affect you, but nevertheless I need
your full attention. I have been, for a few weeks now, writing letters to men like yourself,
though from the point of view of a dog named Steven. Here is one such letter, for you:

> I am Steven and I was born just after the children came home from school. I've
> spent days barking while not knowing why I was barking. On those days I would
> bark and bark, getting hoarse and tired, knowing that I did not know why I was
> barking, all the while guessing that I would be able to figure it out later.

> Yesterday I was running under a hundred tall elms, planted in a row. I was running
> toward a clearing where the grass in the light was chartreuse and soft, and while
> running, eyes glassy from the cold air, I thought of my sister, who was taken from
> me all those years ago, before her eyes had opened. My fur looks like sandpaper
> but is luxurious to touch.

> I still do not know why I bark. Right now, when it's been overcast for a week or so,
> I feel good, I feel rested, like I never want to bark again. But soon enough I will
> find myself barking, barking until I am hoarse, unable to stop barking oh God the
> people stare at me like I'll bark myself to death.

I guess it's back to work for you now, Mr. Miller.

D.

Daniel O'Mara
5811 Mesa Drive, #216
Austin, TX
78731

THE BEES

by DAN CHAON

GENE'S SON FRANKIE wakes up screaming. It has become frequent, two or three times a week, at random times: midnight—3 a.m.—five in the morning. Here is a high, empty wail that severs Gene from his unconsciousness like sharp teeth. It is the worst sound that Gene can imagine, the sound of a young child dying violently—falling from a building, or caught in some machinery that is tearing an arm off, or being mauled by a predatory animal. No matter how many times he hears it he jolts up with such images playing in his mind, and he always runs, thumping into the child's bedroom to find Frankie sitting up in bed, his eyes closed, his mouth open in an oval like a Christmas caroler. Frankie appears to be in a kind of peaceful trance, and if someone took a picture of him he would look like he was waiting to receive a spoonful of ice cream, rather than emitting that horrific sound.

"Frankie!" Gene will shout, and claps his hands hard in the child's face. The clapping works well. At this, the scream always stops abruptly, and Frankie opens his eyes, blinking at Gene with vague awareness before settling back down into his pillow, nuzzling a little before growing still. He is sound asleep, he is always sound asleep, though even after months Gene can't help leaning down and pressing his ear to the child's chest, to make sure he's still breathing, his heart is still going. It always is.

There is no explanation that they can find. In the morning, the child doesn't

Spanish Cross for Ciudad Rodrigo

remember anything, and on the few occasions that they have managed to wake him in the midst of one of his screaming attacks, he is merely sleepy and irritable. Once, Gene's wife Karen shook him and shook him, until finally he opened his eyes, groggily. "Honey?" she said. "Honey? Did you have a bad dream?" But Frankie only moaned a little. "No," he said, puzzled and unhappy at being awakened, but nothing more.

They can find no pattern to it. It can happen any day of the week, any time of the night. It doesn't seem to be associated with diet, or with his activities during the day, and it doesn't stem, as far as they can tell, from any sort of psychological unease. During the day, he seems perfectly normal and happy.

They have taken him several times to the pediatrician, but the doctor seems to have little of use to say. There is nothing wrong with the child physically, Dr. Banerjee says. She advises that such things are not uncommon for children of Frankie's age group—he is five—and that more often than not, the disturbance simply passes away.

"He hasn't experienced any kind of emotional trauma, has he?" the doctor says. "Nothing out of the ordinary at home?"

"No, no," they both murmur, together. They shake their heads, and Dr. Banerjee shrugs.

"Parents," she says. "It's probably nothing to worry about." She gives them a brief smile. "As difficult as it is, I'd say that you may just have to weather this out."

But the doctor has never heard those screams. In the mornings after the "nightmares," as Karen calls them, Gene feels unnerved, edgy. He works as a driver for the United Parcel Service, and as he moves through the day after a screaming attack, there is a barely perceptible hum at the edge of his hearing, an intent, deliberate static sliding along behind him as he wanders through streets and streets in his van. He stops along the side of the road and listens. The shadows of summer leaves tremble murmurously against the windshield, and cars are accelerating on a nearby road. In the treetops, a cicada makes its trembly, pressure-cooker hiss.

Something bad has been looking for him for a long time, he thinks, and now, at last, it is growing near.

When he comes home at night everything is normal. They live in an old house in the suburbs of Cleveland, and sometimes after dinner they work together in the small patch of garden out in back of the house—tomatoes, zucchini, string beans, cucumbers—while Frankie plays with Legos in the dirt. Or they take walks around the neighborhood, Frankie riding his bike in front of them, his training wheels recently removed. They gather on the couch and watch cartoons together, or play board games, or draw pictures with crayons. After Frankie is asleep, Karen will sit at the kitchen table and study—she is in nursing school—and Gene will sit outside on the porch, flipping through a newsmagazine or a novel, smoking the cigarettes that he has promised Karen he will give up when he turns thirty-five. He is thirty-four now, and Karen is twenty-seven, and he is aware, more and more frequently, that this is not the life that he deserves. He has been incredibly lucky, he thinks. Blessed, as Gene's favorite cashier at the super-market always says. "Have a blessed day," she says, when Gene pays the money and she hands him his receipt, and he feels as if she has sprinkled him with her ordinary, gentle beatitude. It reminds him of long ago, when an old nurse had held his hand in the hospital and said that she was praying for him.

Sitting out in his lawn chair, drawing smoke out of his cigarette, he thinks about that nurse, even though he doesn't want to. He thinks of the way she'd leaned over him and brushed his hair as he stared at her, imprisoned in a full body cast, sweating his way through withdrawal and D.T.'s.

He had been a different person, back then. A drunk, a monster. At nineteen, he'd married the girl he'd gotten pregnant, and then had set about to slowly, steadily, ruining all their lives. When he'd abandoned them, his wife and son, back in Nebraska, he had been twenty-four, a danger to himself and others. He'd done them a favor by leaving, he thought, though he still felt guilty when he remembered it. Years later, when he was sober, he'd even tried to contact them. He wanted to own up to his behavior, to pay the back child-support, to apologize. But they were nowhere to be found. Mandy was no longer living in the small Nebraska town where they'd met and married, and there was no forwarding address. Her parents were dead. No one seemed to know where she'd gone.

Karen didn't know the full story. She had been, to his relief, uncurious about his previous life, though she knew he had some drinking days, some bad times. She knew that he'd been married before, too, though she didn't know the extent of it, didn't know that he had another son, for example, didn't know that he had left them one night, without even packing a bag, just driving off in the car, a flask tucked between his legs, driving east as far as he could go. She didn't know about the car crash, the wreck he should have died in. She didn't know what a bad person he'd been.

She was a nice lady, Karen. Maybe a little sheltered. And truth to tell, he was ashamed—and even scared—to imagine how she would react to the truth about his past. He didn't know if she would have ever really trusted him if she'd known the full story, and the longer they knew one another the less inclined he was to reveal it. He'd escaped his old self, he thought, and when Karen got pregnant, shortly before they were married, he told himself that now he had a chance to do things over, to do it better. They had purchased the house together, he and Karen, and now Frankie will be in kindergarten in the fall. He has come full circle, has come exactly to the point when his former life with Mandy and his son, DJ, had completely fallen apart. He looks up as Karen comes to the back door and speaks to him through the screen. "I think it's time for bed, sweetheart," she says softly, and he shudders off these thoughts, these memories. He smiles.

He's been in a strange frame of mind lately. The months of regular awakenings have been getting to him, and he has a hard time getting back to sleep after an episode with Frankie. When Karen wakes him in the morning, he often feels muffled, sluggish—as if he's hung over. He doesn't hear the alarm clock. When he stumbles out of bed, he finds he has a hard time keeping his moodiness in check. He can feel his temper coiling up inside him.

He isn't that type of person anymore, and hasn't been for a long while. Still, he can't help but worry. They say that there is a second stretch of craving, which sets in after several years of smooth sailing; five or seven years will pass, and then it will come back without warning. He has been thinking of going to A.A. meetings again, though he hasn't in some time—not since he met Karen.

It's not as if he gets trembly every time he passes a liquor store, or even as if he has a problem when he goes out with buddies and spends the evening drinking soda and non-alchoholic beer. No. The trouble comes at night, when he's asleep.

He has begun to dream of his first son. DJ. Perhaps it is related to his worries about Frankie, but for several nights in a row the image of DJ—aged about five—has appeared to him. In the dream, Gene is drunk, and playing hide and seek with DJ in the yard behind the Cleveland house where he is now living. There is the thick weeping willow out there, and Gene watches the child appear from behind it and run across the grass, happily, unafraid, the way Frankie would. DJ turns to look over his shoulder and laughs, and Gene stumbles after him, at least a six-pack's worth of good mood, a goofy, drunken dad. It's so real that when he wakes, he still feels intoxicated. It takes him a few minutes to shake it.

One morning after a particularly vivid version of this dream, Frankie wakes and complains of a funny feeling—"right here," he says—and points to his forehead. It isn't a headache, he says. "It's like bees!" he says. "Buzzing bees!" He rubs his hand against his brow. "Inside my head." He considers for a moment. "You know how the bees bump against the window when they get in the house and want to get out?" This description pleases him, and he taps his forehead lightly with his fin-gers, humming, "zzzzzzz," to demonstrate.

"Does it hurt?" Karen says.

"No," Frankie says. "It tickles."

Karen gives Gene a concerned look. She makes Frankie lie down on the couch, and tells him to close his eyes for a while. After a few minutes, he rises up, smiling, and says that the feeling has gone.

"Honey, are you sure?" Karen says. She pushes her hair back and slides her palm across his forehead. "He's not hot," she says, and Frankie sits up impa-tiently, suddenly more interested in finding a matchbox car he dropped under a chair.

Karen gets out one of her nursing books, and Gene watches her face tighten with concern as she flips slowly through the pages. She is looking at Chapter Three: Neurological System, and Gene observes as she pauses here and there, skimming down a list of symptoms. "We should probably take him back to Dr. Banerjee again," she says. Gene nods, recalling what the doc-tor said about "emotional trauma."

"Are you scared of bees?" he asks Frankie. "Is that something that's bother-ing you?"

"No," Frankie says. "Not really."

When Frankie was three, a bee stung him above his left eyebrow. They had been out hiking together, and they hadn't yet learned that Frankie was "moderately allergic" to bee stings. Within minutes of the sting, Frankie's face had begun to distort, to puff up, his eye welling shut. He looked deformed. Gene didn't know if he'd ever been more frightened in his entire life, running down the trail with Frankie's head pressed against his heart, try-ing to get to the car and drive him to the doctor, terrified that the child was dying. Frankie himself was calm.

Gene clears his throat. He knows the feeling that Frankie is talking about—he has felt it himself, that odd, feathery vibration inside his head. And in fact he feels it again, now. He presses the pads of his fingertips against his brow. Emotional trauma, his mind murmurs, but he is thinking of DJ, not Frankie.

"What are you scared of?" Gene asks Frankie, after a moment. "Anything?"

"You know what the scariest thing is?" Frankie says, and widens his eyes, miming a frightened look. "There's a lady with no head, and she went walking through the woods, looking for it. 'Give... me... back... my... head....'"

"Where on earth did you hear a story like that!" Karen says.

"Daddy told me," Frankie says. "When we were camping."

Gene blushes, even before Karen gives him a sharp look. "Oh, great," she says. "Wonderful."

He doesn't meet her eyes. "We were just telling ghost stories," he says, softly. "I thought he would think the story was funny."

"My God, Gene," she says. "With him having nightmares like this? What were you thinking?"

It's a bad flashback, the kind of thing he's usually able to avoid. He thinks abruptly of Mandy, his former wife. He sees in Karen's face that look Mandy would give him when he screwed up. "What are you, some kind of idiot?" Mandy used to say. "Are you crazy?" Back then, Gene couldn't do anything right, it seemed, and when Mandy yelled at him it made his stomach clench with shame and inarticulate rage. I was trying, he would think, I was trying, damn it, and it was as if no matter what he did, it wouldn't turn out right. That feeling would sit heavily in his chest, and eventually, when things got worse, he hit her once. "Why do you want me to feel like shit," he had said through clenched teeth. "I'm not an asshole," he said, and when she rolled her eyes at him he slapped her hard enough to knock her out of her chair.

That was the time he'd taken DJ to the carnival. It was a Saturday, and he'd been drinking a little so Mandy didn't like it, but after all—he thought—DJ was his son, too, he had a right to spend some time with his own son, Mandy wasn't his boss even if she might think she was. She liked to make him hate himself.

What she was mad about was that he'd taken DJ on the Velocerator. It was a mistake, he'd realized afterward. But DJ himself had begged to go on. He was just recently four years old, and Gene had just turned twenty-three, which made him feel inexplicably old. He wanted to have a little fun.

Besides, nobody told him he couldn't take DJ on the thing. When he led DJ through the gate, the ticket-taker even smiled, as if to say, "Here is a young guy showing his kid a good time." Gene winked at DJ and grinned, taking a nip from a flask of Peppermint Schnapps. He felt like a good Dad. He wished his own father had taken him on rides at the carnival!

The door to the Velocerator opened like a hatch in a big silver flying saucer. Disco music was blaring from the entrance and became louder as they went inside. It was a circular room with soft padded walls, and one of the workers had Gene and DJ stand with their backs to the wall, strapping them in side by side. Gene felt warm and expansive from the Schnapps. He took DJ's hand, and he almost felt as if he were glowing with love. "Get ready, kiddo," Gene whispered. "This is going to be wild."

The hatch door of the Velocerator sealed closed with a pressurized sigh. And then, slowly, the walls they were strapped to began to turn. Gene tightened on DJ's hand as they began to rotate, gathering speed. After a moment the wall pads they were strapped to slid up, and the force of velocity pushed them back, held to the surface of the spinning wall like iron to a magnet. Gene's cheeks and lips seemed to pull back, and the sensation of helplessness made him laugh.

At that moment, DJ began to scream. "No! No! Stop! Make it stop!" They were terrible shrieks, and Gene grabbed the child's hand tightly. "It's all right," he yelled jovially over the thump of the music. "It's okay! I'm right here!" But the child's wailing only got louder in response. The scream seemed to whip past Gene in a circle, tumbling around and around the circumference of the ride like a spirit, trailing echos as it flew. When the machine finally stopped, DJ was heaving with sobs, and the man at the control panel glared. Gene could feel the other passengers staring grimly and judgmentally at him.

Gene felt horrible. He had been so happy—thinking that they were finally having themselves a memorable father and son moment—and he could feel his heart plunging into darkness. DJ kept on weeping, even as they left the ride and walked along the midway, even as Gene tried to distract him with promises of cotton candy and stuffed animals. "I want to go home," DJ cried, and "I want my Mom! I want my Mom!" And it had wounded Gene to hear that. He gritted his teeth.

"Fine!" he hissed. "Let's go home to your Mommy, you little crybaby. I swear to God, I'm never taking you with me anywhere again." And he gave DJ a little shake. "Jesus, what's wrong with you? Lookit, people are laughing at you. See? They're saying, 'Look at that big boy, bawling like a girl.'"

* * *

This memory comes to him out of the blue. He had forgotten all about it, but now it comes to him over and over. Those screams were not unlike the sounds Frankie makes in the middle of the night, and they pass repeatedly through the membrane of his thoughts, without warning. The next day, he finds himself recalling it again, the memory of the scream impressing his mind with such force that he actually has to pull his UPS truck off to the side of the road and put his face in his hands: Awful! Awful! He must have seemed like a monster to the child.

Sitting there in his van, he wishes he could find a way to contact them—Mandy and DJ. He wishes that he could tell them how sorry he is, and send them money. He puts his fingertips against his forehead, as cars drive past on the street, as an old man parts the curtains and peers out of the house Gene is parked in front of, hopeful that Gene might have a package for him.

Where are they? Gene wonders. He tries to picture a town, a house, but there is only a blank. Surely, Mandy being Mandy, she would have hunted him down by now to demand child support. She would have relished treating him like a deadbeat dad, she would have hired some company who would garnish his wages.

Now, sitting at the roadside, it occurs to him suddenly that they are dead. He recalls the car wreck that he was in, just outside Des Moines, and if he had been killed they would have never known. He recalls waking up in the hospital, and the elderly nurse who had said, "You're very lucky, young man. You should be dead."

Maybe they are dead, he thinks. Mandy and DJ. The idea strikes him a glancing blow, because of course it would make sense. The reason they'd never contacted him. Of course.

He doesn't know what to do with such premonitions. They are ridiculous, they are self-pitying, they are paranoid, but especially now, with their concerns about Frankie, he is at the mercy of his anxieties. He comes home from work and Karen stares at him heavily.

"What's the matter?" she says, and he shrugs. "You look terrible," she says.

"It's nothing," he says, but she continues to look at him skeptically. She shakes her head.

"I took Frankie to the doctor again today," she says, after a moment, and Gene sits down at the table with her, where she is spread out with her textbooks and notepaper.

"I suppose you'll think I'm being a neurotic mom," she says. "I think I'm too immersed in disease, that's the problem."

Gene shakes his head. "No, no," he says. His throat feels dry. "You're right. Better safe than sorry."

"Mmm," she says, thoughtfully. "I think Dr. Banerjee is starting to hate me."

"Naw," Gene says. "No one could hate you." With effort, he smiles gently. A good husband, he kisses her palm, her wrist. "Try not to worry," he says, though his own nerves are fluttering. He can hear Frankie in the backyard, shouting orders to someone.

"Who's he talking to?" Gene says, and Karen doesn't look up.

"Oh," she says. "It's probably just Bubba." Bubba is Frankie's imaginary playmate.

Gene nods. He goes to the window and looks out. Frankie is pretending to shoot at something, his thumb and forefinger cocked into a gun. "Get him! Get him!" Frankie shouts, and Gene stares out as Frankie dodges behind a tree. Frankie looks nothing like DJ, but when he pokes his head from behind the hanging foliage of the willow, Gene feels a little shudder—a flicker—something. He clenches his jaw.

"This class is really driving me crazy," Karen says. "Everytime I read about a worst-case scenario, I start to worry. It's strange. The more you know, the less sure you are of anything."

"What did the doctor say this time?" Gene says. He shifts uncomfortably, still staring out at Frankie, and it seems as if dark specks circle and bob at the corner of the yard. "He seems okay?"

Karen shrugs. "As far as they can tell." She looks down at her textbook, shaking her head. "He seems healthy." He puts his hand gently on the back of her neck and she lolls her head back and forth against his fingers. "I've never believed that anything really terrible could happen to me," she had once told him, early in their marriage, and it had scared him. "Don't say that," he'd whispered, and she laughed.

"You're superstitious," she said. "That's cute."

He can't sleep. The strange presentiment that Mandy and DJ are dead has lodged heavily in his mind, and he rubs his feet together underneath the covers, trying to find a comfortable posture. He can hear the soft ticks of the old electric typewriter as Karen finishes her paper for school, words rattling out in bursts that remind him of some sort of insect language. He closes his eyes, pretending to be asleep when Karen finally comes to bed, but his mind is ticking with small, scuttling images: his former wife and son, flashes of the photographs he didn't own, hadn't kept. They're dead, a firm voice in his mind says, very distinctly. They were in a fire. And they burned up. It is not quite his own voice that speaks to him, and abruptly he can picture the burning house. It's a trailer, somewhere on the outskirts of a small town, and the black smoke is pouring out of the open door. The plastic window frames have warped and begun to melt, and the smoke billows from the trailer into the sky in a way that reminds him of an old locomotive. He can't see inside, except for crackling bursts of deep orange flames, but he's aware that they're inside. For a second he can see DJ's face, flickering, peering steadily from the window of the burning trailer, his mouth open in a unnatural circle, as if he's singing.

He opens his eyes. Karen's breathing has steadied, she's sound asleep, and he carefully gets out of bed, padding restlessly through the house in his pajamas. They're not dead, he tries to tell himself, and stands in front of the refrigerator, pouring milk from the carton into his mouth. It's an old comfort, from back in the days when he was drying out, when the thick taste of milk would slightly calm his craving for a drink. But it doesn't help him now. The dream, the vision, has frightened him badly, and he sits on the couch with an afghan over his shoulders, staring at some science program on television. On the program, a lady scientist is examining a mummy. A child. The thing is bald— almost a skull but not quite. A membrane of ancient skin is pulled taut over the eyesockets. The lips are stretched back, and there are small, chipped, rodentlike teeth. Looking at the thing, he can't help but think of DJ again, and he looks over his shoulder, quickly, the way he used to.

The last year that he was together with Mandy, there used to be times when DJ would actually give him the creeps—spook him. DJ had been an unusually skinny child, with a head like a baby bird and long, bony feet, with toes that seemed strangely extended, as if they were meant for gripping. He can remember the way the child would slip barefoot through rooms, slinking, sneaking, watching, Gene had thought, always watching him.

It is a memory that he has almost, for years, succeeded in forgetting, a memory he hates and mistrusts. He was drinking heavily at the time, and he knows now that alcohol had grotesquely distorted his perceptions. But now that it has been dislodged, that old feeling moves through him like a breath of smoke. Back then, it had seemed to him that Mandy had turned DJ against him, that DJ had in some strange way almost physically transformed into something that wasn't Gene's real son. Gene can remember how, sometimes, he would be sitting on the couch, watching TV, and he'd get a funny feeling. He'd turn his head and DJ would be at the edge of the room, with his bony spine hunched and his long neck craned, staring with those strangely oversized eyes. Other times, Gene and Mandy would be arguing and DJ would suddenly slide into the room, creeping up to Mandy and resting his head on her chest, right in the middle of some important talk. "I'm thirsty," he would say, in imitation baby-talk. Though he was five years old, he would play-act this little toddler voice. "Mama," he would say. "I is firsty." And DJ's eyes would rest on Gene for a moment, cold and full of calculating hatred.

Of course, Gene knows now that this was not the reality of it. He knows: He was a drunk, and DJ was just a sad, scared little kid, trying to deal with a rotten situation. Later, when he was in detox, these memories of his son made him actually shudder with shame, and it was not something he could bring himself to talk about even when he was deep into his twelve steps. How could he say how repulsed he'd been by the child, how actually frightened he was. Jesus Christ, DJ was a poor wretched five-year-old kid! But in Gene's memory there was something malevolent about him, resting his head pettishly on his mother's chest, talking in that sing-song, lisping voice, staring hard and unblinking at Gene with a little smile. Gene remembers catching DJ by the back of the neck. "If you're going to talk, talk normal," Gene had whispered through his teeth, and tightened his fingers on the child's neck. "You're not a baby. You're not fooling anybody." And DJ had actually bared his teeth, making a thin, hissing whine.

He wakes and he can't breathe. There is a swimming, suffocating sensation of being stared at, being watched by something that hates him, and he gasps, choking for air. A lady is bending over him, and for a moment he expects her to say, "You're very lucky, young man. You should be dead."

But it's Karen. "What are you doing?" she says. It's morning, and he struggles to orient himself—he's on the living room floor, and the television is still going.

"Jesus," he says, and coughs. "Oh, Jesus." He is sweating, his face feels hot, but he tries to calm himself in the face of Karen's horrified stare. "A bad dream," he says, trying to control his panting breaths. "Jesus," he says, and shakes his head, trying to smile reassuringly for her. "I got up last night and

I couldn't sleep. I must have passed out while I was watching TV."

But Karen just gazes at him, her expression frightened and uncertain, as if something about him is transforming. "Gene," she says. "Are you all right?"

"Sure," he says, hoarsely, and a shudder passes over him involuntarily. "Of course." And then he realizes that he is naked. He sits up, covering his crotch self-consciously with his hands, and glances around. He doesn't see his underwear or his pajama bottoms anywhere nearby. He doesn't even see the afghan, which he had draped over him on the couch while he was watching the mummies on TV. He starts to stand up, awkwardly, and he notices that Frankie is standing there in the archway between the kitchen and the living room, watching him, his arms at his sides like a cowboy who is ready to draw his holstered guns.

"Mom?" Frankie says. "I'm thirsty."

He drives through his deliveries in a daze. The bees, he thinks. He remembers what Frankie had said a few mornings before, about bees inside his head, buzzing and bumping against the inside of his forehead like a windowpane they were tapping against. That's the feeling he has now. All the things that he doesn't quite remember are circling and alighting, vibrating their cellophane wings insistently. He sees himself striking Mandy across the face with the flat of his hand, knocking her off her chair; he sees his grip tightening around the back of DJ's thin, five-year-old neck, shaking him as he grimaced and wept; and he is aware that there are other things, perhaps even worse, if he thought about it hard enough. All the things that he'd prayed that Karen would never know about him.

He was very drunk on the day that he left them, so drunk that he can barely remember. It was hard to believe that he'd made it all the way to Des Moines on the interstate before he went off the road, tumbling end over end, into darkness. He was laughing, he thought, as the car crumpled around him, and he has to pull his van over to the side of the road, out of fear, as the tickling in his head intensifies. There is an image of Mandy, sitting on the couch as he stormed out, with DJ cradled in her arms, one of DJ's eyes swollen shut and puffy. There is an image of him in the kitchen, throwing glasses and beer bottles onto the floor, listening to them shatter.

And whether they are dead or not, he knows that they don't wish him well. They would not want him to be happy—in love with his wife and child. His normal, undeserved life.

* * *

When he gets home that night, he feels exhausted. He doesn't want to think anymore, and for a moment, it seems that he will be allowed a small reprieve. Frankie is in the yard, playing contentedly. Karen is in the kitchen, making hamburgers and corn on the cob, and everything seems okay. But when he sits down to take off his boots, she gives him an angry look.

"Don't do that in the kitchen," she says, icily. "Please. I've asked you before."

He looks down at his feet: one shoe unlaced, half-off. "Oh," he says. "Sorry."

But when he retreats to the living room, to his recliner, she follows him. She leans against the door frame, her arms folded, watching as he releases his tired feet from the boots and rubs his hand over the bottom of his socks. She frowns heavily.

"What?" he says, and tries on an uncertain smile.

She sighs. "We need to talk about last night," she says. "I need to know what's going on."

"Nothing," he says, but the stern way she examines him activates his anxieties all over again. "I couldn't sleep, so I went out to the living room to watch TV. That's all."

She stares at him. "Gene," she says after a moment. "People don't usually wake up naked on their living room floor and not know how they got there. That's just weird, don't you think?"

Oh, please, he thinks. He lifts his hands, shrugging—a posture of innocence and exasperation, though his insides are trembling. "I know," he says. "It was weird to me, too. I was having nightmares. I really don't know what happened."

She gazes at him for a long time, her eyes heavy. "I see," she says, and he can feel the emanation of her disappointment like waves of heat. "Gene," she says. "All I'm asking is for you to be honest with me. If you're having problems, if you're drinking again, or thinking about it. I want to help. We can work it out. But you have to be honest with me."

"I'm not drinking," Gene says, firmly. He holds her eyes, earnestly. "I'm not thinking about it. I told you when we met, I'm through with it. Really." But he is aware again of an observant, unfriendly presence, hidden, moving along the edge of the room. "I don't understand," he says. "What is it? Why would you think I'd lie to you?"

She shifts, still trying to read something in his face, still, he can tell, doubting him. "Listen," she says, at last, and he can tell she is trying not to cry. "Some guy called you today. A drunk guy. And he said to tell you that he had a good time hanging out with you last night, and that he was looking forward to seeing you again soon." She frowns hard, staring at him as if this last bit of damning information will show him for the liar he is. A tear slips out of the corner of her eye and along the bridge of her nose. Gene feels his chest tighten.

"That's crazy," he says. He tries to sound outraged, but he is in fact suddenly very frightened. "Who was it?"

She shakes her head, sorrowfully. "I don't know," she says. "Something with a 'B.' He was slurring so badly I could hardly understand him. B. B. or B. J. or…"

Gene can feel the small hairs on his back prickling. "Was it DJ?" he says, softly.

And Karen shrugs, lifting a now teary face to him. "I don't know!" she says, hoarsely. "I don't know. Maybe." And Gene puts his palms across his face. He is aware of that strange, buzzing, tickling feeling behind his forehead.

"Who is DJ?" Karen says. "Gene, you have to tell me what's going on."

But he can't. He can't tell her, even now. Especially now, he thinks, when to admit that he'd been lying to her ever since they met would confirm all the fears and suspicions she'd been nursing for—what?—days? weeks?

"He's someone I used to know a long time ago," Gene tells her. "Not a good person. He's the kind of guy who might… call up, and get a kick out of upsetting you."

They sit at the kitchen table, silently watching as Frankie eats his hamburger and corn on the cob. Gene can't quite get his mind around it. DJ, he thinks, as he presses his finger against his hamburger bun, but doesn't pick it up. DJ. He would be fifteen by now. Could he, perhaps, have found them? Maybe stalking them? Watching the house? Gene tries to fathom how DJ might have been causing Frankie's screaming episodes. How he might have caused what happened last night—snuck up on Gene while he was sitting there watching TV and drugged him or something. It seems farfetched.

"Maybe it was just some random drunk," he says at last, to Karen. "Accidentally calling the house. He didn't ask for me by name, did he?"

"I don't remember," Karen says, softly. "Gene…"

And he can't stand the doubtfulness, the lack of trust in her expression. He strikes his fist hard against the table, and his plate clatters in a circling echo. "I did not go out with anybody last night!" he says. "I did not get drunk! You can either believe me, or you can…"

They are both staring at him. Frankie's eyes are wide, and his puts down the corn cob he was about to bite into, as if he doesn't like it anymore. Karen's mouth is pinched.

"Or I can what?" she says.

"Nothing," Gene breathes.

There isn't a fight, but a chill spreads through the house, a silence. She knows that he isn't telling her the truth. She knows that there's more to it. But what can he say? He stands at the sink, gently washing the dishes as Karen bathes Frankie and puts him to bed. He waits, listening to the small sounds of the house at night. Outside, in the yard, there is the swingset, and the willow tree—silver-gray and stark in the security light that hangs above the garage. He waits for a while longer, watching, half-expecting to see DJ emerge from behind the tree as he'd done in Gene's dream, creeping along, his bony hunched back, the skin pulled tight against the skull of his oversized head. There is that smothering, airless feeling of being watched, and Gene's hands are trembling as he rinses a plate under the tap.

When he goes upstairs at last, Karen is already in her nightgown, in bed, reading a book.

"Karen," he says, and she flips a page, deliberately.

"I don't want to talk to you until you're ready to tell me the truth," she says. She doesn't look at him. "You can sleep on the couch, if you don't mind."

"Just tell me," Gene says. "Did he leave a number? To call him back?"

"No," Karen says. She doesn't look at him. "He just said he'd see you soon."

He thinks that he will stay up all night. He doesn't even wash up, or brush his teeth, or get into his bedtime clothes. He just sits there on the couch, in his uniform and stocking feet, watching television with the sound turned low, listening. Midnight. 1 a.m.

He goes upstairs to check on Frankie, but everything is okay. Frankie is asleep with his mouth open, the covers thrown off. Gene stands in the doorway, alert for movement, but everything seems to be in place. Frankie's turtle sits motionless on its rock, the books are lined up in neat rows, the toys put away. Frankie's face tightens and untightens as he dreams.

2 a.m. Back on the couch, Gene startles, half-asleep as an ambulance passes in the distance, and then there is only the sound of crickets and cicadas. Awake for a moment, he blinks heavily at a rerun of *Bewitched*, and flips through channels. Here is some jewelry for sale. Here is someone performing an autopsy.

In the dream, DJ is older. He looks to be nineteen or twenty, and he walks into a bar where Gene is hunched on a stool, sipping a glass of beer. Gene recognizes him right away—his posture, those thin shoulders, those large eyes. But now, DJ's arms are long and muscular, tattooed. There is a hooded, unpleasant look on his face as he ambles up to the bar, pressing in next to Gene. DJ orders a shot of Jim Beam—Gene's old favorite.

"I've been thinking about you a lot, ever since I died," DJ murmurs. He doesn't look at Gene as he says this, but Gene knows who he is talking to, and his hands are shaky as he takes a sip of beer.

"I've been looking for you for a long time," DJ says, softly, and the air is hot and thick. Gene puts a trembly cigarette to his mouth and breathes on it, choking on the taste. He wants to say, I'm sorry. Forgive me. But he can't breathe. DJ shows his small, crooked teeth, staring at Gene as he gulps for air.

"I know how to hurt you," DJ whispers.

Gene opens his eyes, and the room is full of smoke. He sits up, disoriented: for a second he is still in the bar with DJ before he realizes that he's in his own house.

There is a fire somewhere: he can hear it. People say that fire "crackles," but in fact it seems like the amplified sound of tiny creatures eating, little wet mandibles, thousands and thousands of them, and then a heavy, whispered whoof, as the fire finds another pocket of oxygen. He can hear this, even as he chokes blindly in the smoky air. The living room has a filmy haze over it, as if it is atomizing, fading away, and when he tries to stand up it disappears completely. There is a thick membrane of smoke above him, and he drops again to his hands and knees, gagging and coughing, a thin line of vomit trickling onto the rug in front of the still chattering television.

He has the presence of mind to keep low, crawling on his knees and elbows underneath the thick, billowing fumes. "Karen!" he calls. "Frankie!" but his voice is swallowed into the white noise of diligently licking flame. "Ach," he chokes, meaning to utter their names.

When he reaches the edge of the stairs he sees only flames and darkness above him. He puts his hands and knees on the bottom steps, but the heat pushes him back. He feels one of Frankie's action figures underneath his palm, the melting plastic adhering to his skin, and he shakes it away as another bright burst of flame reaches out of Frankie's bedroom for a moment. At the top of the stairs, through the curling fog he can see the figure of a child watching him grimly, hunched there, its face lit and flickering. Gene cries out, lunging into the heat, crawling his way up the stairs, to where the bedrooms are. He tries to call to them again, but instead, he vomits.

There is another burst that covers the image that he thinks is a child. He can feel his hair and eyebrows shrinking and sizzling against his skin as the upstairs breathes out a concussion of sparks. He is aware that there are hot, floating bits of substance in the air, glowing orange and then winking out, turning to ash. The air thick with angry buzzing, and that is all he can hear as he slips, turning end over end down the stairs, the humming and his own voice, a long vowel wheeling and echoing as the house spins into a blur.

And then he is lying on the grass. Red lights tick across his opened eyes in a steady, circling rhythm, and a woman, a paramedic, lifts her lips up from his. He draws in a long, desperate breath.

"Shhhhh," she says, softly, and passes her hand along his eyes. "Don't look," she says.

But he does. He sees, off to the side, the long black plastic sleeping bag, with a strand of Karen's blond hair hanging out from the top. He sees the blackened, shriveled body of a child, curled into a fetal position. They place the corpse into the spread, zippered plastic opening of the body bag, and he can see the mouth, frozen, calcified, into an oval. A scream.

THREE MEDITATIONS
ON DEATH

by WILLIAM T. VOLLMANN

I.
CATACOMB THOUGHTS

DEATH IS ORDINARY. Behold it, subtract its patterns and lessons from those of the death that weapons bring, and maybe the residue will show what violence is. With this in mind, I walked the long tunnels of the Paris catacombs. Walls of earth and stone encompassed walls of mortality a femur's-length thick: long yellow and brown bones all stacked in parallels, their sockets pointing outward like melted bricks whose ends dragged down, like downturned bony smiles, like stale yellow snails of macaroni—joints of bones, heads of bones, promiscuously touching, darkness in the center of each, between those twin knucklespurs which had once helped another bone to pivot, thereby guiding and supporting flesh in its passionate and sometimes intelligent motion toward the death it inevitably found—femurs in rows, then, and humeri, bones upon bones, and every few rows there'd be a shelf of bone to shore death up, a line of humeri and femurs laid down laterally to achieve an almost pleasing masonry effect, indeed, done by masonry's maxims, as interpreted by Napoleon's engineers and brickmen of death, who at the nouveau-royal command had elaborated and organized death's jetsam according to a sanitary aesthetic. (Did the Emperor ever visit that place? He was not afraid of death—not even of causing it.) Then there were side-chambers walled with bones likewise crossed upon bone-beams; from

German Medal for South-West Africa, 1904-6

these the occasional skull looked uselessly out; and every now and then some spiritual types had ornamented the facade with a cross made of femurs. There had been laid down in that place, I was told, the remains of about six million persons—our conventional total for the number of Jews who died in the Holocaust. The crime which the Nazis accomplished with immense effort in half a dozen years, nature had done here without effort or recourse, and was doing.

I had paid my money aboveground; I had come to look upon my future. But when after walking the long arid angles of prior underground alleys I first encountered my brothers and sisters, calcified appurtenances of human beings now otherwise gone to be dirt, and rat-flesh, and root-flesh, and green leaves soon to die again, I felt nothing but a mildly melancholy curiosity. One expects to die; one has seen skeletons and death's heads on Halloween masks, in anatomy halls, cartoons, warning signs, forensic photographs, photographs of old SS insignia, and meanwhile the skulls bulged and gleamed from walls like wet river-boulders, until curiosity became, as usual, numbness. But one did not come out of the ground then. Bone-walls curled around wells, drainage sockets in those tunnels; sometimes water dripped from the ceiling and struck the tourists' foreheads—water which had probably leached out of corpses. A choking, sickening dust irritated our eyes and throats, for in no way except in the abstract, and perhaps not even then, is the presence of the dead salutary to the living. Some skulls dated to 1792. Darkened, but still not decayed, they oppressed me with their continued existence. The engineers would have done better to let them transubstantiate. They might have been part of majestic trees by now, or delicious vegetables made over into young children's blood and growing bones. Instead they were as stale and stubborn as old arguments, molds for long dissolved souls, churlish hoardings of useless matter. Thus, I believed, the reason for my resentment. The real sore point was that, in Eliot's phrase, "I had not thought death had undone so many"; numbness was giving way to qualmishness, to a nauseated, claustrophobic realization of my biological entrapment. Yes, of course I'd known that I must die, and a number of times had had my nose rubbed in the fact; this was one of them, and in between those episodes my tongue glibly admitted what my heart secretly denied; for why should life ought to bear in its flesh the dissolving, poisonous faith of its own inescapable defeat? Atop bony driftwood, skulls slept, eyeholes downward, like the shells of dead hermit crabs amidst those wracked corpse-timbers. This was the necrophile's beach, but there was no ocean except the ocean of earth overhead from which those clammy drops oozed and dripped. Another cross of bone, and then the inscription—

SILENCE, MORTAL BEINGS—

VAIN GRANDEURS, SILENCE—

words even more imperious in French than I have given them here, but no more necessary, for the calcified myriads said that better than all poets or commanders. In superstition the carcass is something to be feared, dreaded and hated; in fact it deserves no emotion whatsoever in and of itself, unless it happens to comprise a souvenir of somebody other than a stranger; but time spent in the company of death is time wasted. Life trickles away, like the water falling down into the catacombs, and in the end we will be silent as our ancestors are silent, so better to indulge our vain grandeurs while we can. Moment by moment, our time bleeds away. Shout, scream, or run, it makes no difference, so why not forget what can't be avoided? On and on twisted death's alleys. Sometimes there was a smell, a cheesy, vinegary smell which I knew from having visited a field-morgue or two; there was no getting away from it, and the dust of death dried out my throat. I came to a sort of cavern piled up to my neck with heaps of bones not used in construction: pelvic bones and ribs (the vertebrae and other small bones must have all gone to discard or decay). These relics were almost translucent, like seashells, so thin had death nibbled them. That smell, that vinegar-vomit smell, burned my throat, but perhaps I was more sensitive to it than I should have been, for the other tourists did not appear to be disgusted; indeed, some were laughing, either out of bravado or because to them it was as unreal as a horror movie; they didn't believe that they'd feature in the next act, which must have been why one nasty fellow seemed to be considering whether or not to steal a bone—didn't he have bones enough inside his living meat? He must not have been the only one, for when we came to the end and ascended to street level we met a gainfully employed man behind a table which already had two skulls on it, seized from thieves that day; he checked our backpacks. I was happy when I got past him and saw sunlight—almost overjoyed, in fact, for since becoming a part-time journalist of armed politics I am not titillated by death. I try to understand it, to make friends with it, and I never learn anything except the lesson of my own powerlessness. Death stinks in my nostrils as it did that chilly sunny autumn afternoon in Paris when I wanted to be happy.

In the bakeries, the baguettes and pale, starchy *mini-ficelles,* the croissants and *pains-aux-chocolats* all reminded me of bones. Bone-colored cheese stank from other shops. All around me, the steel worms of the Metro bored through other catacombs, rushing still-living bones from hole to hole. In one of the bookshops on the Rue de Seine I found a demonically bound volume of Poe whose endpapers were marbled like flames; the plates, of course, hand-colored by the artist, depicted gruesomely menacing skeletons whose finger-bones snatched and clawed. I spied a wedding at the Place Saint-Germain, whose church was tanned and smoked by time to the color of cheesy bones; I saw the white-clad bride—soon to become yellow bones. The pale narrow concrete sleepers of railroads, metallic or wooden fence-rails, the model of the spinal column in the window of an anatomical bookshop, then even sticks, tree trunks, all lines inscribed or implied, the world itself in all its segments, rays, and dismembered categories became hideously cadaverous. I saw and inhaled death. I tasted death on my teeth. I exhaled, and the feeble puffs of breath could not push my nausea away. Only time did that—a night and a day, to be exact—after which I forgot again until I was writing these very words that *I must die.* I believed but for a moment. Thus I became one with those skulls which no longer knew their death. Even writing this, picking my letters from the alphabet's boneyard, my *o*'s like death's-heads, my *i*'s and *l*'s like ribs, my *b*'s, *q*'s, *p*'s, and *d*'s like ball-ended humeri broken in half, I believed only by fits. The smell came back into my nose, but I was in Vienna by then—whose catacombs, by the way, I decided not to visit—so I went out and smelled espresso heaped with fresh cream. The writing became, as writing ought to be, informed by choreographies and paradigms which mediated that smell into something more than its revolting emptiness. I take my meaning where I can find it; when I can't find it, I invent it. And when I do that, I deny meaninglessness, and when I do *that* I am lying to myself. Experience does not necessarily lie, but that smell is not an experience to the matter which emits it. Death cannot be experienced either by the dead or the living. The project of the Parisian workmen, to aestheticize, to arrange, and thus somehow to transform the objects of which they themselves were composed, was a bizarre success, but it could have been done with stale loaves of bread. It affected bones; it could not affect death. It meant as little, it said as little, as this little story of mine. It spoke of them as I must speak of me. I can read their meaning. Death's meaning I cannot read. To me death is above all things a smell, a very bad smell, and that, like the skeletons which terrify children, is not death at all. If I had to smell it more often, if I had to work in the catacombs, I would think nothing of it. And a few years or decades from now, I will think nothing about everything.

II.
AUTOPSY THOUGHTS

It shall be the duty of the coroner to inquire into and determine the circumstances, manner, and cause of all violent, sudden or unusual deaths...

California state code, sec. 27491[1]

Aldous Huxley once wrote that "if most of us remain ignorant of ourselves, it is because self-knowledge is painful and we prefer the pleasures of illusion."[2] That is why one brushes off the unpleasantly personal lesson of the catacombs. But we can extend the principle: Not only self-knowledge hurts. Consider the black girl whom an investigator pulled from a dumpster one night. Her mouth was bloody, which wasn't so strange; she could have been a homeless alcoholic with variceal bleeding. But, shining the flashlight into that buccal darkness, the investigator caught sight of a glint—neither blood nor spittle sparkling like metal, but metal itself—a broken-off blade. In her mouth, which could no longer speak, lay the truth of her death. The investigator couldn't give her her life back, but by this double unearthing—the knife from the corpse, the corpse from the stinking bin—he'd resurrected something else, an imperishable quantity which the murderer in his fear or fury or cold self-ishness meant to entomb—namely, the fact of murder, the reality which would have been no less real had it never become known, but which, until it was known and proved, remained powerless to do good. —What good? Quite simply, determining the cause of death is the prerequisite for some kind of justice, although justice, like other sonorous concepts, can produce anything from healing to acceptance to compensation to revenge to hypocritical clichés. At the chief medical examiner's office they knew this good—knowing also that the job of turning evidence into justice lay not with them but with the twelve citizens in the jury box—what coroners and medical examiners do is necessary but not sufficient. Probably the black woman's family had figured that out, if there *was* any family, if they cared, if they weren't too stupefied with grief. The morgue would be but the first of their Stations of the Cross. (Afterward: the funeral parlor, the graveyard, perhaps the courtroom, and always the empty house.) Dealing with them was both the saddest and the most important part of the truth-seeker's job: as I said, knowledge hurts. Dr. Boyd Stephens, the Chief Medical Examiner of San Francisco, would later say to me: "One of the things I hoped you'd see was a family coming in here grieving. And when it is a crime of violence, when someone has her son shot during a holdup, that makes it very hard; that's a tremendous emotional blow." I myself am very glad that I didn't see this. I have seen it enough. In the catacombs death felt senseless, and for the investigator who found the black woman, the moral of death remained equally empty, as it must whether the case is suicide, homicide, accident, or what we resignedly call "natural causes." Twenty-six years after the event, a kind woman who had been there wrote me about the death of my little sister. I was nine years old, and my sister was six. The woman wrote: "I remember you, very thin, very pale, your shoulders hunched together, your hair all wet and streaming sideways. You said, 'I can't find Julie.'" She wrote to me many other things that she remembered. When I read her letter, I cried. Then she went on: "I am tempted to say that Julie's drowning was a 'senseless death' but that's not true. I learned the day she died that there are realms of life in which the measure of sense and nonsense don't apply. Julie's death exists on a plane where there is no crime and no punishment, no cause and effect, no action and reaction. It just happened." Fair enough. Call it morally or ethically senseless, at least. (I don't think I ever wrote back; I felt too sad.) Only when *justice itself* condemns someone to death, as when a murderer gets hanged or we bombard Hitler's Berlin or an attacker meets his victim's lethal self-defense, can we even admit the possibility that the perishing had a point. Principled suicides also mean something: Cato's self-disembowelment indicts the conquering Caesar who would have granted clemency, and whose patronizing power now falls helpless before a mere corpse. But most people (including many suicides, and most who die the deaths of malicious judicial *in*justice) die the death of accident, meaninglessly and ultimately anonymously discorporating like unknown skulls in catacombs—and likewise the black woman in the dumpster. No matter that her murderer had a reason—she died for nothing; and all the toxicology and blood spatter analyses in the world, even if they lead to his conviction, cannot change that. The murderer's execution might mean something; his victim's killing almost certainly will not.

FROM THE WHITE HEARSE TO THE VIEWING ROOM

In fiscal year 1994–95, slightly more than eight thousand people died in San Francisco County. Half of these deaths could be considered in some sense questionable, and reports on them accordingly traveled to Dr. Stephens's office, but in three thousand cases the doubts, being merely pro forma, were eventually cleared, signed off by physicians—that is, explained circumstantially if not ontologically. The remaining 1,549 deaths became Dr. Stephens's problem. His findings for that year were: 919 natural deaths, 296 nonvehicular accidents, 124 suicides, ninety-four homicides, thirty mysterious cases, six sudden infant death syndromes, and eighty vehicular fatalities, most of which involved pedestrians, and most of which were accidents (there were six homicides and one suicide).[3] And now I'm going to tell you what his people did to reach those findings. In San Francisco they had a white ambulance, or hearse as I might better say, which was partitioned between the driver's seat and the cargo hold, and the cargo hold could quickly be loaded or unloaded by means of the white double doors, the inside of which bore an inevitable reddish-brown stain: anything that touches flesh for years must get corrupted. It smelled like death in there, of course, which in my experience is sometimes similar to the smell of sour milk, or vomit and vinegar, or of garbage, which is to say of the dumpster in which the murdered girl had been clumsily secreted. A horizontal partition subdivided battered old stainless steel stretchers into two and two. Because San Francisco is hilly, the stretchers, custom-welded years before by a shop just down the street, were made to be stood upright, the bodies strapped in, and rolled along on two wheels. "Kind of like a wheelbarrow in a way," one stretcher man said. This might be the last time that the dead would ever again be vertical, as they serenely travelled, strapped and sheeted, down steep stairs and sidewalks. The ambulance pulled up behind Dr. Stephens's office, in a parking lot that said AMBULANCES ONLY. Out came each stretcher. Each stretcher went through the door marked NO ADMITTANCE, the door which for those of us whose hearts still beat might better read NO ADMITTANCE YET. Inside, the body was weighed upon a freight-sized scale, then wheeled into the center of that bleak back room for a preliminary examination, and fingerprinted three times (if it still had fingers and skin), with special black ink almost as thick as taffy. Finally it was zipped into a white plastic bag to go into the fridge overnight.[4] If the death might be homicide, the investigators waited longer—at least twenty-four hours, in case any new bruises showed up like last-minute images on a pale sheet of photographic paper floating in the developer, as might happen when deep blood vessels had been ruptured. Bruises were very important. If the body of a man who seemed to have hanged himself showed contusions on the face or hands, the investigators would have to consider homicide.[5]

By now perhaps the family had been told. In the big front room that said ABSOLUTELY NO ADMITTANCE I heard a man say, "Yes, we have Dave. I'm so sorry about what happened to Dave." If the family came, they would be led down a narrow corridor to a door that said VIEWING ROOM. The viewing room was private and secret, like the projectionist's booth in a movie theater. It had a long window that looked out onto another very bright and narrow room where the movie would take place, the real movie whose story had already ended before the attendant wheeled in the former actor. The movie was over; Dr. Stephens needed the family to verify the screen credits. They only saw the face. There was a door between the viewing room and the bright and narrow room, but someone made sure to lock it before the family came, because they might have tried to embrace this thing which had once been someone they loved, and because the thing might not be fresh anymore or because it might have been slammed out of personhood in some hideous way whose sight or smell or touch would have made the family scream, it was better to respect the love they probably still felt for this thing which could no longer love them, to respect that love by respecting its clothes of ignorance. The people who worked in Dr. Stephens's office had lost their ignorance a long time ago. They blunted themselves with habit, science, and grim jokes—above all, with necessity: if the death had been strange or suspicious, they had to cut the thing open and look inside, no matter how much it stank.

A Solomonic parable: Dr. Stephens told me that once three different mothers were led into the viewing room one by one to identify a dead girl, and each mother claimed the girl as hers, with a desperate relief, as I would suppose. I know someone whose sister was kidnapped. It's been years now and they've never found her. They found her car at the side of the road. My friend used to live with her sister. Now she lives with her sister's clothes. From time to time the family's private detective will show her photographs of still another female body partially skeletonized or not, raped or not, and she'll say, "That's not my sister." I know it would give her peace to be able to go into a viewing room and say (and *believe*), "Yes, that's Shirley." Those three mothers must all have given up hoping that their daughters would ever speak to them or smile at them again. They wanted to stop dreading and start grieving. They didn't want to go into viewing rooms any more. And maybe the glass window was dirty, and maybe their eyes were old or full of tears. It was a natural mistake. But one mother was lucky. The dead girl was really her daughter.

THE INNOCENT METERMAID

To confirm that identification, someone at Dr. Stephens's office had already looked inside the dead woman's mouth, incidentally discovering or not discovering the gleam of a knife-blade, observed her dental work, and matched it to a dentist's files. Somebody had fingerprinted her and found a match; somebody had sorted through her death-stained clothes and come up with a match. Starting with flesh and cloth, they had to learn what the mothers didn't know. The meter maid didn't know, either, and I am sure she didn't want to know. A young man eased some heroin into his arm—maybe too much, or maybe it was too pure (heroin just keeps getting better and better these days). He died and fell forward, his face swelling and purpling with lividity. The meter maid didn't know, I said. Even after he began to decompose, she kept putting parking tickets on his windshield.

"I'M A HAPPY CUSTOMER"

A stinking corpse, pink and green and yellow, lay naked on one of many parallel downsloping porcelain tables each of which drained into a porcelain sink. The man's back had hurt. Surgery didn't help, so he took painkillers until he became addicted. The painkillers proving insufficiently kind, he started mixing them with alcohol. When the white ambulance came, there were bottles of other people's pills beside his head. He was not quite forty.

"Everything's possible," said one morgue attendant to another, leaning against a gurney, while the doctor in mask and scrubs began to cut the dead man open. "You're limited only by your imagination." I think he was talking about special-effects photography. He had loaned his colleague a mail-order camera catalog.

Meanwhile the dagger tattooed on the dead man's bicep trembled and shimmered as the doctor's scalpel made the standard Y-shaped incision, left shoulder to chest, right shoulder to chest, then straight down the belly to the pubis. The doctor was very good at what he did, like an old Eskimo who I once saw cutting up a dying walrus. The scalpel made crisp sucking sounds. He peeled back the chest-flesh like a shirt, then crackled the racks of ribs, which could almost have been pork. His yellow-gloved hands grubbed in the scarlet hole, hauling out fistfuls of sausage-links—that is, loops of intestine. Then he stuck a hose in and left it there until the outflow faded to pinkish clear. Beset by brilliant lavender, scarlet, and yellow, the twin red walls of rib-meat stood high and fragile, now protecting nothing, neatly split into halves.

The dead man still had a face.

The doctor syringed out a blood sample from the cavity, sponged blood off the table, and then it was time to weigh the dead man's organs on a hanging balance, the doctor calling out the numbers and the pretty young pathology resident chalking them onto the blackboard. The lungs, already somewhat decomposed, were indistinct masses which kept oozing away from the doctor's scalpel. "Just like jello," he said sourly.

The right lung was larger than the left, as is often the case with right-handed people. Another possible cause: the dead man had been found lying on his right side, a position which could have increased congestion in that lung. Either way, his death was meaningless.

His heart weighed 290 grams. The doctor began to cut it into slices.

"This vessel was almost entirely occluded with atherosclerosis," explained the resident. "He used a lot of drugs. Cocaine hastens the onset of atherosclerosis. We get lots of young people with old people's diseases."

That was interesting to know and it meant something, I thought. In a sense, the investigators understood the dead man. I wondered how well he'd been understood before he died.

"God, his pancreas!" exclaimed the doctor suddenly. "That's why he died." He lifted out a purple pudding which spattered blood onto the table.

"What happened?" I asked.

"Basically, all these enzymes there digest blood. This guy was hemorrhagic. The chemicals washed into his blood vessels and he bled. Very common with alcoholics."

Out came the liver now, yellow with fatty infiltrations from too much alcohol. "See the blood inside?" said the doctor. "But the pancreas is a sweetbread. The pancreas is a bloody pulp. Blood in his belly. Sudden death. We got lucky with him—he's an easy one. This is a sure winner."

Quickly he diced sections of the man's organs and let them ooze off his bloody yellow-gloved fingers into amber jars. The pathology and toxicology people would freeze them, slice them thinner, stain them, and drop them onto microscope slides, just to make sure that he hadn't overdosed on something while he bled. Meanwhile the doctor's knowledge-seeking scalpel dissected the neck, to rule out any possibility of secret strangulation. Many subtle homicides are misdiagnosed as accidents by untrained people, and some accidents look like murders. The doctor didn't want that to happen. Even though he'd seen the pancreas, he wanted to be as thorough as he could to verify that there was no knife-blade in the mouth, that all the meaning had come out.

—"Okay, very good," he grunted. Then the attendant, who I should really call a forensic technician, sewed the dead man up, with the garbage bag of guts already stuck back inside his belly. His brain, putrefying, liquescent, had already been removed; his face had hidden beneath its crimson blanket of scalp. The attendant sewed that up, too, and the man had a face again.

"I'm a happy customer," said the doctor.

OF JOKES AND OTHER SHIELDS

If the doctor's wisecracks seem callous to you, ask yourself whether you wouldn't want to be armored against year after year of such sights and smells. Early the next morning I watched another doctor open up an old Filipino man who, sick and despondent, had hanged himself with an electric cord. I have seen a few autopsies and battlefields before, but the man's stern, stubborn stare, his eyes glistening like black glass while the doctor, puffing, dictated case notes and slashed his guts (the yellow twist of strangle-cord lying on an adjacent table) gave me a nightmare that evening. This doctor, like his colleague, the happy customer, was doing a good thing. Both were *proving* that neither one of these dead men had been murdered, and that neither one had carried some contagious disease. Like soldiers, they worked amidst death. Green-stained buttocks and swollen faces comprised their routine. They had every right to joke, to dull themselves. Those who can't do that don't last.

Strangely enough, even their job could be for some souls a shelter from sadder things. Dr. Stephens himself used to be a pediatric oncologist before he became coroner in 1968. "At that time, we lost seventy-five percent of the children," he said. "Emotionally, that was an extremely hard thing to do. I'd be dead if I stayed in that profession."

The thought of Dr. Stephens ending up on one of his own steel tables bemused me. As it happens, I am married to an oncologist. She goes to the funerals of her child patients. Meanwhile she rushes about her life. Embracing her, I cherish her body's softness which I know comprises crimson guts.

EVIDENCE

The little cubes of meat in the amber jars went across the hall to pathology and to toxicology: underbudgeted realms making do with old instruments and machines which printed out cocaine-spikes or heroin-spikes on the slowly moving graph paper which had been state of the art in the 1960s. But after all, how much does death change? Ladies in blue gowns tested the urine samples of motorists suspected of driving while intoxicated, and with equal equanimity checked the urine of the dead. Had they, or had they not, died drunk? The drunken motorist who died in a crash, the drunken suicide who'd finally overcome his fear of guns (in 17th-century Germany, the authorities encouraged condemned criminals to drink beer or wine before the execution), the drunken homicide victim who'd felt sufficiently invincible to provoke his murder— such descriptors helped attach reason to the death. Meanwhile, the blue-gowned ladies inspected the tissue samples that the doctors across the hall had sent them. I saw a woman bent over a cutting board, probing a granular mass of somebody's tumor, remarking casually on the stench. If the stomach was cancerous, if the liver was full of Tylenol or secobarb, that comprised a story, and Dr. Stephens's people were all the closer to signing off that particular death certificate.

In her gloved hands, a lady twirled a long, black-bulbed tube of somebody's crimson blood. On a table stood a stack of floppy disks marked POLICE CASES. Here was evidence, information, which might someday give birth to meaning. Kidneys floated in large translucent white plastic jars. They too had their secret knives-in-the-mouth—or not. They might explain a sudden collapse—or rationalize the toxic white concentration of barbiturates in the duodenum, if the decedent's last words did not. In San Francisco one out of four suicides left a note. Some of the laconic ones might leave unwitting messages in their vital organs. "I would say that about twenty-five percent of the suicides we have here are justified by real physical illness," Dr. Stephens told me. "We had one gentleman recently who flew in from another state, took a taxi to the Golden Gate Bridge, and jumped off. Well, he had inoperable liver cancer. Those are *logical* decisions. As for the others, they have transient emotional causes. A girl tells a boy she doesn't want to see him anymore, so he goes and hangs himself. No one talked to him and got him over to the realization that there are other women in the world."

Look in the liver then. Find the cancer—or not. That tells us something.

"And homicide?" I asked. "Does that ever show good reason?"

"Well I've seen only a few justified homicides," Dr. Stephens replied. "We handle a hundred homicides a year, and very few are justified. They're saving their family or their own lives. But the vast majority of homicides are just a waste, just senseless violent crimes to effect punishment."

And accident? And heart attack, and renal failure? No reason even to ask. From the perspective of the viewing room, it is all senseless.

DEATH CAN NEVER HURT YOU UNTIL YOU DIE

On that Saturday morning while the doctor was running the hanged man's intestines through his fingers like a fisherman unkinking line, and the forensic tech, a Ukrainian blond who told me about her native Odessa, was busily taking the top of his head off with a power saw, I asked: "When bodies decompose, are you at more or less of a risk for infection?"

"Oh, the T.B. bacillus and the AIDS virus degrade pretty quickly," said the doctor. "They have a hard time in dead bodies. Not enough oxygen. But staph and fungus grow... The dead you have nothing to fear from. It's the living. It's when you ask a dead man's roommate what happened, and the dead man wakes up and coughs on you."

He finished his job and went out. After thanking the tech and changing out of my scrubs, so did I. I went back into the bright hot world where my death awaited me. If I died in San Francisco, there was one chance in five that they would wheel me into Dr. Stephens's office. Although my surroundings did not seem to loom and reek with death as they had when I came out of the catacombs—I think because the deaths I saw on the autopsy slabs were so grotesquely singular that I could refuse to see myself in them,[6] whereas the sheer mass and *multiplicity* of the catacomb skulls had worn down my unbelief— still I wondered who would cough on me, or what car would hit me, or which cancer might already be subdividing and stinking inside my belly. The doctor was right: I would not be able to hurt him then, because he'd be ready for me. Nor would his scalpel cause me pain. And I walked down Bryant Street wondering at the strange absurdity of my soul, which had felt most menaced by death when I was probably safest—how could those corpses rise up against me?—and which gloried in removing my disposable mask and inhaling the fresh air, letting myself dissolve into the city with its deadly automobiles and pathogen-breathers, its sailboats and bookstores; above all, its remorseless *futurity*.

III.
SIEGE THOUGHTS

And now, closing my eyes, I reglimpse tangents of atrocities and of wars. I see a wall of skulls in the Paris catacombs. Likewise I see the skulls on the glass shelves at Choeung Ek Killing Field.[7] In place of the tight wall of catacomb skulls gazing straight on at me, sometimes arranged in beautiful arches, I see skulls stacked loosely, laid out on the glass display shelves in heaps, not patterns—although it would give a deficient impression to omit the famous "genocide map" a few kilometers away in Phnom Penh; this is a cartographic representation of all Cambodia, comprised of murdered skulls. At Choeung Ek, they lie canted upon each other, peering and grinning, gaping and screaming, categorized by age, sex and even by race (for a few Europeans also died at the hands of the Khmer Rouge). Some bear cracks where the Khmer Rouge smashed those once-living heads with iron bars. But to my uneducated eye there is nothing else to differentiate them from the skulls of Paris. The Angel of Death flies overhead, descends and kills, and then he goes. The relics of his work become indistinguishable, except to specialists such as Dr. Stephens, and to those who were there. (I remember once seeing a movie on the Holocaust. When the lights came on, I felt bitter and depressed. It seemed that the movie had "reached" me. And then I saw a man I knew, and his face was very pale and he was sweating. He was a Jew. He was really there. The Nazis had killed most of his family.) *Before* the Angel strikes, of course, the doomed remain equally indistinguishable from the lucky or unlucky ones who will survive a little longer. Death becomes apprehensible, perhaps, only at the moment of dying.

To apprehend it, then, let's approach the present moment, the fearful time when they're shooting at you and, forgetting that your life is not perfect, you crave only to live, sweat, and thirst a little longer; you promise that you'll cherish your life always, if you can only keep it. Thus near-death, whose violence or not makes no difference. A woman I loved who died of cancer once wrote me: "You will not be aware of this but it is the anniversary of my mastectomy and I am supposed to be happy that I survived and all that. Actually it has been a terrible day." She'd forgotten, like me; she'd shrugged death off again, not being godlike enough to treasure every minute after all. The first time I survived being shot at (maybe they weren't shooting at me; maybe they didn't even see me), I pledged to be happier, to be grateful for my life, and in this I have succeeded, but I still have days when the catacombs and Dr. Stephens's autopsy slabs sink too far below my memory, and I despise and despair at life. Another fright, another horror, and I return to gratitude. The slabs rise up and stink to remind me of my happiness. A year before her terrible day, the one I'd loved had written: "They had to use four needles, four veins last time. I cried as they put the fourth needle in. My veins are not holding up. I vomited even before leaving the doctor's office and then spent four days semi-conscious, vomiting. I thought very seriously about immediate death. Could I overdose on the sleeping pills, I wondered… My choices aren't that many and I would like to be there to hate my daughter's boyfriends." I remember the letter before that on pink paper that began, "I know I said I wouldn't write. I lied. I've just been told this weekend that I have invasive breast cancer and will have a mastectomy and removal of the lymph nodes within the week. I am scared to death. I have three small kids… I am not vain. I do not care about my chest but I do want to live… So, tell me. This fear—I can smell it—is it like being in a war?"—Yes, darling. I have never been terminally ill, but I am sure that it is the same.

In one of her last letters she wrote me: "There was definitely a time when I thought I might die sooner rather than later—it took me a while to believe that I would probably be okay. It still doesn't feel truly believable but more and more I want it to be the case—mostly because I want to raise my interesting and beautiful children and because I want to enjoy myself… My hair grew back to the point that I no longer use the wig."

In another letter she wrote me: "Here are the recent events in my life. I am not unhappy with them but they do not compare with being shot at and losing a friend and perhaps they will amuse you. I set up a fish tank in my study… I got the kids four fish. They named only one. I told them once they had learned to clean and change the tank and feed the fish and explain how gills work, then they could get a guinea pig. I am not into pets, preferring children. The one catfish in the tank is in great distress and swims around madly looking for a way to die."

When I close my eyes, I can see her as she looked at seventeen, and I can see her the way she was when she was thirty-four, much older, thanks in part to the cancer—bonier-faced, with sparse hair, perhaps a wig, sitting on the steps beside her children. I never had to see her in Dr. Stephens's viewing room. I never saw her body rotting. I'll never see her depersonalized skull mortared into a catacomb's wall. Does that mean I cannot envision death, her death? The six million death's heads under Paris weigh on me much less than her face, which you might call too gaunt to be beautiful, but which was still beautiful to me, which only in a photograph will I ever see again.

But—again I return to this—her death was meaningless, an accident of genetics or environment. No evil soul murdered her. I am sad when I think about her. I am not bitter.

I am sad when I think about my two colleagues in Bosnia who drove into a land-mine trap. Their names were Will and Francis. I will write about them later. At the time, because there were two distinct reports and holes appeared in the windshield and in the two dying men, I believed that they were shot, and when armed men approached I believed that I was looking at their killers. Will I had known only for two days, but I liked what I knew of him. Francis was my friend, off and on, for nineteen years. I loved Francis. But I was never angry, even when the supposed snipers came, for their actions could not have been personally intended. We were crossing from the Croatian to the Muslim side; the Muslims were sorry, and such incidents are common enough in war.

But now I open a letter from my Serbian friend Vineta, who often had expressed to me her dislike of Francis (whom she never met) on the grounds of his Croatian blood, and who after commenting in considerable helpful and businesslike detail on my journalistic objectives in Serbia, then responded to my plans for the Muslim and Croatian sides of the story (my items seven and eight) as follows: "You see, dear Billy, it's very nice of you to let me know about your plans. But, I DON'T GIVE A SHIT FOR BOTH CROATS AND MUSLIMS!" At the end of her long note she added this postscript: "The last 'personal letter' I got was two years ago, from my late boyfriend. The Croats cut his body into pieces in the town of B—— near Vukovar. His name was M——." Then she wrote one more postscript: "No one has a chance to open my heart ever again."

This is what violence does. This is what violence is. It is not enough that death reeks and stinks in the world, but now it takes on inimical human forms, prompting the self-defending survivors to strike and to hate, rightly or wrongly. Too simple to argue that nonviolent death is always preferable from the survivors' point of view! I've heard plenty of doctors' stories about the families of dying cancer patients who rage against "fate." Like Hitler, they'd rather have someone to blame. "Everybody's angry when a loved one dies," one doctor insisted. "The only distinction is between directed and undirected anger." Maybe so. But it *is* a distinction. Leaving behind Dr. Stephens's tables, on which, for the most part, lie only the "naturally" dead with their bleeding pancreases, the accidentally dead, and the occasional suicide, let us fly to besieged Sarajevo and look in on the morgue at Kosevo Hospital, a place I'll never forget, whose stench stayed on my clothes for two days afterward. Here lay the homicides. I saw children with their bellies blown open, women shot in the head while they crossed the street, men hit by some well-heeled sniper's anti-tank round.[8] Death joked and drank and vulgarly farted in the mountains all around us, aiming its weapons out of hateful fun, making the besieged counter-hateful. Every morning I woke up to chittering bullets and crashing mortar rounds. I hated the snipers I couldn't see because they might kill me and because they were killing the people of this city, ruining the city in every terrible physical and psychic way that it could be ruined, smashing it, murdering wantonly, frightening and crushing. But their wickedness too had become normal: this was Sarajevo in the fourteenth month of the siege. Needs lived on; people did business amidst their terror, a terror which could not be sustained, rising up only when it was needed, when one had to run. As for the forensic doctor at Kosevo Hospital, he went home stinking of death, and, like me, sometimes slept in his clothes; he was used to the smell, and his wife must have gotten used to it, too, when she embraced him. (Meanwhile, of course, some people had insomnia, got ulcers or menstrual disturbances, went prematurely gray.[9] Here, too, undirected anger might surface.[10] Political death, cancer death, it's all the same.

The night after Will and Francis were killed, a U.N. interpreter from Sarajevo told me how she lost friends almost every week. "You become a little cold," she said very quietly. "You have to." This woman was sympathetic, immensely kind; in saying this she meant neither to dismiss my grief nor to tell me how I ought to be. She merely did the best thing that can be done for any bereaved person, which was to show me her own sadness, so that my sadness would feel less lonely; but hers had wearied and congealed; thus she told me what she had become. Like Dr. Stephens and his crew, or the backpack inspector at the catacombs, like my friend Thion who ferries tourists to Choeung Ek on his motorcycle, I had already begun to become that way. Sarajevo wasn't the first war zone I'd been to, nor the first where I'd seen death, but I'll never forget it. The morgue at Kosevo Hospital, like the rest of Sarajevo, had had to make do without electricity, which was why, as I keep saying, it stank. I remember the cheesy smell of the Paris catacombs, the sour-milk smell of Dr. Stephens's white hearse; after that visit to Kosevo Hospital my clothes smelled like vomit, vinegar, and rotting bowels. I returned to the place where I was staying, which got its share of machine gun and missile attacks, and gathered together my concerns, which did not consist of sadness for the dead, but only of being scared and wondering if I would eat anymore that day because they'd shot down the U.N. flight and so the airport was closed and I'd already given my food away. Death was on my skin and on the other side of the wall—maybe my death, maybe not; trying to live wisely and carefully, I granted no time to my death, although it sometimes snarled at me. Ascending from the catacombs I'd had all day, so I'd given death all day; no one wanted to hurt me. But in Sarajevo I simply ran; it was all death, death and death, so meaningless and accidental to me.

I wore a bulletproof vest in Mostar, which did get struck with a splinter of something which rang on its ceramic trauma plate, so to an extent I had made my own luck, but Will, who was driving, discovered that his allotted death was one which entered the face *now*, diagonally from the chin. His dying took forever (I think about five minutes). Vineta said that I had been cowardly or stupid not to end his misery. I told her that journalists don't carry guns. Anyhow, had I been in his seat, my bulletproof vest would have done me no good.

The woman I loved simply had the wrong cells in her breast; Vineta's boyfriend had fought in the wrong place at the wrong time, and perhaps he'd fought against the Croats too ferociously or even just too well.[11] For the woman I loved, and for me in Sarajevo, the Angel of Death was faceless, but Vineta's tormenting Angel of Death had a Croatian face; she hated "those Croatian bastards." Vineta, if I could send the Angel of Death away from you, I would. Maybe someone who knows you and loves you better than I can at least persuade your Angel veil his face again so that he becomes mere darkness like the Faceless One of Iroquois legends, mere evil chance, "an act of war," like my drowned sister's Angel; and then your anger can die down to sadness. Vineta, if you ever see this book of mine, don't think me presumptuous; don't think I would ever stand between you and your right to mourn and rage against the Angel. But he is not Francis. Francis was good. I don't like to see him stealing Francis's face when he comes to hurt you.

The Angel is in the white hearse. Can't we please proceed like Dr. Stephens's employees, weighing, fingerprinting, cutting open all this sad and stinking dross of violence, trying to learn what causes what? And when the malignity or the sadness or the unpleasantness of the thing on the table threatens to craze us, can't we tell a callous joke or two? If I can contribute to understanding how and why the Angel kills, then I'll be, in the words of that doctor who swilled coffee out of one bloody-gloved hand while he sliced a dead body with the other, "a happy customer." Hence this essay, and the larger work from which this is extracted. For its many failures I ask forgiveness from all.

NOTES

[1] Medical Examiner's Office, City and County of San Francisco, *Digest of Rules and Regulations* [pamphlet], June 1996.

[2] Aldous Huxley, *The Perennial Philosophy* (San Francisco: Harper Colophon Books, 1970 repr. of 1944 ed.).

[3] Medical Examiner's Office, City and County of San Francisco, annual report, July 1, 1994–June 30, 1995, pp. 9, 36.

[4] Stylists frown upon the passive construction. But I fail to see what could be more appropriate for dead bodies.

[5] For this information on ante- and postmortem contusions I have, as so often, relied on Lester Adelson, *The Pathology of Homicide: A Vade Mecum for Pathologist, Prosecutor, and Defense Counsel*, Springfield, Illinois: Charles C. Thomas, 1974.

[6] Fresh death or old death, it was not my death, and I shrugged it off. In the catacombs they were so anonymous, with such clean carapaces, that it seemed they'd all died "naturally." At the medical examiner's office, some had died accidentally or strangely, a few had ended themselves, like that old man who'd hanged himself with the electric cord, and every now and then the odd murder case was wheeled in. Looking into the hanged man's stare, I'd felt a little creepy. But to protect me from it, Dr. Stephens had established the doors marked NO ADMITTANCE and POSITIVELY NO ADMITTANCE. As I sit here now, trying to refine these sentences, the only dead thing I can see is a spider glued to my windowpane by its withered web. For the most part I see cars in motion on the wide road, glorious trees, people walking down the sidewalk. The doughnut stand where a juvenile homicide occurred a couple of years ago now glows with sugar and life. I remain as yet in the land of the living, and will not believe in my death.

[7] I went there twice, and the second was more horrifying than the first. Here those technical-political details don't matter.

[8] For a description of this place, see "The Back of My Head," in *The Atlas* (p. 5).

[9] Fanon found these psychosomatic symptoms in Algeria, and mentions that they were very common "in the Soviet Union among the besieged populations of towns notably in Stalingrad" (*The Wretched of the Earth*, pp. 290–93).

[10] For one of Fanon's patients, an Algerian who survived a mass execution conducted by the French because "there's been too much talk about this village; destroy it," the Angel of Death wore everyone's face: "You all want to kill me but you should set about it differently. I'll kill you all as soon as look at you, big ones and little ones, women, children, dogs, donkeys..." (op. cit., pp. 259–61).

[11] Martin Luther King insisted in his funeral for victims of the Birmingham bombing that "history has proven over and over again that unmerited suffering is redemptive. The innocent blood of these little girls may well serve as the redemptive force that will bring new light to this dark city" (King, *Testament of Hope,* p. 221; "Eulogy for the Martyred Children," September 1963). As for me, I don't believe that such redemption occurs very often.

YET ANOTHER EXAMPLE
OF THE POROUSNESS
OF CERTAIN BORDERS
(VIII)

by David Foster Wallace

THEN JUST AS I WAS being released in late 1996 Mother won a small product liability settlement and used the money to promptly go get cosmetic surgery on the crow's feet around her eyes. However the cosmetic surgeon botched it and did something to the musculature of her face which caused her to look scared all the time. You doubtless know the way someone's face looks in the split second just before they begin to scream. That was now Mother. It turns out that it only takes a minuscule slip of the knife one way or the other in this procedure and now you look like someone in the shower scene of Hitchcock. So, she went and had more cosmetic surgery to try to correct it. But the 2nd surgeon also botched it and the appearance of fright became even worse. Especially around the mouth. She asked for my candid appraisal and I felt as if our relationship demanded nothing less. Her crow's feet indeed were things of the past but now her face was a chronic mask of insane terror. Now she looked more like Elsa Lanchester when Elsa Lanchester 1st lays eyes on her prospective *"mate"* in the 1935 classic, *Bride of Frankenstein*. Now after the 2nd botched procedure even sunglasses were no longer of much help because still there was the issue of the gaping mouth and mandibular distention and the visible neck tendons and so forth. So, now she was involved in yet another lawsuit and when she regularly took the bus to the lawyer she'd chosen's office I escorted her. We rode at the bus's front in one of the two longer seats which face sideways instead of straight ahead. We had learned the "hard way" not to sit farther back in the rows of more regular seats which face ahead because of the way certain bus passengers would visibly react when they boarded and performed the seemingly reflexive action as they began to move down the aisle to a seat of briefly scanning the sea of faces facing them from the narrow rows of seats and would suddenly see Mother's distended soundlessly screaming face appearing to gaze back at them in abject horror. There were three or four embarrassing incidents and interactions before I applied myself to the issue and evolved a better seated location. Nothing in sources sufficiently explains why people perform the scan of the faces when they 1st board though on my anecdotal view it appears to be a defensive reflex species wide. Nor am I a good specimen to sit beside if she wanted to be inconspicuous because of the way my face usually towers above all others in the crowd. Physically I am a large specimen and have distinctive coloration, to look at me you would never know that I have such a studious bend. There also are the goggles worn and specially constructed gloves for field work, it is far from impossible to find specimens on a public bus even though surveys as yet have yielded no fruit. No it is not as if I actively "enjoy" riding with her while she exerts her will power trying not to allow the self-consciousness about the chronic expression to make it even more terror stricken, or "look forward" to sitting in a would-be-ostentatious reception area reading Rotary newsletters three times per week. It is not as if I do not have plenty of other things and studies to occupy my time. But what is one to do, the terms of my probation involve Mother's sworn statement to assume liability as my "custodian." But anyone privy to the reality of life together since the 2nd surgery would agree that the reality was the other way around because, due to despondency and fear of people's reaction she is all-but-incapable of leaving the house and can answer the lawyer's wheedling summonses to his office only with my presence and protection throughout the long ride. Also I have never liked direct sunlight and burn with great ease. This time the lawyer smells a windfall if and when he can get Mother in a courtroom and let a jury see for itself the consequence of the cosmetic surgeons' negligence. I also carry a briefcase at all times since my own case. One today could call a briefcase a "sematic accessory" to warn off predators. Since the original negligence I've primarily become immunized to Mother's chronic expression of horror but even so am myself made uncomfortable by some's reaction to us visually. A bus' circular steering wheel is not only larger but is set at an angle more horizontal than any taxi, private car, or police cruiser's wheel I have seen and the driver turns the wheel with a broad all-body-motion which is resemblant to someone's arm suddenly sweeping all the

material off a broad surface in a sudden fit of emotion. And the long and perpendicular seats in the front comprise a good vantage from which to watch the
driver wrestle with the bus. Nor did I have anything against the boy in any
way. Nor is there anything in any state, county, or local ordinance restricting
what varieties you can work with or stipulating in any way that cultivating
more than a certain number of them constitutes reckless endangerment or a
hazard to the community at large. If the appointment is in the morning the
driver also keeps a newspaper folded in a hutch by the automatic coin or token
box which he tries to scan while idling at stoplights although it is not as
though he will get much of his daily reading done that way. He was only nine
which was repeatedly stressed as if his youth and innocence in any way
strengthened any charge of negligence on my own part. A common Asian
species has not only the sematic ventral insignia but a red line straight down
the back, "...as if from a bursting seam" leading to its indigenous name, *Red
Line on Back.*" Standardized Testing has confirmed that I have both a studious
bend and outstanding retention in study which she would not even deny. The
theory I have evolved is, the morning driver scans his newspaper and wearily
refolds and replaces it in the hutch in order to unconsciously communicate the
boredom and contempt he feels in his paid job and a clinical-or-court-appointed-
psychologist might diagnose the driver's newspaper as an unconscious "Cry for
help." Our customary seat is the long perpendicular seat on the same side as
the bus's door minimizing the likelihood that someone boarding will have a
sudden frontal view of her chronic mask of insane terror. This too being a lesson we learned the "hard" way. The only comedic interlude was, that when the
1st surgery's bandages came off and they brought her the mirror at first one
could not verify whether the frightened mien in fact was a simple natural
defensive reaction to what she was seeing in the mirror or if it itself was what
she saw. Mother herself who is a decent-hearted if vain, bitter, and timid older
woman who is not a colossus of the roads of the Intellect to put it blatantly,
could not even determine at first if the look of abject terror there was her reaction or the stimulus and, if a reaction then a reaction to what exactly and so
forth. The cosmetic surgeon himself was leaning forwards against the white
wall with his face to the wall a behavioral reaction which signaled, "Yes" there
was "an objective" problem with the results of the cosmetic surgery. The bus is
because we have no car, a situation this new attorney says he can now remedy
in spades. The whole thing was carefully contained and screened off and even
the State conceded that if he had not been up fiddling around on the roof of
someone else's garage there is no way he could have come in contact with them

in any form. This factored into the terms of probation. Sometimes, however it's 1/2 amusing on the public conveyance to see the way passengers upon catching any glimpse of her frightened expression then will reflexively turn to look out whatever window to them Mother appears to be reacting to. Her fear of the phylum *arthropodae* is long-standing which is why she never went into the garage and could contend "*ignorantia facti excusat*," a point of law. Ironically also hence her constant spraying of R—d© despite my impatient pointing-out that these species are long resistant to resmethrin and trans-d Allenthrin. (The active ingredients in R—d©.) Granted "widow" bites are a bad way to go because of the neurotoxin involved hence prompting a physician all the way in 1933 to comment, "I do not recall having seen more abject pain manifested in any other medical or surgical condition" whereas, the painless *loxoceles* or "Recluse" toxin only causes necrosis and sloughing of the bitten area. Recluses however exhibiting a natural aggression which widows never share unless actively disturbed. Which he did. The bus' interior is flesh-colored-plastic with endless advertisements for legal and medical services running horizontally above the bus' windows. The ventilation varies according to such criteria as fullness. The phobia becomes so extreme she will carry a can in her handbag until I always find it before leaving and firmly say, "*No!*" In one or two regret-table moments of insensitivity about it also I have quipped to her about taking the bus all the way through Santa Monica into the city itself and auditioning her as an "extra" in one of the many movies in which crowds of extras are paid to look up in supposed terror of a Special Effect which is only later inserted into the movie through computerized design. Which I sincerely do regret, after all I'm all the support she has. To my mind though it is quite a stretch to say that an area of instability in a twenty-year-old-garage roof equals failing to exercise due diligence or care. Whereas, Hitchcock and the other classics used cruder early Special Effects but to terrifying results. To say nothing of him trespassing and having no business up there anyway. In the deposition. To say nothing of claiming that not foreseeing a trespasser falling through a dry rot-ted portion of the garage roof and wholesale wrecking a complex and expen-sive tempered glass container complex and crushing or otherwise disturbing a great many specimens and naturally due to the mishap allowing some decon-tainment and penetration of the surrounding neighborhood amounts to my failing due exercise of caution. This then is my argument for preferring the "classics" of older film terror. Declining to ever place or slide the briefcase under the seat I keep it in my lap throughout the frequent rides. My position throughout the lengthy proceedings was a natural deep regret for the kid and his family but that the horror of what happened as a result of his fall did not justify hysterical or trumped-up-charges of any kind. Quality counsel would have been able to translate this reasoning into effective legal language in legal briefs and arguments "*in camera.*" But of course the reality is counsel proves to be abundant if you are the aggressor but not if you are merely the prey, they're parasites, cable television is infested with their commercials urging the viewer to wait patiently for the opportunity to attack, "...handled on a percentage basis, no fee of any kind if you are the aggressor!" One could see them come right out of the Woodwork after Mother's original product liability mishap. No one even knows for certain how the neurotoxin works to produce such abjectly horrible pain in larger mammals, science is baffled as to evolutionarily what advantage there is for a venom well in excess of required for this unique but common specimen to subdue its prey. Science is often confounded both by the luminous "widow" and the more banal-looking-Recluse. Plus the ones who say they will really get down in the dirt of the trench and really fight for you are *Sleaze balls* such as this supposed Oxnard negligence "*specialist*" Mother has lined up. In another context the hysteria would have almost been humorous, any area as unkempt as our garage's neighborhood will be naturally infested with them in all the clutter and run-down-homes. Clutter is their natural "element," specimens of varied size are to be found in basement corners, beneath shelves of utility rooms, "linen" closets, in the infinite crevices of cast-away-litter and unkempt weeds. In the right angles of most house's shaded sides. Hence the clear goggles and polyurethane gloves are indispensable even in the shower whose right angles can be infested in just so many hours. Or outside the speeding bus in the palm trees people stand naively beneath in the shade to await the bus, "rent a ladder and check the under sides of those fronds sometime!" one is tempted to shout from the window. Once conditioned to know what to look for they are often almost everywhere, "*hiding*" in plain sight. This very area and also further inland both contain the more exotic species of "red" widow whose ventral hour-glass is brown or black as well as one of the Hemisphere's two "brown" species in the further-inland-desert regions. The "red" widow's red lacks the spellbinding luster of the familiar "black" variety, it is more a dull or matte red, and they are rare and both specimens escaped in his mishap and have not been reacquired. Here as so often in the arthropod realm, the female dominates as well. To be honest Mother's pain and suffering appeared somewhat inflated in the original product liability claim and she in reality coughs far less than during her deposition. Far be it from me however to deny her. But scientifically a large mammal would have to inhale a great deal of resmethrin or d-trans Allenthrin for permanent damage to result which did impact the modesty of Mother's settlement. The facts are less than a centimeter either way is the only difference between smooth youthful eyes and the chronic expression of Vivian Leigh in the shower in the 1960 classic of that name. The briefcase is aerated at select tiny points in each corner and 2.5 dozen polystyrene chocks distributed throughout the interior can protect the contents from jostling or trauma. Her new case's complexity is exactly how to distribute the liability claim between the original cosmetic surgeon whose negligence gave her the frightened eyes and forehead and the 2nd whose "repair"'s callous butchery left her with a chronic mask of abject terror and suffering that now can only cause confrontation in the case of someone in the opposing long perpendicular "sideways" seat directly behind the bus's driver because the sole exposure to liability of Mother's seat here is that any such individual in the opposing seat hence will have the vantage of gazing frontally at us throughout the bus ride. And "he" will on some occasions, if predisposed by environmental conditioning or temperament appear to think the "cause" of the expression is me—with my size and distinctive mark, etc—in that I have kidnapped this terrified-looking-middle-aged-woman or behaved in a somehow threatening manner toward her saying, "Ma'am is there some problem" or, "Why don't you just leave the lady alone?" as she sinks into her scarf in self-conscious-fear over "his" reaction but my own evolved defensive response is to calmly smile and raise my gloves in puzzled amusement as if to say, "Why who knows why anyone wears the public expression they do my good fellow let us not leap to conclusions based on incomplete data!" Her original liability was that a worker at the assembly plant actually glued a can's nozzle on backward. A clear-cut-case of failing to exercise due care. The 5th condition of the settlement was never to even mention again the name of the common household spray in any connection to the liability-suit which I am resolved to honor on her behalf, the "law is the law." There was never one moment of consideration of using the settlement to repair the garage roof or to rehabilitate the damaged interior I have to say. I have been on several 1st dates but there was insufficient chemistry, Mother is blackly cynical in matters of the heart. Recently as the bus left Casitas Springs as I looked down to check I saw accidentally protruding from one of the ventilation holes at the case's corner the very slender tip of a black jointed leg, it was moving about slightly and had the same luminous coloration as the rest of the specimens, moving tentatively in an exploratory way. Unseen against the more banal black of the briefcase's side. Unseen by Mother whose expression I must ironically say would not change in the least.

Even if I opened up the entire case right here on my lap and tipped it out into the central aisle allowing rapid spreading-out and penetration of the contained environs. This worse-case-scenario would only occur if one confronts some duo of young "*punks*" or would-be-toughs in the long opposing seat facing us whose reaction to Mother's chronic expression might be an aggressive challenging returned stare or a hostile, "What the 'fuck' are you looking at." It is ironically for just such a case that I am her public escort, with my imposing size and goggles one can tell beneath the face's insane rictus she believes I can protect her which is good.

Peter I. Bijur
Chief Executive Officer
Texaco
2000 Westchester Avenue
White Plains, NY
10650

Dear Mr. Bijur,

Greetings. I am a resident of Austin, Texas, who is writing to you under the guise of a dog named Steven. Steven is an Irish setter. This here is Steven:

> Before we lived in this house a family of four did. They were named the Clutters, and were of course disturbed by the book of Truman's. I asked once if they were related but they ignored me. I have read Mr. Capote's book and liked it a great deal.

> I sometimes bark. Sometimes I talk to people about my barking; I feel that it's a problem. Or rather, I feel that other people feel it's a problem, which becomes, for me, a problem. When I see headlights in the rear view window I feel menaced. My brother's name is Jonathan and he barks more than I do, but we never bark at the same time because why would we both need to be barking at the same time? I've bitten him so hard I tasted his alkaline blood. Hooo!

> I once ate a pizza. I'm not supposed to eat pizza, because I am a dog, but I don't know who makes rules like this, who can eat what. I ate the pizza and was fine. I looked at a solar eclipse and was fine. I jumped from the roof once and was hardly hurt at all. Maybe I'll never die. I'm a fast dog!

> I bark all night at least once a month. In cars I'm quiet. I run around trees like a stick in a current around rocks that are smooth. Hoooo! Hooooo! Yeah you got me now, yeah! Man I wish you could have seen all this.

Mr. Bijur, you are too kind. Keep up the work.

D.

Daniel O'Mara
5811 Mesa Drive, #216
Austin, TX
78731

THE REPUBLIC OF MARFA

by SEAN WILSEY

ISOLATION

IN THE MIDDLE of what's known as Far West Texas, there is Marfa: a hardscrabble ranching community in the upper Chihuahuan desert, sixty miles north of the Mexican border, that inhabits some of the most beautiful and intransigent countryside imaginable: inexhaustible sky over a high desert formed in the Permian period and left more or less alone since. It's situated in one of the least populated sections of the contiguous United States, known locally as *el despoblado* (the uninhabited place), a twelve-hour car-and-plane trip from the east coast, and seven from the west. It is nowhere near any interstates, major cities, or significant nonmilitary airfields; it hosts an active population of dangerous animals and insects (a gas station clerk died of a spider bite the summer I first visited); and its 2,424 inhabitants represent the densest concentration of people in a county that covers over 6,000 square miles—an area larger than the states of Connecticut and Rhode Island combined. The isolation is such that if you laid out the islands of the Hawaiian archipelago, and the deep ocean channels that separate them, on the road between Marfa and the East Texas of strip shopping and George Bush Jr., you'd still have one hundred miles of blank highway stretching away in front of you.

I've been in regular contact with the place since the summer of 1996—when my girlfriend, Daphne, was a reporter for the local weekly, the *Big Bend*

Excellence in Mining Service Medal

Sentinel—visiting as often as possible, and witnessing some of the often volatile ways the town's 2,424 people come together; having coalesced, through strange endeavor and coincidence, into a sort of city-state of cattlemen, artists, writers, fugitives, smugglers, free-thinkers, environmentalists, soldiers, and secessionists—making Marfa home to what must be the most uncompromised contemporary art museum in the world; and, nineteen months ago, when a local teenager tending goats on a bluff above the nearby Rio Grande was shot by a Marine patrol, the site of the first civilian killing by American military personnel since Kent State.

Marfa is the name of the family servant in *The Brothers Karamazov*, the book a railway overseer's wife was reading when an unnamed water stop became a town in 1881. This frontierswoman was reading the book a year after its initial publication in Russian, the same year Billy the Kid was shot dead in nearby New Mexico, and during the extended period of border uneasiness that followed the Mexican-American war. But such circumstances are typically Marfan. The town attracts the bizarre: some of the first documentation of the area comes from Indian and pioneer accounts, in the 1800s, of flashing, mobile, seemingly animate luminescences on the horizon—the Marfa Mystery Lights, unexplained optical phenomena that are still observed from a pull-off on the outskirts of town, where a crowd seems to appear every night to socialize. And until the mid-'70s the lights were the main attraction. Then the minimalist artist Donald Judd moved to Marfa, exiling himself from what he termed the "glib and harsh" New York art scene, in order to live in a sort of high plains laboratory devoted to building, sculpture, furniture design, museology, conservation, and a dash of ranching, until his death in 1994.

Last April the Chinati Foundation, a contemporary art museum Judd founded in the late '70s, and named after a nearby mountain range, invited architects and artists to come to Marfa and discuss the future of collaboration between the two disciplines. Billed as a symposium, it was more like a conflagration. Among the participants were Frank Gehry, whose Guggenheim Museum had recently opened in Bilbao, Spain (architect Philip Johnson has since declared it "the greatest building of our time"); the Swiss architects Jacques Herzog and Pierre de Meuron, engaged in a massive and controversial expansion of the Tate Gallery in London; the light and space artist Robert Irwin, who had just taken an unexpected creative detour and designed the garden for the Getty Center in Los Angeles; Roni Horn, a wily New York conceptualist who sculpts with words (she's plastic-cast adjectives that describe both emotions and weather and embedded them in the structure of a German meteorological bureau); and the pop artist (and deadpan comedian) Claes Oldenburg. This group spent two days in *el despoblado* showing slides and talking about their work, while two art historians—James Ackerman from Harvard, a hoary emeritus type, and Michael Benedikt from the University of Texas, a searing and somewhat humorless postmodernist—weighed in in a critical capacity, paid homage to Donald Judd, and attempted to shut everyone up. Daphne (her last name is Beal) had assignments to write about it for a couple of architecture magazines, and I went along. They were expecting six hundred people, and I was curious to observe what a 25 per cent increase in Marfa's population might produce—the equivalent of two million ranchers suddenly arriving for a weekend in Manhattan.

Marfa sits in what seems like ground zero of an ancient impact site—a wide plain with mountain ranges surrounding it at an equidistant remove of about thirty miles. To the west lie the Sierra Vieja, to the north the Davis. The Glass, Del Norte, and Santiago (as well as an extinct volcano) are to the east, the Chinati to the south. These mountains run down to the high desert of cacti and yellow grassland around Marfa, framing an oceanic West Texas sky, with virtually nothing in the way of buildings or tall trees to interrupt it. The result is a big basin full of light and dry heat, where every object takes on a peculiar definition; shapes clarified and detailed, shadows standing out in perfect relief.

The town itself is a rectangle sixteen blocks high by twenty wide, with Mexican and Anglo cemeteries (separated by a fence) on the west end, a golf course (highest elevation in Texas) on the east, and satellite neighborhoods protruding to the south and northeast like radar arrays. It contains unexpected delfs and shadows, grand old homes behind tree-shaded lawns, century-old structures whose adobe disintegrates at any elemental provocation, and disused industrial buildings with aluminum siding that ticks in the heat. It operates in a state of oblivion to all the high-concept art that is made and displayed there. The two restaurants, Mike's and Carmen's, are full of ranchers, workmen, and border patrol. The two bars do decent business—there's no open-container law in Texas, and both have takeout windows. The streets are wide and for the most part empty.

In order to get to Marfa you fly into either El Paso or Midland/Odessa. Of course, there's almost never a direct flight, so after landing in Dallas or Houston you get on a small twin-prop plane. When Daphne flew down to work at the *Sentinel* the editors met her in Midland. After shaking hands she ran into the bathroom and vomited. When I went down to visit I couldn't wait till landing and had to throw up on the plane.

UNFORCED EXCOMMUNICATION,
FORCED COMMUNICATION

Donald Judd, a cantankerous Scotsblood Midwesterner with a fondness for kilts, had all the fame, respect, and financial recompense a visual artist could hope for when he relegated his five-story cast-iron residence in SoHo to the status of a pied-à-terre and abandoned New York for Marfa in 1976.

This was a man with a hankering for space—not to say empire. A book devoted exclusively to Judd's many homes and buildings, *Donald Judd Spaces*, runs to more than one hundred pages and contains fifteen different *beds* (less than half the total). Judd held that a bed should always be convenient to a place people might even passingly abide. When he arrived in Marfa he set up residence in two WWI aircraft hangers and proceeded to buy the bank, a three-hundred-acre former cavalry base (now the Chinati Foundation), three ranches (with a total acreage of 38,000), a mohair warehouse, the Safeway, the Marfa Hotel, a handful of light-manufacturing and commercial buildings, six homes from around the turn of the century, and the Marfa hot springs. By the early '90s he was planning on bottling Marfa water (which is said to contain traces of natural lithium), shipping it to New York, and selling it at Dean and Deluca.

Judd's philosophy was both ascetic and profligate—a paradoxical combination of simplicity and mass consumption. He bought everything he could lay his hands on with money from art he'd made with his own two hands. He had an almost feudal arrangement with Marfa, employing a workforce that for a time outnumbered the municipal payroll (and over which I've always unfairly—I have no evidence of such a thing—imagined him exercising some kind of *droit du seigneur*, what with all those beds). Because of the controlled surroundings he created by purchasing whole buildings and stretches of land, his art in Marfa ingeniously extends its own boundaries to include entire rooms, structures, and vistas.

The Brothers Karamazov is a novel about a murder and a family's convoluted relations, played out in a small town. The transposition from the novel's unnamed Russian village to present day Marfa is an easy one to make. The way the brothers talk to each other—in grandiloquent outbursts of "excitement" or grave silences full of "strain"—reminds me of how Marfans communicate. Much of the town's emotion, as expressed in the *Sentinel*'s letters column, is reminiscent of that in the book. One man, writing about Marfa's segregated Anglo/Mexican cemetery, declared it "a slap in the face to humanity." A woman, dissecting an exploitative nuclear waste agreement Texas signed with some eastern states, concluded "We could have made this same compact with a dog."

Marfa's mood is Dostoyevsky's. The book and the town contain the same sort of devotion, and the same sort of outrage.

In Marfa, the people are restrained, disinclined to conversation, courteous, fractious, and, when they wish to be, extremely generous. There is also a good deal of public eccentricity. A woman roams the streets, roads, and surrounding desert with all her possessions tied to the back of a pack animal. Sometimes she's way out on the blacktop between Marfa and the mountains. Other times she's ambling through town, taking a short cut across the concrete apron of the Texaco station. She sleeps out in the open, wherever she happens to be when the sun sets, and bears more than a passing resemblance to another character from *The Brothers Karamazov*, Stinking Lisaveta, who wandered Dostoyevsky's small-town back alleys, sleeping "on the ground and in the mud." Marfans call her the "Burro Lady." And she's one of many descriptions and details in the novel that apply almost word-for-word to Marfa. (Although, according to legend, the Burro Lady, unlike Stinking Lisaveta, does have a companion of sorts. A rogue steer drifts through the countryside—the symbol of an unpunished frontier crime. It's supposed to be immortal, and, as a sort of harbinger, it only shows itself to cursed souls: a brand covering its entire flank, from shoulder to rump, reads "MURDER.")

The town is also a place where mundane interactions unexpectedly take turns for the surreal. Daphne and I once got our car fixed by a gas station attendant who, when I told him I smelled something weird when the car got hot, simply said, "Let's take a look at that *sum*-bitchie," popped the hood, rooted around for awhile, ripped something that looked like a dead snake out of the engine with a flourish (it turned out to be the a/c belt), threw it over his shoulder, and chuckled "re-paired." In a travelogue by Scottish novelist Duncan McLean, something distinctly Marfan happens when the author checks out of the El Paisano, the only hotel in town:

> I stubbed my toe against some clunky bit of litter lying on the sidewalk. It

went skittering away in front of me and stopped a metre ahead, long glint-ing barrel pointing straight at me: A GUN. Next thing I knew I was back at the Paisano's desk, banging on the bell and babbling away to the clerk… "It's out there, a pistol, come on, come on"…

The clerk ducked through a hatch in the counter and walked out of the lobby….

"There," I said. "See it?"…

He held up a hand for me to stay, took a step forward, and peeped over my shoulder-bag.

"Ha!" He exhaled.

"What is it?"

He leant over, snatched up the pistol, and turned back towards me.

"You call this a gun?" he said, and laughed.

"Eh… yeah."

He flicked some kind of catch, then pushed the revolving magazine out sideways.

"This ain't no real gun," he said.

"What then? An imitation?"

He tilted up the pistol so a shower of little silver bullets fell out and on to his palm.

"This here's a lady's gun," he said… "Couldn't kill shit."

When Daphne first arrived, and was living at Chinati, a cowboy gave her a lift into town in his truck. He was a craggy guy in his late fifties who broke horses and raised livestock. When the conversation turned to why he'd settled in Marfa twenty years before, he said it was because the town had a "genius loci." It was an expression neither of us had ever heard before, and when we looked it up we found it strangely faithful to the peculiarity that animates the town. In Latin, it means "genius of the place." "Genius," (says the OED) when applied to a locale, indicates "a presiding deity or spirit."

It's true—something about the landscape, the strange goings-on, the bal-ance between population and depopulation, lends credence to the belief that Marfa didn't just happen this way—that some unseen force presides.

RENEGADE TENDENCIES

The *Big Bend Sentinel* arrives in New York a couple weeks after it's printed in

Pecos (one hundred miles to the north, the nearest town with a printer). The core of its news is crime and the border, with a lot of art, armed forces (jet training for the German and U.S. air forces occurs in county airspace), sports, agriculture, and animal husbandry thrown in. The *Sentinel* covers all of these subjects with curiosity and seriousness, and after a few years of reading it, I'm starting to think it's possible to learn more about the state of the world from a carefully reported small paper than from any other source.

Here are some of the stranger, more significant recent stories:

In 1996, people with multiple chemical sensitivity, a disease whose sufferers take ill when exposed to synthetic materials, began living in the hills near Marfa and building an all-natural commune—until the members of a yearly Bible retreat (one of the oldest of its kind) arrived upwind and began their annual spraying of Malathion, a DDT-style pesticide that caused the Chemical Sensitives to become violently ill, and engage with the religious group in a small war of ideology and incommunication. Compassion for the sick was ultimately rejected, because it was inconvenient to pray with the mosquitoes.

On a spring night in 1997 a band of Marines on a drug interdiction sortie (part of what locals call the "militarization" of the U.S.-Mexico border) spent twenty minutes tracking Esequiel Hernandez Jr., a young goatherd who carried a vintage WWI rifle to keep coyotes away from his flock. For some reason Hernandez raised the rifle, in what evidence shows to have been the opposite direction from the marines, one of whom then shot him "in self-defense." The boy bled to death for twenty minutes before the soldiers summoned help. When a deputy sheriff arrived the Marines said that Hernandez hurt himself "falling into a well." Unfortunately, soldiers have been a constant presence in the county since the Reagan administration circumvented a law prohibiting military involvement in domestic law-enforcement, and this event, though it enraged the populous, has had little long-term impact on the situation. Last fall the defense department, which still denies any wrongdoing, paid the Hernandez family more than $1 million and washed its hands.

Over the last four years the Texas Low-Level Radioactive Waste Disposal Authority has attempted to push through legislation for a nuclear dump less than two-hundred miles west of Marfa, on a site that, aside from being both a geological fault line and a watershed for the Rio Grande, is inhabited by an impoverished, not particularly educated populace, key members of which proved amenable to various forms of bribery. The dump looked like a neatly done deal, until an unlikely group of zealous activists (one of them Gary Oliver, the *Sentinel*'s excellent—and legally blind—cartoonist) galvanized the entire six-county area of Far West Texas, as well as a large delegation from the Mexican government, and the measure was defeated. It seemed like a miracle.

A few months ago a local man survived a gas explosion which blew off his roof and knocked down the walls of his house—a story I followed from mystery occurrence, to medical emergency, to amazing recovery, to possible criminal prosecution (he was trying to gas himself, which made the property damage negligent), and, lately, into the real estate column.

About every other week there's a four-hundred-pound bale of marijuana found on the roadside, an ad taken out by the county informing someone they are "Hereby Commanded" to appear in court, or a violent fugitive on the lam. (Fugitives are another Dostoyevskian touch. In *The Brothers Karamazov*, there is "a horrible convict who had just escaped from the provincial prison, and was secretly living in our town.") The bank in Van Horn, about one hundred miles to the west, went through a period in 1996 when it was robbed every few weeks. Former Marfa Sheriff Rick Thompson is serving a life sentence for smuggling more than a ton of cocaine out of Mexico—he's referred to as "the cocaine sheriff." The Unabomber, whose brother owns property in the area, carried on a lengthy and passionate correspondence with a Mexican campesino just over the border.

The *Sentinel* also contains an outspoken, thoughtful, varied, occasionally bombastic opinion section, with letters from the likes of "Crazy Bear," George "Pepper" Brown (who for some reason is the honorary mayor of Wellfleet, Mass., though he lives near Marfa, and his letters to Robert Halpern, the *Sentinel*'s editor, all begin "Roberto, amigo"), and many members of the large Mexican-American community—names like Lujan and Cabezuela are characteristic—published side-by-side with a sort of rustic philosophical observation-cum-chitchat column called "Wool Gathering," by Mary Katherine Metcalfe Earney. "Wool Gathering" is filed from the retirement home, and can take some strange turns. One meandering edition about a pleasant visit to Delaware and Philadelphia, seeing lapsed Marfans, ended like this, "On the return to Dallas and in between planes, I was stabbed in the hand by an angry woman..."

On the back page there's a section for classified ads and public notices. There's a column for mobile homes, a column for garage sales, a column of miscellany ("about 20 goats, all sizes"), and a half page of real estate. Daphne and I often check to see what houses are going for (usually around $60,000 for a few acres and a couple bedrooms). We imagine moving down to Marfa, becoming some sort of ranch hands, reporting for the *Sentinel* or the daily paper in San Angelo, a town of 100,000 about two hundred miles to the northeast, which used to pick up her stories, and living in the "Judd way," which we've convinced ourselves involves a pure ascetic harmony with the surroundings.

In fact, Donald Judd, for all his land-grabbing, became something of a holy man. His masterpiece in Marfa is an installation of one hundred milled aluminum boxes—each of the exact same volume (about that of a restaurant stove), but with wildly different interiors, full of sloping metal planes and odd angles. The boxes fill two former artillery sheds that he opened up to the Texas plains with huge windows along their sides, and capped with Quonset roofs. During the day the sheds fill with sun and the boxes warp and change and reflect the landscape. At night they turn liquid in the moonlight. In the distance, between the sheds and the far-off silhouette of the Chinati mountains, Judd placed fifteen rectangular boxes, each about ten feet tall, which further link the site to the landscape. This was the artist's favorite (Karamazovian) story about the piece: After a tour, a Jesuit priest turned to him and said, "You and I are in the same business."

And Chinati, just outside town, also seems pulled from *The Brothers Karamazov*, resembling the "neighboring monastery" that "crowds of pilgrims… from thousands of miles, come flocking to see" with Judd—or the spirit of Judd—the presiding elder, called Zosima in the book, responsible for the "great glory" that has come to the place.

By the time he died, Judd had changed from a sculptor into an almost monastic figure. He was living in deep seclusion, on the remotest of his ranches in the high desert, without electricity, close to the border, surrounded by books on art, philosophy, history, and local ecology. "My first and largest interest is in my relation to the natural world," he wrote during this period. "All of it, all the way out. This interest includes my existence… the existence of everything and the space and time that is created by the existing things."

DESERT PICNICS

Approaching Marfa the temperamentality in the local landscape quickly becomes apparent. There's an old cowboy poem about a "place where mountains float it the air," which may be a reference to the mirages that the dry Marfan climate is known to produce. A local man recalls seeing "the entire [nearby] town of Valentine appearing in the morning sky." Another claims to have seen "the apparition of a Mexican village in the still-light sky just after sunset." It rarely rains, but when it does the sky is transformed, going from its usual big serene blue to the purple-black of a deep bruise—and letting loose so much precipitation that water suddenly runs in rivers through the streets. You can see it all coming a hundred miles off, like a train down a straight line of track. At night there's a great heaping feast of stars, and meteor showers— "like confetti" is how Daphne puts it—are a regular event.

Sometimes the sun is so bright that you can't see. I first noticed this while driving back from Balmorhea, a town with a vast spring-fed swimming pool (and ranch-hand brothels) over the mountains about fifty miles north of Marfa. It's typical in Far West Texas to drive one hundred miles just to have something to do, the way the rest of the country goes to the movies, and in Balmorhea Daphne and I'd run into some other people from Marfa and spent the day talking in the shade. Coming back, Daphne drove and I stared out the window. As we started coming out of the flatland, up through the Davis Mountains, where the two-lane road twists through a canyon and the desert terrain gives way a bit, I noticed a tree, a salt cedar or something—the first green I'd seen since leaving the pool—standing out with a sort of fluorescent brightness against the canyon's brown rock and scrub. When I pulled off my sunglasses the color disappeared. With a naked eye the tree looked pale, burnt, and exhausted—almost translucent. The sunlight was so strong that it was shining right through it. But when I put the sunglasses back on the light receded and the tree reappeared—standing out like it was on fire.

Besides the sparse trees, which are more common in town, the terrain supports myriad cacti: yucca and cholla in abundance, but also the odd horse crippler (a nasty, horizontally inclined weed that looks like an unsprung bear trap); nopolito, a cactus with flat pads that are de-spined and sold in fruit bins outside the gas stations; ocotillo, a subaquatic-looking plant with wavy tentacles and sharp thorns that suggests an octopus crossed with a blowfish; and lots of juniper and mesquite. The cholla, or prickly pear, is a thicker, less primordial variant on the ocotillo, with leaves like a pineapple's, and the yucca is a bush with aloe-like spines, each about two feet long. When yucca bloom, a seven-foot rod shoots out of the center and bursts into a brilliant yellow flower that stands out brightly, like a flare in the landscape, sunglasses or no.

There are four roads out of Marfa. One leads to Valentine, a comatose place with a post office that receives bags of mail in early February from all over the country, to be reposted before the fourteenth. A second leads to Shafter, a ghost town waiting for either the governor's order to abolish it or the price of silver to hit $6 an ounce (it's now at $5.30), so as to make it worthwhile for an interested mining concern to tap a vein that was abandoned during World War II. The third road leads to the area's only theater, in Alpine, and the campus of Sul Ross State University, which offers degrees in Range Animal Science and is the birthplace of intercollegiate rodeo. The last leads to Fort Davis, a boutique town with an observatory dedicated to the spectroscopic analysis of light.

Technically, there's a fifth road, through Pinto Canyon, which leads out of Marfa to the southwest, in the direction of Judd's main ranch, and winds up on the border in a town called Ruidosa (though "town" is an exaggeration, as there isn't a single amenity in Ruidosa, besides the road; it's more like an encampment). Leaving Marfa down Pinto Canyon, you see a sign that reads, PAVEMENT ENDS 32 MILES. My one experience driving the length of this road was unnerving in the extreme. About an hour out, halfway between Marfa and the Rio Grande, having seen no other cars, we decided to stop where the road crossed a dry creek-bed. This was long after the pavement had ended. The scenery looked a lot like the ocean floor. The temperature was in the nineties. We'd packed a picnic of avocado sandwiches, Lone Star beer, and some local cheese called *osadero*; we spied some tired-looking bushes—the only non-cactus shade in sight—and figured to have lunch under them. After shutting the car off we trudged about four hundred feet down the dry creek bed (I was thinking *flash-flood*, which is something the area's known for). Away from the road—which was only a spit through the wilderness at this point—we set down our cooler and got out our food. We started to eat without saying much of anything—the silence was so immense it suppressed any conversational impulse.

The picnic was scuttled fifteen minutes later when we heard the sound of someone trying to hotwire our car. The starter whined, but the engine wouldn't catch. We looked at each other for an instant, and then jumped up and started tearing back up the creek bed, afraid of being stuck out there more than whatever we might find. I got there first, in a gasping, adrenaline choked rush, and found the car sitting where we'd left it, and with no one in sight. Daphne ran back, packed up our stuff, and we got the hell out of there fast. Whoever was out in that desert on foot, crossing into the US, had to want a car with Texas plates— *bad*. All we could think was that they gave up trying when they heard us crashing down the creek, thinking to avoid a confrontation: even if the motor caught, the car was headed towards Mexico, and with the road disintegrating into sharp rubble and cacti a foot to either side, there was no obvious way to turn it around.

* * *

For the symposium, we came in from the south, via Shafter, and after checking into the Thunderbird Motel, we dragged some chairs outside and watched the motor court fill up with rental cars. Since the Thunderbird's amenities include a plentiful ice machine, we filled a cooler we'd brought and sat out on a concrete walk beneath an overhang for half an hour. Then we went to check out the town. Rob Weiner, Judd's old assistant, who used to spend his every waking hour with Judd and has stayed on in Marfa, stopped his car to say hello. He knew Daphne well when she lived there, and we became friends after I first visited. His causticity and sense of amusement about most things Marfan is combined with a huge knowledge and passion for the place, and if Marfa turns into an art community, he'll have a lot to do with it. He told us that we might be able to stay in a foundation building later that weekend.

At an ad-hoc Chinati Foundation store, which was selling books on all the lecturers in the symposium as well as on the work of artists Judd admired and permanently installed in Marfa (Claes Oldenburg, Dan Flavin, Carl Andre, Richard Long, Ilya Kabakov, and John Chamberlain), we fell into conversation with our first non-Marfan, a half-American-Indian reporter from the *Houston Press* named Shaila. She had driven from Houston and was camping out in the Marfa trailer park.

"Gehry is God," she told us.

Not in Marfa, I thought. *God's Judd.*

After that we went by the paper to see Robert Halpern and his wife Rosario, who were busy with an issue but invited us to dinner with the newspaper staff, their kids, and Rusty Taylor, the former chief of police, all of whom had recently been involved in a characteristically unusual chapter in Marfa history.

In July 1996, a photograph in the *Sentinel* showed a tall, lean, rangy-looking man with a circle of white hair wearing a T-shirt that said "Ask Me about The Republic of Texas." This was Richard McLaren, described by his neighbors as "capable of tremendous violence," a man who, arguing a legal technicality in an 1845 annexation document, considered himself chief ambassador, consul general, and sovereign of the independent nation of Texas. McLaren had become a bullying presence in the hills north of Marfa, given to threats and harassment, filing false liens against property, passing bogus scrip, and accumulating weapons. That day he and his followers were having a picnic in celebration of "captive nations week," a propaganda occasion established under Eisenhower in the late '50s to foster dissent under communist dictatorships. In the background could be seen two police cruisers: Rusty Taylor, a couple dozen Texas rangers and other lawmen were keeping an eye on the situation.

Less than a year later, in the spring of 1997, three R.O.T. conscripts, dressed in camouflage and carrying assault weapons, stalked through the mountains from McLaren's trailer home to the house of his nearest neighbors, Joe Rowe—former president of the local neighborhood association—and his wife Margaret Ann. When they arrived in the yard they opened fire on the house, sending shrapnel into Mr. Rowe's shoulder, then burst through the door and struck him with a rifle butt, breaking his arm. With the Rowes subdued, the intruders made some long-distance calls, took all the food they could carry (leaving $40 as compensation), and brought their hostages back to McLaren's trailer, from which the group issued a communiqué describing the action as reprisal for the arrest earlier that morning of another Republic of Texas member, Robert Scheidt, on charges of carrying illegal weapons. McLaren declared war on the United States, and named the Rowes as his first prisoners. Showing considerable restraint, police in Marfa agreed to release Scheidt in exchange for the Rowes, and a trade was made that left the group isolated in their trailer, several miles up a dirt road, surrounded by SWAT teams and Texas rangers.

McLaren had prepared for such an occasion by digging a series of bunkers and stockpiling more than sixty pipe bombs, a dozen or so gasoline cans, ten long rifles, several pistols, and five hundred to seven hundred rounds of ammunition. He swore to fight to the end, and issued a grandiloquent statement evoking the diary of William B. Travis, commander at the Alamo in 1836: "Everyone has chosen to stay and hold the sovereign soil of the Republic and its foreign missions. I pray reinforcements arrive before they overrun the embassy." He would wage an Alamo-style fight to the death. He would kill as many officers as possible. As police reinforcements continued to arrive, McLaren got on the shortwave radio and broadcast: "Mayday! Mayday! Mayday! Hostiles are invading the Republic of Texas embassy. We have hostiles in the woods."

After a few days, though, McLaren began to soften. He conceded that he could surrender if the rules of war were applied and the U.S. agreed to treat him under the rules of the Geneva Convention, allowing an appeal to the United Nations. This eventually led to his signing a "Texas-wide cease-fire document," essentially an unconditional surrender, with a proviso that the embassy be respected, which he understood to mean that the Republic flag, a lone yellow star on a blue field, would continue to fly—it was lowered and replaced by the Texas flag, in what a local fireman described as an "Iwo Jima-style ceremony."

McLaren and four others lay down their weapons (though, arriving in Marfa, one of them shouted, "I was captured, not surrendered, and I'm ashamed I didn't die"). Two other members went renegade and retreated into the hills with rifles and small arms. They were pursued by hounds, all of which they shot. Helicopters then tracked the pair into more remote terrain, and when they were fired upon, police snipers shot back and killed one man. The other, Richard Keyes III, who had quit a job at a Kansas bathroom-equipment manufacturer just weeks before these events, managed to escape. He basically evanesced. And now, almost twenty months later, he still has not been found. One newspaper called him "a West Texas version of D. B. Cooper," a hijacker in the early '70s who parachuted out of a 727 with $200,000 in ransom money and was never heard from again.

But a reporter for *Mother Jones* magazine *has* heard from Keyes, or a man claiming (quite credibly) to be Keyes. He defended the attack on the Rowes, and noted that after inflicting wounds they'd subsequently called a doctor, who'd refused to help, because "he was concerned about a house full of armed fruitcakes." Touching on the fact that the kidnappers had left the Rowes payment for food and phone calls, the man declared "They were fully compensated for what happened, except for the fact that they had a rather bad day." He also said that he was safely outside the United States, which, in McLaren terms, probably means he's still in Texas.

As for McLaren, before the surrender he made sure that his international cease-fire agreement also included a conjugal visit with a woman he'd "married" a short time before, in a service binding only under the laws of the Republic of Texas. She was also under arrest for her involvement in the siege, so following arraignment by the Marfa Justice of the Peace, Cinderella Gonzalez, the two were put in the same cell.

In the lonely days that followed, while awaiting trial, McLaren took to writing florid letters to the *Sentinel*, calling his "challenge to gain national independence… the best-executed legal presentation that has ever been accomplished in the 20th century." He also described his predicament in Marfa as that of a "prisoner of war" being held in the "king's jails." More than a few locals have expressed disappointment that he was not killed during the siege. Though McLaren is going to be away for a long time, some neighbors fear that Keyes might return and retake the embassy.

As Daphne and I left the *Sentinel* and stepped onto Highland Avenue, the main street in town, we could see the old courthouse, with its cupola, coffered ceiling, and yard of sprawling almond trees. It's crowned by a statue of justice, which, legend has it, lost her scales sometime in the '20s, after a hungover cowboy, fresh out of jail and reunited with his six-guns, shot them out of her hands, yelling, "Thar ain't no justice in this goddamn county."

CONFLAGRATIONS

The next morning, six hundred artists, art historians, architects, critics, journalists, and a few townspeople assembled under the corrugated tin roof of a former ice plant in a neighborhood called *Salsipuedes* ("get out if you can"). The place was so full that they'd dragged in extra chairs from the local veterans society with phrases like "AMVETS Salutes USO Post 65 with Pride" stenciled on their backs. Opening the proceedings, James Ackerman, the art historian from Harvard, tried to temper the Judd idolatry by describing the artist as a man "at war" with architecture, given less to collaboration than to "fulminations against architecture in our time."

A big man was seated across the aisle from me. It was Frank Gehry, looking a lot like somebody's Palm Springs grandfather. He was wearing old loafers that needed a shine, a white button-down shirt, gray suit pants, and a sport jacket. When the architect Jacques Herzog—thin, hip, dressed with a Swiss meticulousness, completely in black, Gehry's aesthetic opposite—got up to give a detailed lecture, I watched Gehry. Herzog explained the process of "tattooing" photographs to concrete in order to give his buildings variegated surfaces. He'd been talking for half an hour when an El Paso-bound train came by and drowned him out for a minute. I glanced over at Gehry. He seemed aggravated. When Herzog resumed lecturing and began a long series of slides on the expansion of the Tate Gallery, Gehry, brow furrowed, started fidgeting with a pencil. The next time I looked, he was up and gone. Herzog continued lecturing for a few minutes until the director of Chinati suddenly cut him off. It seemed like Gehry had heard enough from his competition and put an end to it.

That afternoon, an ornery vibe intensified, and some Judd-style "fulminating" commenced when the artists took the stage. Robert Irwin, opening his lecture with a sustained tangent about art history, endeavored to make it clear that he didn't believe in anything beyond modernism. "*Post*modernism: If that isn't a red herring I'll kiss your ass," he hollered. He then proceeded to slam Richard Meier, the principal architect on the Getty Center project, saying, "I chewed him up and left him for dead... Though you'd never define a collaboration in that way."

It was around this time that I heard a groan. It wasn't Gehry, but Shaila, from the *Houston Press*, who had fainted from the slowly intensifying heat. Daphne had to help her outside. When Shaila filed her piece she would blame the incident on side effects associated with her stay in the Marfa trailer park, and its limited culinary options: "the smell of my own road fare farts." But at the time we were happily unaware of her condition.

And during all this commotion Irwin didn't ever slow down. Animated with a sort of giddy, profane enthusiasm, the artist reveled in some of the stranger details of his work. He described his relations with his horticultural consultants on the Getty Center garden as "spending a lot of time going to nurseries and hugging each other." As evidence of his attention to minutiae he said that he'd made certain that benches in the garden would "feel good on your ass." He then explained that he'd fashioned the stream that runs through the garden with heavy stonework because "I didn't want it to look like some gay bathroom." With this a disapproving rumble came over the ice plant. (Later, when questioned about the gay bathroom comment, Irwin was both apologetic and cagey. "I don't get out much. I'm an artist," he explained.)

The next speaker, Michael Benedikt, the postmodernist, riveted Irwin through his spectacles and said, "Modernism is male and macho. And that's the problem with it."

After castigating Irwin, Benedikt called the work of making art a "religious project," and delivered a lecture that delved into the Old Testament. In Benedikt's mind, the burning bush that Moses encountered in the desert was, like successful art, "burning with its own authenticity." Then we were released for dinner at Chinati.

Standing in line for food, a man was saying, "We need to maximize returns for the whole Marfa concept." This was Judd's old lawyer, John Jerome. Dinner was brisket and Shiner Bock beer in the Arena, a former army gymnasium that Judd rehabilitated. It's difficult to say what exactly the "Marfa concept" might be. For Judd it meant control: of his surroundings, of his art, of the company he kept. As the Russian installation artist Ilya Kabakov noted, "When I first came to Marfa, my biggest impression was the unbelievable combination of estrangement, similar to a holy place, and at the same time of unbelievable attention to the life of the works there. For me it was like some sort of Tibetan monastery; there were no material things at all, none of the hubbub of our everyday lives. It was... a world for art." (Although I don't think that's what Jerome meant.)

But Kabakov's presence in Marfa alters the concept significantly. Kabakov, whose installation is completely different from all the other major pieces in Marfa, was an underground artist in the Soviet Union who began to exhibit in the West only in the late '80s. In the early '90s Judd invited him to come to Marfa and do a piece. Kabakov was "astounded." The haunting result is "School No. 6," a replica of an entire communist-era Russian grade school— desks, display cases, lesson plans, Cyrillic text books, musical instruments— installed in a Chinati barracks, exposed to the elements, and encouraged to decay. "Of course there was nothing more awful than the Soviet school, with all of its discipline, abomination, and militarization," he has said of the work. "But now that that system has collapsed and left behind only ruins, it evokes the same kind of nostalgic feelings as a ruined temple." It also has its serene, even spiritual overtones. As he describes it: "The entire space of the school is flooded with sunshine and quiet. Sunny squares lie on the school floor. The blue sky is visible in the empty apertures. From all of this, the neglect reigning all around does not seem so cheerless and depressing." The installation plays the trick of turning Marfa into Russia. And Kabakov's description of its mood is akin to one in *The Brothers Karamazov* wherein the youngest brother repeatedly recalls his mother's face, but always in "the slanting rays of the setting sun (these slanting rays he remembered most of all)."

In discussing another one of his installations Kabakov's has said that "everything that we see around us, everything that we discover in our past, or which could possibly comprise the future—all of this is a limitless world of projects." Though he seems to mean it somewhat ironically, the statement pairs nicely with Judd's writing about his interest in the natural world, "all of it, all the way out." A radically different interpretation of the same artistic impulse.

So Kabakov is also part of the "Marfa concept."

And the concept—no matter which of the seminal events or legends in the town's history one follows—always has to do with light.

Light, in fact, is Marfa's last name. Marfa *Ignatievna*—meaning daughter of Ignatius, which, according to a dictionary of names, is derived from the Latin word *ignis*, meaning fire. Ignatievna can be broken down to mean "daughter of fire." According to Dostoyevsky, the character is "not a stupid woman," and early in *The Brothers Karamazov* she gives rise to "a strange, unexpected, and original occurrence"—the birth of a boy that her superstitious husband fears, calls a "dragon"—fire-breathing, presumably—and refuses to care for. When the baby dies, Marfa takes it stoically. Aside from not being stupid, she's a stoical lady—two desirable qualities in a frontierswoman. And since the woman who named the town after this character must have been reading the book in the original Russian—the first translation, into German, wasn't until 1884, and the English version didn't appear until 1912—she could not have been unaware of the name's significance.

After going through the food line, Daphne and I sat down with some of the staff and artists in residence at Chinati, who were talking about how the Lannan Foundation was almost finished renovating two homes it had bought to house writers who receive its literary awards. An English poet would be arriving in a month. (He's there now, putting aside the poetry, evidently, to write a book called *Marfan.*) The other major piece of art news was the receipt of Chinati's first NEA grant, toward the renovation of six old U-shaped army barracks, to house a piece that light artist Dan Flavin planned with Judd and completed designing after Judd's death, when Flavin was on his own deathbed, in 1996. There was also talk about Robert Irwin maybe taking a spare building and making a piece from light-capturing scrim veils.

After dinner the evening migrated to Lucy's Bar, where, as the sun went down in Marfa's austere big-sky setting, the gathering's most imposing participant, Frank Gehry, was given a wide, somewhat awestruck berth. Ray, the owner, even allowed him to stand in an off-limits-to-customers spot beside the bartender (blocking the sink). Eventually he left for the dilapidated old El Paisano Hotel, where he was the most famous guest since James Dean spent a week during the shooting of the film *Giant.* As Lucy's started to break up, people either headed home or out to see the Marfa Lights.

The Marfa Lights, not unlike Frank Gehry, are a fairly aloof phenomenon— mostly appearing at a hard-to-quantify distance from a roadside pull-off, near the site of an old military airfield. To most observers they look like a distant swarm of fireflies, constantly changing direction and flashing on and off in random patterns. But there are wild exceptions to this aloofness. In various accounts the lights are animate and even intelligent. They metastasize, hide behind one another, change color, bounce across the desert "like basketballs," line up for aircraft "like runway lights," and pursue lone motorists between Marfa and Alpine. (Robert Halpern told me about a guy who was descended upon and pursued by a pair of Marfa lights, blazing incandescently, all the way to the town limits, after which he swore that he would never leave Marfa again, and hasn't.) Though the most reliable place to see them is the viewing site, overlooking a vast swath of desert between Marfa and Alpine—where a weather-beaten historical marker details various explanations ("campfires, phosphorescent minerals, swamp gas, static electricity, St. Elmo's fire, and 'ghost lights'")—the lights have been known to stray as far away as the Dead Horse Mountains, sixty miles to the east, the hills near Ruidosa, an equal distance to the southwest, and the Davis Mountains, the location of McDonald Observatory, one of the country's most sophisticated stargazing facilities, thirty miles due north. According to Marfan Lee Bennett, author of some of the boosterish material promoting the annual Lights Festival (an excuse for yearly outdoor concerts), even the observatory is mystified by the lights phenomenon: "One night they trained one of their telescopes on the viewing site until they spied some of the glowing lights. Everyone working that night saw them. They pinpointed the location. The next day, they traveled to that exact spot, certain they would find the source. What did they find? Grass, rocks, dirt. That's it. Nothing else."

Though this history may be a little loose with the facts, more than a few serious science teams have visited the site over the years, eventually arriving at one or more of the hazy explanations engraved on the historical marker. Folktales stretching back to the 19th century explain them as everything from restless Indian spirits to the campfires of perished settlers. Most often close-up observers compare the lights to combustion. "It was a ball of fire," said a motorist of the light that kept pace with her car for ten miles on the way to Alpine. "I saw three big balls of fire lined up" reported a woman of lights she witnessed hovering by the side of the road outside town. A former Alpine resident once stopped at the viewing site on a spring night and saw thirteen lights "coming through the field like little fireballs... and rolling out onto the road." Hallie Stillwell, an Alpine rancherwoman and justice of the peace, spotted some on her property and saw them "die down and then come up again, brighter. They looked like flames." Less credible information comes from a recluse living off in the hills around Shafter, who calls them "agents of Satan" and claims that "they walk up the side of the mountain" near his house; and a bit of hearsay in which the lights are supposed to have incinerated a truck belonging to a pair of investigating scientists, rendering the men, in the words of a Sul Ross University English professor, "idiots from that day on."

Lee Bennett also contributes this story to the Lights Festival material:

> I'm the local historian. So when someone in town dies, the families usually give me pieces of history that may have been collected by that person. Well, a special lady on a ranch west of town had kept a little tiny notebook of

writings about the local flora and fauna and the general environment out here. But one entry especially caught my attention. She wrote in her own handwriting about driving down an old canyon road—a good 20 miles from the usual viewing site—many years ago. She was rather new to the area, and when she looked to her right she saw Chinati Mountain. "Isn't that a pretty big mountain?" she asked. Her friend replied that it was one of the highest around. "And there's a road coming down it?" she asked, amazed. Her friend looked at her strangely and answered, "There's no road coming down off Chianti." "Then why do I see lights coming quickly down that mountain?" The entry went on to describe several lights that shot down the side of the mountain, directly toward them. They danced in the canyon and moved right up to the hood of the car. In her own words she wrote, "I felt so special. We were never afraid. In fact, we had sort of a warm feeling."

There have also been a good many lights posses—debunkers who go out to "get them" and always return humiliated. In the '70s a corporation that figured the site for a uranium cache funded various futile investigations. In the '80s a science professor from Sul Ross University gathered a large party of students and volunteers to converge on the lights, with walkie-talkies and spotter planes to coordinate their maneuvers. But whenever a group got close the lights would wink out or move rapidly out of range. A geologist from Fort Worth named Pat Keeney visited Marfa on business and became fascinated with the lights. Hoping to find their source, he conducted a series of experiments in order to rule out car headlights and other man-made luminosity, and then managed to triangulate the area of the remaining unexplained lights. He then returned with another geologist, Elwood Wright, and together the two drove out on a small ranch road where they encountered a pair of lights moving nearby. Keeney published this account of what happened next:

> They looked like they were moving at about a hundred-fifty to two-hundred miles per hour, but of course I had no way of measuring that. The lights spooked some horses, almost ran into them. Those horses started kicking and running through a cactus patch, trying to get away. The lights came to the edge of this road and stopped. Several times I had seen lights around this old hangar they had on the airbase. Well, one of these lights took off for that hangar, but the other one stayed there by the side of the road. It kept moving around a bush, kind of like it knew we were trying to get near it. It

seemed to possess intelligence—it was like that thing was smarter than we were. It was making us feel pretty stupid. It was perfectly round, about the size of a cantaloupe, and it moved through that bush like it was looking for something. When the light stopped moving, it would get dimmer, but as it moved, it got brighter. Finally, it pulled out in the middle of the road about twenty yards from us and just hovered there. I had left the engine running, and Elwood said, "Put it in gear and floorboard it. We'll run over it." All of a sudden it got real bright and took off like a rocket.

Marfa mayor Fritz Kahl dismisses most accounts of up-close encounters as "asinine stories" (though he has a certain deference for Keeney). Many years prior to his mayoralty Kahl was a military flight instructor at Marfa Field, and he took after the lights one night in a World War II fighter trainer. Unable to ever get close, he banished them from his thoughts (like most saner Marfans have). "The best way to see the lights is with a six-pack of beer and a good looking woman," he says today.

Still, the lights are out there, and on most weekends (as on the first night of the symposium) people assemble by the roadside while the sun goes down, and stay on into the evening. Only after midnight does the crowd thin out and return the road to the circumstances under which most reports of close encounters have occurred.

> Some say that the place was bewitched... during the early days of the settlement; others, that an old Indian chief, the prophet or wizard of his tribe, held his powwows there before the country was discovered... Certain it is, the place still continues under the sway of some witching power, that holds a spell over the minds of the good people... They are given to all kinds of marvelous beliefs; are subject to trances and visions, and frequently see strange sights, and hear music and voices in the air... stars shoot and meteors glare oftener across the valley than in any other part of the country.

This is not a description of Marfa, but in every detail it could be. It is how Washington Irving describes Westchester, New York, the environs where the Headless Horseman prowled. And for the late-night driver traveling between Marfa and Alpine, there is always a certain identification with Ichabod Crane's hoping to make it through Sleepy Hollow, with Paisano Pass, where the lights tend to disappear, subbing in for the church bridge where the Horseman "vanished in a flash of fire."

* * *

On the last day of the symposium, the big boys, Gehry and Oldenburg, spoke. And the odd, inflammatory statements continued. "I'm for an art that doesn't sit on its ass in a museum," Oldenburg declared. He and his wife and collaborator Coosje van Bruggen took turns at the lectern, one talking while the other hit the button for the slide projector. Van Bruggen described the typical architect's ideas about the position sculpture takes in relation to architecture as "nothing more than a turd on the sidewalk." Like Irwin the day before, they seemed all fired up. Among their slides was a proposed sculpture of two giant copper toilet floats to be installed on the Thames, near the location of Jacques Herzog's Tate Gallery (for which they soon expressed unequivocal disdain). By the time Gehry took the stage there was tension in the air.

"Don Judd hated my work," said Gehry, who seemed to find perverse pleasure in the fact. It may have been the spare setting that provoked him, but he made a point of defending the Guggenheim from the charge of upstaging the art it displays (the antithesis of anything that can be said of the unadorned spaces and clean vistas of Judd's Marfa installations), insisting that "artists want their work in an important place." (Again, not exactly the "Marfa concept.") Gehry then talked about his other recent work, like a seafood restaurant topped with a fish that he'd deliberately turned to face the windows of a neighboring five-star hotel. "The owner told me he didn't want 'em looking up the *asshole* of a fish," Gehry explained. Future projects included the Condé Nast cafeteria in New York (a sketch conveying Gehry's idea of a Condé Nast employee showed a leggy woman in a short skirt and shades, blowing a kiss), and a massive gateway for the city of Modena, Italy. Modena's mayor originally offered a design budget of $1 million for the project, "but you get a few people back and forth and that won't hardly cover airfare," said Gehry. "And I ain't gonna stay in no El Paisano Hotel in Modena."

At the end of the lectures the participants gathered together around a long Donald Judd table to discuss each other's work and riff on the theme. It didn't take long for the ideological lines to clarify. Irwin fired a final salvo at critics who engage in "ass-kissing." Coosje van Bruggen lit into Jacques Herzog for his Tate Gallery expansion, calling the whole thing "a pity." Pissed off, Herzog glared out at the audience and said, "It's not bullshit." But before he could go on, he was interrupted by the artist Roni Horn, who stole the moment by remarking, "All this architecture is really about sex." The audience banged its steel chairs, and a beaming Gehry raised his fists above his head like a prize fighter.

"And on that note," Horn said, "I'm going back to New York." Everyone applauded as Gehry and Irwin strode off stage with her, trailed by Herzog (waving a dismissive hand at van Bruggen). The remaining artists soon followed. "The panel has defected," said the moderator. The only ones left on stage were the academics, who were still talking to each other into the microphones.

That afternoon, once everyone had left town, Daphne went running and I went back to Lucy's Bar. I heard a local guy tell the bartender he'd "never seen so many people in black." The bartender told him, "We had the most famous architect in the world in here!" I ordered a Lone Star and heard the bartender tell another customer, "We thought we'd sell a lot of Mexican beer—but all they wanted was Lone Star."

Something in Marfa had *riled up* a lot of architects, artists, and academics. Six hundred of us had been treated to tongue-lashings, dressing downs, fully amplified upbraiding, storming, and railing—not what anyone had expected out of a symposium. In this vexed atmosphere rumors were circulating about an old feud between an art photographer and the Judd estate breaking into a full-blown multimillion dollar lawsuit (broken in the *Sentinel* the next week).

On the surface, of course, Marfa had hosted celebrated artists and architects. But the way it struck me was that *they* had hosted *Marfa*. Marfa had *got into* them. And they had behaved... accordingly: cantankerously, radically, wonderfully, badly, generously, absurdly; *in extremis*. Like Marfans.

Some other notable people who've come through Marfa:

> Katherine Anne Porter
> John Waters
> Denis Johnson
> Dennis Quaid
> Martha Stewart
> David Kaczynski
> W.S. Merwin
> Neil Armstrong
> Gwyneth Paltrow
> Holly Brubach

James Caan
Selena
Elvis.

I wish I could say that the place nourishes artists. It may. But I think it does something stranger. The relationship seems less friendly—more volatile. (I can imagine it destroying some.) Katherine Anne Porter, who lived there as a girl (Judd's son, Flavin, now lives in her house), loathed it. Elvis played a dance nearby and never came back. A cave in the wilderness near the town of Terlingua was a refuge for David Kaczynski, the Unabomber's brother. And W.S. Merwin, who is fascinated with the lights, would rather no one else know about it.

It seems that the best places for artists are places that *are* themselves; have a certain innate self-confidence—burn with that authenticity that Benedikt was talking about. And Marfa is what it is. Less Kabakov's "world for art," perhaps, than a provocative place for all kinds of impulses: creative, destructive, uncharted—by all means authentic.

And it's got better things to do than become aware of its unself-consciousness. Within the next year there may be a hundred-man crew of silver miners in nearby Shafter, drilling on a ten-to-fifteen-year timetable, and eating at Carmen's next to the likes of Seamus Heaney, A.R. Ammons, or William Trevor—all three men are on the small list of Lannan grantees eligible for Marfa residencies. The Entrada al Pacifico, a trade corridor opened up by NAFTA, is altering the regional economy, with border crossings in the county up 100 per cent in the last year. Hydroponic tomatoes are being cultivated in massive greenhouses just outside the city limits, turning Marfa into a desert town that exports water, just as Judd wanted. (It's a bizarre sight: huge glass and steel superstructures, sucking away at the aquifer. Though there's undeniably something Marfan about it.) The border patrol, for better or worse, is bolstering its forces in Marfa. Newcomers have bought back the hot springs, and a handful of other buildings from the Judd estate, restoring the former to public use. An ATM was installed this January (the one Marfa had a few years ago was decommissioned, because it never caught on—but this one may). Things are happening. By no means moribund, Marfa is a viable town on its own terms. As Robert Halpern told me by email the other day, "Pretty much most of the folks who are moving here as well as us locals are reading from the same sheet of music: A town has to change and grow or it dies. Marfa will survive in spite of us all."

And, of course, "mystery lights" is not a bad description of these people who continually pass through Marfa. People like Irwin, Kabakov, Judd, and

Peter Reading, the inaugural Lannan grantee, an oft-inebriated everyman's skeptic, with a tab at Lucy's, who likes to kick around Chinati muttering about how much all the damn boxes cost; or, in characteristic Marfan style, provoke his benefactors by bragging of his residency, "I am required to do nothing. This suits me." But many others also seem to find their way to Marfa. A few weeks after the symposium, a *conjunto* accordionist, Santiago Jimenez Jr., who, along with his brother Flaco, is one of the more revered traditionalists on the Tex-Mex scene, paid a visit. He walked around town playing for old folks, the community center, veterans, whoever wanted to listen. Fantastic pictures of him doing sessions with local musicians kept appearing in the paper. I don't know how long he was around, but he seemed to just stay and stay and stay—through about four issues of the *Sentinel*, becoming a part of the town. And then he winked out and was gone.

For our last night, Rob Weiner at the Chinati Foundation said we could move out of the Thunderbird Motel and into a foundation building. Fortunately, part of Donald Judd's philosophy about beds also pertains to having one in most every gallery. We wound up in the John Chamberlain Building, a 30,000-square foot former mohair warehouse full of sculptures made out of crushed cars. "You'll find it interesting," Rob said. At 2 a.m., I awoke with a start. The windows were shaking, the air vibrating, and roars and whistles seemed to be coming straight from the bathroom. It got louder and louder until I was sure something was going to come crashing through the door. "Get up!" I shouted. "It's the ghost of Donald Judd!" And the El Paso-bound train shot by.

FLUSH

by JUDY BUDNITZ

I CALLED MY SISTER and said: What does a miscarriage look like?

What? she said. Oh. It looks like when you're having your period, I guess. You have cramps, and then there's blood.

What do people do with it? I asked.

With what?

The blood and stuff.

I don't know, she said impatiently. I don't know these things, I'm not a doctor. All I can tell you about anything is who you should sue.

Sorry, I said.

Why are you asking me this? she said.

I'm just having an argument with someone, that's all. Just thought you could help settle it.

Well, I hope you win, she said.

I went home because my sister told me to.

She called and said: It's your turn.

No, it can't be, I feel like I was just there, I said.

No, I went the last time. I've been keeping track, I have incontestable proof, she said. She was in law school.

But Mich, I said. Her name was Michelle but everyone called her Mich, as in Mitch, except our mother, who thought it sounded obscene.

Lisa, said Mich, don't whine.

I could hear her chewing on something, a ball-point pen probably. I pictured her with blue marks on her lips, another pen stuck in her hair.

It's close to Thanksgiving, I said, why don't we wait and both go home then?

You forget—they're going down to Florida to be with Nana.

I don't have time to go right now. I have a job, you know. I do have a life.

I don't have time to argue about it, I'm studying, Mich said. I knew she was sitting on the floor with her papers scattered around her, the stacks of casebooks sprouting yellow Post-its from all sides, like lichen, Mich in the middle with her legs spread, doing ballet stretches.

I heard a background cough.

You're not studying, I said. Neil's there.

Neil isn't doing anything, she said. He's sitting quietly in the corner waiting for me to finish. Aren't you, sweetheart?

Meek noises from Neil.

You call him sweetheart? I said.

Are you going home or not?

Do I have to?

I can't come over there and make you go, Mich said.

The thing was, we had both decided, some time ago, to take turns going home every now and then to check up on them. Our parents did not need checking up, but Mich thought we should get in the habit of doing it anyway. To get in practice for the future.

After a minute Mich said: They'll think we don't care.

Sometimes I think they'd rather we left them alone.

Fine. Fine. Do what you want.

Oh all right, I'll go.

I flew home on a Thursday night and though I'd told them not to meet me at the airport, there they were, both of them, when I stepped off the ramp. They were the only still figures in the terminal; around them people dashed with garment bags, stewardesses hustled in pairs wheeling tiny suitcases.

My mother wore a brown coat the color of her hair. She looked anxious. My father stood tall, swaying slightly. The lights bounced off the lenses of his glasses; he wore jeans that were probably twenty years old. I would have liked to be the one to see them first, to compose my face and walk up to them unsuspected like a stranger. But that never happened—they always spotted me before I saw them, and had their faces ready and their hands out.

Is that all you brought? Just the one bag?

Here, I'll take it.

Lisa honey, you don't look so good. How are you?

Yes, how are you? You look terrible.

Thanks, Dad.

How are you, they said over and over, as they wrestled the suitcase from my hand.

Back at the house, my mother stirred something on the stove and my father leaned in the doorway to the dining room and looked out the window at the backyard. He's always leaned in that door-frame to talk to my mother.

I made that soup for you, my mother said. The one where I have to peel the tomatoes and pick all the seeds out by hand.

Mother. I wish you wouldn't do that.

You mean you don't like it? I thought you liked it.

I like it, I like it. But I wish you wouldn't bother.

It's no bother. I wanted to.

She was up until two in the morning pulling skin off tomatoes, my father said, I could hear them screaming in agony.

How would you know, you were asleep, my mother said.

I get up at five thirty every morning to do work in the yard before I go in to the office, he said.

I looked out at the brown yard.

I've been pruning the rose bushes. They're going to be beautiful next summer.

Yes, they will.

Lisa, he said, I want you to do something for me tomorrow, since you're here.

Sure. Anything.

I want you to go with your mother to her doctor's appointment. Make sure she goes.

Okay.

She doesn't have to come, my mother said. That's silly, she'll just be bored.

She's supposed to get a mammogram every six months, my father said, but she's been putting it off and putting it off.

I've been busy, you know that's all it is.

She's afraid to go. She's been avoiding it for a year now.

Oh stop it, that's not it at all.

She always finds a way to get out of it. Your mother, the escape artist.

She crossed her arms over her chest. There was a history. Both her mother and an aunt had had to have things removed.

It's the same with all her doctors, my father said. Remember the contact lenses?

That was different. I didn't need new contacts.

She stopped going to her eye doctor for fifteen years. For fifteen years she was wearing the same contacts. When she finally went in, the doctor was amazed, he said he'd never seen anything like it, they don't even make contact lenses like that anymore. He thought she was wearing dessert dishes in her eyes.

You're exaggerating, my mother said.

Mich I mean Lise, my father said. He's always gotten our names confused; sometimes, to be safe, he just says all three.

She's afraid to go because of the last time, he said.

What happened last time? I said.

I had the mammogram pictures done, she said, and then a few days later they called and said the pictures were inconclusive and they needed to take a second set. So they did that and then they kept me waiting for the results, for weeks, without telling me anything, weeks where I couldn't sleep at night and I kept your father up too, trying to imagine what it looked like, the growth. Like the streaks in bleu cheese, I thought. I kept feeling these little pains, and kept checking my pulse all night. And then finally they called and said everything was fine after all, that there was just some kind of blur on the first pictures, like I must have moved right when they took it or something.

You were probably talking the whole time, my father said. Telling them how to do their job.

I was probably *shivering*. They keep that office at about forty degrees and leave you sitting around in the cold in a paper robe. The people there don't talk to you or smile; and when they do the pictures they mash your breast between these two cold glass plates like a pancake.

My father looked away. He had a kind of modesty about some things.

My mother said to me: All those nights I kept thinking about my mother having her surgery; I kept feeling for lumps, waking up your father and asking him to feel for lumps.

Leah, my father said.

He didn't mind that. I think he might have enjoyed it a little.

Please.

Didn't you?

Promise me you'll go, he said.

She's not coming, she said.

The next day we drove to the clinic an hour early. My mother had the seat drawn as close to the steering wheel as she could get it; she gripped the wheel with her hands close together at twelve o'clock. She looked over at me as often as she looked out at the road.

There were squirrels and possums sprawled in the road, their heads red smears.

It's something about the weather, my mother said, makes them come out at night.

Oh.

We're so early, my mother said, and we're right near Randy's salon. Why don't we stop in and see if he can give you a haircut and a blowout?

Not now.

He wouldn't mind, I don't think. I talk about you whenever I go see him to have my hair done. He'd like to meet you.

No.

If you just got it angled on the sides, here, and got a few bangs in the front—

Just like yours, you mean.

You know, I feel so bad for Randy, he looks terrible, circles under his eyes all the time, he says his boyfriend is back in the hospital. Now whenever I go to get my hair cut, I bake something to bring him, banana bread or something. But I think the shampoo girls usually eat it all before he can get it home.

That's nice of you.

I worry about him. He doesn't take care of himself.

Yes.

Why are you still getting pimples? You're twenty-seven years old, why are you still getting pimples like a teenager?

Not everyone has perfect skin like you, I said. Green light. Go.

I do not have perfect skin, she said, bringing her hands to her face.

Both hands on the wheel please. Do you want me to drive?

No, I don't. You must be tired.

I touched my forehead. Small hard bumps like Braille.

She drove. I looked at the side of her face, the smooth taut skin. I wondered when she would start to get wrinkles. I already had wrinkles. On my neck, I could see them.

So, how is it going with this Piotr?

He's all right.

Still playing the—what was it? Guitar?

Bass guitar.

She turned on the radio and started flipping through stations. Maybe we'll hear one of his songs, she said brightly.

I said: I told you he was in a band. I didn't say they were good enough to be on the radio.

Oh. I see. So the band's just for fun. What else does he do?

Nothing. Yet.

So. What kind of name is Piotr? Am I saying it right?

Polish, I said.

I did not feel like telling her that only his grandmother lived in Poland; his parents were both born in Milwaukee, and he had grown up in Chicago and had never been to Poland; Piotr was a name he had given himself; he was not really a Piotr at all, he was a Peter with pretensions and long hair. I did not tell her this.

A black car cut into the lane in front of us. My mother braked suddenly and flung her right arm out across my chest.

Mother! Keep your hands on the wheel!

I'm sorry, she said, it's automatic. Ever since you kids were little....

I'm wearing a seatbelt.

I know honey, I can't help it. Did I hurt you?

No, of course not, I said.

When we reached the parking garage my mother rolled down her window but couldn't reach; she had to unfasten her seatbelt and open the car door in order to punch the button and get her parking ticket. I looked at her narrow back as she leaned out of the car, its delicate curve, the shoulder blades like folded wings under her sweater, a strand of dark hair caught in the clasp of her gold necklace. I had the urge to slide across the seat and curl around her. It only lasted for a second.

She turned around and settled back into her seat and the yellow-and-black-striped mechanical bar swung up in front of the car, and I tapped my feet impatiently while she slammed the door shut and rolled up the window. Now she was fiddling with her rearview mirror and straightening her skirt.

Come on, I said, watching the bar, which was still raised but vibrating a little.

Relax honey, that thing isn't going to come crashing down on us the minute we're under it. I promise you.

I know that, I said, and then closed my eyes until we were through the gate and weaving around the dark oil-stained aisles of the parking lot. I would have liked to tell her about some of the legal cases Mich had described to me: freak accidents, threshing machines gone awry, people caught in giant gears or conveyor belts and torn limb from limb, hands in bread slicers, flimsy walkways over vats of acid. Elevator cases, diving board cases, subway train cases, drowning-in-the-bathtub cases, electrocution-by-blender cases. And then there were the ones that were just called Act of God.

 I didn't tell her.

Remember where we parked, she said.

Okay.

But she did not get out of the car right away. She sat, gripping the wheel.

I don't see why we have to do this, she said. Your father worries...

He'll be more worried if you don't go, I said, and anyway there's nothing to worry about because everything's going to be fine. Right? Right.

If there's something wrong I'd just rather not know, she said to her hands.

We got out; the car shook as we slammed the doors.

She was right about the clinic. It was cold, and it was ugly. She signed in with the receptionist and we sat in the waiting room. The room was gray and bare, the chairs were old vinyl that stuck to your thighs. The lights buzzed and seemed to flicker unless you were looking directly at them.

We sat side by side and stared straight ahead as if we were watching something, a movie.

There was one other woman waiting. She had enormous breasts. I could not help noticing.

I took my mother's hand. It was very cold, but then her hands were always cold, even in summer, cool and smooth with the blue veins arching elegantly over their backs. Her hand lay limply in mine. I had made the gesture thinking it was the right thing to do, but now that I had her hand I didn't know what to do with it. I patted it, turned it over.

My mother looked at me strangely. My hand began to sweat.

There was noise, activity, somewhere, we could hear voices and footsteps, the crash and skid of metal, the brisk tones of people telling each other what to do. But we could see nothing but the receptionist in her window and the one woman who looked asleep, sagging in her chair with her breasts cupped in her arms like babies.

I need to use the restroom, my mother said and pulled her hand away.

The receptionist directed us down the hall and around the corner. We went in, our footsteps echoing on the tiles. It was empty, and reeked of ammonia. The tiles glistened damply.

Here, do something with yourself, my mother said and handed me her comb. She walked down to the big handicapped stall on the end and latched the door.

I combed my hair and washed my hands and waited.

I looked at myself in the mirror. The lights were that harsh relentless kind that reveal every detail of your face, so that you can see all sorts of flaws and pores you didn't even know you had. They made you feel you could see your own thoughts floating darkly just under your skin, like bruises.

Mother, I said. I watched her feet tapping around.

Lisa, she said, there's a fish in the toilet.

Oh, please.

No, I mean it. It's swimming around.

You're making it up.

No I'm not. Come see for yourself.

Well, it's probably just some pet goldfish someone tried to flush.

It's too big to be a goldfish. More like a carp. It's bright orange. Almost red.

You're seeing things—maybe it's blood or something, I said; then I wished I hadn't. The clinic was attached to the county hospital; all sorts of things were liable to pop up in the toilets—hypodermic needles, appendixes, tonsils.

No, no, it's a fish, it's beautiful really. It's got these gauzy fins, like veils. I wonder how it got in here. It looks too large to have come through the pipes. It's swimming in circles. Poor thing.

Well then come out and use a different one, I said. I suddenly started to worry that she was going to miss her appointment. You're just stalling, I said.

Come in and see. We have to save it somehow.

I heard her pulling up her pantyhose, fixing her skirt. Then she unlatched the door to the stall and opened it. She was smiling. Look, she said.

I followed her into the stall.

Come see, she said. Together we leaned over the bowl.

I saw only the toilet's bland white hollow, and our two identical silhouettes reflected in the water.

Now where did he go? my mother said. Isn't that the strangest thing?

We looked at the empty water.

How do you think he got out? she said. Look, you can see, the water's still moving from where he was. Look, look—little fish droppings. I swear. Lisa honey, look.

My mother is going crazy, I thought. Let's go back to the waiting room, I said.

But I still have to use the bathroom, she said.

I stood by the sink and waited. You're going to miss your appointment, I said. I watched her feet. Silence.

I was making her nervous. I'll wait for you in the hall, I said.

So I left, leaned against the wall, and waited. And waited. She was taking a long time. I started to wonder if she had been hallucinating. I wondered if something really was wrong with her, if she was bleeding internally or having a weird allergic reaction. I didn't think she was making it all up; she couldn't lie, she was a terrible, obvious liar.

Mother, I called.

Mom, I said.

I went back into the bathroom.

She was gone.

The stall doors swung loose, creaking. I checked each cubicle, thinking she might be standing on the toilet seat, with her head ducked down the way we used to avoid detection in high school. In the handicapped stall the toilet water was quivering, as if it had just been flushed. I even checked in the cabinets under the sink and stuck my hand down in the garbage pail.

I stood there, thinking. She must have somehow left and darted past me without my noticing. Maybe I had closed my eyes for a minute. She could move fast when she wanted to.

Had she climbed out the window? It was a small one, closed, high up on the wall.

She had escaped.

I walked slowly down the halls, listening, scanning the floor tiles.

I thought of her narrow back, the gaping mouth of the toilet, pictured her slipping down, whirling around and vanishing in the pipes.

I tried to formulate a reasonable question: Have you seen my mother? A woman, about my height, brown hair, green eyes? Nervous-looking? Have you seen her?

Or were her eyes hazel?

I came back to the waiting room with the question on my lips, I was mouthing the words she's disappeared, but when I got there the receptionist was leaning through the window calling out in an irritated voice: Ms. Salant? Ms. Salant? They're ready for you, *Ms. Salant.*

The receptionist was opening the door to the examining rooms; the nurses and technicians were holding out paper gowns and paper forms and urine sample cups, Ms. Salant, Ms. Salant, we're waiting, they called; people were everywhere suddenly, gesturing impatiently and calling out my name.

So I went in.

Later I wandered up and down the rows of painted white lines in the lot. I had forgotten where she parked the car. When I finally came upon it I saw her there, leaning against the bumper. For a moment I thought she was smoking a cigarette. She didn't smoke.

When I drew closer I saw that she was nibbling on a pen.

We got in the car and drove home.

All of a sudden I thought of something I wanted to pick up for dinner, she said at one point.

Some fish? I said.

We drove the rest of the way without speaking.

So how did it go today, ladies? my father said that evening.

My mother didn't say anything.

Did you go with her? he asked me. Yeah, I said.

So, you'll hear results in a few days, right? he said with his hand on my mother's back.

She looked away.

Right, I said.

She looked at me strangely, but said nothing.

I told them not to but they both came to the airport Sunday night when I left.

Call me when you get the news, all right? I said.

All right, she said.

I wanted to ask her about the fish in the toilet, whether it had really been there. Whether she had followed the same route it had. But I couldn't work myself up to it. And the topic never came up by itself.

We said good-bye at the terminal. My hugs were awkward. I patted their backs as if I were burping babies.

I told them to go home but I knew they would wait in the airport until the plane took off safely. They always did. I think my mother liked to be there in case the plane crashed during take-off so she could dash onto the runway through the flames and explosions to drag her children from the rubble.

Or maybe they just liked airports. That airport smell.

I had a window seat; I pushed my suitcase under the seat in front of me. A man in a business suit with a fat red face sat down next to me.

I wondered if my mother even knew what I had done for her. I had helped her escape. Although at the time I hadn't thought of it that way; I hadn't really thought at all; I had gone in when I heard my name, automatic school-girl obedience, gone in to the bright lights and paper gowns and people who kneaded your breasts like clay. I began to feel beautiful and noble. I felt like I had gone to the guillotine in her place, like Sydney Carton in *A Tale of Two Cities*.

I called Piotr when I got home. I'm back, I said.

Let me come over, he said, I'll make you breakfast.

It's seven thirty at night.

I just got up, he said.

My apartment felt too small and smelled musty. I'd been gone three days but it seemed longer. Piotr came and brought eggs and milk and his own spatula—he knew my kitchen was ill-equipped for anything but sandwiches.

He seemed to have grown since I last saw him, and gotten more hairy; I looked at the hair on the backs of his hands, the chest hair tufting out of the collar of his T-shirt.

He took up too much space. As he talked his nose and hands popped out at me huge and distorted, as if I were seeing him through a fish-eye lens. He came close to kiss me and I watched his eyes loom larger and larger and blur out of focus and merge into one big eye over the bridge of his nose.

I was embarrassed. My mouth tasted terrible from the plane.

What kind of pancakes do you want? he asked.

The pancake kind, I said.

He broke two eggs with one hand and the yolks slid out between his fingers.

I can do them shaped like snowmen, he said, or rabbits or flowers.

He was mixing stuff up in a bowl; flour slopped over the edges and sprinkled on the counter and the floor. I'll have to clean that up, I thought.

Round ones please, I said.

There was butter bubbling and crackling in the frying pan. Was that pan mine? No, he must have brought it with him—it was a big heavy skillet, the kind you could kill someone with.

He poured in the batter, it was thick and pale yellow; and the hissing butter shut up for a while. I looked in the pan. There were two large lumpy mounds there, side by side, bubbling inside as if they were alive, turning brown on the edges.

He turned them over and I saw the crispy undersides with patterns on them like the moon; and then he pressed them down with the spatula, pressed them flat and the butter sputtered and hissed.

There was a burning smell.

I'm not feeling very hungry right now, I said.

But I brought maple syrup, he said. It's from Vermont, I think.

The pan was starting to smoke. Pushing him aside, I took it off the flame and put it in the sink. It was heavy; the two round shapes were now charred and crusted to the bottom.

Well, we don't have to eat them, he said. He held out the bottle of syrup. Aunt Jemima smiled at me. She looked different, though. They must have updated her image; new hairstyle, outfit. But that same smile.

There's lots of stuff we can do with syrup, he said, it's a very romantic condiment.

He stepped closer and reached out and turned the knob on the halogen lamp. His face looked even more distorted in the dimness.

What? I said. Where did you get such a stupid idea?

Read it somewhere.

I'm sorry, I'm just not feeling very social tonight, I said. Peter, I said.

Oh come on.

I missed my parents very much suddenly. You're so insensitive, I said. Get out.

Hey, I *am* sensitive. I'm *Mr.* Sensitive. I give change to bums. Pachelbel's Canon makes me cry like a baby.

Like a what? I said.

Why are you screaming at me? he said.

Don't let the door hit you in the ass on the way out, I said. I thought I was being smart and cutting. But he took it literally; he went out and closed the door behind him with great care.

My sister called later that night.

So how were they? she asked.

Fine, I said. Same as always.

Your voice sounds funny; what happened? she said.

Nothing.

Something's wrong. Why don't you ever tell me when something's wrong?

There's nothing, Mich.

You never tell me what's going on; when you think I'll worry about something you keep it to yourself.

I tell you everything.

Well then, tell me what was wrong with you earlier this fall.

Nothing... I don't know... there's nothing to tell.

That was the truth. All that happened was I got tired of people for a while. I didn't like to go out, didn't shower, and didn't pick up the phone except to call my office with elaborate excuses. The smell of my body became comforting, a ripe presence, nasty but familiar. I lay in bed telling myself that it was just a phase, it would pass. Eventually the bulb on my halogen lamp burned out and after two days of darkness I ventured out to buy a new one. The sunlight out on the street did something to my brain, or maybe it was the kind bald man who sold me the bulb. I went back to work.

So how are you? How's Neil?

Oh we broke up, she said. We had a big fight, and he couldn't see that I was right and he was wrong. It was high drama, in a restaurant with people watching, us screaming and stuff, and this fat waitress pushing between us using her tray as a shield and telling us to leave. So we finished it outside on the street, I made my points, one two three, and did my closing arguments. If we were in court I would have won.

I'm sorry, I said. Why didn't you tell me right away?

Oh, I didn't want you feeling bad for me. I'm glad, really. Small-minded jerk. Did I ever tell you he had all this hair on his back? Gray hair, like a silverback gorilla.

Yes, well. I don't know that I'll be seeing Piotr any more either.

That's too bad.

No, it's not.

* * *

That night as I lay in bed I thought of my mother and I felt my body for lumps the way she said she felt hers, and I put two fingers to the side of my throat. And I began to think of her and think of an undetected cancer, spreading through her body unnoticed. It began to dawn on me that I had done a very stupid thing.

I thought of her lying in bed beside my father at that moment, oblivious to the black thing that might be growing and thickening inside her, maybe in tough strands, maybe in little grainy bits, like oatmeal. She would avoid thinking about it for another six months or a year or two years; she'd deny it until her skin turned gray and she had tentacles growing out of her mouth and her breasts slid from her body and plopped on the floor like lumps of wet clay. Only when all that happened would she give in and say, Hmmm, maybe something is wrong, maybe I should see a doctor after all.

I lay awake for most of the night.

At one point I got up to use the bathroom, and as I sat on the toilet in the dark I suddenly became convinced that there was something horrible floating in the water below me. I was sure of it. A live rat. Or a length of my own intestines lying coiled bloody in the bowl. I sat there afraid to turn on the light and look, yet couldn't leave the bathroom without looking.

I sat there for half an hour, wracked with indecision. I think I fell asleep for a bit.

And when I finally forced myself to turn on the light, turn around and look—I was so convinced there would be something floating there that I was horribly shocked, my stomach lurched to see only the empty toilet.

I went back to work on Tuesday.

Did I miss anything? I asked one of the men.

You were gone? he said.

I didn't know his name; all the men who worked there looked alike. They were all too loud, and had too much spit in their mouths.

I had a cubicle all my own, but I dreamed of an office with a door I could close.

A few days later my father called. Your mother heard the results from the clinic, he said, the mammogram was fine.

That's great, I said.

She doesn't seem happy about it, he said, she's acting very strange.

Oh, I said.

What's going on, Lisa? he said. There's something fishy going on here.

Nothing, I said. Ask your wife, I said. Can I talk to her?

She just dashed out for an appointment, told me to call you. She said you'd be relieved.

Yes.

I'm going to call your sister now, she was waiting to hear. Or do you want to call her?

I'll do it, I said.

It seemed strange to me then that I would need to call Mich; a phone call implied distance, but our family seemed so close and entwined and entangled that we could hardly tell each other apart. Why should you need a phone to talk to someone who seems like she's living inside your skin?

We both went home for Christmas.

Later Mich visited them.

Then I visited.

Then it was Mich's turn again.

When I called home during Mich's visit my father said: Your mother was due for another mammogram, so I sent Lisa with her to make sure she goes.

You mean you sent Mich, I said. I'm Lisa.

Yes, right, you know who I mean.

A few days later my father called, his voice sounding strained. Your mother talked to the mammography clinic today, he said, but she won't tell me anything. She's been in her room, crying. She's been talking on the phone to your sister for an hour. I guess the doctors found something, but I'll let you know when we know for sure.

Okay.

I hung up and called Mich.

Hello, she said. She sounded like she was choking on one of her pens.

Mich, I said, it's yours, isn't it?

She sighed and said: It's ridiculous, but I thought I was doing her a favor, I thought I was sparing her some worry.

You went in for her, didn't you?

You know, Mich said, she's more worried about this than if she was the one with a lump in her breast. She feels like it's her lump, like it was meant for her, like she gave it to me somehow.

That's ridiculous, I said. I felt like I was talking to myself.

Although, you know, if it were possible, I would, Mich said. I mean, if there was somehow a way to magically take a lump out of her breast and put it in mine, I'd do it in a second.

I wish I could do that for you, I said.

Yeah, we could all share it.

One dessert and three forks, I said.

And later as I sat alone on the floor in the apartment I started to lose track of where I stopped and other people began, and I remembered standing in a white room with my breast clamped in the jaws of a humming machine, and I felt for the lump that I thought was mine, and sometimes I thought it was my mother's, and I imagined the mammogram pictures like lunar landscapes. Then I could not remember who had the lump anymore, it seemed we all did, it was my mother's my sister's and mine, and then the phone rang again and I picked it up and heard my father call out as he sometimes did: Leah-Lise-Mich.

A MOWN LAWN

by LYDIA DAVIS

SHE HATED a *mown lawn*. Maybe that was because *mow* was the reverse of *wom*, the beginning of the name of what she was—a *woman*. A *mown lawn* had a sad sound to it, like a *long moan*. From her, a *mown lawn* made a *long moan*. *Lawn* had some of the letters of *man*, though the reverse of *man* would be *Nam*, a bad war. A *raw war*. *Lawn* also contained the letters of *law*. In fact, *lawn* was a contraction of *lawman*. Certainly a *lawman* could and did *mow* a *lawn*. *Law and order* could be seen as starting from *lawn order*, valued by so many Americans. *More lawn* could be made using a *lawn mower*. A *lawn mower* did make *more lawn*. *More lawn* was a contraction of *more lawmen*. Did *more lawn* in America make *more lawmen* in America? Did *more lawn* make *more Nam*? *More mown lawn* made *more long moan*, from her. Or a *lawn mourn*. So often, she said, Americans wanted *more mown lawn*. All of America might be one *long mown lawn*. A *lawn* not *mown* grows *long*, she said: better a *long lawn*. Better a *long lawn* and a *mole*. Let the *lawman* have the *mown lawn*, she said. Or the *moron*, the *lawn moron*.

Christopher M. Connor
Chief Executive Officer
Sherwin-Williams
101 Prospect Avenue NW
Cleveland, OH
44115

Dear Mr. Connor,

You have many important things to do so I will get to the point. I have recently been writing letters to captains of industry, from the point of view of an Irish setter named Steven. Each letter is one-of-a-kind. Here is yours:

> There was a night that I ran like I was swimming in deep back water, but quieter. When I ran past other dogs, dogs I knew, silhouettes now or just legged bushes of black, they looked hollow. Samson's eyes, ice-blue in the daylight, were white and reflective. I went by as if carried by a current, not feeling my feet grabbing at the wet wet grass.

> I was running why because I wanted to feel the air cool the gaps in my fur. The sky was that gray-blue it is when there are clouds out after dark. The houses bent over me and I curved around trees. Damn I'm a fast dog!

> It's so fucking tiring to hear people talk. I hear everything they say, all at once. I mean, every time one of them opens their mouth, I hear them all talking, and hear everything they've all been saying for so long, and it's so much all the same thing, one long angry shrugging complaint. But I say: Hoooo! Hooooooo!

> You know how cheetahs run — how you never see their feet touch the ground? That's me, man — only when I run, my brain is circling my body at the same time — a hula hoop hooping around my head as I run like a fucking hovercraft!

> I'm just in love with all this.

Mr. Connor, I thank you for your time.

Daniel O'Mara
5811 Mesa Drive, #216
Austin, TX
78731

BANVARD'S FOLLY
(Or, HOW DO YOU LOSE A THREE-MILE PAINTING?)

by PAUL COLLINS

"Mister Banvard has done more to elevate the taste for fine arts, among those who little thought on these subjects than any single artist since the discovery of painting and much praise is due him."—*The London Times*

THE LIFE OF JOHN BANVARD is the most perfect crystallization of loss imaginable. In the 1850s, Banvard was the most famous living painter in the world, and possibly the first millionaire artist in history. Acclaimed by millions and by such contemporaries as Dickens, Longfellow, and Queen Victoria, his artistry, wealth, and stature all seemed unassailable. Thirty-five years later, this same man was laid to rest in a pauper's grave in a lonely frontier town in the Dakota Territory. His most famous works were destroyed, and an examination of reference books will not turn up a single mention of his name. John Banvard, the greatest artist of his time, has been utterly obliterated by history. What happened?

In 1830, a fifteen-year-old schoolboy passed out this handbill to his classmates, complete with its homely omission of a fifth entertainment:

BANVARD'S ENTERTAINMENTS
(To be seen at No. 68 Centre Street, between White and Walker.)

Spanish Gold Cross for Vittoria

Consisting of
1st. SOLAR MICROSCOPE
2nd. CAMERA OBSCURA
3rd. PUNCH & JUDY
4th. SEA SCENE
6th. MAGIC LANTERN
Admittance (to see the whole) SIX CENTS.
The *following* are the days of performance, viz:
Mondays, *Thursdays*, and *Saturdays*.
Performance to *commence* at half-past 3 P.M.
JOHN BANVARD, *Proprietor*

Although they were not to know, they were only the first of over two million to witness the showmanship of John Banvard. Visiting Banvard's home museum and diorama, they might have been greeted by his father Daniel, a successful building contractor and a dabbler in art himself. The adventurous son had acquired a taste for sketching, writing, and science—the latter pursuit beginning with a bang when an experiment with hydrogen exploded in the young man's face, badly injuring his eyes.

Worse calamities lay in store. When Daniel Banvard suffered a stroke in 1831, his business partner fled with the firm's assets. Daniel's subsequent death left the family bankrupt. After watching his family's possessions auctioned off, John "lit out for the territories"—to Kentucky, to be exact. Taking up residence in Louisville as a drugstore clerk, he honed his artistic skills by drawing chalk caricatures of customers in the back of the store. His boss, not interested in patronizing adolescent art, fired him. Banvard soon found himself scrounging for signposting and portrait jobs on the docks.

It was here that he met William Chapman, the owner of the country's first showboat. Chapman offered Banvard work as a scene painter. The craft itself was primitive by the standards of later showboats, as Banvard later recalled:

> The boat was not very large, and if the audience collected too much on one side, the water would intrude over the low gunwales into their exhibition room. This kept the company by turns in the un-artist-like employment of pumping, to keep the book from sinking. Sometimes the swells from a passing steamer would cause the water to rush through the cracks of the weatherboarding and give the audience a bathing... They made no extra charge for this part of the exhibition.

The pay proved to be equally unpredictable. But if nothing else, Chapman's showboat gave Banvard ample practice in the rapid sketching and painting of vast scenery—a skill that would prove invaluable later in life.

Deciding that he'd rather starve on his own payroll than on someone else's, Banvard left the following season. He disembarked in New Harmony, Ohio, where he set about assembling a theater company. Banvard himself would serve as an actor, scene painter, and director; occasionally, he'd dash onstage to perform as a magician. He funded the venture by suckering a backer out of his life savings, a pattern of arts financing that would haunt him later in life.

The river back then was still unspoilt—and unsafe. But the crew did last for two seasons, performing Shakespeare and popular plays while they floated from port to port. Few towns could then support their own theater, but they could afford to splurge when the floating dramatists tied up at the docks. Customers sometimes bartered their way aboard with chickens and sacks of potatoes, and this helped fill in the many gaps in the crew's menu. But eventually food, money, and tempers ran so short that Banvard, broke and exhausted from bouts with malarial ague, was reduced to begging on the docks of Paducah, Kentucky. While Banvard was now a toughened showman with years of experience, he was also still a bright, intelligent, and sympathetic teenager. A local theater impresario took pity on the bedraggled boy and hired him as a scenepainter. Banvard, relieved, quit the showboat.

It was a good thing that he did quit—farther downriver, a bloody knife fight broke out between the desperate thespians. The law showed up in the form of a hapless constable, who promptly stumbled through a trap door in the stage and died of a broken neck. With a dead cop on the their hands, the company panicked and abandoned ship; Banvard never heard from any of them again.

While in Paducah, Banvard made his first attempts at crafting "moving panoramas." The panorama—a circular artwork that surrounded the viewer—was a relatively new invention, a clever use of perspective that emerged in the late 1700s. By 1800, it was declared an official art form by the Institut de France. Photographic inventor L.J. Daguerre went on to pioneer the "diorama," which was a panorama of moving canvas panels viewed through atmospheric effects. When Banvard was growing up in Manhattan, he could walk a few blocks to gape at these continuous rolls of painted canvas depicting seaports and "A Trip to Niagara Falls."

Moving into his twenties with the memories of his years of desperate illness and hunger behind him, Banvard spent his spare time in Paducah painting landscapes and creating his own moving panoramas of Venice and Jerusalem; stretched between two rollers and operated on one side by a crank, they allowed audiences to stand in front and watch exotic scenery roll by. Banvard could not stay away from the river for long, though. He began plying the Mississippi, Ohio, and Missouri Rivers again, working as a dry goods trader and an itinerant painter. He also had his eye on greater projects: a diorama of the "infernal regions" had been touring the frontier successfully, and Banvard thought he could improve upon it. During a stint in Louisville, he executed a moving panorama that he described as "INFERNAL REGIONS, nearly 100 feet in length." He completed and sold this in 1841, and it came as a crowning success atop the sale of his Venice and Jerusalem panoramas.

It is not easy to imagine the effect that panoramas had upon their viewers. It was the birth of motion pictures—the first true marriage of the reality of vision with the reality of physical movement. The public was enthralled, and so was Banvard: he had the heady rush of an artist working at the dawn of a new media. Emboldened by his early successes, the twenty-seven-year-old painter began preparations for a painting so enormous and so absurdly ambitious that it would dwarf any attempted before or since: a portrait of the Mississippi River.

When we read of the frontier today, we are apt to envision California and Nevada. In Banvard's time, though, "the frontier" still meant the Mississippi River. A man setting off into its wilds and tributaries would only occasionally find the friendly respite of a town; in between he faced exposure, mosquitoes, and if he ventured ashore, bears. But Banvard had been up and down the river many times now, and had taken at least one trip solo as a traveling salesman. The idylls of river life had its charms and hazards, as he later recalled:

> All the toil, and its dangers, and exposure, and moving accidents of this long and perilous voyage, are hidden, however, from the inhabitants, who contemplate the boats floating by their dwellings and beautiful spring mornings, when the verdant forest, the mild and delicious temperature of the air, the delightful azure of the sky of this country, the fine bottom on one hand, and the romantic bluff on the other, the broad and the smooth stream rolling calmly down the forest, and floating the boat gently forward, present delightful images and associations to the beholders. At this time, there is no visible danger or call for labor. The boat takes care of itself; and little do the beholders imagine how different a scene may be presented in half an hour.

> Meantime, one of the hands scrapes a violin, and others dance. Greetings, or
> rude defiances, or trials of wit, or proffers of love to the girls on shore, or saucy
> messages, are scattered between them and the spectators along the banks.

Banvard knew the physical challenge that he faced and was prepared for it. But
the challenge to his artistry was scarcely imaginable. In the spring of 1842,
after buying a skiff, provisions, and a portmanteau filled with pencils and
sketch pads, he set off down the Mississippi River. His goal was to sketch the
river from St. Louis all the way to New Orleans.

For the next two years, he spent his nights with his portmanteau as a pillow, and his days gliding down the river, filling his sketch pads with river
views. Occasionally, he'd pull into port to hawk cigars, meats, household
goods, and anything else he could to sell to river folk. Banvard prospered at
this, at one point trading up to a larger boat so as to sell more goods. Recalling
those days to audiences a few years later—with a flair for drama, of course—he
remembered the trying times in between, when he was alone on the river:

> His hands became hardened with constantly plying the oars, and his skin as
> tawney as an Indian's, from exposure to the sun and the vicissitudes of the
> weather. He would be weeks altogether without speaking to a human
> being, having no other company than his rifle, which furnished him with
> his meat from the game of the woods or the fowl of the river... In the latter
> part of the summer he reached New Orleans. The yellow fever was raging in
> that city, but unmindful of that, he made his drawing of the place. The sun
> the while was so intensely hot, that his skin became so burnt that it peeled
> from off the back of his hands, and from his face. His eyes became inflamed
> by such constant and extraordinary efforts, from which unhappy effects he
> has not recovered to this day.

But in his unpublished autobiography, he recalled his travels a bit more benignly:

> The river's current was averaging from four to six miles per hour. So I made
> fair progress along down the stream and began to fill my portfolio with
> sketches of the river shores. At first it appeared lonesome to me drifting all
> day in my little boat, but I finally got used to this.

By the time he arrived back in Louisville in 1844, this adventurer had acquired
the sketches, the tall tales, and the funds to realize his fantastic vision of the

river he had traveled. It would be the largest painting the world had ever known.

Banvard was attempting to paint three thousand miles of the Mississippi from its Missouri and Ohio sources. But if his project was grander than any before, so were the ambitions of his era. Ralph Waldo Emerson, working the New England public lecture circuit, had already urged that "Our fisheries, our Negroes, and Indians, our boasts... the northern trade, the southern planting, the Western clearing, Oregon, and Texas, are yet unsung. Yet America is a poem in our eyes, its ample geography dazzles the imagination..." The idea had been voiced by novelists like Cooper before him, and later on by such poets as Walt Whitman. When Banvard built a barn on the outskirts of Louisville in 1844 to house the huge bolts of canvas that he had custom ordered, he was sharing in this grand vision of American art.

His first step was to devise a tracked system of grommets to keep the huge panorama canvas from sagging. It was ingenious enough to be patented and featured in a *Scientific American* article a few years later. And then, for month after month, Banvard worked feverishly on his creation, painting in broad strokes. Trained in background painting, he specialized in conveying the impression of vast landscapes. Looked at closely, this work held little for the connoisseur trained in conventions of detail and perspective. But motion worked magic upon the rough hewn cabins, muddy banks, blooming cotton-woods, frontier towns, and medicine show flatboats.

During this time he also worked in town on odd jobs, but if he told any-one of his own painting, we have no record of it. Fortunately, though, we have a letter from an unexpected visitor to Banvard's barn. Lieutenant Selin Woodworth had grown up a few houses away from Banvard and hadn't seen him in sixteen years, and he could hardly pass by in the vast frontier without saying hello. When he showed up unannounced at the barn, he was amazed by what maturity had wrought in his childhood friend:

> I called at the artist's studio, an immense wooden building.... the artist himself, in his working cap and blouse, pallet and pencil in hand, came to the door to admit us.... Within the studio, all seemed chaos and confusion, but the lifelike and natural appearance of a portion of his great picture, dis-played on one of the walls in a yet unfinished state.... A portion of this can-vas was wound upon a upright roller, or drum, standing on one end of the building, and as the artist completes his painting he thus disposes of it.
>
> Any description of this gigantic undertaking... would convey but a faint idea of what it will be when completed. The remarkable truthfulness of the

minutest objects upon the shores of the rivers, independent of the masterly and artistical execution of the work will make it the most valuable historical painting in the world, and unequaled for magnitude and variety of interest, by any work that has been heard of since the art of painting was discovered.

This was the creation that Banvard was ready to unveil to the world.

Banvard approached his opening day with the highest of hopes. Residents reading the *Louisville Morning Courier* discovered on June 29, 1846, that their local painter had rented out a hall to show off his work: "Banvard's Grand Moving Panorama of the Mississippi will open at the Apollo Rooms, on Monday evening, June 29, 1846, and continue every evening till Saturday, July 4." A review in the same paper declared that "The great three-mile painting is destined to be one of the most celebrated paintings of the age." Little did the writer of this review know how true this first glimpse was to prove: while it was to be the most celebrated painting of the age, it did not last for the ages.

Opening night certainly proved to be inauspicious. Banvard paced around his exhibition hall waiting for the crowds and the fifty cent admission fees to come pouring in. Darkness slowly fell, and a rain settled in. The panorama stood upon the lighted stage, fully wound and awaiting the first turn of the crank. And as the sun set and rain drummed on the roof, John Banvard waited and waited.

Not a single person showed up.

It was a humiliating debut, and it should have been enough to make him pack up and leave. But the next day saw John Banvard move from being a genius of artistry to a genius of promotion. He spent the morning of the thirtieth working the Louisville docks, chatting to steamboat crews with the assured air of one who'd navigated the river many times himself. Moving from boat to boat, he passed out free tickets to a special afternoon matinee.

Even if they had paid the full fee, the sailors would have got their money's worth that afternoon. As the painted landscape glided by behind him, Banvard described his travels upon the river—a tall tale of pirates, colorful frontier eccentrics, hair-breadth escapes, and wondrous vistas—a tad exaggerated, perhaps, but it still convinced a hall full of sailors that could have punctured his veracity with a single catcall. When he gave his evening performance, crew recommendations to passengers boosted his take to ten dollars—not bad for an evening's work in 1846. With each performance the audience grew, and within a few days he was playing to a packed house.

Flush with money and a successful debut, Banvard returned to his studio and added more sections to the painting and moved it to a larger venue. The crowds continued to pour in, and nearby towns chartered steamboats to see the show. With the added sections, the show stretched to over two hours in length; the canvas would be cranked faster or slower depending on audience response. Each performance was unique, even for a customer who sat through two in a row. The canvas wasn't rewound at the end of the show, so the performances alternated between upriver and downriver journeys.

After a successful shakedown cruise, Banvard was ready to take his "Three-Mile Painting" to the big city. He held his last Louisville show on October 31st and then headed for the epicenter of American intellectual culture: Boston.

Banvard installed his panorama in Boston's Armory Hall in time for the Christmas season. He had honed his delivery to a perfect blend of racy improvisation, reminiscences, and tall tales about infamous frontier brigands. The crank machinery was now hidden from the audience, and Banvard had commissioned a series of piano waltzes to accompany his narration. With creative lighting and the unfurling American landscape behind him, Banvard had created a seemingly perfect synthesis of media.

Audiences loved it. By Banvard's account, in six months 251,702 Bostonians viewed his extraordinary show; at fifty cents a head, he'd made about $100,000 in clear profit. In just one year, he'd gone from a modest frontier sign painter to famous and wealthy man—and probably the country's richest artist. When he published the biographical pamphlet *Description of Banvard's Panorama of the Mississippi River* (1847) and a transcription of his show's music, it brought in even more money. But there was an even happier result to his inclusion of piano music—the young pianist he'd hired, Elizabeth Goodman, soon became his fiancée, and then his wife.

Accolades continued to pour in, culminating in a final Boston performance that saw the Governor, the Speaker of the House, and state representatives in the audience unanimously passing a resolution to honor Banvard. His success was also the talk of Boston's intellectual elite. John Greenleaf Whittier titled a book after it (*The Panorama and Other Poems*) in 1856, and Henry Wordsworth Longfellow wrote about the Mississippi in his epic *Evangeline* after seeing one of Banvard's first Boston performances. Longfellow had never seen the river himself—to him, the painting was real enough to suffice. In fact, Longfellow was to invoke Banvard again in his novel *Kavanaugh*, using him as the standard by which future American literature was to be judged: "We want a national epic that shall correspond to the size of the country; that shall be to all other epics what Banvard's panorama of the Mississippi is to all other paintings—the largest in the world."

There is little doubt that Banvard's "Three-Mile Painting" was the longest ever produced. But it was a misleading appellation. John Hanners—the scholar who has almost single-handedly kept Banvard's memory alive in our time—points out that: "Banvard always carefully pointed out that others called it three miles of canvas... . Since the area in its original form was 15,840 square feet, not three miles in linear measurement."

But perhaps Banvard was in no hurry to correct the public's inflated perceptions of his painting. His fame was now preceding him, and he moved his show to New York City in 1847 to even bigger crowds and greater enrichment; it was hailed there as "a monument of native talent and American genius." Each night's receipts were carted to the bank in locked strong boxes; rather than count the massive deposits, the banks simply started weighing Banvard's haul.

With acclaim and riches came the less sincere flattery of his fellow artists. The artist closest upon Banvard's heels was John Rowson Smith, who had painted a supposed "Four-Mile Painting." For all Banvard's tendencies toward exaggeration, there is even less reason or evidence to believe that his opportunistic rivals produced panoramas larger than his. Still, it was a worrisome trend. Banvard had been hearing for some time of plans by unscrupulous promoters to copy his painting and to then show the pirated work in Europe as the "genuine Banvard panorama." With the US successfully behind him, Banvard closed his New York show and booked a passage to Liverpool.

Banvard spent the summer of 1848 warming up for his London shows with short runs in Liverpool, Manchester, and other smaller cities. Reaching London, the enormous Egyptian Hall was booked for his show. He began by suitably impressing the denizens of Fleet Street papers with a special showing. "It is impossible," *The Morning Advertiser* marveled, "to convey an adequate idea of this magnificent [exhibition.]" *The London Observer* was equally impressed in its review of November 27, 1848: "This is truly an extraordinary work. We have never seen a work... so grand in its whole character." Banvard was rapidly achieving a sort of artistic beatification in the press.

The crowds and the money flowed in yet again. But to truly bring in the chattering classes, Banvard needed something that he'd never had in the United States: the imprimatur of royalty. After much finagling and plotting by Banvard, he was summoned to Windsor Castle on April 11, 1849, for a special performance to Queen Victoria and the royal family. Banvard was already a rich man, but royal approval could make the difference being a mere artistic show-man and an officially respected painter. Banvard gave the performance of his life, delivering his anecdotes in perfect combination with his wife at the piano; at the end, when he gave his final bow to the family assembled at St. George's Hall, Banvard knew that he had made it as an artist. For the rest of his life, he was to look back upon this as his finest hour.

His panorama show was now a sensation, running for a solid twenty months in London to over 600,000 spectators. An enlarged and embellished reprint of his autobiographical pamphlet, now titled *Banvard, or the Adventures of an Artist* (1849), also sold well to Londoners, and his show's waltzes could be heard in many a parlor. He penetrated every level of society; after attending one show, Charles Dickens wrote to him in an admiring letter: "I was in the highest degree interested and pleased by your picture." To the other dwellers of this island nation, whose experience of sailing was often that of stormy seas, Banvard offered the spice of frontier danger blended with the honeyed idylls of riverboat life:

> Certainly, there can be no comparison between the comfort of the passage from Cincinnati, New Orleans, in such a steamboat, and to a voyage at sea. The barren and boundless expanse of waters soon tires upon every eye but a seaman's. And then there are storms, and the necessity of fastening the tables, and of holding onto something to keep in bed. There is the insup-portable nausea of sea sickness, and there is danger. Here you are always near the shore, always see green earth, can always eat, write and study, undisturbed. You can always obtain cream, fowls, vegetables, fruit, fresh meat, and wild game, in their season, from the shore.

Toward the end of these London shows, Banvard found himself increasingly dogged by imitators—there were fifty competing panoramas in the 1849–50 season alone. In addition to longtime rival John Rowson Smith, Banvard now had scurrilous accusations of plagiarism flung at him by fellow expatriate portraitist George Caitlin, a jealous painter who had "befriended" Banvard in order to borrow money. Banvard also found his shows being set upon by the spies of his rivals, who hired art students to sit in the audience and sketch his work as it rolled by.

We know that a form of art has permeated a culture when such cheap imitations appear, and even more so when parodies of these imitations emerge. There is a long-forgotten work in this vein by American humorist Artemus Ward, which was published posthumously as *Artemus Ward, His Panorama* (1869). Ward spent the last years of his life working in London, and had probably attended some of the numerous panoramic travelogues and travesties that darted about in Banvard's wake. His panorama, as shown by illustrations of the supposed stage (which, as often as not, is obscured by a faulty curtain), consists of a discourse on San Francisco and Salt Lake City, often interrupted by crapulous bits of tangential mumbling in small type:

> If you should be dissatisfied with anything here to-night—I will admit you all free in New Zealand—if you will come to me there for the orders.

> This story hasn't anything to do with my Entertainment, I know—but one of the principle features of my Entertainment is that it contains so many things that don't have anything to do with it.

For ads reproduced in the book, Ward munificently assures his audiences that his lecture hall has been lavishly equipped with "new doorknobs." But Banvard's most serious rivals were not such bumblers, and so he had to swing back into action. Locking himself in the studio again, he created another Mississippi panorama. Where the first panorama had been a view of the eastern bank, this new painting depicted the western bank. He then placed the London show in the hands of a new narrator, and toured Britain himself with the second painting for two years, bringing in nearly 100,000 more viewers.

What might Banvard have done with these two paintings had he placed them on stage together? Angled in diagonally from each side to terminate just behind the podium, moving in unison, they would have provided a sort of stereo-optical effect to the audience of floating down the center of the Mississippi River. It would have been the first "surround multimedia." For all of Banvard's innovation, though, there is no record of such an experiment.

Not all of Banvard's time in London was spent on his own art. In his spare hours, he haunted the Royal Museum; he was fascinated by its massive collection of Egyptian artifacts. He soon became a protégé of the resident Egyptologists, and under their tutelage he learned to decipher hieroglyphics—the only American of his time, by some accounts, to learn this skill. For decades afterward, he was able to pull sizable crowds to his lectures on the reading of hieroglyphics.

Banvard moved his show to Paris, where his success continued unabated for another two years. He was now also a family man: a daughter, Gertrude, was born in London, and a son, John Jr., was born in Paris. Having children scarcely slowed down his travels; on the contrary, he left the family to spend the next year on an artistic pilgrimage to the Holy Land. In a reprise of his American journey, he sailed down the Nile and filled up notebooks with sketches. But he no longer had to sleep with these notebooks as a pillow. He was now wealthy enough to travel in comfort, and he bought thousands of artifacts along the way—a task assisted by his unusual ability at translating hieroglyphics.

These travels were to become the basis for yet two more panoramas: one of the Palestine, and the other of a trip down the Nile. Neither were to earn him as much as his Mississippi panorama; the market was now flooded with imitations, and the public was beginning to weary of the panoramic lecture. Even so, Banvard's abilities were greater than ever. As one American reviewer commented in 1854 in *Ballou's Pictorial Drawing Room Companion*:

> Mr. Banvard made a name and fortune by his three mile panorama of the Mississippi. It was one of those cases in which contemporary justice is bestowed upon true merit... His sole teacher in his art is Nature; there are few conventionalisms in his style. His present great work is far superior in artistic merit to his Mississippi—showing his rapid improvement; its effect is enhanced by its great height.

Just eight years after his voyage down the Mississippi, he had become both the most famous living artist in the world and the richest artist in history.

Banvard returned to the US with his family in the spring of 1852. He was a fantastically wealthy man, enough so that he could retire to a castle and casually dabble in the arts for the rest of his life. And at first that's exactly what he did.

The world's most famous artist needed an equally imposing home to live in; accordingly, he bought a sixty-acre lot on Long Island and proceeded to build a replica of Windsor Castle. When the local roads didn't meet the needs of his castle, he simply built one of his own. He dubbed the castle "Glenada" in honor of his daughter, Ada; neighbors, who were alternately aghast and awed by the unheard-of construction expenses being incurred, simply dubbed it "Banvard's Folly."

A reporter touring the site was kinder in his appraisal of Banvard's castle:

> It has a magnificent appearance, reminding you forcibly of some of the quaint old castles nestled among the glens of old Scotland.... There are nine offices on the first floor, as you enter from the esplanade, viz., the drawing room, parlors, conservatory, ante room, servant's room, and several chambers. The second story contains the nursery, school room, guest chambers, bath, library, study, etc., with the servants' rooms in the towers. The basement is occupied with the offices, store rooms, etc. Although the facade extends in front one hundred and fifteen feet, still Mr. Banvard says his castle is not completed, as he plans arranged for adding a large donjon, or keep, to be occupied by his studio, painting-room, and a museum for the reception of the large collection of curiosities which he has gathered in all parts of the world.... It has been proposed to change the name of the place [Cold Spring Harbor] and call it BANVARD...

Not surprisingly, the residents of the town failed to see the charm of this last proposal.

Still, Banvard spent the next decade in relative prosperity and modest continued artistic success. Indeed, his artistic horizons broadened each year. In 1861, he provided the Union military with his own hydrographic charts of the Mississippi River. General Fremont wrote back personally to thank him for his expert assistance. That same year, Banvard provided the illustration for the first successful chromolithograph in America. The process was unique in duplicating both the color and the canvas texture of the original illustration, which Banvard had titled "The Orison." The result was a tremendous success, and helped assure his continued reputation as a technically innovative artist.

Banvard then turned his attention back to his first love: the theater. "Amasis, or, The Last of the Pharaohs" was a massively staged "biblical-historical" drama that ran in Boston in 1864. Banvard had both written the play and painted its enormous scenery, and was gratified by its warm reception among critics. It seemed to him that there was nothing that he could not succeed at.

* * *

Even as Banvard displayed his Egyptian artifacts to guests at Glenada, the role of museum was changing rapidly in America. By 1780, the "cabinet of wonder" kept by wealthy dilettantes had evolved into the first recognizable museum, operated by Charles Peale in Philadelphia. Joined by John Scudder's American Museum in New York, these museums focused on educational lectures and displays—illustrations and examples of unusual natural objects, as well as the occasional memento.

This all changed when P.T. Barnum bought out Scudder's American Museum in 1841. Barnum brought in a carnivalesque element of equal parts spectacle and half-believable fraud—a potent and highly salable concoction of freak shows, dioramas, magic acts, natural history, and the sheer unrepentant bravado of acts like Tom Thumb and "George Washington's nursemaid." Barnum was not an infallible entrepreneur, but he was the shrewdest showman that the country had ever produced. Imitators attracted by Barnum's success soon found themselves crushed under the weight of Barnum's one-upmanship and his endless capacity for hyperbolic advertising.

By 1866, Barnum's total ticket sales were greater than the country's population of thirty-five million. John Banvard, with a castle full of actual artifacts, could scarcely ignore the fortune Barnum was making just a few miles away with objects of much more questionable provenance. Goaded by this, he paid a visit to his old sailing partner William Lillienthal. It had been over fifteen years since the two had floated down the Nile, collecting the artifacts that now formed the core of Banvard's collection.

With Lillienthal's help—and a lot of investors' money—Banvard was going to take on P.T. Barnum. Their venture was precarious from the start. Aside from the daunting task of taking on America's greatest showman, Banvard was hampered by his own inexperience. Years of panoramic touring and a successful play had convinced Banvard that he could run a museum, but he had never really run a conventional business with a staff and a building to maintain. In all his years as a showman, he'd earned millions with the help of only one assistant, a secretary who he eventually fired for stealing a few dollars.

Lillienthal and Banvard financed the Banvard Museum by floating a stock offering worth $300,000. In lieu of cash, they paid contractors and artisans with shares of this stock; other shares were bought by some of the most prominent families in Manhattan. There was one problem, though; Banvard had never registered his business or its stock with the state of New York. No share certificates existed for the stock. Unbeknownst to Banvard's backers, and perhaps to Banvard himself, the shares were utterly worthless.

Flush with the money of the unwary, Banvard's Museum raced toward completion.

When the massive 40,000-square-foot building opened on June 17, 1867, it was simply the best museum in Manhattan. The famous Mississippi panorama was on stage in a central auditorium that seated 2,000 spectators, and there were a number of smaller lecture rooms and displays of Banvard's hand-picked collection of antiquities. The lecture rooms were important, as Banvard had invited in student groups for free to emphasize the family-friendly educational qualities of his museum, as opposed to Barnum's sensationalism. The museum also had one genuine crowd-pleaser built right in: ventilation. Poor auditorium ventilation was a constant complaint dogging panoramist shows, and Banvard took the initiative to install louvres and windows all the way around his auditorium.

P.T. Barnum had met a serious challenger in John Banvard. One week after Banvard's opening, Barnum ran ads in *The New York Times*, crowing that his own museum was "THOROUGHLY VENTILATED! COOL! Delightful!! Cool!!! Elegant, Spacious, and Airy Halls." This was hardly true, of course; Banvard's building was far superior, and Barnum knew it. But Barnum had a grasp of advertising that not even Banvard could match. The rest of the summer was to see America's greatest showmen—and its first entertainment millionaires—locked in an economic struggle to the death.

With each stab at innovation by Banvard, Barnum would parry with inferior copies but superior advertising. Banvard had the Mississippi panorama; Barnum had a Nile panorama, probably copied from Banvard's. Banvard had the real Cardiff Man skeleton; Barnum had a fake. On and on the showmen battled throughout the summer, with the stage and the newspapers as their respective weapons of choice.

The struggle ended with shocking speed. Banvard was in far over his head; creditors were dunning him for payments, and shareholders were furious over the discovery that their stock had been worthless all along. On September 1st— scarcely ten weeks after opening—Banvard's Museum padlocked its doors shut.

Banvard improvised furiously. The building reopened one month later as Banvard's Grand Opera House and Museum. Productions dropped in and out over the next six months—first a leering dance production, then adaptations of *Our Mutual Friend* and *Uncle Tom's Cabin*. None were successful. Unable to make anything work, Banvard finally leased out the building to a group of promoters that included—perhaps to his chagrin—P.T. Barnum.

Banvard spent the next decade with the barest grasp on solvency, and then only by quietly appropriating lease money that should have been going to shareholders and other creditors. He and his wife lived virtually alone on their rambling sixty-acre estate; they were down to one servant for the whole property. After his shoddy treatment of the museum backers, no New Yorker would want to invest in a Banvard enterprise now; he wrote two more plays only to find that no producer would take them.

If his financial ethics were suspect, Banvard's artistic integrity was suffering even more. The innovator had been reduced to plagiarism: first in his history book, *The Court and Times of George IV, King of England* (1875), which was lifted from a book written in 1831; and then again the next year, when he finally managed to write a play that opened in his old museum, now named the New Broadway Theatre. *Corrina, A Tale of Sicily* was not only plagiarized, but it was plagiarized from a living and thoroughly annoyed playwright.

Humiliated and surrounded by creditors, Banvard desperately sought a buyer for his theater. P.T. Barnum, when approached, sent a crushing reply back to his old rival: "No sir!! I would not take the Broadway Theatre as a gift if I had to run it." When Banvard finally did unload his decrepit building in 1879, he had to watch its new owners achieved exactly where he had failed. As Daly's Theatre, the building thrived for decades before finally being torn down in 1920.

Banvard's castle was not to be as long-lived as his museum. Banvard and his wife clung to Glenada for as long as they could, but by 1883, their deep entanglement in bankruptcy forced them to sell it off. It eventually fell to the wrecking ball, and virtually all their other possessions were sold off to meet the demands of creditors. But the Mississippi panorama was spared from the auction block—now worn from nearly forty years of use, and nearly forgotten by public, perhaps it was judged to be worthless anyway.

Banvard and his wife were now both well into their sixties, and with scarcely any money to their name. They packed their few remaining belongings and quietly left New York. The only place left for them was what Banvard had left so long ago: the lonely, far-off American frontier. He was returning as he had left, a poor and forgotten painter.

* * *

It was a deeply humbled and aged John Banvard that arrived in the frontier town of Watertown, in present-day South Dakota. He and his wife, the recent proprietors of a castle, had been reduced to living in a spare room of their son's house. Eugene Banvard was an attorney with some interest in local public works and construction projects, and occasionally the elder Banvard renewed his energies of yore by pitching in with his son on these projects.

For the most part, though, Banvard retreated into his writing. He was to write about 1,700 poems in his life—as many as Emily Dickinson—and like her, he only ever published a few of them. Unlike the more dubious plays and histories that he had "authored," his poems appear to be original to Banvard, and sincere if not particularly innovative efforts. Taking up the pen name of "Peter Pallette," Banvard wrote hundreds of poems during his years in Watertown, becoming the state's first published poet. One of Banvard's more sustained efforts, published in Boston back in 1880 as "The Origin of the Building of Solomon's Temple," centered on the biblical brothers Ornan and Araunah. It opens with a standard Romantic invocation:

> I'll tell you a legend, a beautiful legend;
> A legend an Arab related to me.
> We sat by a fountain beneath a high mountain,
> A mountain that soar'd by the Syrian sea:
> When a harvest moon shewed its silvery sheen,
> Which called into thought the Arabian's theme.

The book's epilogue descends into a miscellany of details about English church building, Egyptian obelisks, and loony speculations about Masonic oaths, a subject of apparently inexhaustible interest to the author.

On a more practical note, Banvard also authored a pocket-sized treatise on *Banvard's System of Short-Hand* (1886)—one of the first books published in the Dakota Territories. He claimed it could it be learned within a week, and that he had been using it for years, keeping in practice by surreptitiously transcribing conversations on buses and ferry boats: "The author acquired the knowledge of shorthand precisely in this manner when he was but a youth.... He has many of these little volumes now in his possession and they have become quite of value as forming a daily journal of these times."

For transcription practice, Banvard included his own poems and pithy maxims, such as, "He jests at scars who never felt a wound." Banvard had felt some wounds himself of late, and more were to come before his strange journey came to an end. But that same year, now into his seventies, he locked himself in his studio one last time, ready to produce a final masterpiece.

Dioramas and panoramas were no longer a novelty by 1886, and Edison's miraculous work in motion pictures was just over the horizon. If the art form hadn't aged well, neither had its greatest proponent—along with the usual infirmities of age and his ruined finances, Banvard's eyesight had worsened with age. His eyes had never been terribly strong since his childhood laboratory mishap. Still, even now he could muster a certain heartiness. "In his mature years his appearance was like that of many Mississippi River pilots," said one contemporary. "A thickset figure, with heavy features, bushy dark hair, and rounded beard."

Nonetheless, Banvard's family was uneasy with his notions of taking the show on the road one last time, as his daughter later recalled: "My mother and the older members of the family were quite averse to his giving [the performance], as they felt his health was too impaired for him to attempt it." If the older members of the family were against it, one can imagine the solace Banvard took in his grandchildren, who were only now seeing the family patriarch revive the art that had made him rich and famous long before they were even born.

For his diorama, Banvard had chosen a cataclysm still in the living memory of many Americans: "The Burning of Columbia." Most of the capital city of South Carolina was burnt to the ground by General Sherman's troops in a daylong conflagration on February 17, 1865. Banvard's rendition of it was by all accounts a magnificent performance. Even more impressively—in an echo of his humble beginnings—Banvard ran the diorama and a massed array of special effects as a one-man show. As one audience member recalled:

> Painted canvasses, ropes, windlasses, kerosene drums, lycopodium, screens, shutters, and revolving drums were his accessories. Marching battalions, dashing cavalry, roaring cannon, blazing buildings, the rattle of musketry, and the din of battle were the products, resulting in a final spectacle beyond belief, when one considers it was a one man show.
>
> I have read of the millions expended in the production of a single modern movie, but when I remember what John Banvard did and accomplished in a spectacular illusion in Watertown, Dakota Territory, more than fifty years ago for an outlay of ten dollars, I am rather ashamed of Hollywood.

For all the spectacle, though, Banvard's day had long passed. Dakota was simply too sparsely populated to support much of a traveling show, and the artist found himself packing away the scrims, drums, and screens for one last time, never to be used again.

A few years later, in 1889, his wife Elizabeth died. They had been married for over forty years; as is so often the case in a long companionship, the spouse followed not long afterward. A visitor to his Watertown grave will scarcely guess from the simple inscription that this had once been the world's richest artist:

JOHN BANVARD

Born

Nov. 15, 1815

Died

May 16, 1891

As word of his death reached newspapers back east and in Europe, editors and columnists expressed amazement: how could this millionaire have died penniless on a lonely frontier? Had they sought to get any answers from his family, though, they would have come up empty-handed. Unable to pay their bills, the Banvards all fled town after the funeral.

In their haste to evacuate their house on 513 Northwest 2nd St., they had left much behind, and an auction was held by creditors. Among John Banvard's remaining possessions was a yellowed scrap of paper listing his unpaid $15.51 bill for his own father's funeral service in 1831. Young John had spent his life haunted by his father's lonely death and humiliating bankruptcy. Sixty years later, still clutching the shameful funeral bill, he had met the same fate.

So where are his paintings?

His early panoramas of the Inferno, Venice, and Jerusalem were lost in a steamboat wreck in the 1840s. A few small panels are scattered across South Dakota; The Robinson Museum, in Pierre, has three. Two more are in Watertown; the Kampeska Heritage Museum has "River Scene with Glenada," while the Mellette Memorial Association has a hint of the "Three-Mile Painting" with "Riverboats in Fog."

And what of the paintings that made his fame and fortune, the ingenious moving panoramas? One grandson, interviewed many years later, remembered playing on the massive rolls when he was little. But after the elder Banvard's death, they lay abandoned to the auctioneer. As Edith Banvard recalled in a 1948 interview: "I understood that part of it was used for scenery... in the Watertown opera house." From there, she conjectured, the rolls may have cut into pieces and sold as theater backdrops. Worn from decades of touring, and torn from their original context as moving pictures, they might have seemed little more than old rags. Not surprisingly, no record is known of what theaters might have done with them.

One persistent account, however, holds that Banvard's masterpieces never left Watertown at all. They were shredded to insulate local houses—and there, imprisoned in the walls, they remain to this day.

CROSS-DRESSER
THE WRITTEN TESTIMONY OF CAPTAIN JEFFREY DUGAN, 418TH SQUADRON BANDIT #573

by GABE HUDSON

MY NAME IS Captain Dugan and at the request/demand of Dr. Barrett, I am writing all this down. She says that only if I write all this down will she be able to make a strong case for me to her superior, Dr. Hertz. I have never actually seen this Dr. Hertz, and so I have to take Dr. Barrett at her word that this Dr. Hertz even exists. Otherwise, Dr. Barrett says, if I don't write down my side of it, then legally they will have no choice but to keep me here at the neuropsych ward at Holloman AFB, because she said that a sane man has nothing to hide, whereas a crazy man is full of secrets. To which I said, "Well I'm sure as hell not crazy." That's when she pushed this pencil and paper across the table and said, "So prove it."

If I am to do myself justice, then I suppose I should start with a thesis remark, and so here it goes: this world is strange, and to me it is all very sinister and miraculous. If you don't agree with me now perhaps you will agree with me by the time you are done reading this. Before I begin it's important to me that I establish credibility, which means I want to say that I'm not nearly as dumb as I look. Because the truth is that how I look is not who I really am (and I'm just not saying this just because I'm short either.) Probably other people have this secret too, that how they look is not who they really are. Though sometimes I forget about this until I look in the mirror and then I'm like, "Oh God, not him again. There must be some mistake." But then I'm like, "Okay, what the hell, might as well: I mean it's not like I have a choice or anything."

Hanoverian Medal for Waterloo

Then I get in my F-117A Stealth Fighter which I call Gracie and fly up into the sky and kill people. Or at least I have, in the Persian Gulf, for which I was awarded the Silver Star, and I'm sure I'll have to kill some more people when I get out of here. Word on the base right now is Somalia's going to be the next hot spot. This is what I do for a living, and I try to have fun with it, since it's my job. I zoom around the earth in a sleek, black, weapon of mass destruction and I'd be lying if I didn't admit that it's a serious rush to be in the cockpit, because when I'm up there in the sky it's like I'm straight out of God's head, a divine thought inside a divine thought bubble, totally invisible.

Except that day when I got my ass shot out of the sky in Iraq and crashed Gracie in the desert. Right in the middle of a ramshackle military compound where I was taken as a POW and sadistically tortured by a one-eared man named The Mule. I didn't feel so invisible then.

Here is where I should mention my curse. This will explain some things. I was born with a gift. Or a curse depending on how you look at it. It's my dreams. My dreams let me see into the future. I know it sounds bizarre but as proof to support this claim I'll tell you that three nights ago I had a dream in which I saw myself wearing a dark blue dress and red high heels (just like I am now) and sitting in a padded room with one arm handcuffed to a chair (just like I am now), writing a document that started, "My name is Captain Dugan and at the request/demand of Dr. Barrett, I am writing all this down." I should also probably mention that that dream had a happy ending because in that dream Dr. Barrett read over my statement proclaiming that I was innocent (which is the same thing I shouted when I felt the MP's tranquilizer dart stick in my hip) and then in the dream Dr. Barrett let me return to active duty (just like you will after you read this) after concluding that if anything I was merely compassionate to a fault, completely sane, and that I am a victim of my wife's vindictive, ridiculous accusation that I am some sort of sicko transvestite pervert.

The mission was supposed to be simple. A routine sortie, clear skies, fly low and blow up some oil refineries south of Nukhayb, and then get the hell out of there. I was sitting around with Captain Jibs and Colonel Cowry under the tent, this was in Khamis Mushait, trying to stay out of the heat, sipping on a cold one when I got the word. I remember downing my beer and standing up in the same motion, and then slamming the bottle on the table and looking at

Jibs and Cowry with a grin and saying, "Back in a jiff boys. Desert Storm calls." Then I hopped in Gracie and hit the wide Arabian sky. Well when I came up on the oil refinery below me I saw three Iraqi soldiers jumping up and down on barrels, waving white flags attached to sticks.

I let them have it. I swooped down and dropped a GBU-10 bomb, and my stomach was lit up with that smoky, mystical sensation you get when you kill something, which is virtually indescribable, though I can say for sure that it's the only time I can feel God really watching me: it's a good way to make Him sit up and take notice. And so there I was, basking in God's gaze, the wreckage smoking below me, when that son-of-a-bitch Iraqi fighter dropped in out of nowhere and tried to *kill me*, shooting my tail wing to tatters.

Gracie skittered forward among the clouds like a bumper car. I was dazed. I smelled smoke. The Emergency Gear Extension handle was stuck. Then I tried to duck and roll but Gracie was shimmying all over the place and I was in a spin, streaking toward the earth like a comet, and I watched in horror on the Multi-Function Display as the desert's giant yellow jaws rose up and then opened wide and swallowed me whole.

When I came to I was strapped in a chair with a light-bulb hanging over my head. There were cracks of sunlight coming through the bamboo walls. After blinking a few times I saw that I was in a small hut with three Iraqi soldiers. This was the place I would come to call The Shack. It had the stink of fear in it. The soldiers were smoking and laughing about something, and one of them had his hands up in front of him, squeezing the air, like there were breasts. Then the one squeezing the air heard me moan and after glancing in my direction put two fingers in his mouth and whistled loud through the tiny barred window in the door. The door swung open and a small man with one ear walked directly up to me and cracked my jaw with a bully-stick. My jaw was instantly dislocated, and I toppled over with the chair to the floor. Through the scream trapped in my head I heard the men laugh, and then the one-eared man said, "Hello. My name is The Mule. I have some questions for you. You will answer, no?"

I gasped for air. It felt like my mouth had been knocked up into my forehead. I tried to say something and the top of my head opened up. I slowly squirmed forward a few feet, knees and elbows, dimly aware that the soldiers were watching my progress with detachment, and I heard one of them chuckle and mutter, "Americana." Finally I pushed my jaw hard up against a wall and then clink, with the sound of a camera shutter, my jaw popped back into place, and the relief flooded up my spine in waves of ecstasy. The relief never really went away after that. So that two hours later when The Mule struck me across the jaw for what seemed like the hundredth time I was almost, but not quite, grateful.

Instead I spit out some teeth.

From there on out it's mostly a blur. Because of the pain, I only remember images and flashes, smells, and finally, the taste of blood in my mouth. The Mule wanted me to make a propaganda videotape.

The Mule said, "If you ever want to see your family again."

The Mule said, "This is not too much to ask. You will be a movie star."

The Mule said, "I am losing my patience, Captain Dugan."

The Mule said, "That looks like it hurts, Captain Dugan."

I didn't say anything. I kept my mouth shut, but not because I was feeling patriotic, because to tell the truth I couldn't care less about my country at that moment, but because I was sure that if I did it, make the videotape, then they wouldn't have any more use for me and they would kill me.

The Mule whipped out this handheld Sears Craftsman electric drill. I had my focus back. He revved the trigger a few times and the drill made a squealing sound. Then he walked over to me and placed the drill to the back of my head. "Perhaps now you make the video?"

I gave him a look. I said, "Please don't do this."

The Mule smiled. "Have it your way, Captain Dugan."

"Please," I said. "No."

Then I felt the bit of the drill push hard against my skull. It was very quiet, and I could see everything, even though I had my eyes closed. All the hairs in The Mule's nose. The three soldiers that were now standing outside The Shack. One of them was thrusting his hips back and forth like he was having sex. The other two were laughing. A vulture flew by overhead. Then I saw The Mule's index finger slowly push down on the orange plastic trigger of the drill, and the roar of the drill's motor was deafening, and I felt the bit push in and break the skin around my skull.

As you can imagine, this thing with my dreams hasn't always been easy. I've never told anyone about it, not my wife, Mrs. Dugan, and certainly not my daughter Libby, when she was alive, may she rest in peace. And of course I don't always like what I see (the future is not always pleasant), but by far the worst part is the guilt. God, the guilt. It's like it's my fault. Which is to say I always end up feeling like these things happened *because* I dreamt them first, like the time my next door neighbor Mr. Gordon's Tricksy turned on him and bit his thumb off. Now it's true I have never liked this Mr. Gordon, given the fact that he got drunk at a neighborhood barbecue last year and grabbed my wife's right breast in front of everyone and said, "Knock knock," and then she, albeit drunk, smiled in a coy way and said, "Who's there," which was of course completely humiliating for me, but that's really beside the point, because it's not like I wished Mr. Gordon would get his thumb bit off. But I dreamt it. And then it happened, and so you tell me, how can I not feel a little bit responsible?

All told, The Mule put six quarter-inch holes in the back of my head. I was barely conscious. When it was all over I remember looking up in a steamy haze as The Mule smiled and said, "You are a very stubborn man, Captain Dugan." I was vaguely aware of him putting my ankles in shackles, which were clamped to a stake in the middle of the floor. Then The Mule said, "Perhaps you will die. Perhaps not. But if not, you will be hungry. And maybe when you're hungry, well maybe then you will make the videotape. Good-bye for now, Captain Dugan," and then he slipped out the door.

After that things went downhill fast. I was alone with my madness. You've heard it all a hundred times before. The whole POW thing. I went to hell and back in my mind. I gave up hope. My soul was a pink worm stuck through its belly with a hook, and I waited for the Angel of Death to come swimming up out of the darkness and swallow it whole.

That was the first day.

The second day was worse. The second day I started hearing my thirteen-year-old daughter Libby's voice. I knew it was an illusion, but still. I was sitting with my back against the wall and there were flies buzzing around my head. I heard Libby's voice say, "Lieutenant Jeff Dugan, this is your daughter speaking. Get a hold of yourself. Snap out of it. Yes, it's true, things don't look good, but I'm here to help. You are a Lieutenant in the United States Air Force, and this is war, so keep your wits about you. A little cunning can carry you through."

I realized Libby's voice wasn't inside my head. I looked up and there standing with her back to the door was Libby. Or at least some sort of wavy version of her. She was surrounded by a white, wavy energy. She was well dressed, with fine leather loafers, off-white hose, and a green cashmere turtleneck. Her nose was, as always, small.

I couldn't believe the stupid tricks my mind was playing on me. "You're kidding right?" I said. "Is this some sort of joke?"

"No, Daddy. It's me. Libby."

I didn't know what to say. "Alright then," I said. "Why are you all wavy?"

"Because," she said, and then she told me everything. She said she was dead. She told me about how her Siamese cat Smoky Joe had run out in front of a red Chevy and how she had saved Smoky Joe, but was hit and killed in the process. When she was through I spoke up.

"This is ridiculous. How I am supposed to believe something like that?" I started beating my head with my fist. "Hello? Hello? I know you're in there brain. I know you're behind this. I expected more from you. Stop it now."

I could tell by the look on Libby's face that she wasn't interested in my cynicism. Her brow was wrinkled and she was chewing on her bottom lip.

"Look. You aren't real. This is a trick, it's the stress. Please go away. I can't take this."

"Come on. I'm here to help, Daddy," she said. "We've got to get you out of here. Mommy can't lose both of us."

I could feel my temper start to rise. "Yeah right. Listen you, whatever the hell you are. You're starting to piss me off."

"Shhhhh. Now that's enough. We don't have time. I have to go now, but I'll be back tomorrow to help you escape," and with that Libby turned and stepped into the wall and passed through it out of sight.

The next morning I woke to someone kicking me in the shins. "Wake up. What are you doing? Sleeping in?" I looked and saw Libby. She was all business. "Okay," she said. "I've been spying in and listening to what they have been saying. Things are getting nuts up there. I think they're planning some sort of attack. The leader seems like a real jerk. You don't want to cross this guy, trust me."

"Ooooh, I'm scared," I said. I pointed to my head. "I've got six holes drilled into my head, and now I've got some wavy figment of my imagination telling me I'm in trouble. Give me a break. What can you tell me about trouble that I don't already know?"

"Daddy, they're going to hang you in the courtyard today. Now. You and some other pilot they captured. They want to make an example of you two, to boost morale before the attack," she said.

"I told you. You're not real." I put my hands over my eyes. "I can't see you."

She kept on. "Okay. So here's what you're going to do. They're coming to get you any minute now. We need to move fast. I'm going to let you out of those shackles. You bend down and act like you're hurt. Then grab the guard's pistol and hit him over the head with it."

I suddenly froze. Because it was true, I could hear the guard rustling his keys on the other side of the door. My mouth went dry.

Two seconds later the guard came in and I was lying on the floor, doubled over, pretending to be in pain. "Oh my God, oh my God," I cried.

There was also the time when I was nine. This dream was much fuzzier than the rest, but when I woke in the dead of night I was sweating, and though I couldn't remember what happened I knew my Mom was in danger. And then the next night, right before dinner, I watched as my mother cut a carrot on the cutting board, and wasn't at all surprised when she looked up to tell me to set the table and sliced off her index finger. On the way to the hospital in the ambulance I kept sobbing, "I'm so sorry. I'm so sorry. I'm so sorry."

But the most disturbing dream of all happened two weeks before I had to ship out to Saudi to fight in the Gulf War. This is extremely difficult for me to talk about even now. The dream was swift and simple. I saw my thirteen-year-old daughter Libby run out in the street and get hit and killed by a red Chevy when she tried to shoo her Siamese cat Smoky Joe out of the way. Smoky Joe lived. Smoky Joe is short for Smoky Joe the Best Kitty Cat in the World.

And so now you understand. Because each of these events—the thing with Mr. Gordon, the thing with my Mom, the thing with Libby—have one thing in common. Each of these things happened in my dream before they happened in reality.

When I burst through the front door of The Shack the sunlight almost split my eyes open but then my pupils shrank and I bounded off toward Gracie. To my horror, as I ran over to Gracie, I spotted Captain Jibs hanging by his neck from a rope in the center of the courtyard. A group of soldiers were standing around with their backs to me, jeering at Jibs, throwing rocks at him and spitting on him. When I reached Gracie I checked behind the seat and all my gear was still there, untouched. I threw on my flak jacket. While I was rifling through my pack I heard a shout and looked up, and there in the doorway of The Shack was the guard rubbing the back of his head. He shouted something in Arabic and pointed at me. The mob around Jibs turned and looked in my direction. There was a moment of silence, and then when they saw me they started screaming and shouting and running.

A siren went off. Dogs started barking.

I took the guard's Beretta 9mm pistol and leapt out of Gracie and ran straight at a parked M60 tank, shooting rounds off left and right, and two men dropped. I ran up the side of the tank and off of it, doing a forward flip, with bullets flying everywhere. I saw a wounded man on the ground reaching for something in his belt. Shot him.

I leapt with my legs wide open and landed on a camel and shouted, "Huyaaa!" and I rode that camel fast and hard into the middle of the windstorm of bullets and swarm of Iraqi soldiers. The Mule appeared directly in my path, and the camel skidded to a halt. The Mule said, "This was very stupid, Captain Dugan," and then lobbed a frag grenade. The grenade was in midair when I ripped off my flak jacket and held it in front of the camel's face. The grenade went off and all the shrapnel bounced off my flak jacket. I think that's when the camel knew that I was a compassionate animal. I shouted, "Little help," and the camel rushed forward and head-butted The Mule.

Looking down at The Mule on the ground in that instant, I felt the strangest sensation in my belly button. It felt like my belly button was wiggling around. It was a widening sensation. When I reached down to touch my belly button I felt a hole in my stomach the size of a silver dollar. My index finger disappeared in the hole, but there was no blood. Just this hole. And then I passed out.

When I came to the camel was galloping over the desert. That was the sound I woke to, the steady bric-a-brac of the camel's hooves on the desert floor. My chest kept bouncing against the camel's hump. The sun was just starting to come up, a blood red squirting over the horizon as if someone had stuck the sun in a juicer, and I could see the faint silver sliver image of the moon on the other side of the sky. When I looked behind me the Iraqi camp was a pinpoint on the horizon. "Thank God," I said. "I almost ate it on that one." But as soon as the words were out of my mouth I realized I had no idea who I was, and I started to panic. I couldn't even remember why I was out here in the desert. I asked myself a question.

When you want to start thinking where do you start?

I didn't know the answer.

My heart jumped up a couple decibels. Still I kept on, riding and pondering my question for as long as I could stand it, but then my brain was suddenly tired from all that thinking, so eventually I figured that until I got my memory back I should keep it simple. The best I could come up with was this: you are a person. You are alive. You are riding a camel.

So I rode through the desert on a camel with no name.

I rode for days and days and days, without food and water. I didn't know where I was going, and hadn't even given it a thought. The sun, that great ball of fire, came up and went down and came up and went down and came up and went down more times than I could count. I watched my haggard shadow do its mindless dance on the desert floor and I watched the horizon.

Once a vicious sandstorm came up in a blur and ate my uniform right off my body. I kept my eyes closed the whole time. The storm came and went. I was completely naked. The camel galloped on like it was in a race against time.

Then one day I looked up and saw ahead of me a palm tree and an oasis of clear blue water. The water shimmered in the heat. My camel had been stumbling throughout the day, and I knew it wasn't long for this world. I considered throwing the camel over my back and carrying him, but I decided against it. I was so thirsty my tongue felt like a balled-up piece of paper in my mouth. I shook my head, and took another look to make sure this wasn't a trick my mind was playing on me. At the sight of the water my camel picked up its pace again, with renewed enthusiasm. It broke into a trot. That camel was amazing. It had a heart of gold. I shouted, "Thata boy! Thata boy!" and the shout came out as a whisper. We were getting closer and closer. I tried to smile but my lips were exhausted.

And then the camel stumbled, faltered, and came crashing down face first, and I was pitched forward, airborne, right to the bank of the oasis. I scraped my knee in the sand. The camel was lying on the ground, floundering like a newborn colt, trying to get back up. It was elegant. It was tragic. I felt like I was witnessing the secret of the universe in the camel's effort. Then it let out a tremendous, "Harrrrumpppp," and its soul flew out toward the world beyond.

I named the camel Applejack.

I know you're thinking what's the point in naming something after it's dead and the answer is: well I don't know. But I did it.

The water was a plate of glass. I don't think I ever saw anything so beautiful as that oasis. When I slipped into the water I could feel the weeks of agony and fear wash off me like a bad cologne. I was clean.

More days passed. This was a time of joy. This was something different than I had ever known. I ate coconuts out of the tree. I didn't understand what was happening, but when I looked at my reflection in the water I thought, "You could be pretty." I let my hair grow out. I put on lipstick that I made from tree sap. I spent most of my time looking down at my reflection. I built a hut out of palm fronds. I made a two-piece bikini bathing suit.

Days days and more days.

Finally I thought: "Alright already. It doesn't really matter who I am, everyone needs love. People sound like a pretty good idea." So I set off on foot. I had been walking for centuries. I turned and looked and saw my footprints in the sand as far back as I could see. The entire desert stretched out before me. One day it snowed. Right there in the desert. I know it sounds weird but it did. I was so relieved to be out of the heat that I ran around catching snowflakes on my tongue. I built a snowman named Bert. I shook the snowman's hand and said, "Hi, Bert," and Bert's arm broke off in my grip. Why had Bert's arm broken off but not mine? I laughed out loud because I was so grateful that I still had two arms. I laughed harder than I have ever laughed. I laughed so hard I almost choked on my beard. It seemed to me that the snowman was laughing too but then Bert said, "Okay. Here's the deal. Your name is Lieutenant Dugan. That's your first clue. People are looking for you. Follow me. I'm going to lead you back to your base."

And that's exactly what Bert did.

Well it turned out I'd been lost in the desert for six months. And back at Khamis Mushait, I got the POW recovery treatment, which was nice, because I certainly was tired. I slept for three days straight. And it was only afterward, when I woke up and called my wife and she told me that six months before Libby had been killed by a red Chevy that everything came flooding back into my mind. Because it was then that I remembered how Libby's ghost had appeared and helped me escape from the compound, and it was only then that I truly understood what happened to me out there, what that thing with my belly button was.

My Dad didn't want me to die, and so he leapt out of his body and forced me into it, because he wanted me to live. My Dad couldn't bear the guilt. That's what that thing with the belly button was. He was leaving his body, and pushing me into it. That's how much my Dad loved me.

So this is me, Libby. I am a thirteen-year-old girl living inside an Air Force Captain's body. It was the only way. I hide my identity from the rest of the people in my life. I conduct myself as an Air Force pilot and I report for duty at Holloman AFB and take Gracie up for training runs. It's not so hard to be a Captain in the Air Force, and plus my Dad's body remembers how to do every-thing, so it's a cinch. And like I said, when I'm up there in the cockpit it's like I'm straight out of God's head, a divine thought inside a divine thought bub-ble, totally invisible. Some times I feel bad for my Mom, because she doesn't know the truth and I can't tell her. She wouldn't believe me if I did anyway. It would just cause her unnecessary pain.

When I got back to Holloman AFB they awarded me a Silver Star and bumped my rank up to Captain. Then my first day home, my Mom drove me out to the cemetery to visit my grave, or should I say the grave where my old body is buried. I forced a tear out for Mom's benefit. The plot was nice. There was an oak tree with a crow in it. On my gravestone it said, "Libby Dugan, Beloved Daughter, Too Good To Be True." Of course sometimes at night Mom tries to get frisky in bed, but I turn her away. She thinks it's because I'm sad, and she tries to talk to me about it. She says, "I know what's bothering you. But we can get past this. Libby's in Heaven now. Life is too beautiful for us to be sad. And we still have each other." But then recently she's started getting mad. She'll start yelling and telling me that the flower inside her is drying up. Well I always change the subject because it makes me feel funny. Or I'll roll out of bed and go out to the back porch and smoke a cigarette.

Smoky Joe is the only one who knew the truth. He followed me every-where, rubbing on my shins and jumping into my lap whenever he got the chance. I guess he was grateful to me for saving his life. Sure I was glad to see him too, but he was also causing me massive problems. Because Mom would come home and see Smoky Joe lying on my chest, and say, "That's weird isn't it, Jeff? I thought Smoky Joe hated you, Jeff. Since you've been home he won't leave you alone." Well I started to suspect that Mom was on to me. She'd give me these funny looks whenever I tied ribbons to Smoky Joe's tail, or gave him Liver Treats. Threads were starting to unravel. My story was coming loose. I couldn't sleep at night, and then I'd look down at the foot of the bed and there would be Smoky Joe, staring at me, purring. So it shouldn't come as any surprise that one brisk morning I accidentally backed over Smoky Joe in our driveway with my Ford Bronco.

Other than that it's all good, and sometimes when Mom's still at work I come home early from the base and lock all the doors to the house and close the curtains and take all the phones off the hook. Then I go to the back of the closet, where I keep some things in a trash bag that I don't want anyone to know about. I tape my penis down between my legs and put on a pair of flowered panties. I put on one of my Mom's dresses and too much lipstick and eyeliner and admire myself in the big mirror in the living room. On special occasions when I imagine that I am going to a royal ball, I put on long white gloves that come up to my elbows. I curtsy, and in my mock elegant voice I say, "And how do you do? You look so lovely tonight dear. Tea? Yes, please. Well, thank you, you are such a darling."

Which is what I was doing today when Mom came home early and walked in on me holding our video camera. When I saw Mom come through the front door I leapt back out of sight and dove into the closet. I guess she saw me because she rushed over and started banging on the door and shouted, "Jeff, I know you're in there. Come out, Jeff. We need to talk. I know what you're doing. I've known about this for weeks. There's no need to hide this anymore, Jeff. I got you on videotape this time. We need to talk!"

Well I started getting nervous, with her banging on the door like that. I was trying to figure a way out of this, where nobody's feelings got hurt, and nobody ended up learning more than he or she needed to know. My mind was on fire. But at least you know I'm not crazy. Dr. Barrett, at least now you know. You make sure you tell this Dr. Hertz as much. You make sure he reads every single word I've written. And surely now you can understand the logic of my thesis remark: this world is strange, and to me it is all very sinister and miraculous.

While I was in the closet I resolved to make a break for it. I was going to bolt out of there and streak over to my Bronco and zoom away before my Mom could see me. But I didn't know that my Mom knew that that was exactly what I would try to do. I didn't know that my Mom had already been in touch with you. I didn't know that when I burst through the closet door and ran out onto the lawn that there would be MPs with tranquilizer guns waiting for me. I didn't know.

THE GIRL WITH BANGS

by ZADIE SMITH

I FELL IN LOVE with a girl once. Some time ago, now. She had bangs. I was twenty years old at the time and prey to the usual rag-bag of foolish ideas. I believed, for example, that one might meet some sweet kid and like them a lot—maybe even marry them—while all the time allowing that kid to sleep with other kids, and that this could be done with no fuss at all, just a chuck under the chin, and no tears. I believed the majority of people to be bores, however you cut them; that the mark of their dullness was easy to spot (clothes, hair) and impossible to avoid, running right through them like a watermark. I had made mental notes, too, on other empty notions—the death of certain things (socialism, certain types of music, old people), the future of others (film, footwear, poetry)—but no one need be bored with those now. The only significant bit of nonsense I carried around in those days, the only one that came from the gut, if you like, was this feeling that a girl with soft black bangs falling into eyes the color of a Perrier bottle must be good news. Look at her palming the bangs away from her face, pressing them back along her hairline, only to have them fall forward again! I found this combination to be good, *intrinsically* good in both form and content, the same way you think of cherries (life is a bowl of; she was a real sweet) until the very center of one becomes lodged in your windpipe. I believed Charlotte Greaves and her bangs to be good news. But Charlotte was emphatically bad news, requiring only eight months to take me entirely apart; the kind of clinically efficient dismembering you see when a bright child gets his hand on some toy he assembled in the first place. I'd never dated a girl before, and she was bad news the way boys can never be, because with boys it's always possible to draw up a list of pros and cons, and see the matter rationally, from either side. But you could make a list of cons on Charlotte stretching to Azerbaijan, and "her bangs" sitting solitary in the pros column would outweigh all objections. Boys are just boys after all, but sometimes girls *really seem to be* the turn of a pale wrist, or the sudden jut of a hip, or a clutch of very dark hair falling across a freckled forehead. I'm not saying that's what they really are. I'm just saying sometimes it seems that way, and that those details (a thigh mole, a full face flush, a scar the precise shape and size of a cashew nut) are so many hooks waiting to land you. In this case, it was those bangs, plush and dramatic; curtains opening on to a face one would queue up to see. All women have a back-stage, of course, of course. Labyrinthine, many-roomed, no doubt, no doubt. But you come to see the show, that's all I'm saying.

I first set eyes on Charlotte when she was seeing a Belgian who lived across the hall from me in college. I'd see her first thing, shuffling around the communal bathroom looking a mess—undone, always, in every sense—with her T-shirt tucked in her knickers, a fag hanging out of her mouth, some kind of tooth-paste or maybe mouthwash residue by her lips and those bangs in her eyes. It was hard to understand why this Belgian, Maurice, had chosen to date her. He had this great accent, Maurice, *elaborately* French, like you couldn't *be* more French, and a jaw line that seemed in fashion at the time, and you could tick all the boxes vis-à-vis personal charms; Maurice was an impressive kind of a guy. Charlotte was the kind of woman who has only two bras, both of them gray. But after a while, if you paid attention, you came to realize that she had a look about her like she just got out of a bed, no matter what time of day you collid-ed with her (she had a stalk of a walk, never looked where she was going, so you had no choice) and this tendency, if put under the heading "QUALITIES THAT GIRLS SOMETIMES HAVE," was a kind of poor relation of "BEDROOM EYES" or "LOOKS LIKE SHE'S THINKING ABOUT SEX ALL THE TIME"—and it worked. She seemed always to be stumbling away from someone else, toward you. A limping figure smiling widely, arms outstretched, dressed in rags, a smouldering city as backdrop. I had watched too many films, possibly. But still: a bundle of pre-cious things thrown at you from a third-floor European window, wrapped loose-ly in a blanket, chosen frantically and at random by the well-meaning owner, slung haphazardly from a burning building; launched at you; it could hurt, this bundle; but look! You have caught it! A little chipped, but otherwise fine. Look what you have saved! (You understand me, I know. This is how it feels. What is the purpose of metaphor, anyway, if not to describe women?)

Now, it came to pass that this Maurice was offered a well-paid TV job in Thailand as a newscaster, and he agonized, and weighed Charlotte in one hand and the money in the other and found he could not leave without the promise that she would wait for him. This promise she gave him, but he was still gone, and gone is gone, and that's where I came in. Not immediately—I am no thief—but by degrees; studying near her in the library, watching her hair make reading difficult. Sitting next to her at lunch watching the bangs go hither, and, I suppose, thither, as people swished by with their food trays. Befriending her friends and then her; making as many nice noises about Maurice as I could. I became a boy for the duration. I stood under the window with my open arms. I did all the old boy tricks. These tricks are not as difficult as some boys will have you believe, but they are indeed slow, and work only by a very gradual process of accumulation. You have sad moments when you wonder if there will ever be an end to it. But then, usually without warning, the hard work pays off. With Charlotte it went like this: she came by for a herbal tea one day, and I rolled a joint and then another and soon enough she was lying across my lap, spineless as a mollusk, and I had my fingers in those bangs—teasing them, as the hairdressers say—and we had begun.

Most of the time we spent together was in her room. At the beginning of an affair you've no need to be outside. And it was like a filthy cocoon, her room, ankle deep in rubbish; it was the kind of room that took you in and held you close. With no clocks and my watch lost and buried, we passed time by the degeneration of things; the rotting of fruit, the accumulation of bacteria, the rising-tideline of cigarettes in the vase we used to put them out. It was a quarter past this apple. The third Saturday in the month of that stain. These things were unpleasant and tiresome. And she was no intellectual; any book I gave her she treated like a kid treats a Christmas present—fascination for a day and then the quick pall of boredom; by the end of the week it was flung across the room and submerged; weeks later when we made love I'd find the spine of the novel sticking into the small of my back, paper cuts on my toes. There was no bed to speak of. There was just a bit of the floor that was marginally clearer than the rest of it. (But wait! Here she comes, falling in an impossible arc, and here I am by careful design in just the right spot, under the window, and here she is, landing and nothing is broken, and I cannot believe my luck. You understand me. Every time I looked at the bangs, the bad stuff went away.)

Again: I know it doesn't sound great, but let's not forget the bangs. Let us not forget that after a stand-up row, a real screaming match, she could look at me from underneath the distinct hairs, separated by sweat, and I had no more resistance. *Yes, you can leave the overturned plant pot where it is. Yes, Rousseau is an idiot if you say so.* So this is what it's like being a boy. The cobbled street, the hopeful arms hugging air. There is nothing you won't do.

Charlotte's exams were coming up. I begged her to look through her reading list once more, and plan some strategic line of attack, but she wanted to do it her way. Her way meant reading the same two books—Rousseau's *Social Contract* and Plato's *Republic* (her paper was to be on people, and the way they organize their lives, or the way they did, or the way they should, I don't remember; it had a technical title, I don't remember that either)—again and again, in the study room that sat in a quiet corner of the college. The study room was meant to be for everyone but since Charlotte had moved in, all others had gradually moved out. I recall one German graduate who stood his ground for a month or so, who cleared his throat regularly and pointedly picked up things that she had dropped—but she got to him, finally. Charlotte's papers all over the floor, Charlotte's old lunches on every table, Charlottes clothes and my clothes (now indistinguishable) thrown over every chair. People would come up to me in the bar and say, "Look, Charlotte did X. Could you please, for the love of God, stop Charlotte doing X, *please?*" and I would try, but Charlotte's bangs kept Charlotte in the world of Charlotte and she barely heard me. And now, please, before we go any further: tell me. Tell me if you've ever stood under a window and caught an unworthy bundle of chintz. Gold plating that came off with one rub; faked signatures, worthless trinkets. Have you? Maybe the bait was different—not bangs, but deep pockets either side of the smile or unusually vivid eye pigmentation. Or some other bodily attribute (hair, skin, curves) that recalled in you some natural phenomenon (wheat, sea, cream). Same difference. So: have you? Have you ever been out with a girl like this?

*　*　*

Some time after Charlotte's exams, after the 2.2 that had been stalking her for so long finally pounced, there was a knock on the door. *My* door—I recall now that we were in my room that morning. I hauled on a dressing-gown and went to answer it. It was Maurice, tanned and dressed like one of the Beatles when they went to see the Maharashi; a white suit with a Nehru collar, his own bangs and tousled hair, slightly long at the back. He looked terrific. He said, "Someone in ze bar says you might have an idea where Charlotte is. I need to see 'er—it is very urgent. Have you seen 'er?" I had seen her. She was in my bed, about five feet from where Maurice stood, but obscured by a partition wall. "No..." I said. "No, not this morning. She'll probably be in the hall for breakfast though, she usually is. So, Maurice! When did you get back?" He said, "All zat must come later. I 'ave to find Charlotte. I sink I am going to marry 'er." And I thought, *Christ, which bad movie am I in?*

I got Charlotte up, shook her, poured her into some clothes, and told her to run around the back of the college and get to the dining hall before Maurice. I saw her in my head, the moment the door closed—no great feat of imagination, I had seen her run before; like a naturally uncoordinated animal (a panda?) that somebody has just shot—I saw her dashing incompetently past the ancient walls, catching herself on ivy, tripping up steps, and finally falling through the swing doors, looking wildly round the dining hall like those movie time-travellers who know not in which period they have just landed. But still she managed it, apparently she got there in time, though as the whole world now knows, Maurice took one look at her strands matted against her forehead, running in line with the ridge-ways of sleep left by the pillows, and said, "You're sleeping with her?" (Or maybe, "You're sleeping with *her?*"—I don't know; this is all reported speech) and Charlotte, who, like a lot of low-maintenance women, cannot tell a lie, said "Er ... yes. Yes" and then made that signal of feminine relief; bottom lip out, air blown upward; bangs all of a flutter.

Later that afternoon, Maurice came back round to my room, looking all the more noble, and seemingly determined to have a calm man-to-man "you see, I have returned to marry her / I will not stand in your way" type of a chat, which was very reasonable and English of him. I let him have it alone. I nodded when it seemed appropriate; sometimes I lifted my hands in protest but soon let them fall again. You can't fight it when you've been replaced; a simple side-step and here is some old/new Belgian guy standing in the cobbled street with his face upturned, and his arms wide open, judging the angles. I thought of this girl he wanted back, who had taken me apart piece by piece, causing me nothing but trouble, with her bangs and her antisocial behaviour. I was all (un)done, I realized. I sort of marvelled at the devotion he felt for her. From a thousand miles away, with a smoldering city as a backdrop, I watched him beg me to leave them both alone; tears in his eyes, the works. I agreed it was the best thing, all round. I had the impression that here was a girl who would be thrown from person to person over years, and each would think they had saved her by some miracle when in actual fact she was in no danger at all. Never. Not even for a second.

He said, "Let us go, zen, and tell 'er the decision we 'ave come to," and I said yes, let's, but when we got to Charlotte's room, someone else was putting his fingers through her curls. Charlotte was always one of those people for whom sex is available at all times—it just happens to her, quickly, and with a minimum of conversation. This guy was some other guy that she'd been sleeping with on the days when she wasn't with me. It had been going on for four months. This all came out later, naturally.

Would you believe he married her anyway? And not only that, he married her after she'd shaved her head that afternoon just to spite us. All of us—even the other guy no one had seen before. Maurice took a bald English woman with a strange lopsided walk and a temper like a gorgon back to Thailand and married her despite friends' complaints and the voluble protest of Aneepa Kapoor, who was the woman he read the news with. The anchorwoman, who had that Hitchcock style: hair tied back tight in a bun, a spiky nose and a vicious red mouth. The kind of woman who doesn't need catching. "Maurice," she said, "you *owe* me. You can't just throw four months away like it wasn't worth a bloody thing!" He emailed me about it. He admitted that he'd been stringing Aneepa along for a while, and she'd been expecting something at the end of it. For in the real world, or so it seems to me, it is almost always women and not men who are waiting under windows, and they are almost always disappointed. In this matter, Charlotte was unusual.

THE HYPNOTIST'S TRAILER

by ANN CUMMINS

A WOMAN, JOSEPHINE, read an ad in the advertiser one day: *Addiction Therapist. Can Cure Anything. Hypnotism; Psychic Massage.* Josephine smoked, and she drank a little bit, too. She decided to give the hypnotist a try. She took her daughter along.

The hypnotist lived and worked in a trailer on a paved lot at the base of Stone Mountain. He was a hairy man but his teeth were straight and his fingernails clipped. His place was sparsely furnished, a rattan couch, a tweedy chair. No little vases, no magazines.

"Let's skip the preliminaries and get right down to it," the hypnotist said. "Do you believe in God?"

"Yes," Josephine said.

"What does he look like?"

This confused her.

"Does he have a beard?"

"Oh, yes."

"I have a beard."

"Yes you do."

"He has long hair and brown eyes, too."

Josephine supposed he did.

In short order, the hypnotist convinced her that she was in the presence of God.

"Do you believe that God can deliver you from your sins? Will you put your trust in the Lord?"

She did. She would.

"Give me a token of your trust, then."

"Token?"

"Something you value. Your purse perhaps."

The daughter—Irene was her name—laughed, and a shadow crossed the hypnotist's face. He glanced at the girl. She was pretty in a trashy way. Her face was white with makeup, and her eyes were lined with green. She wore her hair in a half-shaved, half-dyed style, which he hated. She was a skinny thing, though. He liked skinny things, and he felt a sudden urge to involve her.

"Your daughter was right to laugh," he said. "A purse is just a thing."

Josephine smiled at the girl; Irene rolled her eyes.

"Give me something you truly value," the hypnotist said. He winked at the girl. "Give me your daughter."

Irene laughed. "Yeah, Mom. Give me to him."

"My daughter?" Josephine frowned. Irene caused Josephine countless sleepless nights and tormented days. Josephine looked at the hypnotist who was stroking his beard, eyeing the girl. To her surprise, the man's face began to change—to lose its rough and flabby cheeks and nose, to smooth and tighten.

Suddenly she threw her arms around Irene. "You can't have her!" she hissed.

The hypnotist raised his eyebrows, then looked at his feet.

"It's all my fault she's bad," Josephine whispered.

"I can see that," he whispered back.

Irene slipped out from her mother's grasp. She was pleased to be noticed. But also bored. She began kicking her foot, fidgeting. The hypnotist frowned. Boredom was not good. Boredom broke the mood. He ran his tongue over his teeth, leaned forward, smiled at Josephine, and said, "Give me your belly button."

"What?" Josephine said.

"Give me your navel."

The girl grinned. This she liked.

"Give it to me," he whispered.

The woman looked down. She lifted her shirt, pushed down her skirt, and looked at it. What did he mean, give it to him? Was it like what you did with kids when you pretended to take their noses? She looked at her daughter. Irene nodded. It must be like what you did with kids. Josephine laughed. She reached down and grabbed her belly button. It came off in her hand. She stared at it. It was flat as a penny, but as she watched the ends began to curl up.

"Good," the hypnotist said.

She pushed it against her middle, trying to reattach it. Her ears were ringing. It wouldn't stay.

"Only God can put it back," the hypnotist said. "You see. You didn't trust after all."

"I didn't," she wailed. She held the navel in her right hand. Her throat had thickened, and her temples were throbbing. She felt like crying.

"I will take good care of it because I believe you value it. Do you hear what I'm saying to you, Josephine? I believe you."

She looked at him. "You believe me?"

"I believe you, and I believe in you!" He said this with such conviction that her throat opened, and tears came to her eyes.

"Let me see it for a minute," he said.

"See it?"

"Just for a minute."

"Why?"

"To heal it. It's dying. Look at it."

She opened her hand. The navel had curled up into a little ball. It was brown and wrinkled. Her hand began to shake violently.

"Here." He covered her hand with both of his. "There, there," he said. "Now I have it. It's OK." And he began to stroke it.

She watched closely. At first, she could see no difference, but then she noticed that the color was changing. Was the color changing? Yes. The color was fading, and the thing was growing. It was, with each stroke, flattening out to its original shape, and it was turning a sort of peachish. She smiled. He was fixing it.

"Now," he said. "How's that? Better?"

"Yes," she whispered. She held out her hand, but he did not give it back.

"I want to talk to you about something, Josephine."

"Oh," Josephine said. She sat back in her chair. She knew whatever he was going to say was right. She drank too much. She smoked too much. She laced her fingers over her stomach. Without her navel, she felt naked.

"Did you notice how easily this came off?" She swallowed. "That wouldn't happen in a healthy person." He looked at the daughter. She had her elbow on her knee, her chin in her hand; she was absorbed by something outside the window.

"In a healthy person, the center is vibrant; it's elastic. Shall I show you?" He began to wave his hand over the navel. "Watch it," he whispered. The little thing in the middle of his palm began to throb, and to fill with color. He touched its edges. He licked his finger and ran it around the rim. He looked at the girl. She was really a very pretty girl. He admired the haughty turn of her head, the regal line of her ear, the curve of her jaw—the awkward neck, the long and turtleish neck that would, when she was older and fatter, lose its sinewy grace, but now turned elegantly at the clavicle. He followed the line of her neck, under the skimpy halter to the bare and pointed shoulder, down to the rose tattooed on her arm, back up to the shoulder, and down along the teenage breast which curved nicely, not too full, not too flat, there against the thin cotton. He closed his eyes and ran his finger slowly along the lip of the navel. "Look," he whispered. "Watch me make it grow."

Josephine, watching, saw her navel turn a translucent white, the color of a communion host, a shimmering world from a cold and beautiful night—God's night—and it had grown. When he held it at a certain angle, tilted slightly toward her, she saw the moon, and saw herself reflected in it. It was hers! She laughed.

The hypnotist opened his eyes. He looked at the mother, at her slack jaw and gleaming eyes, and he laughed, too. "Look," he said. He twirled the thing on his finger. "Watch this." He tossed it in the air, and it began to wobble, to redden, and smell a little like perfume. The disc was changing from orange to red to pink, undulating, and Josephine began sliding up and down in her chair, and her skirt hiked up. He stared at her thigh. It was a nasty little thigh, plump and unmuscled, just the way he liked them.

"Stand up," he commanded. "Turn around."

Irene glanced from the window to see her mother dancing in slow, snaky circles, running her tongue over her lips, rubbing her hands over herself. Her mother—a reserved woman. Her mother was from a line of reserved women. Even when she was drunk, her mother would wander around the house tucking things in. But now she began catching her skirt and pulling it up, shimmying up and down, and the man's tongue was resting between his teeth. His eyes were little beads in his face. "Bend over," he whispered. Josephine bent at the waist, shook her head between her knees.

"Mom?" Irene said.

The hypnotist leaned back in his chair, clasped his hands behind his head, and said, "Well, hello, Josephine."

"Hey!" Irene said. The man glanced at the girl. Irene glared stonily at him, and he sneered. He looked her up and down, then looked into her eyes and saw his own reflection, an ugly fat man. He looked closer. Stared into the contempt of Irene's eyes and saw himself as she saw him—a flabby-skinned, dim-eyed, feeble-gummed half man, looked further then and saw the man he would become: his lips began to turn inward, and his skin to hang from his sharpened cheekbones, his eye sockets to protrude, and his eyes to sink. Irene, caught in his stare, saw his shoulders begin to bow, his chest under his shirt to sink, his hands and lips and head to shake. His aged face was a mesh of tiny broken blood vessels, blue and red, and his eyes were pupil-less pools of pain, dank, sludgy bogs oozing tears.

In spite of herself, Irene's young throat constricted, and her heart was moved to pity; she heard a bird call, and began to notice a faint odor in the room.

The hypnotist glanced out the window at the mountain with its nothing-colored surface and stone-cold center, at this scenic stupor where they'd made him park his trailer.

He looked at Josephine, whose face was red, whose eyes were mostly pupil. His heart flexed. He curled his lip.

"OK, now," he whispered, and the woman straightened. She smoothed her skirt, perched on the couch, put her fingers to her lips, glanced cautiously at her daughter who seemed to be listening to something. Josephine shivered.

"OK, now, watch it shrink." Josephine sat back and watched. The hypnotist took down the moon which had been hovering over his head and began to fold it in triangles, each triangle smaller than the last, and when it was the size of his hand, he began to mold it into a glowing sphere. He covered it with his other hand, closed his eyes, opened them, opened his hand, and there was her navel again, a perfect little peach disc, flat as a penny, but with the little spiral in the middle. He smiled and held it out to her. She started to reach for it when he opened his fingers. "Oops," he said. "I dropped it." He laughed an ugly laugh.

"You dropped it?" Josephine said.

"Where'd it go?" he said.

"You dropped it?" she said again, and there was a tremor, something that could have been fear, or perhaps anger, in her voice.

"Where is it?" he said.

Josephine was staring at the floor. "I don't know," she said. She dropped to all fours. She began heaving, then hiccuping and sobbing. "Renie, it's lost."

"What's lost?" Irene shook herself, rubbed her eyes, saw her mother crawling around on the floor. "What's lost?"

He picked his foot up, studied the bottom of his shoe, seemed to scrape something off the bottom, winked at Josephine. He popped the thing in his mouth. Josephine's mouth dropped open and her eyes bulged.

"What's lost?" Irene demanded.

The hypnotist shrugged. "Everything," he said. His right cheek poofed like a chipmunk's. "I have eaten the plum she gave me. It was cold," he said. "So delicious." He opened his mouth, fluttered his purple tongue. And then he swallowed. He sat back and licked his lips. "Another satisfied customer."

Irene scowled. "Nothing's lost, Mom."

Josephine was clutching her stomach as if she had been run through with a sword, and the hypnotist was grinning. When had he felt so good? He leaned forward, shielded his mouth with his hand, and whispered a little secret to Josephine. "She's right, you know. It's not lost. Looky here. It's in the cuff of my pant."

Josephine sagged against the couch. She stared miserably at the little disc he fished from the cuff.

"Let's go, Mom," Irene said.

"Go?" Josephine said. "We can't go."

"She can't go," the hypnotist agreed. "I got her gumption."

But Irene was tired of this. Why had she come? She didn't want to come. Josephine had begged her to come. Be my courage, Josephine had said. She was always having to be Mama's courage. That's what daughters are for, Josephine liked to say.

Irene stood. "I'm going," she said.

"Going?" Josephine said.

Irene, hands fisted, stood over her mother. Josephine, looking up, saw Irene poised for flight. Poised in that if-you-don-t-pay-attention-to-me-right-now-you'll-regret-it stance, and Josephine frowned. Really, the girl had the attention span of a pea! And so rude!

Suddenly, Josephine wanted a drink. She couldn't talk to the girl any more. She wanted a smoke. She began digging around in her purse but then remembered why she was here. Wasn't he supposed to do something about this? She frowned at the man. He leered at her. Her stomach flipped.

But it was getting late, and she wanted a smoke. She stood up. Her legs wobbled, and her head spun. She clutched her purse with both hands and walked carefully to the door. She felt as if her parts didn't quite connect.

"Go?" the hypnotist boomed.

Josephine looked back at him. The man's eyes smoldered, and she shuddered.

"Aren't you forgetting something?" he said.

Josephine moistened her lips. But Irene had her hand on the knob, and when the door opened, Josephine saw the man's eyes grow wide. How sweet, she thought. He doesn't want me to leave.

And I, a married woman.

The air in the room was rotten with perfume. The hypnotist stared at the door. White-knuckled, he gripped his chair. His lips twitched spastically into something that wanted to be, and then was, a smile. "Go?" He threw his head back and laughed. "Need not be present to win!" he shouted.

He looked from the door to the little hairs on his knuckles, turned his left hand over. With eyes half-closed, he gazed at the center of his palm. The skin was yellowish, thick, though as he watched it began to change, to bubble tumor-like. Gradually, the skin tightened and stretched and seemed to crack. A glowing disc, flat as a penny, worried its way to the surface.

The hypnotist held it up to his eye. There was a pinpoint hole at the center, and he stared through it at the door, and laughed again. He tossed the disc into the air, caught it. "Heads or tails?" He slapped it hard onto the back of his hand. "Tails. You lose." He ground the thing into his hand, then watched it emerge on the other side.

Was that the whisper of wheels on pavement? "Back again?" He cocked his head and smiled at the door. But he heard no humming engine. The little disc quivered.

The six o'clock sun filtered through the blinds, scissoring the couch where the woman had sat. The trailer was quiet. He listened for the birds, but the birds never sang in the six o'clock heat. He frowned at the door. "Well aren't you the little flirt," he said.

He got up, walked to the door, opened it, looked out into the cellophane waves that shimmied above the asphalt. Hot, stinky tar bubbled up through cracks at the base of his stoop. There was no one on the lot but him. There was no one in the drive.

"Gone?" he said. He shrugged. "Oh, well."

Really, he blamed himself. He was always going too far. A little rambunctious, that's what he was. Always had been. He chuckled at himself, at the way he was. And he was so sure he'd get lucky today—if not with the girl, then the mom. "Just shows you never can tell," he said.

In the palm of his hand, he held the disc over the asphalt. "If you don't want it," he shouted in the direction of the road, "I don't either." With the index finger of his left, he flicked the disc.

It jiggled.

He flicked it again.

It jiggled.

He pushed it hard with the ball of his thumb, then shook his hand vigorously.

The little peach, grown sticky in the heat, clung to him.

He stepped back into the room, closed the door. His hands were gooey with it. "Down the drain you go," he said, heading toward the bathroom, but stopped. It seemed, somehow, larger. Had it grown? Could it have? Irritated, the thing sat, swollen and flaming, in the ball of his hand, and it smelled! Did it stink? He put it to his nose and sniffed. An odor, surely blood, the suffocating stink of blood-laced perfume, spoiled the air, and his hand itched. He scratched. The thing throbbed. It was a throbbing itch, and his fingers—he saw with horror—were swelling. He tried to make a fist but the fingers, each of them, were red and pregnant and didn't want to close. And perhaps—his eyes weren't so good anymore.

Yes, tiny blue veins laced the crusted edges of the thing in his hand. He began to tremble. When he looked closely he saw that the veins extended beyond the thing and into—into?

Like a small boy, he put his hand behind his back. The birds were singing again. The thing was pulsing. Into him? His ears were ringing.

"Now you see it," he murmured. "Now you don't." He gasped.

It was gone. He felt it leave! He pulled his hand from behind his back. His palm was flat and yellow. He laughed, and then he hiccuped because there it was again, a slimy, pulsing, growing gob.

"Nowyouseeit, nowyoudon't!"

It jiggled, little belly laugh. The birds twittered.

This was wrong. He held it upside down, shook his hand, shook it vigorously, but the more he shook, the bigger it got. He stopped shaking. Sweat beads rolled along his fat lines. She—

Shouldn't have given it. What was she thinking? To give such a thing!

Then why'd you take it, dummy, he couldn't help but think, if you were only going to give it back? All sales final!

He slumped into his chair. He felt like crying, and he felt like laughing. Well, this was something new at least. He stared at the wad in the palm of his hand. "Are you my little wife?" he said. He ran his finger over the thing, which was now, clearly, a translucent, pulsing membrane. He shuddered. "Are you my love?"

FOUR INSTITUTIONAL MONOLOGUES

by GEORGE SAUNDERS

I.
(EXHORTATION)

MEMORANDUM
DATE: Apr 6
TO: Staff
FROM: Todd Bernie
RE: March Performance Stats

I would not like to characterize this as a plea, but it may start to sound like one (!). The fact is, we have a job to do, we have tacitly agreed to do it (did you cash your last paycheck, I know I did, ha ha ha). We have also—to go a step further here—agreed to do the job well. Now we all know that one way to do a job poorly is to be negative about it. Say we need to clean a shelf. Let's use that example. If we spend the hour before the shelf-cleaning talking down the process of cleaning the shelf, complaining about it, dreading it, investigating the moral niceties of cleaning the shelf, whatever, then what happens is, we make the process of cleaning the shelf *more difficult than it really is*. We all know very well that that "shelf" is going to be cleaned, given the current climate, either by you or by the guy who replaces you and gets your paycheck, so the question boils down to: Do I want to clean it happy or do I want to clean it sad? Which would be more effective? For me? Which would accomplish my purpose more efficiently? What is my purpose? To get paid. How do I accomplish that purpose most efficiently? I clean that shelf well and I clean it quickly. And what mental state helps me clean that shelf well and quickly? Is the answer: Negative? A negative mental state? You know very well that it is not. So the point of this memo is: Positive. The positive mental state will help you clean that shelf well and quickly, and thus accomplish your purpose of getting paid.

What am I saying? Am I saying whistle while you work? Maybe I am. Let us consider lifting a heavy dead carcass such as a whale. (Forgive the shelf/whale thing, we have just come back from our place on Reston Island, where there were 1) a lot of dirty shelves, and 2) yes, believe it or not, an actual dead rotting whale, which Timmy and Vance and I got involved with in terms of the clean-up.) So say you are charged with, you and some of your colleagues, lifting a heavy dead whale carcass onto a flatbed. Now we all know that is hard. And what would be harder is, doing that with a negative attitude. What we found, Timmy and Vance and I, is that even with only a neutral attitude, you are talking a very hard task. We tried to lift that whale, while we were just feeling neutral, Timmy and Vance and I, with a dozen or so other folks, and it was a no-go, that whale wouldn't budge, until suddenly one fellow, a former Marine, said what we needed was some mind over matter and gathered us in a little circle, and we had a sort of a chant. We got "psyched up." We knew, to extend my above analogy, that we had a job to do, and we got sort of excited about that, and decided to do it with a positive attitude, and I have to tell you, there was something to that, it was fun, fun when that whale rose into the air, helped by us and some big straps that Marine had in his van, and I have to say that lifting that dead rotting whale onto that flatbed with that group of total strangers was the *high point of our trip*.

So what am I saying? I am saying (and saying it fervently, because it is important): Let's try, if we can, to minimize the grumbling and self-doubt regarding the tasks we must sometimes do around here that maybe aren't on the surface all that pleasant. I'm saying let's try not to dissect every single thing we do in terms of ultimate good/bad/indifferent in terms of morals. The time for that is long past. I hope that each of us had that conversation with ourselves nearly a year ago, when this whole thing started. We have embarked on a path, and having embarked on that path, for the best of reasons (as we decided a year ago) wouldn't it be kind of suicidal to let our progress down that path be impeded by neurotic second-guessing? Have any of you ever swung a sledgehammer? I know that some of you have. I know some of you did when we took out Rick's patio. Isn't it fun when you don't hold back, but just pound down and down, letting gravity help you? Fellows, what I'm saying is, let gravity help you here, in our workplace situation: Pound down, give in to the natural feelings that I have seen from time to time produce so much great energy in so many of you, in terms of executing your given tasks with vigor and without second-guessing and neurotic thoughts. Remember that record-breaking week Andy had back in October, when he doubled his usual number of units? Regardless of all else, forgetting for the moment all the namby-pamby thoughts of right/wrong etc etc, wasn't that something to see? In and of itself? I think that, if we each look deep down inside of ourselves, weren't we each a little envious? God he was really pounding down and you could see the energetic joy on his face each time he rushed by us to get additional clean-up towels. And we were all just standing there like, wow, Andy, what's gotten into you? And no one can argue with his numbers. They are there in the Break Room for all to see, towering about the rest of our numbers, and though Andy has failed to duplicate those numbers in the months since October, 1) no one blames him for that, those were miraculous numbers, and 2) I believe that even if Andy never again duplicates those numbers, he must still, somewhere in his heart, secretly treasure the memory of that magnificent energy flowing out of him in that memorable October. I do not honestly think Andy could've had such an October if he had been coddling himself or entertaining any doubtful neurotic thoughts or second-guessing tendencies, do you? I don't. Andy looked totally focused, totally outside himself, you could see it on his face, maybe because of the new baby? (If so, Janice should have a new baby every week, ha ha.)

Anyway, October is how Andy entered a sort of, at least in my mind, de facto Hall of Fame, and is pretty much henceforth excluded from any real close monitoring of his numbers, at least by me. No matter how disconsolate and sort of withdrawn he gets (and I think we've all noticed that he's gotten pretty disconsolate and withdrawn since October), you will not find me closely monitoring his numbers, although as for others I cannot speak, others may be monitoring that troubling fall-off in Andy's numbers, although really I hope they're not, that would not be so fair, and believe me, if I get wind of it, I will definitely let Andy know, and if Andy's too depressed to hear me, I'll call Janice at home.

And in terms of why is Andy so disconsolate? My guess is that he's being neurotic, and second-guessing his actions of October—and wow, isn't that a shame, isn't that a no-win, for Andy to have completed that record-breaking

October and now to sit around boo-hooing about it? Is anything being changed by that boo-hooing? Are the actions Andy did, in terms of the tasks I gave him to do in Room 6, being undone by his boo-hooing, are his numbers on the Break Room Wall miraculously scrolling downwards, are people suddenly walking out of Room 6 feeling perfectly okay again? Well we all know they are not. No one is walking out of Room 6 feeling perfectly okay. Even you guys, you who do what must be done in Room 6, don't walk out feeling so super-great, I know that, I've certainly done some things in Room 6 that didn't leave me feeling so wonderful, believe me, no one is trying to deny that Room 6 can be a bummer, it is very hard work that we do. But the people above us, who give us our assignments, seem to think that the work we do in Room 6, in addition to being *hard*, is also *important*, which I suspect is why they have begun watching our numbers so closely. And trust me, if you want Room 6 to be an even worse bummer than it already is, then mope about it before, after, and during, then it will really stink, plus, with all that moping, your numbers will go down even farther, which guess what: They cannot do. I have been told in no uncertain terms, at the Sectional Meeting, that our numbers are not to go down any farther. I said (and this took guts, believe me, given the atmosphere at Sectional): Look, my guys are tired, this is hard work we do, both physically and psychologically. And at that point, at Sectional, believe me, the silence was deafening. And I mean deafening. And the looks I got were not good. And I was reminded, in no uncertain terms, by Hugh Blanchert himself, that our numbers are not to go down. And I was asked to remind you—to remind us, all of us, myself included— that if we are unable to clean our assigned "shelf," not only will someone else be brought in to clean that "shelf," but we ourselves may find ourselves on that "shelf," *being* that "shelf," with someone else exerting themselves with good positive energy all over us. And at that time I think you can imagine how regretful you would feel, the regret would show in your faces, as we sometimes witness, in Room 6, that regret on the faces of the "shelves" as they are "cleaned," so I am asking you, from the hip, to try your best and not end up a "shelf," which we, your former colleagues, will have no choice but to clean clean clean using all our positive energy, without looking back, in Room 6.

This all was made clear to me at Sectional and now I am trying to make it clear to you.

Well I have gone on and on, but please come by my office, anybody who's having doubts, doubts about what we do, and I will show you pictures of that incredible whale my sons and I lifted with our good positive energy. And of course this information, that is, the information that you are having doubts, and have come to see me in my office, will go no further than my office, although I am sure I do not even have to say that, to any of you, who have known me these many years.

All will be well and all will be well, etc etc,

Todd Birnie
Divisional Director

II.
(DESIGN PROPOSAL)

It is preferable, our preliminary research has indicated, for some institutional space to be provided, such as corridor, hallway, etc, through which the group may habitually move. Our literature search indicated that a tiled area is preferable, in terms of preventing possible eventual damage to the walls and floors by the group moving through the space. The review of published literature also indicated that it is preferable that this area to move through (henceforth referred to, per Ellis et al., as the "Fenlen Space") be non-linear in areal layout, that is, should include frequent turning options (i.e., side hallways or corners), to give the illusion of what Ellis terms "optional pathway choices." Per Gasgrave, Heller et al., this non-linear areal layout, and the resulting apparent optional pathway choices, create a "Forward-Anticipating" mindset. Per Ellis et al., the Forward-Anticipating mindset (characterized by an Andrew-Brison Attribute Suite which includes "hope," "resolve," "determination," and "sense of mission") results in less damage to the Fenlen Space, as well as better general health for the Temporary Community, which in turn results in significantly lower clinic/medicinal costs.

Also in Ellis et al., the phrase "Forward-Anticipating Temporary Community" (FATC) is defined to designate a Temporary Community which, while moving through a given Fenlen Space, maintains NTEI (Negative Thought External Indicator) values below 3 per person/per hour. A "Non-Forward-Anticipating Temporary Community" (NFATC) is defined as one for which NTEI values are consistently above 3 per person/per hour. NTEIs are calculated using the Reilly Method, from raw data compiled by trained staff observing from inside what are termed "Amstel Booths," one-way mirror locales situated at regular intervals along the Fenlen Space.

For the purposes of this cost proposal, four Amstel Booths have been costed, along with the necessary ventilation/electrical additions.

As part of our assessment, we performed a statistical analysis of the NTEIs for four distinct Fenlen Spaces, using a standard Student's T-test, supplemented with the recently developed Anders-Kiley outlier correction model. Interestingly, the most important component of the Fenlen Space appeared to be what is referred to in the current literature as the Daley Realignment Device (DRD).

The DRD allows for quick changes in the areal layout of the Fenlen Space during time periods during which the Temporary Community is moving through another, remote portion of the Fenlen Space. The purpose of the DRD is to prolong what Elgin et al. term the "Belief Period" in the Fenlen Space; that is, the period during which the Temporary Community, moving through the recently realigned DRD, fails to recognize that the portion of the Fenlen Space being traversed by them has already in fact been traversed by them. Rather, the altered areal layout leads to the conclusion that the portion of the Fenlen Space being traversed is an entirely unfamiliar and previously untraversed place, thus increasing the Temporary Community's expectation that, in time, they will arrive at what Allison and Dewitt have termed the "Preferable Destination." At some facilities, a brief oral presentation is made to the Temporary Community shortly before the Community enters the Fenlen Space, during which it is strongly implied or even directly stated that the Community will be traversing the Fenlen Space in order to reach the Preferable Destination, which is described in some detail, especially vis-à-vis improvements in terms of cold/heat considerations, food considerations, crowding/overcrowding considerations, and/or perceived menace considerations. An "apology" may be made for any regrettable past incidents. It may also be implied that the individuals responsible for these incidents have been dismissed etc etc. Such presentations have been found to be extremely beneficial, significantly minimizing NTEIGs and prolonging the Belief Period, and several researchers have mentioned the enthusiasm with which the Temporary Community typically enters the Fenlen Space following such a presentation.

Should Building Ed Terry wish to supplement its DRD with such a pre-traversing oral presentation, Judson & Associates would be pleased to provide the necessary technical writing expertise, a service we have already provided successfully for nine facilities in the Northeast.

In any event, some sort of DRD is strongly recommended. In a study of a Fenlen Space located in Canton, New Jersey, a device which was not equipped with a DRD, it was reported that, toward the end of Day 1, the Temporary Community went, within a few hours, from a strong FATC (with very low NTEIs, ranging from 0–2 per person/per hour) to a very strong NFATC (with NTEIs as high as 9 per person/per hour). Perhaps the most striking finding of the Canton study was that, once the Temporary Community had devolved from an FATC to a NFATC (i.e., once the Belief Period had expired), NTEI values increased dramatically and catastrophically, until, according to one Amstel Booth observer, the NTEIs were occurring at a frequency that were "essentially impossible to tabulate," resulting in the event being classified as "Chaotic" (on the Elliot Scale), after which the Fenlen Space had to be forcibly cleared of the Temporary Community. In other words, once the Temporary Community perceived the Fenlen Space as a repetitious traversing of the same physical space, morale eroded quickly and, per clinical data, could not be restored. Needless to say, the forcible clearing of a Fenlen Space involves substantial risk and expense, as does the related interruption to the smooth flow of facility operations.

In contrast, since a DRD was added to the Canton facility, no further Chaos Situations have occurred, with one exception, which was later seen to be related to a small fire that occurred within one of the Amstel Booths.

Currently available DRDs range from manually rearranged units (typically featuring wallboard panels with quick-release bolts, which are placed into a floor-embedded grid) to electronic, track-based units which offer a large, practically unlimited range of configurations and are typically integrated using the ChangeSpace™ computer software package. The design we have submitted for Building Ed Terry includes cost estimates for the economical Homeway DRD6 (wallboard-grid model) as well as the higher-end Casio 3288 DRD (track-based, computer-operated unit). For the Homeway unit, we have included approximate costs for the physical labor involved in the manual rearrangement of the DRD. For the purposes of this proposal, we have assumed seven rearrangements a day, with four persons required for each rearrangement. This corresponds with a circumnavigation period of approximately three hours— that is, seven rearrangements a day, precluding the possibility that the Temporary Community would inadvertently encounter areal rearrangements in progress, which has been shown (in Percy et al.) to markedly decrease the belief period, for obvious reasons.

Judson Associates firmly believes that the enclosed proposal more than meets the needs described in your Request for Proposal of January 9. Should you desire further clarification, please do not hesitate to contact either Jim

Warner or myself. We look forward to hearing from you, and to working with you on this exciting and challenging project, and on other projects yet to come.

Sincerely,

Mark Judson
President and CEO
Judson Associates

III.
(A FRIENDLY REMINDER)

We in Knuckles herebuy request that those of you in Sorting refran from calling the Fat Scrap Box the Pizza Hut Box and refran from calling the Bone Scrap Box the Marshmallow Box and refran from calling the Misc. Scrap Box the Dog Food Box because we think that is insulting to our work and workplace in terms of why do you have to make fun of what we all of us do for a living as if it is shameful. Even though it is true that some of our offal might get used for pizza topping and mashmallows and dog food we do not like it when you are saying those names in a sarcasmic voice. Because new hires can be infected by these attitudes which are so negative and soon they will not be working their best but only laughing at your smartass dumb jokes, so in the future use the correct names (Fat Scrap and Bone Scrap and Misc. Scrap) for these boxes if you feel like you have to talk at all while working although also we in Knuckles suggest you just shut up and just work. For example when one of us in Knuckles throws a Knuckle but it misses the belt you do not have to call it a "skidder" or act like you are a announcer on a basketball show by saying whoa he missed the hole. And also you dont have to say Ouch whenever one of our throwed Knuckles goes too far and hits the wall, it is not like the Knuckle could feel that and say Ow, because it is dead dumbass, it cannot feel its leg part hitting the wall, so we know you are being sarcasmic. And we dont think this is funny because when we miss the belt or hit the wall what do we have to do is we have to put down our knives and go get it which takes time. And already we are tired without that extra walking. Because what we do takes real muscle and you can easily see us if you look huffing and breething hard all day in the cold inside air, whereas you, although its true you are all hunched over, we never see you breething hard and you dont even work with knives and so never accidentally cut your friend. Which is why we think you have so much energy for yelling your "funny" taunts that you say at us and have so much energy for making up dumb names of your Belts. So to summarize we do not appreciate all the sarcasmic things that are daily said by you in Sorting in your snotty voices, as it is not something to be ashamed about, people need meat and people like meat, it is good honest work you should be glad you got it, so straighten up and fly right, in other words fucken shut up while working and just do your work silencely and try to appreciate the blessing god give you, like your job of work, it could be worse and is worse for many peeple who have no work

IV.
(93990)

A ten-day acute toxicity study was conducted using twenty male cynomolgous monkeys ranging in weight from 25 to 40 kg. These animals were divided into four groups of five monkeys each. Each of the four groups received a daily intra-venous dose of Borazidine, delivered at a concentration of either 100, 250, 500, or 10,000 mg/kg/day.

Within the high-dose group (10,000 mg/kg/day) effects were immediate and catastrophic, resulting in death within 20 mins. of dosing for all but one of the five animals. Animals 93445 and 93557, pre-death, exhibited vomiting and disorientation. These two animals almost immediately entered a catatonic state and were sacrificed moribund. Animals 93001 and 93458 exhibited vom-iting, anxiety, disorientation, and digging at their abdomens. These animals also quickly entered a catatonic state and were sacrificed moribund.

Only one animal within this high-dose group, animal 93990, a diminutive 26 kg male, appeared unaffected.

All of the animals that had succumbed were removed from the enclosure and necropsied. Cause of death was seen, in all cases, to be renal failure.

No effects were seen on Day 1 in any of the three lower-dose groups (i.e., 100, 250, or 500 mg/kg/day).

On Day 2, after the second round of dosing, animals in the 500 mg/kg/day group began to exhibit vomiting and, in some cases, aggressive behavior. This aggressive behavior most often consisted of a directed shriek-ing, with or without feigned biting. Some animals in the two lowest-dose groups (100 and 250 mg/kg/day) were observed to vomit, and one in the 250 mg/kg/day group (animal 93002) appeared to exhibit self-scratching behav-iors similar to those seen earlier in the high-dose group (i.e., probing and scratching at abdomen, with limited writhing).

By the end of Day 3, three of five animals in the 500 mg/kg/day group had entered a catatonic state and the other two animals in this dose group were exhibiting extreme writhing punctuated with attempted biting and pinching of their fellows, often with shrieking. Some hair loss, ranging from slight to extreme, was observed, as was some "playing" with the resulting hair bundles. This "playing" behavior ranged from mild to quite energetic. This "playing" behavior was adjudged to be typical of the type of "play" such an animal might initiate with a smaller animal such as a rodent, i.e., out of a curiosity impulse, i.e., may have been indicative of hallucinogenic effects. Several animals were observed to repeatedly grimace at the hair bundles, as if trying to elicit a fear behavior from the hair bundles. Animal 93110 of the 500 mg/kg/day group was observed to sit in one corner of the cage gazing at its own vomit while an unaffected animal (93222) appeared to attempt to rouse the interest of 93110 via backpatting, followed by vigorous backpatting. Interestingly, the sole remaining high-dose animal (93990, the diminutive male), even after the second day's dosage, still showed no symptoms. Even though this animal was the smallest in weight within the highest-dose group, it showed no symptoms. It showed no vomiting, disinterest, self-scratching, anxiety, or aggression. Also no hair loss was observed. Although no hair bundles were present (because no hair loss occurred), this animal was not seen to "play" with inanimate objects present in the enclosure, such as its food bowl or stool or bits of rope, etc. This animal, rather, was seen only to stare fixedly at the handlers through the bars of the cage and/or to retreat rapidly when the handlers entered the enclosure with the long poking sticks to check under certain items (chairs, recreational tire) for hair bundles and/or deposits of runny stool.

By the middle of Day 3, all of the animals in the 500 mg/kg/day group had succumbed. Pre-death, these showed, in addition to the effects noted above, symptoms ranging from whimpering to performing a rolling dementia-type motion on the cage floor, sometimes accompanied by shrieking or frothing. After succumbing, all five animals were removed from the enclosure and necropsied. Renal failure was seen to be the cause of death in all cases. Interestingly, these animals did not enter a catatonic state pre-death, but instead appeared to be quite alert, manifesting labored breathing and, in some cases, bursts of energetic rope-climbing. Coordination was adjudged to be adversely affected, based on the higher-than-normal frequency of falls from the rope. Post-fall reactions ranged from no reaction to frustration reactions, with or without self-punishment behaviors (i.e., self-hitting, self-hair-pulling, rapid shakes of head).

Toward the end of Day 3, all animals in the two lowest-dose groups (250 and 100 mg/kg/day) were observed to be in some form of distress. Some of these had lapsed into a catatonic state; some refused to take food; many had runny, brightly colored stools; some sat eating their stool while intermittently shrieking.

Animals 93852, 93881, and 93777, of the 250 mg/kg/day group, in the last hours before death, appeared to experience a brief period of invigoration and renewed activity, exhibiting symptoms of anxiety, as well as lurching, confusion, and scratching at the eyes with the fingers. These animals were seen to repeatedly walk or run into the cage bars, after which they would become agitated. Blindness or partial blindness was indicated. When brightly colored flags were waved in front of these animals, some failed to respond, while others responded by flinging stool at the handlers.

By noon on Day 4, all of the animals in the 250 mg/kg/day group had succumbed, been removed from the enclosure, and necropsied. In every case the cause of death was seen to be renal failure.

By the end of Day 4, only the five 100 mg/kg/day animals remained, along with the aforementioned very resilient diminutive male in the highest dose group (93990), who continued to manifest no symptoms whatsoever. This animal continued to show no vomiting, retching, nausea, disorientation, loss of motor skills, or any of the other symptoms described above. This animal continued to move about the enclosure normally and ingest normal amounts of food and water and in fact was seen to have experienced a slight weight gain and climbed the rope repeatedly with good authority.

On Day 5, animal 93444 of the 100 mg/kg/day group was observed to have entered the moribund state. Because of its greatly weakened condition, this animal was not redosed in the morning. Instead, it was removed from the enclosure, sacrificed moribund, and necropsied. Renal failure was seen to be the cause of death. Animal 93887 (100 mg/kg/day group) was seen to repeatedly keel over on one side while wincing. This animal succumbed at 1300 hrs on Day 5, was removed from the enclosure, and necropsied. Renal failure was seen to be the cause of death. Between 1500 hrs on Day 5 and 2000 hrs on Day 5, animals 93254 and 93006 of the 100 mg/kg/day dose group succumbed in rapid succession while huddled in the NW corner of the large enclosure. Both animals exhibited wheezing and rapid clutching and release of the genitals. These two animals were removed from the enclosure and necropsied. In both cases the cause of death was seen to be renal failure.

This left only animal 93555 of the 100 mg/kg/day dose group and animal 93990, the diminutive male of the highest dose group. 93555 exhibited nearly all of the aforementioned symptoms, along with, toward the end of Day 5, several episodes during which it inflicted scratches and contusions on its own neck and face by attempting to spasmodically reach for something beyond the enclosure. This animal also manifested several episodes of quick spinning. Several of these quick-spinning episodes culminated in sudden hard falling. In two cases, the sudden hard fall was seen to result in tooth loss. In one of the cases of tooth loss, the animal was seen to exhibit the suite of aggressive behaviors earlier exhibited toward the hair bundles. In addition, in this case, the animal, after a prolonged period of snarling at its tooth, was observed to attack and ingest its own tooth. It was judged that, if these behaviors continued into Day 6, for humanitarian reasons, the animal would be sacrificed, but just after 2300 hrs, the animal discontinued these behaviors and only sat listlessly in its own stool with occasional writhing and therefore was not sacrificed due to this improvement in its condition.

By 1200 hrs of Day 5, the diminutive male 93990 still exhibited no symptoms. He was observed to be sitting in the SE corner of the enclosure, staring fixedly at the cage door. This condition was at first mistaken to be indicative of early catatonia but when a metal pole was inserted and a poke attempted, the animal responded by lurching away with shrieking, which was judged normal. It was also noted that 93990 occasionally seemed to be staring at and/or gesturing to the low-dose enclosure, i.e., the enclosure in which 93555 was still sitting listlessly in its own stool occasionally writhing. By the end of Day 5, 93990 still manifested no symptoms and in fact was observed to heartily eat the preferred food and weighing at midday Day 6 confirmed further weight gain. Also it climbed the rope. Also at times it seemed to implore. This imploring was judged to be, possibly, a mild hallucinogenic effect. This imploring resulted in involuntary laughter on the part of the handlers, which resulted in the animal discontinuing the imploring behavior and retreating to the NW corner where it sat for quite some time with its back to the handlers. It was decided that, in the future, handlers would refrain from laughing at the imploring, so as to be able to obtain a more objective idea of the duration of the (unimpeded) imploring.

Following dosing on the morning of Day 6, the last remaining low-dose animal (93555), the animal that earlier had attacked and ingested its own tooth, then sat for quite some time writhing in its own stool listlessly, succumbed, after an episode that included, in addition to many of the aforementioned symptoms, tearing at its own eyes and flesh and, finally, quiet heaving breathing while squatting. This animal, following a limited episode of eyes rolling back in its head, entered the moribund state, succumbed, and was necropsied. Cause of death was seen to be renal failure. As 93555 was removed from the enclosure, 93990 was seen to sit quietly, then retreat to the rear of the enclosure, that is, the portion of the enclosure farthest from the door, where it squatted on its haunches. Soon it was observed to rise and move toward its food bowl and eat heartily while continuing to look at the door.

Following dosing on Day 7, animal 93990, now the sole remaining animal, continued to show no symptoms and ate and drank vigorously.

Following dosing on Day 8, likewise, this animal continued to show no symptoms and ate and drank vigorously.

On Day 9, it was decided to test the effects of extremely high doses of Borazadine by doubling the dosage, to 20,000 mg/kg/day. This increased dosage was administered intravenously on the morning of Day 9. No acute effects were seen. The animal continued to move around its cage and eat and drink normally. It was observed to continue to stare at the door of the cage and occasionally at the other, now-empty, enclosures. Also the rope-climbing did not decrease. A brief episode of imploring was observed. No laughter on the part of the handlers occurred, and the unimpeded imploring was seen to continue for approximately 130 seconds. When, post-imploring, the stick was inserted to attempt a poke, the stick was yanked away by 93990. When a handler attempted to enter the cage to retrieve the poking stick, the handler was poked. Following this incident, the conclusion was reached to attempt no further retrievals of the poking stick, but rather to obtain a back-up poking stick available from Supply. As Supply did not at this time have a back-up poking stick, it was decided to attempt no further poking until the first poking stick could be retrieved. When it was determined that retrieving the first poking stick would be problematic, it was judged beneficial that the first poking stick was now in the possession of 93990, as observations could be made as to how 93990 was using and/or manipulating the poking stick, i.e., effect of Borazadine on motor skills.

On Day 10, on what was to have been the last day of the study, upon the observation that animal 93990 still exhibited no effects whatsoever, the decision was reached to increase the dosage to 100,000 mg/kg/day, a dosage 10 times greater than that which had proved almost immediately lethal to every other animal in the highest-dose group. This was adjudged to be scientifically defensible. This dosage was delivered at 0300 hrs on Day 10. Remarkably, no acute effects were seen other than those associated with injection (i.e., small, bright purple blisters at the injection site, coupled with elevated heart rate and extreme perspiration and limited panic gesturing) but these soon subsided and were judged to be related to the high rate of injection rather than to the Borazadine itself.

Throughout Day 10, animal 93990 continued to show no symptoms. It ate and drank normally. It moved energetically about the cage. It climbed the rope. By the end of the study period, i.e., midnight of Day 10, no symptoms whatsoever had been observed. Remarkably, the animal leapt about the cage. The animal wielded the poking stick with good dexterity, occasionally implored, shrieked energetically at the handlers. In summary, even at a dosage 10 times that which had proved almost immediately fatal to larger, heavier animals, 93990 showed no symptoms whatsoever. In all ways, even at this exceptionally high dosage, this animal appeared to be normal, healthy, unaffected, and thriving.

At approximately 0100 hrs of Day 11, 93990 was tranquilized via dart, removed from the enclosure, sacrificed, and necropsied.

No evidence of renal damage was observed. No negative effects of any kind were observed. A net weight gain of 3 kg since the beginning of the study was observed.

All carcasses were transported off-site by a certified medical waste hauler and disposed of via incineration.

THE DOUBLE ZERO
(WITH APOLOGIES TO SHERWOOD ANDERSON)

by RICK MOODY

MY DAD WAS for Midwestern values; he was for families; he was for a firm handshake; he was for a little awkward sweet-talking with the waitress at the HoJo's. Until he grew to the age of thirty-four he worked at one of those farms owned by a big international corporation that's created from family farms gone defunct. Looked like a chessboard, if you saw it from the air. This was near Bidwell, Ohio. Don't know if it was Archer Daniels Midland, Monsanto, some company like that. The particular spread I'm talking about got sold to developers later. Guess it was more lucrative to sell the plot and buy some other place. The housing development that grew up on that land, it was called Golden Meadow Estates even though it didn't have any meadows. That's where we lived after Dad got laid off. He'd been at the bar down by the railroad when the news came through.

So he took the job at Sears, in the power tools dept. About the same time he met my mom. She'd once won a beauty contest, Miss Scandinavian Bidwell. They got married after dating a long while. My mom, probably on account of her beauty crown, was eager for my dad (and me, too, because I showed up pretty soon) to get some of that American fortune all around her. She was hopeful. She was going to get her some. The single-story tract house over in Golden Meadow Estates, well, it was a pretty tight fit, not to mention falling down, and they were stuck next door to a used-car salesman nobody liked.

I heard a rumor that this guy Stubb, this neighbor, had dead teenagers in the basement. The Buckeye State had a national lead in serial killers, though, so maybe that wasn't any big surprise. My mother convinced my dad that he had to get into some other line of work, where there was a better possibility of advancing. Was he going to spend his whole life selling power tools? Her idea was raising Angora rabbits. He went along with it. They really multiplied, these rabbits, like I bet you've heard. They were my chore, as a matter of fact. You'd get dozens of these cages with rabbits that urinated and shat all over everything if you even whispered at them, and then you had to spin their fur, you know, on an actual loom. If you wanted to make any kind of money at all. I didn't have to spin anything back then. I was too little. But you get the idea. Turned out my mother didn't have the patience for all that.

Next was yew trees. Some chemical in the yew tree was supposed to be an ingredient in the toxins for fighting cancers. Maybe my mother was thinking about that cluster in town. I mean, just about everybody in Golden Meadow Estates sported a wig, and so it wasn't newsworthy later when they found that the development had been laid out on an old chromium dump. Meantime, we actually had a half acre of yew trees already planted on some land rented from the nylon manufacturer downtown, and there were heavy metals there too, must have been fatal to the yew trees. The main thing is they made this chemical, the yew chemical, in the laboratory by the end of the year.

Mom made a play for llamas. She went down to the Bidwell public library. To the business section. Read up about llamas. But what can you do with them anyway? Make a sweater? Well, that's how we settled on ostriches. The ostrich is a poetic thing, let me tell you. Its life is full of dramas. The largest of birds on planet earth. The ostrich is almost eight feet tall and weighs three hundred pounds and it has a brain not too much bigger than a pigeon's brain. It has two toes. It can reach speeds of fifty miles an hour, and believe me, I've seen them do it. Like if you were standing at the far end of the ostrich farm we had, the Rancho Double Zero, and you were holding a Cleveland Indians beer cup full of corn, that ostrich would come at you about the speed an eighteen-wheeler comes at you on the interstate. Just like having a pigeon swoop at you, except that this pigeon is the size of a minivan. The incredible stupidity on the ostrich's face is worth commenting on, too, in case you haven't seen one lately. They're mouth-breathers, or anyhow their beaks always hang open a little bit. That pretty much tells you all you need to know. Lights on, property vacant. They reminded me of a retarded kid I knew in grammar school, Zechariah Dunbar. He's dead now. Anyway, the point is that ostriches are always trying to hold down other ostriches, by sitting on them, in order to fuck these other ostriches, without any regard to whether it's a boy or girl animal they're trying to get next to. And speaking of sex and ostriches, I'm almost sure that the men who worked on my father's farm tried to have their way with the Rancho Double Zero product. With a brain so small, it was obvious that the ostrich would never feel loving congress with some heartbroken Midwestern hombre as any kind of bodily insult. Actually, it's amazing that the pea-sized brain in those ostrich skulls could operate the other end of them. Amazing that electrical transmissions could make it that far, what with that huge bulky midsection that was all red meat, hundreds of pounds of it, as every brochure will tell you, but with a startlingly low fat content. In fact, it tastes like chicken, my grandma said before the choking incident. Okay, it was almost like the ostrich was some kind of bird. But it didn't look like a bird, and when there were three or four hundred of them, running around in a herd at fifty miles an hour, flattening rodents, trying to have sex with each other, three or four hundred of them purchased with a precarious loan from Buckeye Savings and Trust, well, they looked more like conventioneers from some Holiday Inn assembly of extinct species. You expected a mating pair of wooly mammoths or a bunch of saber-toothed tigers to show up any moment.

I'm getting away from the story, though. I really meant to talk about ostrich eggs. After ten years of trying to get the Rancho Double Zero to perform fiscally, my parents had to sell the whole thing and declare bankruptcy. That's the sad truth. And it was no shame. Everybody they knew was bankrupt. Everybody in Bidwell, practically, had a lien on their bank account. When we were done with the Double Zero, we had nothing left but a bunch of ostrich eggs, the kind that my parents used to sell out in front of the farm, under a canopy, for people who came out driving. There were three signs, a quarter-mile apart, SEE THE OSTRICHES! TWO MILES! And then another half-mile. OSTRICH EGGS! FIVE DOLLARS EACH! Then another. FEED THE OSTRICHES! IF YOU DARE!

I remember giving the feeding lecture myself to a couple from back East. They were the only people who'd volunteered to feed the ostriches in weeks. I handed them the Cleveland Indians cups. They were dressed up fine. You can either put some of this corn in your hand and hold it out for the ostriches, but I sure wouldn't do that myself, because I've seen them pick up a little kid and whirl him around like he was a handkerchief and throw him over a fence, bust his neck clean through. Or you can hold out the cup and the ostriches will try to trample each other to death to get right in front of you, and then one of those pinheads will descend with incredible force on you, steal the entire cup away. Or else you can just scatter some corn at the base of the electrified fence there and get the heck out of the way, which is certainly what I'd do if I were you. Who would go from Bidwell to anywhere, I was asking myself, unless they were trying to avoid a massive interstate manhunt? Probably this couple, right here, laughing at the poor dumb birds, probably they were the kind of people who would sodomize an entire preschool of kids, rob a rich lady on Park Avenue, hide her body, grind up some teenagers, and then disappear to manage their investments.

Anyhow, that ranch came and went and soon we were in a used El Dorado with 120,000 miles on it. I was in the backseat, with five dozen ostrich eggs. Dad was forty-eight, or thereabouts, and he was bald, and he was paunchy, and, because of the failure of all the gold-rush schemes, he was discouraged and mean. If he spoke at all it was just to gripe at politicians. He was an independent, in terms of gripes. Just so you know. Nonpartisan. And the only hair left on his ugly head, after all the worrying, was around those two patches just above his ears, just like if he were an ostrich chick himself. Because you know when they came out of the shell, these chicks looked like human fetuses. In fact, I've heard it said that a human being and an ostrich actually share 38 per cent of their DNA, which is pretty much when you think about it. So Dad looked like an ostrich. Or maybe he looked like one of those cancer survivors from Golden Meadow Estates who were always saying they felt like a million bucks even though it was obvious that they felt like about a buck fifty. Mom, on the other hand, despite her bad business decisions, only seemed to get prettier and prettier. She still spent a couple of hours each morning making up her face with pencils and brushes in a color called deadly nightshade.

In terms of volume, one ostrich egg is the equivalent of two dozen of your regular eggs. It's got two liters of liquefied muck in it. That means, if you're a short-order cook, that one of these ostrich eggs can last you a long time. A whole day, maybe. The ostrich shell is about the size of a regulation football, but it's shaped just like the traditional chicken eggshell. Which is something I was told to say to tourists, Note your traditional eggshell styling. The ostrich egg is so perfect that it looks fake. The ostrich egg looks like it's made out of plastic. In fact, maybe the guys who came up with plastics got the idea from looking at the perfection of the ostrich egg. Myself, I could barely eat one of those ostrich eggs without worrying about seeing a little ostrich fledgling in it, because it looked so much like a human fetus, or what I imagined a human fetus looked like based on some pictures I'd seen in the Golden Books

Encyclopedia. What if you accidentally ate one of the fledglings! Look out! They made pretty good French toast, though.

Over the years, my dad had assembled an ostrich freak exhibition. There were lots of genetic things that could go wrong with an ostrich flock, like say an ostrich had four legs, or an ostrich had two heads, or the ostrich didn't have any head at all, just a gigantic midsection. Maybe the number of genetic abnormalities in our stock had to do with how close the farm was to a dioxin-exuding paper plant, or maybe it was the chromium or the PCBs, whatever else. It was always something. The important part here is that the abnormalities made Dad sort of happy and enabled him to have a collection to take away from the Rancho Double Zero, and what's the harm in that. Not a lot of room for me in the back seat, though, what with the eggs and the freaks.

The restaurant we started wasn't in Bidwell, because we had bad memories of Bidwell, after the foreclosure and all. There wasn't much choice but to move farther out where things were cheaper. We landed in Pickleville, where it was real cheap, all right, and where there wasn't anything to do. People used to kill feral cats in Pickleville. There was a bounty on them. Kids learned to obliterate any and all wildlife. Pickleville also had a train station where the out-of-state train stopped once a day. Mom figured what with the train station right nearby there was a good chance that people would want to stop at a family-style restaurant. So it was a diner, Dizzy's, which was the nickname we had given our ostrich chick with two heads. The design of our restaurant was like the traditional style of older diners, you know, shaped like a suppository, aluminum and chrome, jukeboxes at every booth. We lived out back. I was lucky. I got to go to a better school district and fraternize with a better class of kids who called me hayseed and accused me of intimate relations with brutes.

My parents bought a neon sign, and they made a shelf where Dad put his ostrich experiments, and then they got busy cooking up open-faced turkey sandwiches and breaded fish cutlets and turkey hash and lots of things with chipped beef in them. Just about everything in the restaurant had chipped beef in it. Mom decided that the restaurant should stay open nights (she never had to see my dad that way, since he worked a different shift), for the freight trains that emptied out their passengers in Pickleville occasionally. Freight hoboes would come in wearing that hunted expression you get from never having owned a thing and having no fixed address. Sometimes these guys would order an egg over easy, and Dad would attempt to convince them that they should have an ostrich egg. He would haul one of the eggs down, and the hoboes would get a load of the ostrich egg and there would be flourishing of change money, and then these hoboes would be gone.

My guess is that Dad had concluded that most Midwestern people were friendly, outgoing folks, and that, in spite of his failure in any enterprise that ever had his name on it, in spite of his galloping melancholy, he should make a real attempt to put on a warm, entertaining manner with the people who came into the diner. It was a jolly innkeeper strategy. It was a last-chance thing. He tried smiling at customers, and even at me, and he tried smiling at my mother, and it caught on. I tried smiling at the alley cat who lived in the trailer with us. I even tried smiling at the kids at school who called me hayseed. But then an ostrich egg ruined everything.

One rainy night I was up late avoiding homework when I heard a really scary shriek come from the restaurant. An emergency wail that couldn't be mistaken for anything but a real emergency. Made goosebumps break out on me. My dad burst into the trailer, weeping horribly, smashing plates. What I remember best was the fact that my mother, who never touched the old man, caressed the bald part of the top of his head, as if she could smooth out the canals of his worry lines.

It was like this. Joe Kane, a strip-club merchant in Bidwell, was waiting for his own dad, Republican district attorney of Bidwell, to come through on the train that night. There'd been a big case up at the state capital. The train was late and Joe was loafing in the restaurant, drinking coffees, playing through all the Merle Haggard songs on the jukebox. After a couple of hours of ignoring my dad, Joe felt like he ought to try to say something. He went ahead and blurted out a pleasantry, —Waiting for the old man. On the train. Train's running late.

Probably, Dad had thought so much about this body that was right there in front of him, this body who happened to be the son of the district attorney, that he started getting really nervous. A white foam began to accumulate at the corners of his mouth. And like in your chess games that kind of pile outward from the opening, maybe dad was attempting to figure out every possible future conversation with Joe Kane, ahead of time, so he would have something witty to say, becoming, in the process, a complete retard.

He said the immortal words, —How-de-do.

—How-de-do? said Joe Kane. Did anyone still say stuff like this? Did kiddy television greetings still exist in the modern world of schoolyard massacres and religious cults? Next thing you know my father'd be saying poopy diapers, wee-nie roast, tra la la, making nookie. Just so he could conduct his business. He'd locate in his playbook the conversational gambit entitled withering contempt dawns in the face of your auditor, and, according to this playbook, wasn't anything else for him to do but go on being friendly, and he would.

—Uh, well, have you heard the one about how Christopher Columbus, discoverer of this land of ours, was a cheat? Sure was. Said he could make an egg stand on its end, which obviously you can only do when the calendar's on the equinoxes. And when he couldn't make the egg stand, why he had to crush the end of the egg. Maybe it was a hard-boiled egg, I don't know. Obviously, he can't have been that great a man if he had to crush the end of the egg in order to make it stand. I wonder, you know, whether we ought to be having all these annual celebrations in honor of him, since he was a liar about the egg incident. Probably about other things too. He claimed he hadn't crushed the end of the egg when he had. That's not dealing fair.

To make his point, my father took an ostrich egg from the shelf where a half-dozen were all piled up for use at the diner. The counter was grimy with a shellac of old bacon and corn syrup and butterfat and honey and molasses and salmonella. He set the egg down here.

—Helluva egg, Joe Kane remarked. —What is that, some kind of nuclear egg? You make that in a reactor?

—I know more about eggs than any man living, my father mumbled.

—Don't doubt that for a second, Joe Kane said.

—This egg will bend to my will. It will succumb to my powers of magic.

—If you say so.

My dad attempted to balance the ostrich egg on its end without success. He tried a number of times. Personally, I don't get where people thought up this idea about balancing eggs. You don't see people trying to balance gourds or footballs. But people seem like they have been trying to balance eggs since there were eggs to balance. Maybe it's because we all come from some kind of ovum, even if it doesn't look exactly like the kind that my father kept tipping up onto its end in front of Joe Kane, but since we come from some kind of ovum and since that is the closest we can get to any kind of real point of origin, maybe we're all kind of dumb on the subject of ova, although on the other hand, I guess these ova probably had to come from some chicken, and vice versa. Don't get me confused. Joe had to relocate his cup of coffee out of the wobbly trajectory of the shell. A couple of times. My father couldn't get anything going in terms of balancing the ostrich egg and so why did he keep trying?

Next, Dad got down the formaldehyde jars from up on the shelf, and started displaying for Joe Kane some deformed ostriches. In his recitation about the abnormalities he had names for a lot of the birds. He showed Joe the fetus with two heads, Dizzy; she was the sweetest little chick, and then showed Joe one with four legs. He showed Joe two or three sets of Siamese twin ostriches, including the set called Jack 'n' Jill. This pair could run like a bat out of hell. My dad's voice swelled. He was a proud parent. He gazed deeply into yellowed formaldehyde.

Joe Kane tried to figure an escape. He looked like an ostrich himself, right then, a mouth-breather, a shill waiting for the sideshow, where the real freaks, the circus owners themselves, would go to any lengths, glue a piece of bone on the forehead of a Shetland pony and call it a unicorn, for the thrill of separating crowds from wallets. Wasn't there any other place for Joe to take shelter from the buckets of rain falling from the sky? Must have been a lean-to or something. On the good side of the tracks.

—This bird here has two male appendages, and I know a number of fellows would really like it if they had two of those. Imagine all the trouble you could get into with the ladies.

Ever notice how in the Midwest no one ever kisses anyone? That little peck on the cheek people are always giving one another back East? Nice to see you! Much less in evidence here in the Midwest. It accounts for the ostrich farmhands and their romantic pursuits, turned down by wives, just looking for some glancing contact somewhere, with a mouth-breather, if necessary. They came home, these working men, to wives reciting lists of incomplete chores, because of which they'd just get right back into their pickups and head for the drive-thru. They'd sing their lamenting songs into drive-thru microphones. My father had seen a man once slap another man good-naturedly on the shoulder after a friendly exchange about a baseball. This was at a fast-food joint. He was sick with envy right then. And that's why, since he'd just shown Joe Kane an ostrich fetus with two penises, he decided to chuck Joe under the chin, as a sign of neighborly good wishes. My father came out from around the counter—he was a big man, I think I already said, 250 pounds, and over six feet—and as Joe Kane attempted to get up from his stool, my father chucked him under the chin.

—Take a weight off for a second, friend; I'm going to show you how to get an ostrich egg into a Coke bottle. And when the magic's done you can carry this Coke bottle around with you as a souvenir. I'll give it to you as a special gift. Here's how I do it. I heat this egg in regular old vinegar, kind you get anyplace, and that loosens up the surface of the egg, and then I just slip it into this liter bottle of Coke, which I also bought at the mini-mart up the road, and then when it's inside the Coke bottle, it goes back to its normal hardness.

When people ask you how you did it, you just don't let on. Okay? It's our secret. Is that a deal?

What could Joe say? Dad already had the vinegar going on one of the burners. When the egg had been heated in this solution, my dad began attempting to cram the thing into the Coke bottle, to disappointing results. Of course, the Coke bottle kept toppling end over end. Falling behind the counter. Dad would have to go pick it up again. Meantime, the train was about to come in. Hours had passed. The train was wailing through the crossing. My father jammed the ostrich egg, which didn't look like it had loosened up at all, against the tiny Coke bottle opening, without success. Maybe if he had a wide-mouth bottle instead.

—Last time it worked fine.

—Look, I gotta go. Train's pulling in. My dad's —

—Sit down on that stool. Damned if you're going to sit in here for two hours on a bunch of coffees, eighty-five-cent cups of coffee, and that's going to be all the business I'm gonna have all week, you son of a bitch. I know one place I can get this egg to fit. Goddamn you.

And this is where the ostrich egg broke, of course, like a geyser, like an explosion at the refinery of my old man's self-respect. Its unfertilized gunk, pints of it, splattered all over the place, on the counter, the stools, the toaster, the display case of stale donuts. Then Joe Kane, who was already at the door, having managed to get himself safely out of the way, laughed bitterly. My father, his face pendulous with tusks of egg white, reached himself down an additional ostrich egg and attempted to hurl it at Joe Kane. But, come on, that was like trying to be a shot-put champion. He managed to get it about as far as the first booth, where it shattered on the top of a jukebox, obscuring in yolk an entire run of titles by the Judds.

Next thing that happened, of course, was the blood-curdling shriek I already told you about. I'm sorry for it turning up in the story twice, but that's just how it is this time. My father, alone in the restaurant, like the proverbial bear in the trap, screamed his emergency scream, frightened residents of Pickleville for miles around, especially little kids. People who are happy when they're speculating about other people's business, they might want to make a few guesses about that scream, like that my dad was ashamed of himself because the trick with the ostrich egg didn't work, or my dad was experiencing a crisis of remorse because he couldn't ever catch a break. And these people would be right, up to a point, but they'd be missing a crucial piece of information that I have and which I'm going to pass along. My father screamed, actually, because he was experiencing a shameful gastrointestinal problem. That's right. It's not really, you know, a major part of the story, but there was this certain large food company that was marketing some cheese snacks with a simulated fatty acid in them, and that large company was test marketing the cheese snacks guess where? Buckeye State. Where these companies test marketed lots of products for people they thought were uninformed. These cheese snacks were cheap, all right, a real bargain when compared to leading brands, and they had a cheddar flavor. Only problem was, since your large and small intestines couldn't absorb the fatty acid, it was deposited right out of you, usually in amounts close to two or three tablespoons. Right in your briefs, an oily residue that didn't come out in the wash. Depended on how fond you were of the cheese snacks. If you ate a whole bag, it could be worse. So the truth is, on top of having egg on his face, my dad messed his pants. It was a rough day.

You'll be wanting to know how I know all this stuff, all these things, that happened to my father in the restaurant, especially since I wasn't there and since Dad would never talk about any of it. Especially not anal leakage. Wouldn't talk about much at all, after that, unless he was complaining about Ohio State during football season. You'll want to know how I know so much about the soul of Ohio, since I was a teenager when all this happened and was supposed to be sullen and hard to reach. Hey, what's left in this breadbasket nation, but the mystery of imagination? My mother lay in bed, hatched a plan, how to get herself out of this place, how to give me a library of books. One night she dreamed of escaping from the Rust Belt, from a sequence of shotgun shacks and railroad apartments. A dream of a boy in the shape of a bird in the shape of a story, a boy who has a boy who has a boy: each generation's dream cheaper than the last, like for example all these dreams now feature Chuck E. Cheese (A special birthday show performed by Chuck E. Cheese and his musical friends!) or Cracker Barrel or Wendy's or Arby's or Red Lobster or the Outback Steakhouse or Boston Chicken or Taco Bell or Burger King or TCBY or Pizza Hut or Baskin Robbins or Friendly's or Hard Rock Cafe or KFC or IHOP or Frisch's Big Boy. Take a right down by Sam's Discount Warehouse, Midas Muffler, Target, Barnes & Noble, Home Depot, Wal-Mart, Super Kmart, Ninety-Nine Cent Store. My stand's at the end of the line. Eggs in this county they're the biggest darned eggs you ever seen in your whole life.

K IS FOR FAKE

by JONATHAN LETHEM

"The birth of the sad-eyed waifs was in Berlin in 1947 when I met these kids," Mister Keane said. "Margaret asked for my help to learn to paint, and I suggested that she project a picture she liked on a canvas and fill it in like children do a numbered painting. Then the woman started copying my paintings."

While he has sought redress in the courts twice, Margaret Keane has thus far emerged the winner. A lawsuit against her for copyright infringement was dismissed; she then sued Mister Keane for libel for statements he made in an interview with USA Today, and to back her suit, she executed a waif painting in front of the jury in less than one hour. She won a $4 million judgment. Walter Keane declined to participate in the paint-off, citing a sore shoulder.

—*The New York Times*, Feb. 26, 1995

K.'s PHONE RANG while he was watching cable television, an old movie starring the Famous Clown. In the movie the Famous Clown lived in a war-torn European city. The Famous Clown walked down a dirt road trailed, like the Pied Piper, by a line of ragged children. The Famous Clown juggled three lumps of bread, the hardened heels of French loaves. K.'s phone rang twice and then he lifted the receiver. It was after eleven. He wasn't expecting a call. "Yes?" he said. "Is this painter called K.?" "Yes, but I'm not interested in changing my long distance—" The voice interrupted him: "The charges against you have at last been prepared." The voice was ponderous with authority. K. waited, but the voice was silent. K. heard breath resound in some vast cavity. "Charges?" said K., taken aback. K. paid the minimums on his credit cards promptly each month. "You'll wish to answer them," intoned the voice. "We've prepared a preliminary hearing. Meanwhile a jury is being assembled. But you'll undoubtedly wish to familiarize yourself with the charges."

On the screen the Famous Clown was being clapped in irons by a pair of jackbooted soldiers. The ragamuffin children scattered, weeping, as the Famous Clown was dragged away. Through the window beyond K.'s television the cityscape was visible, the distant offices, lights now mostly extinguished, and the nearby apartments, from whose open windows gently arguing voices drifted like mist through the summer air. On the phone the sonorous breathing continued. "Is it possible to send me a printed statement?" said K. He wondered if he should have spoken, whether he had in fact now admitted to the possibility of charges. "No," sighed the voice on the phone. "No, the accused must appear in person; hearing first, then trial. All in due course. In the meantime a defense should be readied." "A defense?" K. said. He had hoped that whatever charges he faced could be cleared by rote and at a remove, by checking a box or signing a check. K. had once pleaded no contest to a vehicular infraction by voicemail. "Press One for No Contest," the recorded voice had instructed him. "Press Two for Not Guilty. Press Three for Guilty with an Explanation." "A defense, most certainly," said the voice on K.'s telephone now. "Be assured, you are not without recourse to a defense." The voice grew suddenly familiar, avuncular, conspiratory. "Don't lose heart, K. That is always your weakness. I'll be in touch." With that K.'s caller broke the connection. More in curiosity than fear K. dialed *69, but his caller's number had a private listing. K. replaced the receiver. On his television the Famous Clown was in shackles in a slant-roofed barracks, his head being shaved by a sadistic commandant. Wide-eyed children with muddy cheeks and ragged hair peered in through a window. In the distance past them a sprawling barbed-wire fence was visible, and at the corner of the fence a high wooden tower topped with a gunnery. K. thumbed the remote. The Sci-Fi channel was in the course of a *Twilight Zone* marathon. A man awoke alone in terror, in sweats, in a shabby black-and-white room. The camera boxed at him, the score pulsed ominously. K. fell asleep, comforted.

The central European Jewish world which Kafka celebrated and ironized

went to hideous extinction. The spiritual possibility exists that Franz Kafka
experienced his prophetic powers as some visitation of guilt...

—*George Steiner*

I consider him guilty... he is not guilty of what he's accused of, but he's guilty
all the same.—*Orson Welles*, on *The Trial*

K. was on his way to visit his art dealer, Titorelli, when the Waif appeared in
the street before him. It was a cold day, and heaps of blackened snow lay everywhere in the street. The Waif wasn't dressed for the cold. The Waif stood shivering, huddled. Titorelli's gallery was in Dumbo (Down Under the Manhattan
Bridge Overpass) and though it was midday the cobblestone streets were
empty of passersby. Above them loomed the corroded pre-war warehouses, once
Mafia-owned, now filled with artists' studios and desirable loft apartments.
The sky was chalky and gray, the chill wind off the East River faintly rank.
The Waif's huge eyes beckoned to K. They gleamed with tears, but no tears
fell. The Waif took K.'s hand. The Waif's grip was cool, fingers squirming in
K.'s palm. Together they walked under the shadow of the vast iron bridge, to
Titorelli's building. K. wanted to lead the Waif to shelter, to warmth. Through
the plate glass window on which was etched Titorelli's name and the gallery's
hours K. saw Titorelli and his art handler, Lilia, animatedly discussing a painting which sat on the floor behind the front desk. K. glanced at the Waif, and
the Waif nodded at K. K. wondered how the Waif would be received by
Titorelli and Lilia. Perhaps in the refrigerator in the back of the gallery a bit of
cheese and cracker remained from the gallery's most recent opening reception,
a small snack which could be offered to the Waif. K. pictured the Waif eating
from a saucer on the floor, like a pet. In his imaginings the Waif would always
be with him now, would follow him home and take up residence there. Now
K. pushed the glass door and they stepped inside. Immediately the Waif
pulled away from K. and ran silently along the gallery wall, moving like a cat
in a cathedral, avoiding the open space at the center of the room. The Waif
vanished through the door into the back offices of the gallery without being
noticed, and K. found himself alone as he approached Titorelli and Lilia. The
art dealer and his assistant contemplated a canvas on which two trees stood on
a desolate grassy heath, framing a drab portion of gray sky. As K. moved closer
he saw that the floor behind the desk was lined with a series of similar paintings. In fact they were each identical to the first: trees, grass, sky. "The subject
is too somber," said Titorelli, waving his hand, dismissing the canvas. Lilia

only nodded, then moved another of the paintings into the place of the first. "Too somber," said Titorelli again, and again, "Too somber," as Lilia presented a third example of the indifferently depicted heathscape. Lilia removed it and reached for another. "Why don't you hang them upside down?" remarked K., unable to bear the thought of hearing Titorelli render his verdict again, wishing to spare Lilia as well. "Upside down?" repeated Titorelli, his gaze still keenly focused on the painting as though he hadn't yet reached a complete judgement. "That may be brilliant. Let's have a look." Then, looking up: "Oh, hello, K." K. greeted Titorelli, and Lilia as well. The assistant lowered her gaze shyly. She had always been daunted and silent in K.'s presence. "Quickly, girl, upside down!" commanded Titorelli. K. craned his neck, trying to see into the back office, to learn what had become of the Waif. "Have you got anything to drink, Titorelli?" K. asked. "There might be a Coke in the fridge," said Titorelli, waving distractedly. K. slipped through the doorway into the back room, where a cluttered tumult of canvases and shipping crates nearly concealed the small refrigerator. K. didn't see the Waif. He went to the refrigerator and opened the door. The Waif was inside the refrigerator. The Waif was huddled, arms wrapped around its shoulders, trembling with cold, its eyes wide and near to spilling with tears. The Waif reached out and took K.'s hand again. The Waif stepped out of the refrigerator and, tugging persistently at K.'s hand, led him to the vertical racks of large canvases which lined the rear wall of the office. Moving aside a large shipping tube which blocked its entrance the Waif stepped into the last of the vertical racks, which was otherwise empty. K. followed. Unexpectedly, the rack extended beyond the limit of the rear wall, into darkness, alleviated only by glints of light which penetrated the slats on either side. The Waif led K. around a bend in this narrow corridor to where the space opened again into a tall foyer, its walls made of the same rough lath which lined the racks, with stripes of light leaking through faintly. In this dark room K. discerned a large shape, a huge lumpen figure in the center of the floor. The glowing end-tip of a cigar flared, and dry paper crackled. As the crackle faded K. could hear the sigh of a long inhalation. The Waif again released K.'s hand and slipped away into the shadows. K.'s eyes began to adjust to the gloom. He was able to make out the figure before him. Seated in a chair was a tremendously fat man with a large, stern forehead and a shock of white eyebrows and beard. He was dressed in layers of overlapping coats and vests and scarves and smoked a tremendous cigar. K. recognized the man from television. He was the Advertising Pitchman.

The Advertising Pitchman was advocate for certain commercial products:

wine, canned peas and pears, a certain make of automobile, et cetera. He loaned to the cause of their endorsement his immense gravity and bulk, his overstuffed authority. "It is good you've come, K.," said the Advertising Pitchman. K. recognized the Advertising Pitchman's voice now as well. It was the sonorous voice on the phone, the voice which had warned him of the accusation against him. "We're overdue to begin preparations for your defense," continued the Pitchman. "The preliminary hearing has been called." The Advertising Pitchman sucked again on his cigar; the tip flared; the Pitchman made a contented sound. The cigar smelled stale. "By any chance did you see a small child—a Waif?" asked K. "Yes, but never mind that now. It is too late to help the child," said the Pitchman. "We must concern ourselves with answering the charges." The Pitchman rustled in his vest and produced a sheaf of documents. He placed his cigar in his lips to free both hands, and thumbed through the papers. "Not now," said K., feeling a terrible urgency, a sudden force of guilt regarding the Waif. He wondered if he could trouble the Pitchman for a loan of one of his voluminous scarves; one would surely be enough to cloak the Waif, shelter it from the cold. "I want to help—" K. began, but the Pitchman interrupted. "If you'd thought of that sooner you wouldn't be in this predicament." The Pitchman consulted the papers in his lap. "Self-absorption is among the charges." K. circled the Pitchman, feeling his way through the room by clinging to the wall, as though he were a small bearing circling a wheel, the Pitchman the hub. "Self-absorption, Self-amusement, Self-satisfaction," continued the Pitchman. K. found himself unable to bear the sound of the Pitchman's voice, precisely for its quality of self-satisfaction; he said nothing, instead continued his groping search, moving slowly enough that he wouldn't injure the Waif should he stumble across it. "Ah, here's another indictment—Impersonation." "Shouldn't that be Self-impersonation?" replied K. quickly. He believed his reply quite witty, but the Pitchman seemed not to notice, instead went on shuffling papers and calling out charges. "Insolence, Infertility, Incompleteness—" By now K. had determined that the Waif had fled the cul-de-sac he and the Pitchman currently inhabited, had vanished back through the corridor behind them, through the gallery racks, perhaps even slipping silently between K.'s legs to accomplish this feat. "See under Incompleteness: Failure, Reticence, Inability to Achieve Consummation or Closure; for reference see also Great Chinese Wall, Tower of Babel, *Magnificent Ambersons*, et cetera," continued the Pitchman. K. ignored him, stepped back into the narrow corridor. "See under Impersonation: Forgery, Fakery, Ventriloquism, Impersonation of the Father, Impersonation of the Gentile, Impersonation of the Genius, Usurpation of the Screenwriter—" K. moved through the corridor back toward the gallery office and the Pitchman's voice soon faded. K. made his way through the glinted darkness of the gallery racks to Titorelli's office. The Waif was nowhere to be seen, but Lilia waited there, and when K. emerged she came near to him and whispered close to his ear. "I told Titorelli I had to go to the bathroom in order to come find you," she said teasingly. "I didn't really have to go." The shyness Lilia exhibited in front of Titorelli was gone now. Her sleek black hair had fallen from the place where it had been pinned behind her ears, and her glasses were folded into her blouse pocket. "Perhaps you've seen a child," said K. "A little— Waif. In tatters. With big eyes. And silent, like a mouse. It would have just run through here a moment ago." Lilia shook her head. K. felt that there only must be some confusion of terms, for Lilia had been standing at the entrance to the racks, apparently waiting for K. "A small thing—" K. lowered his hand to indicate the dwarfish proportions. "No," said Lilia. "We're alone here." "The Waif has been with me in the gallery all this time," said K. "We entered together. You and Titorelli were distracted and didn't notice." Lilia shook her head helplessly. "The Waif is like a ghost," said K. "Only I can see it, it follows me. It must have some meaning." Lilia stroked K.'s hand and said, "What a strange experience. It's practically Serlingesque." "Serlingesque?" asked K., unfamiliar with the term. "Yes," said Lilia. "You know, like something out of *The Twilight Zone.*" "Oh," said K., surprised and pleased by the reference. But it wasn't exact, wasn't quite right. "No, I think it's more—" K. couldn't recall the adjective he was seeking. "Titorelli was very happy with your suggestion," whispered Lilia. She put her lips even closer to his ear, and he felt the warmth of her body transmitted along his arm. "He's hung them all upside down—you'll see when you go back into the gallery. But don't go outside yet." K. was faintly disturbed; he'd intended the remark to Titorelli as a joke. "What about the artist's intentions?" he asked Lilia. "The artist's intentions don't matter," said Lilia. "Anyway, the artist is dead, and his intentions are unknown. He left instructions to destroy these canvases. You've saved them; the credit belongs to you." "There's little credit to be gained turning a thing upside down," said K., but Lilia seemed oblivious to his reflections. She pulled at his collar, then traced a line under his jaw with her finger, closing her eyes and smiling dreamily while she did it. "Do you have any tattoos?" she whispered. "What?" said K. "Tattoos, on your body," said Lilia, tugging his collar farther from his collarbone, and peering into his shirt. "No," said K. "Do you?" "Yes," said Lilia, smiling shyly. "Just one. Do you want to see it?" K. nodded. "Turn around," commanded Lilia. K. turned to face the rear wall of the gallery office.

He wondered if Titorelli was occupied, or if the gallery owner had noticed K.'s and Lilia's absence. "Now, look," said Lilia. K. turned. Lilia had unbuttoned her shirt and spread it open. Her brassiere was made of black lace. K. was nearly moved to fall upon Lilia and rain her throat with kisses, but hesitated: something was evident in the crease between her breasts, a mark or sign. Lilia undid the clasp at the center of the brassiere and parted her hands, so that she concealed and also gently parted her breasts. The tattoo in her cleavage was revealed. It was an image of the Waif, or a child very much like the Waif, with large, shimmering eyes, a tiny, downturned mouth, and strawlike hair. Looking more closely, K. saw that the Waif in the tattoo on Lilia's chest also bore a tattoo: a line of tiny numerals on the interior of the forearm. "I should go," said K. "Titorelli must be wondering about us." "You can visit me here anytime," whispered Lilia, quickly buttoning her shirt. "Titorelli doesn't care." "I'll call," said K., "or email—do you email?" K. felt in a mild panic to return to the front of the gallery, and to pursue the Waif. "Just email me here at the gallery," said Lilia. "I answer all the emails you send, anyway. Titorelli never reads them." "But you answer them in Titorelli's voice!' said K. He was distracted from his urgency by this surprise. "Yes," said Lilia, suddenly dropping her voice in impersonation to a false basso, considerably deeper than Titorelli's in fact, but making the point nonetheless. "I pretend to be a man on the internet," she said in the deep voice, dropping her chin to her neck and narrowing her nostrils as well, to convey a ludicrous satire of masculinity. "Don't tell anyone." K. kissed her cheek quickly and rushed out to the front of the gallery, where he found Titorelli adjusting the last of the small landscapes in its place on the wall. The paintings were hung upside down, and they lined the gallery now. "There you are," said Titorelli. He thrust a permanent marker into K.'s hand. "I need your signature." "Did you see a—a child, a Waif?" said K., moving to Titorelli's desk, wanting to sign any papers quickly and be done with it. "A wraith?" said Titorelli. "No, a Waif, a child with large, sad eyes," said K. "Where are the papers?" K. looked through the front window of the gallery and thought he saw the Waif standing some distance away, down the snowy cobblestone street, huddled again in its own bare arms and staring in his direction. "Not papers," said Titorelli. "Sign the paintings." Titorelli indicated the nearest of the upside-down oils. He tapped his finger at the lower right-hand corner. "Just your initial." In irritation K. scrawled his mark on the painting. "I have to go—" he said. The Waif waited out in the banks of snow, beckoning to him with its sorrowful, opalescent eyes. "Here," said Titorelli, guiding K. by the arm to a place beside the next of the inverted heathscapes. K. signed. Outside, the Waif had turned away. "And the next," said Titorelli. "All of them?" asked K. in annoyance. Outside, the Waif had begun to wander off, was now only a speck barely visible in the snowy street. "Please," said Titorelli. K. autographed the remaining canvases, then headed for the door. "Perhaps now we can market these atrocities," said Titorelli. "If they move I'll have her paint a few more; she can do them in her sleep." "I'm sorry," said K., doubly confused. Market atrocities? Paint in her sleep? Outside, the Waif had vanished. "Isn't the painter of these canvases dead?" K. asked. "Not dead," said Titorelli. "If you really think she can be called an artist. Lilia is responsible for these paintings." Outside, the Waif had vanished.

> Citizen Kafka
> —name of punk band on flyer, San Francisco, circa 1990

As the babyfaced wunderkind awoke one morning from uneasy dreams he found himself transformed in his bed into a three-hundred-pound advertising pitchman.

As Superman awoke one morning from a Red K Dream he found himself transformed in his bed into two Jewish cartoonists.

As the laughing-on-the-outside clown awoke one morning from uneasy dreams he found himself transformed in his bed into a gigantic crying-on-the-inside clown.

As the painter of weeping children awoke one morning from uneasy dreams he found himself transformed in his bed into his own defense attorney, a man who in his previous career in Hollywood had himself been accused of charlatanism, plagiarism, and dyeing Rita Hayworth's hair black. Great, he thought, this is just what I need. He found that he was so heavy he had to roll himself out of bed.

As Modernism awoke one morning from uneasy dreams it found itself transformed in its bed into a gigantic Postmodernism.

The Waif didn't have a bed.

Gregor Samsa ducked into a nearby phone booth. "This looks," he said, "like a job for a gigantic insect."

In my masterwork I wanted to portray the unsolved problems of mankind; all rooted in war, as that vividly remembered sight of the human rats amid the rubble of Berlin so poignantly signified... endless drawings, the charcoal sketches lay scattered along the years. Each in its groping way had helped lead me to this moment...

—Walter Keane, in *Walter Keane: Tomorrow's Master Series*

I've come up against the last boundary, before which I shall in all likelihood again sit down for years, and then in all likelihood begin another story all over again that will again remain unfinished. This fate pursues me.

—Kafka, *Diaries*

On a gray spring morning before K.'s thirty-first birthday K. was summoned to court for his trial. He hadn't thought a trial so long delayed would ever actually begin, but it had. Go figure. K. was escorted from his apartment to the court by a couple of bailiffs, men in black suits and dark glasses and with grim, set expressions on their faces that struck K. as ludicrous. "You look like extras from the *X-Files*!" he exclaimed, but the bailiffs were silent. They held K.'s arms and pressed him close from both sides, and in this manner K. was guided downstairs and into the street. In silence the bailiffs steered K. through indifferent crowds of rush-hour commuters and midmorning traffic jams of delivery trucks and taxicabs, to the new Marriott in downtown Brooklyn. A sign in the lobby of the Marriott said: "Welcome Trial of K., Liberty Ballroom A/B," and in smaller letters underneath: "A Smoke-Free Building." K. and the bailiffs moved through the lobby to the entrance of the ballroom which now served as a makeshift court. The ballroom was already packed with spectators, who broke into a chorus of murmurs at K.'s appearance at the back of the room. The bailiffs released K.'s arms and indicated that he should precede them to the front of the court, where judge and jury, as well as prosecuting and defending attorneys, waited. K. moved to the front, holding himself erect to indicate his indifference to the craning necks and goggling eyeballs of the spectators, his deafness to their murmurs. As he approached the bench K. saw that his defending attorney was none other than the Advertising Pitchman. The Pitchman levered his bulk out of his chair and rose to greet K., offering a hand to shake. K. took his hand, which was surprisingly soft and which retreated almost instantly from K.'s grip. Now K. saw that the prosecuting attorney was the Famous Clown. The Famous Clown was dressed in an impeccable three-piece suit and tremendously wide, pancakelike black shoes which were polished to a high gloss. The Famous Clown remained in his seat, scowling behind bifocal lenses at a sheaf of papers on his desk, pretending not to have noticed K.'s arrival. Seated at the high bench in the place of a judge was the Waif. The Waif sat on a tall stool behind the bench. The Waif wore a heavy black robe, and on its head sat a thickly curled wig which partly concealed its strawlike thatch of hair but did nothing to conceal the infinitely suffering black pools of its eyes. The Waif toyed with its gavel, seemingly preoccupied and indifferent to K.'s arrival in the courtroom. K. was guided by the Pitchman to a seat at the defense table, where he faced the Waif squarely, the Prosecuting Clown at his right. The jurors sat at a dais to K.'s left, and he found himself resistant to turning in their direction. K. wanted no pity, no special dispensation. "Don't fear," stage-whispered the Pitchman. He winked and clapped K.'s shoulder, conspiratory and garrulous at once. "We've practically ended this trial before it's begun," the Pitchman said. "I've exonerated you of nearly all of the charges. Incompleteness, for one. It turns out their only witnesses were the Unfinished Chapters and the Passages Deleted by the Author. They were prepared to put them on the stand one after another, but I disqualified them all on grounds of character." "Their character was deficient?" asked K. "I should say so," boasted the Pitchman, arching an eyebrow dramatically. "Why, just have a look at them. You've left them woefully underwritten!"

K. hadn't understood himself to be the *author* of the Unfinished Chapters and the Passages Deleted by the Author, but rather a fictional character, one subject to the deprivations of being underwritten himself. However, one glance at the Unfinished Chapters and the Passages Deleted by the Author, all of whom sat crowded together in the spectators' gallery, muttering resentfully and glaring in K.'s direction, told K. that they did not themselves understand this to be the case. The Unfinished Chapters held themselves with a degree of decorum, their ties perhaps a little out-of-fashion and certainly improperly knotted, but they at least wore ties; the Passages Deleted by the Author were hardly better than unwashed rabble. Still, K.'s instinct was for forgiveness. He reflected that for Chapters and Passages alike it must have been bitter indeed to be denied their say in court after so long. "Additionally," continued the Pitchman, "you've been cleared of the various charges of Impersonation, Ventriloquism, Usurpation, and the like." "How was this achieved?" asked K., a little resentfully. "Which other witnesses had to be smeared in order that I not need defend myself in this matter in which, incidentally, I am entirely innocent?" The Pitchman was undeterred, and said with a guttural chuckle, "No, not witnesses. This was a side bargain with my counterpart on the opposite aisle." K. glanced at the Famous Clown, who just at that moment was staring across at the Advertising Pitchman with poisonous intensity, even as he readjusted his false buck teeth. K. heard a sharp and rhythmic clapping sound and saw that the Famous Clown was slapping his broad, flat shoes against the floor beneath his desk. The Pitchman seemed not to notice or care. He said, "Let's just say you're not the only one in this room with skeletons in his closet—perhaps I should say with a dressing room full of masks and putty noses." The Pitchman groped his own bulbous proboscis, and grew for one moment reflective, even tragic in his aspect. "I speak even for myself..." He seemed about to digress into some reminiscence, then apparently thought better of it and waved his hand. "Still, congratulations would be premature. One charge against you remains—a trifle, I'm sure. This charge you can eradicate with a few swift brushstrokes." "How with brushstrokes?" asked K. "You stand charged with Forgery," said the Pitchman. "Patently absurd, I know, yet it is the only jeopardy that still remains. A woman has stepped forward and claimed your work as her own. I negotiated with the prosecution a small demonstration before the jury, knowing how this opportunity to clear yourself directly would please you." "A demonstration?" asked K. "Yes," chuckled the Pitchman. "One hardly worthy of your talents. A hot-dog eating contest would be more exalted. Regardless, it should provide the flourish these modern show trials require." K. saw now that the bailiffs had dragged two painting easels to the front of the courtroom and erected them before the Waif's bench. Blank canvases were mounted on each of the easels, and two sets of brushes and two palettes of oils were made available on a table to one side. The Waif was now rolling the handle of its gavel back and forth across the desktop, in an uncharacteristic display of agitation. "A masterpiece isn't required," said the Pitchman. "Merely a display of competence, of facility." "But who is this woman?" asked K. "Here she is now," whispered the Pitchman, nudging K.'s shoulder. K. turned. The woman who had entered the courtroom was Lilia, Titorelli's art handler. There was a buzz from the jury box, like a small hive of insects. Lilia wore a prim white smock and a white painter's hat. Her gaze was fiercely determined, her eyes never lighting on K.'s. "Go now," whispered the Pitchman. "A sentimental subject would be best, I think. Something to stir the hearts of the jurors." K. stood. He saw now that the jury box was full of ragged children, much like the Waif who stood now in its robes and clapped its gavel to urge the painters to commence the demonstration. Lilia seized a brush and began immediately to paint, first outlining two huge orbs in the center of the canvas. K. wondered if they were breasts, then saw that in fact they were two enormous, bathetic eyes: Lilia was initiating a portrait of the

Waif. K. moved for the table. As he reached to take hold of a brush he felt a sudden clarifying pain in the shoulder where the Pitchman had nudged him a moment before, a pain so vivid that he wondered if he would be at all able to paint, or even to lift his arm; it now felt heavy and inert, like a dead limb. Lilia, meanwhile, continued to work intently at her easel.

(Note: It is here the fragment ends. Nevertheless, I believe this sequence, taken in conjunction with the completed chapters which precede it, reveals its meaning with undeniable clarity.— Box Dram, Editor)

> I don't like that ending. To me it's a "ballet" written by a Jewish intellectual before the advent of Hitler. Kafka wouldn't have put that after the death of six million Jews. It all seems very much pre-Auschwitz to me. I don't mean that my ending was a particularly good one, but it was the only possible solution. —Orson Welles, on *The Trial*

See K. awaken one morning from righteous dreams to find himself transformed in his bed into a caped superhero: Holocaust Man!

See Holocaust Man stride forth in the form of the golem, with a marvelously powerful rocklike body and the Star of David chiseled into its chest!

See Holocaust Man and his goofy sidekick, Clown Man, defeat Mister Prejudice, Mister Guilt, Mister Tuberculosis, Mister Irony, Mister Paralysis, and Mister Concentration Camp!

See Holocaust Man and Clown man lead a streaming river of tattered, orphaned children to safety across the battlefields of Europe!

Laugh on the outside! Cry on the inside!

THE DAYS HERE

by KELLY FEENEY

1.

THE HOTEL IS CALLED the Longacre. It is not the kind of place where people introduce themselves. The only way to learn anyone's name is to listen when they are called to the telephone. The announcements are infrequent; they jangle the hollow quiet of the all-beige dining room.

I eat dinner, alone, while it is still light, with a view of the tennis courts where no one ever plays. Some nights I take a sleeping pill at dinner. It makes me feel benevolent. I love the waiter. He brings water to the table—room temperature, no ice—in a perfect, clear cylinder.

Some nights I eat in my room, at my desk. I get nervous waiting for room service. I straighten up the room, making sure I have something to give as a tip. I stare at the door and look at my watch. I am afraid I will look like an amateur, even though I have some experience being waited upon in this way.

The rooms here are pleasant but inert, with worn wooden furniture in streamlined silhouettes, netlike curtains affording little privacy, and slightly faded bedspreads in yellow and turquoise. The palette emulates the decor of the famous sanitarium in Paimio, Finland, and is intended to promote respiratory health. Cleanliness used to be a big part of the rest-cure. I read about it in the "Legendary Longacre" brochure. Another hallmark of the "cheerful-punitive style" is the relentless use of tatami floor mats. They torture my feet with excessive tickling.

The brochure also discusses the difference between the invalid and the convalescent diet (different kinds of broths), warns against improper food combinations, and plaintively observes that "Crumbs in the bed are the greatest enemy to the patient's comfort." The mineral springs dried up a long time ago, and then the movie stars stopped coming in their private planes. These days the overgrown airstrip is mostly a field of red-tipped grass.

In the spirit of the history of the place, I take two baths a day and eat crackers in bed at night.

2.

I tried everything. I tried concentrating on a single far-off object, I tried writing my name in the air until I could do it forward and backward. I tried seminars and haircuts, I even tried looking myself up in the phone book. The more earnestly I sought a cure, the worse it became. I waited for her to die for so long I do not know what else to wait for. I cannot look at pictures of her or read things she wrote. I am no good at making adjustments.

It began in February; it always does. Someone would forget my birthday, and then I'd vow to improve myself.

I started drinking a kind of tea made from boiled sticks that cost eighteen dollars a pound. I pressure-cooked grains. I ate difficult, blood-cleansing vegetables. "Sing a happy song each day," the brochure said.

Or it wasn't February. It might have been spring or fall. I couldn't look at anything anymore, not cars or buildings or sunsets, couldn't say anything funny about the things I hated. Bad taste was everywhere and had to be put down. Whole continents shoved into the ocean, everything must go.

After breakfast, I'd move casually up the attic stairs, checking for squirrels. Often there would be a big, red-eyed, smelly thing in the trap. The trap was called Hav-a-hart, my personal motto. I'd put the thing in the trunk of my car and drive to work. One morning my boss arrived as I was teetering on a snow bank along the edge of the driveway with my captive. Jumping out of his Saab, he complimented me on an unremarkable aspect of my attire. He seemed bewildered by the sight of me. I released the squirrel, who actually spat on me before skittering out of the cage. Something saintly overcame me atop that snow bank, in spite of my dislike of bosses and rodents. For a moment I felt kind and unafraid, twelve miles from my attic. Maybe it was the diet.

At lunchtime, five days a week, I drove to town in a big hurry, trying to make every light. I'd read back issues of *Opera News* in the waiting area of the Child Study Center. I tried to care about opera. Will I ever be too old to see a shrink at the Child Study Center, I'd wonder.

After my appointment, it always seemed that I had to buy a baby gift. The woman at the store smiled at me, because of the seventeen baby gifts I bought there in three years. Did she know about the special burden of the childless? One day I bought a tiny velour hooded tunic with matching pants. Something fit for a small pasha, I mused. I also got a votive candle for myself, one with a picture of a ladder ("La Escalera") in colored glitter. I had been told to burn candles and breathe a lot.

I was on a new regime involving ornate food combinations and oriental pickles. There were foods to enjoy, foods to enjoy occasionally, and foods to avoid. Besides the regimen, there was nothing to do. Nothing to do but engage in soulless avoidance: of caffeine, alcohol, nightshades, subtropical fruits, and electricity. I was hoping for health. A clear, voiceless way of thinking.

3.

Returning to the room after a morning walk around the old resort, I find the bed made. It is crisp-looking, fiercely tucked in. How thrilling to be cared for. In order to get into bed I must pry open the covers and wedge myself in, careful to lie flat as possible between the pressed linens, taking shallow breaths. A little confinement is probably good. Didn't the Puritans torture suspected witches and adulteresses by laying boards on their chests and piling heavy stones until they extracted a confession? Adding stones and asking questions, gradually crushing ribs and lungs.

4.

My boss's marriage was complicated, he told me. Difficult. I didn't want to know about it, didn't want to hear precisely how difficult or complicated it was. But since I possess a naturally watery and sympathetic manner, I listened. He was in a churlish mood because he had bumped his head on the copier. His monogrammed cuff peeked out from beneath his sport coat. This was a yellow tie day. (I kept a private tally of how many he wore in a month.) I slouched in my chair, hoping to appear more intelligent than I felt. His lips were puffy, his eyes bulged well past their sockets. His neck looked as if it might burst open any moment. I listened as long as I thought appropriate, really thinking about office supplies.

At the office I waited for all kinds of things. I waited for FedEx and UPS I waited for the mail, for 11 o'clock and then 3 o'clock and the excuse of going home at the end of the day. But mostly I waited for Mrs. Albrecht to die.

5.

The decaying hotel reminds me of the things I can't see, of the things I don't know to want. I pace around the vacant swimming pool, weaving a path among the disused cabanas. A rose branch scratches my arm; the hotel preys upon my nervous torpor. The light is sometimes perfect in the late afternoons, sweet and pink and solemn. It is the familiar light of lost opportunity.

I came here, decided to come here, as a bet, a kind of joke with myself. My back was hurting and I wanted to go some place where I could lie very still all day. No one believed I had an actual pain. No one thought it warranted room service.

The people at the front desk perhaps do not believe that I am a good person, someone who wants to be healthy. They see me check for messages nearly every hour, trying to feel that I belong in this hotel.

The clerk looks over his reading glasses at me. He does not approve of how I linger in the common room every Saturday, stuck to the celery-colored ottoman, becoming overly involved in the secrets being revealed by the famous chefs on PBS. Puffed pastry has 729 layers, I learned.

One night in my room I am startled by headlights bending their tracks across the bed. The refracted angles of light span my chest and the right side of my face. Is this company? But the car drives past. The lights slip back through the window as carelessly as they came.

6.

I think about what the office must be like when I'm not there. Does everyone still dash into their offices, slamming doors behind them? Do they stay in there a long time, bending and unbending paper clips?

The office, the Foundation, it's called, is in a suburban raised-ranch. When you open the door you see straight upstairs into the kitchen and right down to the office at the same time. The house displays its cheapness unself-consciously. That quality, and the yellow DEAD END sign across the street, always seemed unlucky. Another piece of bad luck is that I worked there thirteen years and some people said I look just like my boss' wife, only thinner.

Now that I'm not there I float up the stairs, above the flimsy metal railing, and peer around the hall corner to see who's there. Mrs. Albrecht's bedroom is now the new person's office. A desk is where her bed once was. I pass into the kitchen where the chrome tea kettle reflects in convex miniature the paintings on the wall behind me. An entire world of yellow squares. I move quietly, cloudlike, down the hall, into what used to be the nurse's room and is now my boss' office. It has been abandoned for an afternoon tennis date. The mail teeters in tall piles. The computer screen burns with the text of an essay he's writing. After Mrs. Albrecht's husband died, a Polish nurse named Yadwiga ran screaming from this room, never to return, because of a ghost.

The phone lights up; downstairs someone is making a call.

7.

Mrs. Albrecht, the woman who kept her husband's foundation going, refused to die for a long time. The year before, the second or third time we thought she was going to die, we FedExed photographs and a draft obituary to the *Times*. She was ninety-three and had a fever of 108. Our actions did not feel hasty. When she finally did die, just when it seemed she would dwindle indefinitely in her bed upstairs, she died in her sleep. I hope she didn't call out for someone who wasn't there.

The writer staffing the arts desk that morning normally wrote about antiques. Her name was Elita, and she asked about the cause of death. "She was ninety-four, she died in her sleep," I said. "She had been failing for a long time."

"The *Times* always specifies the cause of death. What does the police report say?"

"Police report?" I said.

"You didn't call the police? In New York we have to call the police. Do you have a death certificate?"

I could tell I was making a bad impression on Elita, reluctant writer of art obituaries.

"The death certificate says natural causes, old age."

Elita asked if she could speak to my boss. "Of course," I said. "But what about her photograph? You will run that picture of her, won't you?"

"No. Look, we didn't print a picture of her husband when he died, and he was a lot more famous. We like to be consistent."

I put her on hold. I began to feel sorry for any other somewhat-famous widows whose deaths were being reported on Elita's shift.

Charcot-Marie-Tooth disease is a hereditary disorder of the peripheral nervous system characterized by weakness and atrophy, but she did not die of it. She had lymphoma and lost all her hair when she was seventy-seven, but she didn't die of that either. Last year she had a record-breaking fever, and she did not die of that.

She lived through the fever. No one knows why.

I know I went into her room to look at her while waiting for the funeral director to arrive, but I can't remember if I kissed her. I always imagined that I'd want to. I remember the fifty-four white drip-dry blouses in the closet. And two long rows of specially made suede oxfords, the kind with the fringed flap covering the laces. The shoes weighted her withered feet as they dragged the ground. They kept her from floating up.

8.

The days begin early at the hotel because I can't stop thinking about Mrs. Albrecht. It is a problem that cannot be solved awake or asleep. What was the story of her life, why should I try to recollect it, what was she to me?

What do you want to know about her? That she was famous or disciplined, that she did or did not walk with a limp? She was famous, famous enough to have her picture taken but not famous enough always to have it published. And she was disciplined, she hated stopping for lunch. She did walk with a limp (people thought she had rickets) and missed out on all the dances at the Bauhaus. She could not climb a flight of stairs without making a sound so she never became a sneaky person. She preferred the warming up of the orchestra to the actual performance. She loved that in America glasses of water always came with ice and pillowcases without buttons. She did not believe in voting or sunsets. She preferred counting volcanoes and assassinations. She knew that she could not have every single thing worth having in life, so she did not try to.

I cannot remember what I said to her, I cannot remember if I said goodbye the last time I saw her alive. She told me about the crossing once, I remember later on someone told me she often lied about it. I have forgotten most of what she said, except that she threw up almost continuously, the seas were stormy and the trip took longer than usual. When they arrived she was a slim and somewhat minor celebrity in a fur coat. After gathering around her husband for several minutes the reporters suddenly exclaimed, "Hey, let's get one with the wife!"—as if it were a new idea to photograph a man and a woman together on the deck of a ship.

9.

I can hear the guests next door shower and listen to television in the mornings and at night. The voices sound wobbly, twisting through sheetrock and the thin fiberglass shower unit. Water thunders through the hollow bathroom. It is familiar, but surprising. I would like to wash my hair, but I just washed it a few hours ago in a small campaign to divide the day into segments of less and less to do.

I walk through the woods in a thin kind of daylight and feel transparent, or insubstantial, except for the occasional bare branch slapping my coat sleeve. I picture myself in the landscape, in a panorama of inaction.

This is supposed to be about a woman and a hotel, why she went, what she did there. How did she get there? Was there a journey involved? Her gray raincoat, her straight black hair, her eyes, slightly hooded, what will become of her?

Every day something empties out: air, light, the possibility of telling a story, having a story, or recording the boredom. Why do we say we're "bored to tears"? What are we mourning?

I project the dreamed movie of my life, somewhere in the future of enframement, nothing broken, everything continuous, at the center of a spinning landscape, or sinking in a cool green pool after lunch.

10.

Mrs. Albrecht liked me as much as she could bear to like anyone young, female, and ambulatory. She said I was noisy, that my real name was "Boom-boom." Mornings she sat in her wheelchair, shrouded in an enormous white terrycloth robe, staring at a boiled egg. A plastic sip cup of coffee mixed with Ensure trembled in her hand. With excruciating deliberateness, the cup moved toward her mouth. She drank. She swallowed some. She coughed in a serious way several times, but I was used to this and knew not to be alarmed. I'd stand behind her, to her right, looking at my shoes, hoping she wouldn't comment on them. I'd say "Good morning! How are you?" and wait for a response.

Even when the windows were open, the faint smell of urine was every-where. Her ears and hands and nose seemed to get larger all the time, or was it that the rest of her was shrinking?

"What do you hate?" I'd ask her.

"That skirt you're wearing."

"Sorry you don't like it." On this particular day it was leopard-printed denim, short, and had been on sale for nine dollars.

"Hello, pussycat," she said.

11.

I have been told that when you die you cannot breathe, not even through a straw. There are things I'll never be able to do again, things I used to be able to do without concentrating. Time isn't endless and shadowy anymore. From now on, time will be an insanely narrow and ill-conceived corridor connecting nothing. And instead of those romantic shadows, I'll see only a headache-inducing glare.

The present is very close and often makes me feel faint. I see those bright spots dancing. Everywhere I look the spots want to look, too. I am learning to tolerate it. This is what it is like to look for the future.

12.

Dear Mrs. Albrecht:

Hotel stationery is romantic. The idea of it is romantic. You would approve of the bony, lowercase lettering across the bottom:

h o t e l   l o n g a c r e .

Last night I dreamt that I could not sleep because you were lying in the other bed, propped against an enormous pile of mittens, wearing the white terrycloth robe you were buried in. I was afraid to close my eyes. I was afraid to go near you. I woke myself up, certain that everything was my fault.

I remember one night when I was five telling my mother that I was afraid to fall asleep because the world could end during the night and I might not wake up. She told me not to worry, that I'd be in heaven before I knew what happened. A while later when I was still awake in her bed, unable to be comforted by thoughts of a place as scary as heaven, she said, "You know dear, rest is eighty percent of sleep."

It's not that I think of you as being asleep, because I know death is not really like sleep. It's just that when the doctor announced that you died "in your sleep," I wondered how we'd ever know if that was true. You might have awakened because you were feeling bad, and then died. You might have been lying there, looking at that painting that hung opposite your bed, the one Joseph made in the '40s that was supposed to be an abstract allegory of your marriage. (I always wished it had been painted in something more than black, white, and gray.) Maybe the TV was on in the nurse's room and no one heard you calling.

Monday is a popular day to die. The promise of the weekend is past, the dread of another week before. When you were learning English you walked through a field in North Carolina explaining to Joseph that "pasture" was the opposite of "future." I think of that all the time.

I don't go to your house anymore. I try not to drive anywhere near it, in fact. I still have the key to the front door, and I know where everything is inside. The beaver coat, the one you wore in the newspaper photo taken on the S.S. Europa, still hangs in the hall closet. And even though your bedroom is now an office, that little statue of Isis remains on the bookshelf.

I do drive to the cemetery from time to time. I sit there with the windows rolled down looking at the mail, or balancing my checkbook. I don't get out of the car, though, and I know you wouldn't mind.

Who says goodbye to paintings, I wonder. No one driving by its shoebox exterior could tell that 818 Larchwood Drive contained a great collection of modern art. Before leaving I tried to memorize your husband's paintings, as alike as Easter eggs, nested squares of color. Did you tell me they reminded you of hearts beating? Your own work is a kind of ancient writing, loosely woven glyphs painstakingly plotted on a loom. Solemn and hardly ever ethereal, always weighted by the labor of weaving, and impossible to memorize.

The day I left the Foundation I told myself I would go back sometime, that part of me would always be at my desk, looking up out of the basement window. Or I'm in your studio, sitting at the aluminum work table where we sat when I helped steady your hand while you signed your name a few hundred times. Sometimes I picture you in your wheelchair at the top of the stair, waiting in a Chanel knock-off and smelling of L'Origan a full hour before a visitor was due to arrive. It was from that post above the railing that you used to call down to us. That's where you ordered us to cut off a branch of a tree in the front yard because it blocked your view of the mailbox.

On my last day at the Foundation I sorted some of your old letters at the table in your soothing white kitchen. Four small paintings, yellow and orange squares within squares, hung opposite me. I loved them as if they were related to me, but they were the blankest faces I have ever seen.

I have always loved air mail, a ghostly form of travel. Some of the envelopes were pale blue with navy-and-red-striped edges. Aerogrammes from Brazil bore exotic yellow and green slash marks. In them you wrote about painting the kitchen, about the days seeming long, about the unpleasantness of working with wool in August. You wondered whether Joseph remembered to wear his hat on cool days, or took his vitamin pill. Your English was peculiar, cadenced, careful. The complete text of one letter was simply "Without news—."

I touched the linen-patterned Formica, the vinyl dinette chairs, and what you always referred to as the "first Chemex coffee pot in North America," grateful that if people don't go on indefinitely, at least objects do.

13.

If I have lunch early at the hotel the day is ruined, but sometimes this can't be helped. If the day is going to be bad, it's better just to get it over with. Have lunch early, have dinner early, go to sleep early.

Hotel rooms are easier to be in than rooms in houses or offices. You're supposed to be inert in hotels, supposed to watch *Cujo* dubbed into Dutch on TV, or stare at the view if there is one, one that you either can or cannot afford. You are not supposed to make your bed or clean up after yourself. You're supposed to pick up the phone and ask the people who wait on the other end to bring you mineral water and baskets of fruit. Complain if the peaches are too hard and the rolls are stale. And where is the bathrobe you asked for yesterday?

I used to go more places, I have been in other hotels, much livelier than this one. I have been in many hotels trying to forget what I am doing there. In Spain or Italy I drank too much and said things that made a lot of well-dressed people laugh. The next day I couldn't remember what the joke was.

I would like to tell you that I have danced in circles of lamplight outside the Congress Hall in Nuremberg, that I have crawled the pilgrim's route to the church of Hagia Sophia in Istanbul, that I have run cold water over my wrists to keep from fainting in Algeria, but I have not done these things. I have stayed in my hotel room in Cologne, afraid to venture out to a restaurant in the evening, eating an entire cake bought from a bakery for my supper.

I slide through cities and buildings and plazas and mountain ranges, talking to no one. It is cheaper this way, but sadder. There is no comfort. This is how it starts.

SOLICITATION

by REBECCA CURTIS

I WAS WAITING for my lover—I would say boyfriend, but my boyfriend reminds me to say lover, not boyfriend, because we are in school and boyfriend sounds silly for a person in school—and it was late. When my bell rang I thought—here's my lover!—so I opened my top-door, and at the bottom of the stair I saw the face of the crack lady, although of course I didn't know yet who she was.

I'm your neighbor, the crack lady called up through the glass, I live next door.

Now I had a neighbor who lived next door and he was black and his name was Tim, and I liked Tim very much, so when the crack lady said she lived next door I believed her. I did not want to be rude to a friend of Tim's.

You know Tim? I said.

I'm your neighbor, the crack lady said. I live next door.

So I walked down the stairs and I opened the bottom door, the one that goes outside, and then we were body to body.

I need your help, the crack lady said. I need your help real bad.

Yes, I said.

She explained that she needed diapers for her baby, who was out of diapers, and that she needed my help to get the diapers. She said, Sister, I need your help.

Medal to the Hero of Abkhazia

323

I knew we were not sisters. But it was nice of her to say so, and if what she really wanted was crack, I thought I would force her to have diapers instead by going with her to the store, which was only one block away, and which stays open until long after midnight.

The street was crispy and our feet made a fine noise stepping together.

So you know Tim? I said.

Who's Tim? she said.

Tim is my neighbor next door, I said. Don't you live next door?

I'm new, she said.

At the store we went together, my neighbor and I, to the diaper aisle. Everyone saw us together in the diaper aisle, looking at the diapers. I felt that in some sense this made me her mother. I'm gonna get some diapers to last a while, my neighbor said, touching a pack of mega-bonus-diapers.

Please don't, I said. I don't have much money. Please get the cheap diapers.

All right, she said. She chose some diapers. These are the cheap diapers, she said.

They were not the cheap diapers but we took them to the register.

At the counter the counter-boy looked at us funny. I did not think anything was so funny. I did not like his funny look.

I need a receipt, my neighbor said.

Do you need a receipt? The counter boy said to me.

That made me angry. He had heard us ask for a receipt.

Yes, I said, we need a receipt. I thought it was something to do with welfare, that if you were on welfare, you had to have receipts.

My neighbor left me outside the store. She took a cigarette butt from the butt-can. I need a cigarette, she said.

Good night, I said. I went to my house. I sat on my couch and felt alone. By the time my lover rang my doorbell, I knew I had been fooled.

What's with the diapers? my lover said.

Nothing, I said.

She already brought them back, he said.

Well, I said. It's a very crispy night.

I don't like you living on this street, he said. I'll be happy when you live with me, on my street.

The next night I was sitting with my lover. We were watching a movie about basketball. When the bell rang I thought—here she is! But when I looked down from the top-door I saw a man at the bottom who I had not seen before.

I went downstairs. Hi, I said.

Is your boyfriend home? he said.

My lover? I said.

Yes, he said. Is he home?

Yes, I said. I went upstairs. He wants to speak with you, I said.

While my lover went down, I sat on the couch and waited. I heard their voices—like trucks on a highway—I could not hear their words.

My lover came back. What did he say? I said.

He wanted two dollars, my lover said.

Did he want the two dollars for crack? I said.

For milk, my lover corrected. He wanted two dollars for milk.

Oh, I said. Milk-man, I said. Then, Do you know him? I did not understand.

No, my lover said. I do not know him. My lover laid back on the couch. He started the movie about basketball which he had stopped before. They know this house, my lover said, and they know you live in it, and I do not like you living on this street. I'll be happy when you live with me, on my street.

Okay, I said.

Now I do live with my lover on my lover's street. It is a very pretty street, much prettier than my old street, and the snow has begun to collect itself so that we may have a white holiday.

This morning, well noon, that is when we wake up, since we are awake late at night, our doorbell rang. Can you get that? said my lover (who generally likes to answer the door but was naked), I'm naked.

At the door was a man. He was a shaggy man waring a red wool hat. He looked a lot like the father in *A Time to Kill*—he had eyebrows of wrath and an ivory smile. Got any bottles today? he said.

Sorry, I said. I shut the door.

Who was that? said my lover, pulling on pants.

Bottle-man, I said.

Oh, he said, Bottle-man.

I stood there.

I opened the door. The bottle-man was down the street, wheeling a shopping cart toward the house of our neighbor. Hey! I said.

He turned. Got bottles? He rolled toward me.

I carried two cases of bottles from the kitchen and I put them on the porch. Wait, I told the bottle-man, who stood on the porch with his cart, there's more.

What are you doing? my lover said.

It's Christmas, I said. It's the holiday. I picked up two more cases and carried them out. The bottle-man was waiting on the porch. I was glad to give him so many boxes of bottles.

Happy crack! I said.

He shrugged. Happy crack to you, too, he said.

Inside, I was happy, but my lover, no longer naked, was not happy.

You are weird, my lover said.

Was he a crack-man? I said.

No, he said. He's a bottle-man.

Oh, I said.

Now I am often confused. Crack-man, bottle-man, father, neighbor, crack-lady, sister, mother, boyfriend, lover, pretty-street, crack-street, all these distinctions are slick and leave their colors on one another, but I have the idea that one white day soon my God will speak, and then my headphones may save my life.

THE KAUDERS CASE

by ALEKSANDAR HEMON

I.
VOLENS-NOLENS

I MET ISIDORA in college, at the University of Sarajevo, in 1985. We both trans-
ferred to the general literature department: she from philosophy, I from engineering. We met in the back of a Marxism class. The Marxism professor had his
hair dyed hell-black, and often spent time in mental institutions. He liked to
pontificate about man's position in the universe: man was like an ant holding on
to a straw in a Biblical flood, he said, and we were too young to even begin to
comprehend it. Isidora and I, thus, bonded over tear-inducing boredom.

Isidora's father was a well-known chess analyst, good friends with Fischer,
Kortchnoy, and Tal. He reported from world-championship matches, and wrote
books about chess—the most famous one, an item in every chess-loving household,
was a book for beginners. Sometimes when I visited Isidora, she would be helping
her father with correcting the proofs. It was a tedious job of reading back tran-
scripts of chess games to each other (K e-4; R d5; c8-b7; etc), so they would occasionally sing the games, as if performing in a chess musical. Isidora was a licensed
chess judge, and she traveled the world with her father, attending chess tourna-
ments. She would often come back with stories about the strange people she had
met. Once, in London, she met a Russian immigrant named Vladimir, who told
her that Kandinsky was merely a Red Army officer who ran a workshop of anony-

mous artists and then appropriated their paintings as his own, becoming the great Kandinsky. In any case, the world outside seemed to be a terribly interesting place.

We were bored in Sarajevo. It was hard not to be. We had ideas and plans and hopes that, we thought, would change the small-city staleness, and ultimately the world. We always had unfinished and unfinishable projects: once we started translating a book about Bauhaus, never finished the first paragraph; then a book on Hieronimus Bosch, never finished the first page—our English was not very good, and we had neither dictionaries nor patience. We read and talked about Russian futurism and constructivism, attracted to the revolutionary possibilities of art. Isidora was constantly thinking up performances, in which, for instance, we showed up at dawn somewhere with a hundred loaves of bread and made crosses out of them. It had something to do with Hlebnikov, the poet, as the root of his name: *hleb* was the common word for bread in many Slavic languages. We never did it, of course—just showing up at dawn was a sufficient obstacle. Isidora did stage several performances, involving her friends (I never took part) who cared less about the hidden messages of the performance than the possibility of the random passer-by heckling them in a particularly menacing Sarajevo way.

Eventually, we found a socialist-youth institution and, with it, a way to act upon some of our revolutionary fantasies. The socialist-youth institution gave us a space, ensured that we had no interest in getting paid, and made clear that we were not to overstep the borders of decent public behavior and respect for socialist values. A few more friends joined us (Gusa, living in London now; Goga, in Philadelphia; Bucko, still in Sarajevo). We adorned the space with slogans handpainted on bedsheets sewn together: "The fifth dimension is being created!" was one of them, straight from a Russian futurist manifesto. There was an anarchy sign (and a peace sign, for which I am embarrassed now, but it was a concession to the socialist-youth people with hippie pasts), and Kasimir Malevich crosses. We had to repaint some of the crosses, as they alluded to religion in the blurry eyes of the socialist-youth hippies. This place of ours was called Club Volens-Nolens, a ludicrously pretentious name.

We hated pretentiousness, so the name was a form of self-hatred. Planning the opening night, we had fierce discussions whether to invite the Sarajevo cultural elite, idle people who attended the opening of boxes, and whose *cultureness* was conveyed by wearing cheap Italian clothes bought in Trieste or from smugglers working the streets. One proposal was to invite them, but to put barbed wire everywhere, so their clothes would be ripped. Even better, we could do the whole opening in complete darkness, except for a few stray dogs with flashlights attached to their heads. It would be nice, we agreed, if the dogs started biting the guests. But we realized that the socialist hippies would not go for that, as they would have to invite some socialist elite, to justify the whole project. We settled for inviting the elite, along with local thugs and people some of us grew up with, and generally people who had no interest in culture whatsoever. We hoped that at the very least a few fights might break out, bloodying an elite nose or two.

Alas, it was not to happen. No dogs, no bites, no fights—the opening was attended by a lot of people, who all looked good and behaved nicely.

Thereafter we had programs every Friday. One Friday, there was a panel discussion on alcoholism and literature with all the panelists drunk, and the moderator the drunkest of all. Another Friday there were two comic-book artists, whose drawings we exhibited. One of them got terribly drunk and locked himself in the bathroom and would not come out, as the audience waited. After a couple of hours of our lobbying and outright begging, he left the bathroom and faced the audience, only to holler at them: "People! What is wrong with you? Do not be fooled by this." We loved it. Then there was the time when we showed a movie, called *The Early Works*, which had been made in the sixties and banned almost everywhere in Yugoslavia and never shown in Sarajevo, as it belonged to a group of movies, known as the Black Wave, which painted not so rosy a picture of socialism. It was one of those sixties movies, heavily influenced by Godard, in which young people walk around junkyards, discuss comic books and revolution, and then make love to mannequins. The projectionist—who was used to showing soft-core porn, where narrative logic didn't matter—switched the reels, showing them out of order, and nobody noticed except the director, who was present, but tipsy. We organized a performance of John Cage music, the only one ever in Sarajevo, by which I mean we played his records, including one with a composition performed by twelve simultaneously screeching radios and another with the infamous "4:33"—a stretch of silence on the record supposed to provide time for the audience to create its own inadvertent, incidental music. The audience, however, consisting by this time mainly of idle elite, was getting happily drunk—we'd heard that music many times before. When the performer, who came from Belgrade, forgoing a family vacation at the peril of divorce, stepped in front of the microphone, the audience was uninterested. Nobody had asked him to perform Cage in years, so he didn't care. The few audience members who glanced at the stage saw a hairy man eating an orange and a banana in front of the microphone, performing, unbeknownst to almost everybody, the John Cage composition appropriately titled, "An Orange and a Banana."

It was irritating not to be irritating to the elite, so even on the nights when we just spun records, the goal was to inflict pain: Gusa, the DJ, played Frank Zappa and Yoko Ono screaming plus Einsturzende Neubauten, the fine artists who used chainsaws and drill machines to produce music, all at the same time and at a high volume. The elite was undeterred, though their numbers declined. We wanted them all to be there and to be there in severe mental pain. This concept, needless to say, did not fly too well with the socialist hippies.

The demise of Club Volens-Nolens (which I might as well confess means "willy-nilly" in Latin) was due to "internal differences." Some of us thought we had made too many compromises: the slide down the slippery slope of bourgeois mediocrity (the socialist version) clearly began when we gave up the stray dogs with flashlights. Before we called it all off, we contemplated having stray dogs, this time rabid, for the closing night. But Club Volens-Nolens went out with a whimper, rather than a mad bark.

We sank back into general ennui. I busily wrote self-pitying poetry, hundreds of dreadful poems, eventually amounting to one thousand, the subjects of which flip-flopped between boredom and meaninglessness, with a dash of generic hallucinatory images of death and suicide. I was a nihilist, living with my parents. I even started thinking up an Anthology of Irrelevant Poetry, calculating that it was my only hope of ever getting anthologized. Isidora wanted to assemble the anthology, but nothing came of it, although there was clearly irrelevant poetry everywhere around us. There was nothing to do, and we were quickly running out of ways to do it.

II.
THE BIRTHDAY PARTY

Isidora's twentieth birthday was coming up, and she—ever disinclined to do it the usual way—did not want it to be a booze-snacks-cake-somebody-fucking-in-the-bathroom thing. She thought that it should have a form of performance. She couldn't decide whether it should be modeled on a "Fourrieristic orgy" (the idea I liked), or a Nazi cocktail party, as frequently rendered in the proper movies of the socialist Yugoslavia: the Germans, all haughty, decadent bastards, throwing a lavish party, it being 1943 or so, while local whores and "domestic traitors" licked their boots, except for a young Communist spy who infiltrated the inner circle, and who would make them pay in the end. For some unfortunate reason, the Nazi party won over the orgy.

The birthday party took place on December 13, 1986. Men donned black shirts and swastikas and had oil in their hair. Women wore dresses that reasonably approximated gowns, except for my teenaged sister, who was cast as a young Communist girl, so she wore a girly Communist dress. The party was supposed to be set in Belgrade, sometime in the early forties, with all the implicit decadence, as seen in the movies. There were mayo swastikas on sandwiches; there was a sign on the wall saying "In Cock We Trust"; there was a ritual burning of Nietzsche's *Ecce Homo* in the toilet; my sister—being a young Communist—was detained in the bedroom, which was a makeshift prison; Gusa and I fought over a bullwhip; Veba, who lives in Montreal now, and I sang pretty, sad Communist songs, about fallen strikers, which we did at every party; I drank vodka out of a cup, as I was cast as a Ukrainian collaborator. In the kitchen we discussed the abolishment of the Tito cult, still running strong, and the related state rituals. We entertained the idea of organizing demonstrations: I would be looking forward, I said, to smashing some store windows, as some of them were ugly, and, besides, I really liked broken glass. There were people in the kitchen and at the party whom I didn't know, and they listened carefully. The morning after, I woke up with a sense of shame that always goes with getting too drunk. I took a lot of citric acid and tried to sleep, but the sense of shame wouldn't go away for a while, and, in fact, is still around.

The following week I was cordially invited over the phone to visit the State Security—a kind of invitation you cannot decline. They interrogated me for thirteen hours straight, in the course of which I learned that all other people who attended the party visited or were going to visit the warm State Security offices. Let me not bore you with the details—let's just say that the good-cop-bad-cop routine is transcultural, that they knew everything (the kitchen listeners listened well), and that they had a big problem with the Nazi thing. I foolishly assumed that if I explained to them that it was really just a performance, a bad joke perhaps, and if I skipped the kitchen demonstration-fantasies, they would just slap our wrists, tell our parents to whup our asses and let us go home, to our comfy nihilistic quarters. The good cop solicited my opinion on the rise of fascism among the youth of Yugoslavia. I had no idea what he was talking about, but strenuously objected to the existence of such tendencies. He didn't seem too convinced. As I was sick with a flu, I frequently went to the State Security bathroom—no keys on the inside, bars on the window—while the good cop was waiting outside, lest I cut my wrist or bang my head on the toilet bowl. I looked at myself in the mirror and thought: "Look at this dim, pimply face, the woozy eyes—who can possibly think I am a fascist?" They let us all go, eventually, our wrists swollen from slapping.

A few weeks later the Sarajevo correspondent of the Belgrade daily *Politika*—

which was soon to become the voice of the Milosevic regime—received an anonymous letter describing a birthday party at the residence of a prominent Sarajevo family, where Nazi symbols were exhibited and values belonging to the darkest recesses of history were extolled. The rumor started spreading around Sarajevo, the world capital of gossip. The Bosnian Communist authorities, often jitterbugging to the tunes from Belgrade, confidentially briefed its members at closed Party meetings, one of which was attended by my mom, who nearly had a heart attack when she realized that her children were at the party. In no time letters started pouring in to Sarajevo media, letters from concerned citizens, some of whom were clearly part-time employees of the State Security, unanimously demanding that the names of the people involved in organizing a Nazi meeting in Sarajevo be released, and that the cancerous growth on the body of socialism be dealt with immediately and mercilessly.

Under the pressure of the obedient public, the names were finally provided: there was a TV and radio broadcast roll-call in January 1987, and the papers published the list the next day, for those who missed it the night before. Citizens started organizing spontaneous meetings, which produced letters demanding severe punishment; university students had spontaneous meetings, recalling the decadent performances at Club Volens-Nolens, concluding with whither-our-youth questions; Liberation-War veterans had spontaneous meetings, whereby they expressed their firm belief that work had no value in our families, and they demanded more punishment. My neighbors turned their heads away, passing me by; my fellow students boycotted an English-language class because I attended it, while the teacher quietly wept in the corner. Some friends were banned by their parents from seeing us—the Nazi-party nineteen, as we were labeled. Even some who had attended the cursed party avoided meeting the others, including my girlfriend. I watched the whole thing, as if reading a novel in which one of the characters—an evil, nihilistic motherfucker—carried my name. His life and my life intersected, indeed overlapped. At some point I started doubting the truth of my being. What if, I thought, I was the only one not seeing what the world was really like? What if I was the dead-end of perception? What if my reality was someone else's fiction, rather than his reality being my fiction?

Isidora, whose apartment was searched, all her papers taken, fled to Belgrade and never came back, but some of us who stayed pooled our realities together. Goga had her appendix taken out, and was in the hospital, where nurses scoffed at her, and Gusa, Veba, and I became closer than ever. We attended the spontaneous meetings, all in the vain hope that somehow our presence there would provide some reality, explain that it was all a bad joke, and that, after all, it was nobody's business what we did at a private party. Various patriots and believers in socialist values played the same good-cop-bad-cop games at those meetings. At a Communist Party meeting that I crashed, as I was not invited, because I was never a member, a guy named Tihomir (which could be translated as Quietpeace) played the bad cop. He yelled at me: "You spat at my grandfather's bones!" and then moaned in disbelief when I suggested that this was all just plain ridiculous, all while the Party secretary, a nice young woman, kept saying: "Quiet, Tihomir."

The Party, however, was watching how we behaved. Or so I was told by a man who came to our home, sent by the County Committee of the Party, to check up on us. "Be careful," he said in an avuncular voice, "they are watching you very closely." In a flash I understood Kafka. Years later, the same man came to buy some honey from my father (my father was, at the time, brazenly dealing honey out of our home). He didn't talk about the events regarding the birthday party, except to say, "Such were the times." He told me that his twelve-year-old daughter wanted to be a writer, and showed me a poem she had written, which he proudly carried in his wallet. The poem was really the first draft of a suicide note, as the first line read: "I do not want to live, as nobody loves me." He said that she was too shy to show him her poems—she would drop them, as if accidentally, so he could find them. I remember him walking away burdened with buckets of honey. I hope his daughter is still alive.

The scandal fizzled out when a lot of people realized that the level of the noise was inversely proportional to the true significance of the whole thing. We were scapegoated, as the Bosnian Communists wanted to show that they would nip in the bud any attempt at questioning socialist values. Besides, there were larger, far more serious scandals that were to beset the hapless Communist government. Within a few months, the government was unable to quell rumors about the collapse of the state company Agrokomerc, whose head, friends with Communist big-shots, created his miniempire on nonexistent securities, or the socialist version thereof. And there were people who were being arrested and publicly castigated for saying things that questioned Communist rule. Unlike ourselves, those people knew what they were talking about: they had ideas, rather than confused late-adolescent feelings. We had been our own stray dogs with flashlights, and then Animal Control arrived.

But for years after, I ran into people who were still convinced that the birthday party was a fascist event, and who were ready as ever to send us to the gallows. Understandably, I did not always volunteer information about my involvement. Once, up in the wilderness of a mountain near Sarajevo, while called up in

Army Reserve, I shared the warmth of a campfire with drunken reservists who all thought that the birthday party people should have at least been severely beaten. I wholeheartedly agreed—indeed I claimed, perversely, that they should have been strung up, and got all excited about it. Such people, I said, should be publicly tortured. I became someone else, I inhabited my enemy for a short time, and it was a feeling both frightening and liberating. Let's drink to that, the reservists said.

Doubts about the reality of the party persisted. It did not help matters that Isidora did eventually become a downright, unabashed fascist. Belgrade in the nineties was probably the most fertile ground for the most blood-thirsty fascism. She had public performances that celebrated the tradition of Serbian fascism. She dated a guy who was a leader of a group of Serbian volunteers, cutthroats and rapists, known as the White Eagles, who operated in Croatia and Bosnia. She wrote a memoir entitled *The Fiancée of a War Criminal*. Our friendship ceased at the beginning of the nineties, and I keep doubting my sense of reality—maybe the fascist party was concocted by her fascist part, invisible to me. Maybe I didn't see what she saw, maybe I was a pawn in her chess musical. Maybe my life was like one of those images of the Virgin Mary that show up in the frozen food section of a supermarket in New Mexico or some such place—visible only to the believers, ridiculous to everyone else.

III.
THE LIFE AND WORK OF ALPHONSE KAUDERS

In 1987, in the wake of the birthday party fiasco, I started working at a Sarajevo radio station, for a program geared toward younger urban people. It was called Omladinski Program (The Youth Program), and everyone there was very young, with little or no radio experience. I failed the first audition, in the spring, as the noise from the party still echoed in the station's studios, but was accepted in the fall, despite my mumbling, distinctly unradiophonic voice. I did this and that at the station, mainly writing dreadful film reviews and invectives against government idiocy and general stupidity, then reading them on the air. The radio heads gave the program considerable leeway, as the times had politically changed, but also because we could still easily take a fall, if need be, as we were all young nobodies.

What is important is that I was allotted three minutes a week, on my friends' pretty popular show, which I used to air my stories. The timeslot was called "Sasha Hemon Tells You True and Untrue Stories" (SHTYTUS). Some of the stories I read on the air were shorter than the jingle for SHTYTUS. Some of them embarrassed my family—already thoroughly embarrassed by the birthday party—because I had a series of stories about my cousin, a Ukrainian, in which he, for example, somehow lost all his limbs and lived a miserable life, until he got a job in a circus, where elephants rolled him around the ring like a ball, night in, night out.

Around that time, I wrote the story "The Life and Work of Alphonse Kauders." It was clear that it was unpublishable, as it made fun of Tito, contained a lot of lofty farts, and involved Hitler and Goebbels and such as characters. At that time, most literary magazines in Yugoslavia were busily uncovering this or that national heritage, discovering writers whose poems would later become war songs. I broke up the story into seven installments, each of which could fit into the three allotted minutes of SHTYTUS, and then wrote an introduction for each—all suggesting that I was a historian and that Alphonse Kauders was a historical figure and the subject of my extensive and painstaking research. One of the introductory notes welcomed me upon my return from the archives of the USSR, where I had dug up revealing documents about Kauders. Another informed the listeners that I had just come back from Italy, where I was a guest at the convention of the Transnational Pornographic Party, whose party platform was, naturally, based on the teachings of the great Alphonse Kauders. A third introduction quoted letters from nonexistent listeners who praised me for exhibiting the courage necessary for a historian, and proposed that I be appointed head of the radio station.

Most of the time, I had a sense that nobody knew what I was doing, as nobody listened to SHTYTUS, apart from my friends (Zoka and Neven, now in Atlanta and London, respectively) who generously gave me the time on the show, and the listeners who had no time to change the station as the whole thing was just too short. Which was okay with me, as I had no desire to upset the good cop or the bad cop again.

After all seven installments were broadcast individually, I decided to record the whole Kauders saga, reading it with my mumble-voice, still fondly remembered as one of the worst voices ever broadcast in Bosnia, and provided some historical sound effects: Hitler's and Stalin's speeches, Communist fighting songs, *Lili Marlen*. We broadcast the whole thing straight up, no breaks, for twenty-some minutes—a form of radio-suicide—on Zoka and Neven's show. I was their guest in the studio, still pretending that I was a historian. With straight faces and solemn voices, Zoka and Neven read the listeners' letters, all of which were phony. One demanded that I and people like me be strung up for defiling the sacred memories. Another demanded more respect for horses (as

Alphonse Kauders hated horses). Another objected to the representation of Gavrilo Princip, the assassin of the Austro-Hungarian Archduke Franz Ferdinand, and asserted, contrary to my research, that Princip *absolutely did not* pee his pants while waiting at a Sarajevo street corner to shoot the Archduke.

With that, we opened the phone lines to listeners. I had thought that a) nobody really listened to the Kauders series, and b) those who listened found it stupid, and c) that those who believed it was true were potheads, simpletons, and demented senior citizens, for whom the lines between history, fantasy, and radio programs were already pathologically blurred. Hence I did not prepare for questions or challenges or further manipulation of dubious facts. The phones, however, were on fire, for an hour or so, live on the air. The vast majority of people bought the story, and then had many a tricky question or observation. A physician called and claimed that one cannot take out one's own appendix, as I claimed Kauders had done, which obviously stands to reason. A man called and said that he had in his hand the *Encyclopedia of Forestry*—where Kauders was supposed to be covered extensively—and there was no trace of him in it. There were other questions, but I cannot remember them, as I had entered the trance of fantasy-making. I came up with plausible answers, never laughing for a moment. I inhabited the character completely, fearing all the while that my cover might be blown, fearing—as I suspect actors do—that the audience could see the real, phony me behind the mask, that my performance was completely transparent. I did manage to dismiss the fear of the good cop or the bad cop (probably the bad cop) calling in and ordering me to instantly come down to State Security headquarters. But the weirdest fear of all was that someone might call in and say: "You know nothing about Kauders. I know far more than you do—here is the true story!" Kauders became real at that moment—he was my Virgin Mary, appearing in the sound-proof studio glass, behind which there was an uninterested sound engineer and a few people sparkling with the electricity of excitement. It was an exhilarating moment, when fiction ruptured reality and then overran it, much akin to the moment when the body rose from Dr. Frankenstein's surgical table and started choking him.

For days, even years, after, people stopped me and asked: "Did Kauders really exist?" To some of them I said yes, to some of them I said no. But the fact of the matter is that there is no way of really knowing, as Kauders really did exist for a flicker of a moment, like those subatomic particles in the nuclear accelerator in Switzerland, just not long enough for his existence to be recorded. The moment of his existence was too short for me to determine whether he was a mirage, a consequence of reaching the critical mass of collective delusion, or whether he had appeared to let me know that my life had been exposed to the radiation of his malevolent aura.

My Kauders project was an attempt to regain reality. I had blissfully persisted in believing I was a real person until I became a fictional character in someone else's story about the birthday party. I wanted Kauders—a fictional character—to enter someone else's reality and spoil the party by becoming real. After finding myself on the wrong side of the mirror, I threw Kauders back into it, hoping to break it, but he just flew right through and ran off, no longer under my control. I do not know where he might be now. Perhaps he is pulling the strings of fact and fiction, of untruth and truth, making me write stories that I foolishly believe I imagine and invent. Perhaps one of these days I am going to get a letter signed by A.K. (as he, of course, liked to sign his letters), telling me that the whole fucking charade is over, that my time of reckoning has come.

David I. Fuentes
Chief Executive Officer
Office Depot
2200 Old Germantown Road
Delray Beach, FL
33445

Dear Mr. Fuentes,

Recently, I have been writing letters to other large-company CEOs, all from the point of view of an Irish setter named Steven. For you, though, I will be writing as a small bird, probably a hummingbird, named Buck. Here goes:

> When I was young and hungry always, my mother left me and my siblings alone as she hopped around the field, looking for food and sticks with which to line our nest. When she was gone we opened our mouths, waiting for food, our eyes green-blue peas covered with the thinnest pink skin.

> When she was gone we sometimes taught each other songs. I don't remember any of the songs, or why we sang them. Months later we all flew away and I never saw any of them again, my siblings or mother. We small birds are unsentimental because we can fly!

> But you know what? I'm not actually a small bird. I am a dog named Steven. I could never fool you — I'm a fast goddamn dog and I run around trees like a rocket-seeking rocket. Hoooo! Hoooooo! I don't need any bird, any small bird asking for food! No way, man! I'm running and running on the dry hot grass and it's like I never want to bark again, if I can just keeping running. If I can keeping running, turning like a skier, staying low, I'll never want to just bark and bark and bark — oh sweet Jesus, let me keep running! I'm just so fucking afraid of getting tired, you know, man?

Mr. Fuentes, your attention is appreciated.

D.

Daniel O'Mara
5811 Mesa Drive, #216
Austin, TX
78731

TEDFORD AND THE
MEGALODON

by JIM SHEPARD

HE'D BROUGHT SOME books with him on the way out, but had lost the lot of them on the transfer to the smaller boat. One of the lifting pallets had upset and spilled the crate down the side of the ship. His almanac had been saved, for which he was thankful.

Among the losses had been his Simpson and his Eldredge; his *Osteology and Relationships of Chondrichthyans*; his *Boys' Book of Songs*, Balfour's *Development of Elasmobranch Fishes*, and, thrown in from his childhood, his Beadle Boys' Library, including *Wide Awake Ned; the Boy Wizard*.

Above his head, interstellar space was impossibly black. That night he wrote in his almanac, *Velvet set with piercing bits of light*. There seemed to be, spread above him, some kind of galactic cloud arrangement. Stars arced up over one horizon and down the other. The water nearest the ice seemed disturbingly calm. Little wavelets lapped the prow of the nearest kayak. The cold was like a wind from the stars.

Thirty-three-year-old Roy Henry Tedford and his little pile of provisions were braced on the lee side of a talus slope on a speck of an island at somewhere around degree of longitude 146 and degree of latitude 58, seven hundred miles from Adélie Land on the Antarctic Coast, and four hundred from the nearest landfall on any official map: the unprepossessing dot of Macquarie Island to the east. It was a fine midsummer night in 1923.

Mauritanian Medal of Honor

His island, one of three ice-covered rocks huddled together in a quarter-mile chain, existed only on the hand-drawn chart that had brought him here, far from those few shipping lanes and fishing waters this far south. The chart was entitled, in Heuvelmans's barbed-wire handwriting, alongside his approximation of the location, *The Islands of the Dead.* Under that Heuvelmans had printed in block letters the aboriginal word *Kadimakara,* or "Animals of the Dreamtime."

Tedford's provisions included twenty-one pounds of hardtack, two tins of biscuit flour, a sack of sweets, a bag of dried fruit, a camp-stove, an oilskin wrap for his almanac, two small reading-lanterns, four jerry cans of kerosene, a waterproofed one-man tent, a bedroll, a spare coat and gloves, a spare set of Wellington boots, a knife, a small tool set, waterproofed and double-wrapped packets of matches, a box camera in a specially made mahogany case in an oilskin pouch, a revolver, and a Bland's .577 Axite Express. He'd fired the Bland's twice, and both times been knocked onto his back by the recoil. The sportsman in Melbourne who'd sold it to him had assured him that it was the closest thing to field artillery that a man could put to his shoulder.

He was now four hundred miles from sharing a wish, or a word, or a memory. If all went well, it might be two months before he again saw a friendly face. Until she'd stopped writing, his mother had informed him regularly that it took a powerful perversity of spirit to send an otherwise intelligent young man voluntarily into such a life.

His plan looked excellent on paper. He'd already left another kayak, with an accompanying supply depot, on the third or westernmost island, in the event bad weather or high seas prevented his return to this one.

He'd started as a student of J.H. Tate's in Adelaide. Tate had assured himself of volunteers for his fieldwork by making a keg of beer part of his collection kit, and had introduced Tedford to evolutionism and paleontology, enlivening the occasional dinner party by belting out, to the tune of "It's a Long Way to Tipperary":

It's a long way from Amphioxus,
It's a long way to us;
It's a long way from Amphioxus
To the meanest human cuss.
Farewell, fins and gill slits,
Welcome, teeth and hair—
It's a long long way from Amphioxus,
But we all came from there!

Tedford had been an eager acolyte for two years and then had watched his enthusiasm stall in the face of the remoteness of the sites, the lack of monetary support, and the meagreness of the finds. Three months for an old tooth, as old Tate used to put it. Tedford had taken a job as a clerk for the local land survey- or, and his duties had exposed him to a panoply of local tales, whispered sto- ries, and bizarre sightings. He'd found himself investigating each, in his free time, in search of animals known to local populations but not to the world at large. His mode was analysis, logical dissection, and reassembly, when it came to the stories. His tools were perseverance, an appetite for observation, a toler- ance for extended discomfort, and his aunt's trust fund. He'd spent a winter month looking for bunyips, which he'd been told inhabited the deep water- holes and roamed the billabongs at night. He'd found only a few fossilized bones of some enormous marsupials. He'd been fascinated by the paringmal, the "birds taller than the mountains," but had uncovered them only in rock paintings. He'd spent a summer baking on a blistering hardpan awaiting the appearance of the legendary cadimurka.

All that knocking about had become focused on the day that a fisherman had shown him a tooth he'd dredged up with a deep sea net. The thing had revealed itself to be a huge whitish triangle, thick as a scone, the root rough, the blade enamel-polished and edged with twenty or so serrations per centimeter. The heft had been remarkable: that single tooth had weighed nearly a pound.

Tedford had come across teeth like it before, in Miocene limestone beds. They belonged, Tate had assured him, to a creature science had identified as *Carcharodon Megalodon*, or Great Tooth, a recent ancestor of the Great White Shark, but nearly three times as large: a monster shark, with jaws within which a tall man could stand without stooping, and a stout, oversized head. But the tooth that Tedford held in his hand was *white*, which meant it came from an animal either quite recently extinct, or not extinct at all.

He'd written up the find in the *Tasmanian Journal of Natural Science*. The editor had accepted the piece but refused its inflammatory title.

A year later nearly to the day, his eye had been caught by a newspaper account of the Warrnambool Sea Monster, christened for the home port of eleven fishermen and a boy, in three tuna boats, who had refused to go to sea for several days. They'd been at work at certain far-off fishing grounds that only they had discovered, which lay beside a shelf plunging down into very deep water, when an immense shark, of unbelievable proportions, had surfaced among them, taking nets, one of the boats, and a ship's dog back down with it. The boy in the boat that had capsized had called out, "Is that the fin of a great fish?" and then everything had gone topsy-turvy. Everyone had been saved from the vortex except the dog. They'd been unanimous that the beast had been something the like of which they'd never seen. In interviews conducted in the presence of both the local Fisheries Inspector and one B. Heuvelmans, dentist and naturalist, the men had been questioned very closely, and had all agreed upon the details, even down to the creature's length, which seemed absurd: at least sixty-five feet. They'd agreed that it was at least the length of the wharf shed back at their bay. The account made clear that these were men used to the sea and to all sorts of weather, and to all sorts of sharks, besides. They had seen whale sharks and basking sharks. They recounted the way the sea had boiled over from the thing's surfacing and its subsequent submersion. This was no whale, they'd insisted; they'd seen its terrible head. They'd agreed on everything: the size of its dorsal, the creature's staggering width, its ghostly whitish color. What seemed most to their credit, in terms of their credibility, was their flat refusal to return to the sea for nearly a week, despite the loss of wages involved: a loss they could ill afford, as their wives, also present for the interviews, pointed out.

It had taken him a week to get away, and when he'd finally gotten to Warrnambool no one would speak to him. The fishermen had tired of being the local sport, and had told him only that they wished that anyone else had seen the thing rather than them.

He'd no sooner been back at his desk when other stories had appeared. For a week, there'd been a story every morning, the relevance of which only he apprehended. A small boat had been swamped south of Tasmania, in calm seas, its crew missing. A ninety-foot trawler had struck a reef in what was charted as deep water. A whale carcass, headless and bearing trenchlike gashes, had washed ashore near Hibbs Bay.

As soon as he could get away, he took the early coach back to Warrnambool and looked up B. Heuvelmans, the dentist, who turned out to be an untidy cockatoo of a man holed up in a sanctuary at the rear of his house, where he'd built himself a laboratory. As he explained impatiently to Tedford, in the afternoons he retired there, unavailable to his patients' pain and devoted to his entomological and zoological studies, many of which lined the walls. The room was oppressively dark and close. Dr. Heuvelmans was secretary to the local Scientific Society. Until recently he'd been studying a tiny but monstrous-looking insect found exclusively in a certain kind of dung, but since the fishermen's news, the Sea Monster story had entirely obsessed him. He sat in a rotating chair behind a broad table covered with books, maps, and diagrams, and suggested they do what they could to curtail Tedford's visit, which could hardly be agreeable to Tedford, and was inexpressibly irksome to his host. While he talked, he chewed on the end of what he assured Tedford was a dentifricial root. He sported tiny, horn-rimmed sunglasses and a severely pointed beard.

He wanted no help and he was perfectly content to be considered a lunatic. His colleagues only confirmed his suspicion that one of the marvels of Nature was the resistance which the average human brain offered to the introduction of knowledge. When it came to ideas, his associates stuck to their ruts until forcibly ejected from them. Very well. That ejection would come about soon enough.

Had he information beyond that reported in the newspapers? Tedford wanted to know.

That information alone would have sufficed for him, Heuvelmans retorted; his interviews at least had demonstrated to his satisfaction that if he believed in the beast's existence he did so in good company. But in fact, he *did* have more. At first he would proceed no further upon that point, refusing all direct inquiry. The insect he'd been studying was apparently not eaten by birds because of a spectacularly malodorous or distasteful secretion, which began to rise faintly from the man's clothing the longer Tedford sat in the stuffy little room.

But the longer Tedford did sit, mildly refusing to stir, the more information the excitable Belgian brought forth. He talked of a fellow tooth-puller who'd befriended some aborigines up near Coward Springs and Bopeechee and who'd reported that they spoke of hidden islands to the southeast infused with the spirit of the deep upwellings, something terrible, something malevolent, something to be avoided. He'd reported that they had a word for "shark that devours the sea." He displayed a piece of fisherman's slate—from a boat he said had gone entirely missing—on which was written "Please help us. Find us soon before we die."

Finally, when Tedford apparently seemed insufficiently impressed, he'd gone into a locked cabinet with a great flourish and had produced a tooth—white—identical to the tooth Tedford had been shown. The Warrnambool fishermen had pulled it from the tatters of their net-line, he said.

Moreover, the dentist said, working the dentifricial root around his back molars, he'd found the fishing grounds. And with them, the islands.

Tedford had been unsuccessful at concealing his shock and excitement.

The job had taken him a couple of weeks, Heuvelmans had gone on, but on the whole he was quite set up by his overall ingenuity and success. He was traveling there in a matter of days, to positively identify the thing, if not catch it. Could Tedford accompany him? Not by a long chalk.

What they were talking about, Heuvelmans mused, after they'd both had sufficient time to ponder the brutality of his refusal, would be second only to the Sperm Whale as the largest predator the planet had ever produced. He then lapsed into silence with the look of a man peering into deep space.

When Tedford finally asked what sort of weapons he intended to bring, the man quoted Job: "He esteemeth iron as straw, and brass as rotten wood." And when his guest responded, "Am I to understand that you're proceeding unarmed?" Heuvelmans said only merrily, "He maketh the deep to boil like a pot."

Tedford had taken his leave intending to return the next day, and the next, and the next, but had come back the following morning to discover Heuvelmans already gone, on, as his housekeeper put it, "a sea-voyage." He never returned.

Tedford finally asked the housekeeper to notify him if there was any news, and two weeks after that the good woman wrote to say that part of the stern of the ship her master had contracted, the *Tonny*, had floated ashore on the Tasmanian coast.

He'd prevailed upon the housekeeper to give him access to the sanctuary—in order that he might help solve the mystery of the poor man's disappearance—and there discovered, in the course of tearing the entire place apart, the man's notes, a copy of the precious map: everything. On one of the three islands there was said to be a secret opening, a hidden entry to a sort of lagoon otherwise completely encircled by rock and ice. He was to look for light-blue ice along the water level, under a half-dome overhang, to paddle up to that place, and to push through what he found. That would be his private gate into the unknown.

It had reached the point at which his friends had noticed that the great majority of his expressions reflected discontent, and he'd started speaking openly about being crowded round by an oppressive world. Everything had been herded into a few narrow margins; everything had been boxed up and organized. What was zoology—or paleontology—but an obsessive reordering of the boxes? Finding what science insisted wasn't there—that was the real contribution.

He liked to believe that he was the sort of man who viewed the world with an unprejudiced eye and judged it in a reasonable way. In letters to those few undemanding correspondents who'd remained in touch, he described himself as suppliant before the mysteries of Nature.

He felt more frequently as though his only insight was his desire to be left alone. Passing mirrors, he noticed that his bearing was that of someone who'd seen his share of trouble and expected more on the way.

He didn't find himself to be particularly shy. When addressed he always responded. He had proposed to one woman, and she had visibly recoiled, and replied that their friendship had been so good and so pleasant that it would have been a pity to have spoiled it.

His first memory was of beating on the fireplace hob with a spoon. Asked by his father what he thought he was doing, he replied, "I'm playing pretty music."

His mother, whose family had made a fortune in shipbuilding, was prone to remarks like, "I have upgraded my emeralds, down through the years."

As a boy he'd felt his head to be full of pictures no one else could see. It was as if the air had been heavy-laden with strange thoughts and ideas. He'd grown up on an estate far outside of their little town, with his brother Freddy as his closest and only friend. Freddy had been two years older. They'd trapped bandicoots and potoroos in the understory of eucalyptus stands, and Freddy had taught him how to avoid getting nipped by jew lizards and scaly-foots. They'd ridden each other everywhere on the handlebars of their shared bicycle, and worked together on chores. They couldn't have been more different in their parents' eyes: tall and fair Freddy, who'd announced at the age of fourteen that he'd been called upon to minister to lost souls in the interior, once he came of age; and the diminutive Roy, with a mat of brown hair he'd never fully wrestled into order and a tendency to break jars of preserves or homemade wine just from restlessness. Freddy had helped out at the local hospital, while Roy had collected filthy old bones and left them lying around the house. Freddy's only failing, in fact, seemed to have been his inability to more fully transform his brother.

Until it all went smash, the day before Roy's fourteenth birthday, when Freddy, on an errand to the lumber mill, somehow had pitched into the circular saw and had been cut open from sternum to thigh. He'd lived for two days. His brother had visited him twice in the hospital, and each time Freddy had ignored him. Just before he had died, in Roy's presence, he had asked their mother if she could hear the angels singing. She had fallen to weeping again, and had told him she couldn't. "What a beautiful city," he had responded. And then he had died.

Tedford's father had never mentioned the accident again. His mother had talked about it only with her sister and a close cousin. They'd had one other daughter, Mina, who had caught a chill and died at the age of seven.

His father had become the kind of man who disappeared the moment attention was directed elsewhere. He seemed to leave just for the sensation of motion. He had developed a way of lingering on a word, kneading it for its sadness. His mother had evolved the belief that Providence put such people as Freddy on Earth to make everyone happy, and then to open everyone's eyes to certain virtues once they were gone.

Tedford had been found a month after the accident, asleep in the road with a mouthful of raw onion, and a paring knife in his hand.

No one had ever talked to him about his brother's refusal to see him. And until his brother had died, he would have said that his life story had been the story of a nuisance.

Dawn came like a split along the horizon. The first night had gone well, he thought, peering out of his tent flap. He'd even slept. While he pulled on his over-clothes the walls of the tent bucked and filled in the wind. His arms and back ached from the previous day's paddling. Cold damp air filled his sleeves and the back of his shirt.

The night before it had occurred to him, the moment he'd extinguished his reading-lantern, that for the next two months he would be as far from human aid as he would be on the moon. If he ran into serious mishap, only his own qualities would save him.

Old Tate had used to remark, often after having noted some particularly odd behavior on Tedford's part, that there were as many different kinds of men in the world as there were mothers to bear them and experiences to shape them, and in the same wind, each gave out a different tune. Tedford had slowly discovered himself to be unfit for life in the land-surveyor's office as he had gradually come to understand his inability to express to anyone else the awful resiliency the image of *Carcharodon Megalodon* had taken on in his psyche.

The creature inhabited dreams that did not even feature marine settings. He'd once pronounced its name in church services. As far as *Carcharodon Megalodon* was concerned, he was still a caveman, squatting on his haunches and bewitched by the magic-conjuring representation he himself had drawn on the wall.

But if he were acting like a schoolboy, at least he'd resolved to address the problem, and see Life as it was, for its own sake, prepared to take the consequences. Lacing up his boots, he reasoned to himself that he wanted to see the animal itself, and not his fear and delight in it.

Fifteen million years ago, such monsters had been the lords of creation, the lords of time; then they'd remained nearly unchanged throughout the ages, carrying on until there were only a few stragglers hanging on the very edge of annihilation. Life had gone on around them, leaving them behind. The monsters science knew about, and the ones it didn't. The formation of the northern ice caps and the extension of the southern during the Pleistocene had resulted in the drastic lowering of the sea level, exposing the continental shelves around Australia and Antarctica and trapping all sorts of marine life in the deep pockets of isolated water. Tedford was convinced that in a few of those deep pockets—adjacent to the cold, nutrient-rich bottom current that seemed to originate along the edge of Antarctica, to flow north to all the other continents of the world—his quarry resided, surfacing every so often in the same remote feeding-zones.

What percentage of the sea's *surface* had been explored? Never mind its abyssal depths—and meanwhile, dunderheads who plowed back and forth across the same sea-lanes with their roaring engines announced with certainty that there was nothing unusual to see in the ocean. Outside of those narrow water-lanes, upon which everyone traveled, it was all darkness. He was in an unexplored area the size of Europe. He was in a region of astounding stories. And he had always lived for astounding stories.

His first day of searching came up a bust when a cresting wave swamped his kayak a few feet from camp. He spent the bulk of the afternoon shivering and beating his arms and having to disassemble and examine the camera for water damage. His second day was scotched when he slipped on an icy slope outside his tent and badly sprained an ankle. The third dawned gray and ominous and turned to an ice storm in the time it took him to outfit his kayak. The fourth dawned bright and clear and he lay in his tent, cold and wet, his ankle throbbing, unwilling to even believe that things were beginning to turn around.

He finally roused himself and hurried into his outer clothes and spent some time in the blinding sunlight chipping the glaze of ice off his kayak's control surfaces. He breakfasted on some dried fruit and tea. The sea was calm. He loaded the camera and rifle in their oilskin pouches into the storage basket on the kayak's prow, hung his compass around his neck, put his map-packet in his jacket pocket, settled into his seat, and shoved off from the ice with his paddle. His little tent seemed to be awaiting his return.

He traveled east along the lee side of the island. It was larger than he'd realized. He saw streaks of guano on some of the rocks but otherwise no sign of life. The paddling seemed to help the pain in his ankle, and the ice slipped by at a walking speed. Every so often he had to skirt what looked like submerged ice-reefs.

The easternmost island unveiled itself through a torus-shaped mist. From what he could see in his bobbing little boat, it looked to be the largest of the three. The seas around it displayed more chop, perhaps from the open ocean beyond. He spent the remainder of the day circling it twice, each time more slowly. He saw no light blue ice, no half-dome overhang, no hidden entry. Upon completion of the second full circuit, he despaired, and immediately upbraided himself for his lack of pluck.

The sun was getting low. To the south, in the far distance, ice-fields stretched from horizon to horizon, with peaks towering higher than mast-heads.

He bobbed back and forth for a bit in the gathering swell, stymied, and then paddled a hundred yards or so offshore and began his circuit again, from a different perspective.

Halfway around on the northern side he spied a bit of yellow fifty feet up on an ice-shelf. He considered various approaches to it for some minutes, trying to calm his excitement, paddling this way and that, and finally puzzled out what looked like a workable route. He lost another half hour trying to find a secure tie-up. When he finally began climbing, he had only an hour or so of sunlight left.

Even with his ankle, it was an easier climb than he'd hoped. At the top he came upon a recent encampment sheltered in the lee of a convex wall of ice-covered rock. There were meat tins and an old bottle. It looked as if the contents of a small leather bag had been burned. Only two notebooks and a stylographic pencil were left. The notebooks were empty.

He assumed all of this was Heuvelmans's work. Perhaps he'd had the ship he'd contracted wait some distance away while he'd made the rest of the journey alone.

But what to make of it? He crouched among the tins, feeling himself maddeningly unable to concentrate. It was only when he stood, aware that the light was failing at such a rate that he had to leave without delay, that he saw the rock cairn, arranged in an arrow-shape, pointing to the west, and the island from which he'd come.

He spent the evening in his bedroll listening to his tent walls buffet madly in the wind, and trying to devise a method of measuring the salinity of his little bay. The morning revealed the interior canvas to be tapestried with thin sheets of ice crystals in fantastic designs.

Sunrise was a prismatic band in the east, violet near the water and shading to golden above. He found it difficult to conceive that along that violet line, steamers ran, and men talked about the small affairs of life.

He'd secured a packet from Hobart on the southeastern coast of Tasmania for the trip across the south Indian Ocean. In spite of the steamships and railways and motor cars, the whole place had felt close to the end of the earth, especially at night. Tedford had prowled around in his sleeplessness, and in the last hours before dawn, the hills around the docks had emanated with layers of unearthly noises. He'd spent a little time in some pubs but had found a general state of disinterest in science to be the case among the fishermen and dockhands. His ship had left in the predawn darkness of his third day in the town, and he remembered thinking as it pulled away from its moorings that he was now up to his neck in the tureen.

Three mackintoshed figures had been walking the quay alongside his ship in a thin, cold rain. He'd thought of calling out to them a last word, and had dismissed the notion. He'd seen big ships and little ships on his way out of the harbor, some with their deck-lights burning and some in darkness except for the riding lights upon their mainstays. He'd been able to make out the names of a few of them as his ship's light had passed over their overhanging sterns or bows. Lighters and small craft had been crowded into their darker shadows. Near a steamship's funnel, a great lamp had illuminated some coaling basins and the sides of a wharf.

Once the sun was up, he had passed the time imagining that every wave had its twin, and singling one out and searching for its mate. The islands had revealed themselves only a few miles west of Heuvelmans's coordinates, and he'd arranged his pickup date, descended the ship's ladder into his heaving kayaks, at that point lashed together, had given the ship's mate a cheery wave, and had set off from the hull. He'd looked back only once, and the ship had disappeared by that point.

He opened a tin and made sure of his breakfast. While he ate he observed how the snow around his campsite organized itself into little crescents, as though its lee sides had been scooped out with tablespoons.

How he'd liked life, he wanted to think—every bit of it, the colored and the plain, the highlights and the low! He wondered whether the mere feel of things—common things, all sorts of things—gave anyone else the intensities of contentment that they provided him.

He thought he would start with the windward side before the breeze picked up. When he set off, a petrel winged past overhead, in a leisurely manner: the first sign of life. A half an hour later he noted, out to sea, the steam-puff fountains blown into the air by the exhalations of whales.

Again he circled the entire island without finding anything. This time he repeated the circle even closer to the shore, however, his kayak often bumping and scraping on rocks. In a protected hollow, he found another arrow, this one hastily carved into the rock. It pointed the way into an unpromisingly narrow backwater, which, when he maneuvered it, opened a bit into an odd kind of anteroom. The water below him seemed to drop off into infinity. The wavelet sounds were excessively magnified in the enclosed space. Way below, he could make out thick schools of dull green fish, two to four feet long, which he assumed to be rock cod.

Before him was a wall of ice thirty feet high. He bumped and nudged his kayak back and forth. The wind played tricks down the natural chimney. He could see no opening, and he sat.

But in the late morning, when the sun cleared the opposite wall above him, it illuminated, through the ice, a ridge about ten feet high, in the middle of which a six-foot-wide fissure had opened. The ice in frozen cascade over the fissure turned a pearl blue.

He hacked at it and it came away in slabs which dunked themselves and swirled off in eddies. He kept low, poled his way in with his oar, and the mouth of a great blue cavern opened on his right hand.

When he passed clear of the cavern it was as though his vision was drowned in light. The sun rebounded everywhere off snow and ice. It took him minutes, shading his eyes, to get his bearings.

He was in an ice-walled bay, square in shape, perhaps four hundred yards across. The water seemed even deeper than it had before, and suffused with a strange cerulean light. There was no beach, no ledge. At their apex, the walls looked to be seventy feet high.

The atmosphere above them seemed to have achieved a state of perfect visibility. Away from the sun, in a deep purple sky, a single star was shining. The taste of the air was exhilarating.

He waited. He circled the bay. He felt a silent and growing desire for lunch. Schools of big fish roiled and turned, everywhere he looked in the depths.

He'd wait all day, if necessary. He'd wait all night. His kayak drifted to and fro, his paddle shipped and dripping from the blade, while he double-checked his rifle and his lantern. He removed his camera from its case.

The fish-schools continued to circle and chase themselves about, every so often breaking the surface. He waited. Halfway through the afternoon the detonations of an ice fall boomed off to the west. The sun started to dip. The shadows in the little bay seemed to grow cooler. He suppered on some hardtack and a sip of water.

There was a great upwelling that he rode, like a liquid dome; and then calm. He put a hand on his camera and then his rifle's stock as well. His pulse eventually steadied. A pale moon rose, not very high above the ice wall. While he watched, it acquired a halo. The temperature was dropping. His breath was pluming out before him.

He judged he'd been in the bay, floating, for six hours. His legs were stiff and his bum sore. When he rotated his foot, his ankle lanced and radiated with pain.

He'd been lucky with the weather, he knew. The South Pole was the Southern Hemisphere's brew vat of storms.

The darkness was now more complete. He switched on his lantern. As he swung it around, shadows became stones, or shards of ice. The water was as motionless as indigo glass, until he lifted his paddle and began to stroke with it, and every stroke sent more and more ripples across the shining surface.

As he paddled, he reiterated for himself what Tate had taught him regarding the cardinal features of Life: the will to live, the power to live, the intelligence to live, and the adaptiveness to overcome minor dangers. Life carried itself forward by its own momentum, while its mode was carved and shaped by its battle with its environment.

He sang a song his father had sung to him, while he paddled:

Over his head were the maple buds
And over the tree was the moon,
And over the moon were the starry studs
That dropped from the Angels' shoon.

He stopped and drifted once again, turning his bow so he could gaze at his wake. Freddy had always referred to him as Old Moony because of his daydreaming. Tedford carried in his almanac, back at his campsite, his membership card in the Melbourne Scientific Society and his only photograph of his brother: a murky rendering of a tall, sweet-looking boy with pale hair.

Above him the southern lights bloomed as green and pink curtains of a soap-bubble tenuousness. He could see the stars through them. The entire eastern sky was massed with auroral light. Draperies shimmered across it.

There in his bay, uplifted on the swell of the round earth, he could see how men had come to dream of Gardens of Eden and Ages of Gold. He wondered more things about *Carcharodon Megalodon* than he could have found out in a lifetime of observation; more than he had tools to measure. All that he could attend to now was a kind of dream noise, huge and muted, that the bay seemed to be generating, resonant on the very lowest frequencies. That, and a kind of emotional mirage of himself as the dying man taking his leave. He considered the picture as if from high on the ramparts of ice, and found it to be oddly affecting. The cold was insistent and he felt his every fibre absorbed in it, his consciousness taken up in some sort of ecstasy of endeavour. The air felt alive with its innumerable infinitesimal crystallizations. His ankle throbbed.

He fancied he heard submarine sounds. Then, more distinctly, the stroke of something on the surface. His lantern revealed only the after-turbulence.

He paddled over. In the moonlight, splashes made silvery rings. He would have said he was moving through a pool of quicksilver.

The moon disappeared and left him in darkness. He glided through it, close enough to whatever had surfaced to taste a mephitic odor upon the air.

For the first time he was frightened. He kept his lantern between his legs and shipped his paddle and pulled his Bland's to him by the stock. This thing was the very figure of the terrifying world around him, of the awfulness of nature.

The surface of the bay began to undulate. His little craft rocked and bobbed accordingly, in the darkness. He was very near the end but he had not, and would not, lose good cheer. Things had come out against him, but he had no cause for complaint.

Why had his brother refused to see him? Why had his brother refused to see him? Tears sprang to his eyes, making what little light there was sparkle.

The moonlight reemerged like a curtain raised upon the bay. Above it, the stars appeared to rise and fall on a canopy inflated by wind. But there was no wind, and everything was perfectly still. Everything was silent. His heart started beating in his ears.

The water alone dipped and swirled. Just below the surface, shoals of fish panicked, scattering like handfuls of thrown darts.

He caught sight of a faint illumination in the depths. As it rose, it took the shape of a fish. The illumination was like phosphorescence, and the glimmer gave it obscure, wavering outlines.

There was a turbulence where the moon's reflection was concentrated and then a rush of water like a breaking wave as the shark surged forward and up.

The body towered over Tedford's head. He lost sight of the ice wall behind it in the spray.

It was as if the bottom itself had heaved surfaceward. The run-up of its splash as it dove sent his kayak six or seven feet up the opposite wall, and he was barely able to keep his seat. He lost both his rifle and his lantern.

The backwash carried him to the middle of the bay. He was soaked, and shaking. Seawater and ice slurried around his legs. He experienced electric spikes of panic. His camera bobbed and tipped nearby in its oilskin pouch, and then sank. A wake, a movement started circling him. The dorsal emerged, its little collar of foam at its base, and flexed and dripped, itself as tall as a man. The entire animal went by like a horrible parade. He estimated its length at fifty feet. Its thickness at twelve. It was a trolley car with fins.

It turned on its side, regarding him as well, its eye remarkable for its size and its blackness against the whiteness of the head, hobgoblin-like. It sank, dwindling away to darkness, and then, deep below, reemerged as a vast and gaping circle of teeth coming up out of the gloom.

Where would Tedford have taken his find, had he been able to bring it back? Who understood such a creature's importance? Who understood loss? Who understood separation? Who understood the terrors of inadequacy laid bare? The shark's jaws erupted on either side of Tedford's bow and stern, curtains of spray shattering outward, turning him topsy-turvy, spinning him to face the moon, leaving him with a flash of Jonah-thought, and arresting him an instant short of all for which he had hoped, and more.

CONTRIBUTORS

K. KVASHAY-BOYLE's stories have appeared in *The Best American Non-Required Reading* and *Politically Inspired*. She is a graduate of the Iowa Writer's Workshop, and a Pushcart Prize nominee.

ARTHUR BRADFORD is the author of *Dogwalker*, the director of *How's Your News?*, a documentary, and an O. Henry Award winner.

KEVIN BROCKMEIER has been included in three O. Henry Awards anthologies; he has also received an NEA Grant and many other prizes. His books include *Things That Fall from the Sky* and *The Truth About Celia*.

JUDY BUDNITZ's short story collection, *Flying Leap*, was a *New York Times* Notable Book of the Year. Her newest collection is *Nice Big American Baby*.

DAN CHAON's collection, *Among the Missing*, was a finalist for the National Book Award in 2001 and appeared on many year-end ten-best lists. His stories have been included in *Best American Short Stories*, *The Pushcart Prize*, and the *O. Henry Prize Stories*.

PAUL COLLINS is the founder and editor of The Collins Library, dedicated to unusual and out-of-print literature. He has written two memoirs, *Sixpence House* and *Not Even Wrong*, and, most recently, *The Trouble with Tom*.

ANN CUMMINS has published stories in *The New Yorker*, the *Sonora Review*, and many other publications, and released a collection, *Red Ant House*. She lives in California and Arizona.

REBECCA CURTIS's fiction has appeared in *The New Yorker* and *Harper's*. She has

served as fiction editor of *Salt Hill Journal* and been nominated for a Pushcart Prize.

AMANDA DAVIS passed away in 2003. She left two books of fiction: a collection of short stories, *Circling the Drain*, and *Wonder When You'll Miss Me*, a novel. She received the New York Public Library Young Lions Award and fellowships from the Bread Loaf Writers Conference and Yaddo. She is sorely missed by us at McSweeney's, and friends of books everywhere.

LYDIA DAVIS has translated work by Sartre, Simenon, and Foucault, and has published several short story collections, including *Break It Down* and *Samuel Johnson Is Indignant*. She has received the Guggenheim Fellowship and the MacArthur award.

KELLY FEENEY has written perfromance pieces and art criticism. She lives in Colorado.

IAN FRAZIER is a frequent contributor to *The New Yorker*. His most recent collection, of essays on angling, is *The Fish's Eye*.

GLEN DAVID GOLD is the author of *Carter Beats the Devil*, a *New York Times* Notable Book of 2001.

ALEKSANDAR HEMON's work appears regularly in *The New Yorker* and *Granta*. *Nowhere Man* is his most recent novel; his first was *The Question of Bruno*.

SHEILA HETI has recently published a new novel, *Ticknor*. She is also the author of *The Middle Stories*, a story collection.

A.M. HOMES is the author of *Music for Torching, The Safety of Objects,* and several other books. She has written for *The New*

York Times and *The New Yorker.* She teaches at Columbia.

GABE HUDSON's first novel, *Dear Mr. President*, was named a Best Book of the Year by *GQ* and *The Village Voice.* It was also a PEN/Hemingway finalist. He teaches at Princeton.

PAUL LA FARGE has written three novels; *The Facts of Winter* is his newest. In 2002, he was a Guggenheim Fellow.

JONATHAN LETHEM is the author of *The Fortress of Solitude*, as well as five other novels, a novella, two story collections, and an essay collection, *The Disappointment Artist.*

SARAH MANGUSO is the author of *The Captain Lands in Paradise* and the forthcoming *Siste Viator.* She lives in Brooklyn and teaches at the Pratt Institute.

RICK MOODY's newest novel is *The Diviners;* his other books include *Demonology, Purple America, The Ice Storm,* and *Garden State.*

GEORGE SAUNDERS is the author of *Pastoralia, CivilWarLand in Bad Decline,* and, most recently, *The Brief and Frightening Reign of Phil.* He lives and teaches in Syracuse, New York.

JIM SHEPARD has written six novels—his latest is *Project X*—and two story collections, and edited several anthologies. His fiction has appeared in *The Atlantic Monthly, Tin House,* and *The New Yorker.*

ZADIE SMITH is the author of two novels, *White Teeth* and *The Autograph Man;* two new books, *On Beauty* and *Fail Better,* will be published soon.

WILLIAM T. VOLLMANN's seven-volume treatise on violence, *Rising Up and Rising Down*, was published in 2004. He has written more than a dozen other books, including his newest story collection, *Europe Central.*

DAVID FOSTER WALLACE's newest book is the non-fiction collection *Consider the Lobster.* He has written nine other books, including *Oblivion* and *Infinite Jest.*

SEAN WILSEY recently published a memoir, *Oh the Glory of It All.* His writing has appeared in *The Los Angeles Times* and *The London Review of Books.*

STORIES: ISSUES 1 – 10
Alphabetized by author

[*continued from page 4*] silly to read these words when applied to good fiction, for the users of these labels forget so much about the history of fiction; they deny the fact that a very large percentage of the books that are remembered and cherished today— from *Don Quixote* to *Ulysses*—were and still remain formally inventive. If we can only remember—oh lord if only!—that art should be allowed to innovate, that the traditional can exist side-by-side with the experimental, then we will all foster a far more healthy environment for the creation of great books. Let us hope that the dark cloak that covers the world of new fiction will soon be lifted, and again we will walk in the light that allows the new. ¶ Now for the story of ISSUE 7: This one had a rubber band around it. For no good reason, I went back to the single-story, single-booklet idea of Issue 4, though this time there would be no boxes. Instead, we went with the notion of a raw book. We took the exact sort of carboard that would be used for the cover of a book, and left it raw, without paper, cloth, any garnish at all. We wrapped that cover around the nine booklets inside, and now needed a way to keep it all together. My original idea was to use a belt-like thing, as schoolkids used to have. This was not feasible, so at some point the idea of the rubber band—which would have to be a very thick and sturdy rubber band—was arrived at. Did Oddi procure and send to Brooklyn a number of rubber bands, from which I had to choose? They did. The choice was then made. A month or so later, the booklets were printed and were being placed inside the cardboard covering, and there was one problem. I got a call from Arni, our Icelandic (though New Jersey-based) representative at Oddi, and he began with a hesitant little laugh, which he used whenever he encountered a problem that was both funny and perplexing. In this case, he called to say that there would be a problem with the rubber bands, as they were. He explained that the rubber bands had been sent to Oddi—from where, I can't remember — in a box full of white powder. The powder keeps the rubber from sticking to itself, of course, and is used even for small-scale rubber-band boxes. This powder, though, would be a problem, Arni explained, given that a few weeks before, anthrax had been found in a certain post office, and in a few other US government offices, and there was a near-panic in every mailroom in the United States. "But we have an idea," Arni said. "It will delay the shipment a few days, but it will work, I think." I asked him what that idea was. "We are going to wash the rubber bands." Wash them? "Yes, wash them. We are going to wash them in a washing machine." This is indeed what they did. They took 15,000 rubber bands and washed them in washing machines. When Issue 7 arrived, it looked wonderful, but the rubber bands were darker than they would otherwise have been. Water does that to rubber. ¶ I could go on, but we won't. Below, and in the pages that follow, for no good reason, we will be reprinting the copyright sections of the first five issues of McSweeney's, because Eli Horowitz, our young managing editor, thought it would be a good idea. Blame him. But first, we would like to thank him: Thank you, Eli Horowitz, because before your arrival, McSweeney's was sort of a mess sometimes, and now it runs smoother, it runs cleaner—you are our gas-powered engine, Eli Horowitz. While we're at it, we need to thank Barb Bersche, our publisher, for she also made sure that McSweeney's, which was destined for financial ruin, did not disappear. Without her leadership, we would have been without her leadership. We are also nothing without Dave Kneebone, without Heidi Meredith, without Jordan Bass, Evany Thomas, Andrew Leland, Diane Vadino, and the editors, editors-at-large and copy editors of the past, including Todd Pruzan, Sean Wilsey, Gabe Hudson, Chris Gage, and Lawrence Weschler. We benefited greatly from the pre-Barb leadership of Sarah Min, our first publisher, who bailed water from one end of the boat as we were poking holes in the other. She was a master at keeping us afloat, and we missed her the moment she left. We have been indebted over the years to the design genius of Elizabeth Kairys—who designed Issue 8 and assisted in many others—and to the many other designers, Brian McMullen among them, who helped clarify our ideas. Thank you also to all the interns and other helpers who will be mentioned below, in the staff sections of all of these copyright pages, which as we approach the bottom of the page, we really are second guessing. Can we really include this sort of thing? Eli thinks we should, since these sections tell the sort-of-interesting story of a little magazine as it goes from being very very little to only little. May we always be this small. We thank you for helping.

f) Good; g) Pretty Good; h) Cloying, but Editable; i) Editable in a Pinch; j) Rewritable; k) Will Go Through Five Versions and Get Worse; l) Not at All Worth the Trouble, Despite the Amusing Cover Letter. 2. If your work addresses issues of race or class, please indicate to which race and/or class you belong. Manuscripts will not be returned under any circumstances and only stand a chance of response if they arrive accompanied by a SASE, which will more likely be cannibalized for the stamp and discarded. Send submissions to the address listed above, or email them to mcsweeneys@earthlink.net. For a copy of McSweeney's writers' guidelines, visit the website of *Foreign Policy* at www.foreignpolicy.com. TO ANSWER YOUR QUESTION: this journal, of which 2,500 copies were made, cost $4,109 to print (approx. $1.64 copy). Shipping to and from Iceland, where this was most assuredly printed, was about $1,400, bringing the total bill to about $5,509, which was offset in part by a meaningful donation by one of the journal's contributors, but the majority of which was fronted by the makers of McSweeney's, who sincerely believe they will break even, according to the following math: After giving away a good number of copies to those we wish to impress, we expect to sell somewhere in the neighborhood of 1,500 copies through bookstores and mail-order solicitations. At $8 a pop, we take home between $6 (mail-order) and $4 (bookstores) per, which means about $7,500 in revenue, giving us a tidy little profit about $1,991, which we plan to Invest Responsibly in the Stock Market. This journal was typeset using a small group of fonts that you already have on your computer, with software you already own. STAFF: Adrienne Miller, Todd Pruzan, and Christopher Matthew. Thanks also to Courtney Eldridge and Peter Garfield. DESIGN ASSISTANCE provided by Elizabeth Kairys. EDITED by David Eggers.

ISSUE TWO:

COPYRIGHT ©1999 TIMOTHY McSWEENEY'S BLUES-JAZZ ODYSSEY, *until recently known as* TIMOTHY McSWEENEY'S QUARTERLY CONCERN, *and often confused with* TIMOTHY McSWEENEY'S FATUOUS EMBARRASSMENT, TIMOTHY McSWEENEY'S GLOBAL APOLOGY, T. McSWEENEY'S UNFORTUNATE INCIDENT and TIMOTHY McSWEENEY: UNBOUND. *Also rumored to fraternize openly with* TIMOTHY McSWEENEY'S INTERNET TENDENCY, *which is of course known in the South and West as* TIMOTHY McSWEENEY'S INTERNET PRONG, *but which will be known, from April 3, 1999, on, as* TIMOTHY McSWEENEY'S ELECTRONIC NEWSPAPER. All rights are reserved by McSWEENEY'S, unless they are held by the authors in question, in which case those people are welcome to them, as if we care. McSWEENEY'S is published quarterly by the makers of tight velour shirts. SUBSCRIPTIONS ARE AVAILABLE. They cost $28 for one year, or four issues, whichever comes first. Canadian subscriptions are $34. English, Australian, European— subscriptions for you people are $38. All subscriptions are fulfilled promptly and with enthusiasm. Specifically: On the day that McSWEENEY'S receives your envelope, which will be pushed through the mail slot at the bottom of the stairs of the McSWEENEY'S compound, a McSWEENEY'S representative will either a) take the envelope(s) and run up his stairs—he runs up stairs, still, cannot help but run up stairs, hurry or no—and open it on his kitchen counter; or b) take the envelope with him as he walks up the slope on his way to one of his many interesting and vitally important daily errands. In either case, whether in the kitchen or on 7th Avenue, he will eagerly open the envelope, hoping that the new subscriber has written an amusing note, or is someone he went to high school with, or has ordered one of the McSWEENEY'S T-shirts, which for some reason have not yet been moving. If there is no amusing note, and he is not en route to an interesting and vital errand, he will take the envelope(s) and go up to his bedroom, and sit cross-legged on the filthy red-carpeted floor, where he fulfills the subscriptions. He will put the new subscriber's(s') envelope(s) on a pile with the rest of the new subscribers' envelopes—those envelopes having arrived in the two to three days previous—and will set to work in fulfilling them. First, though, he will have to go back downstairs, to the kitchen pantry, because he has forgotten to procure a stack of copies of the journal. He will lean into the pantry, on the floor of which sit boxes (actually, now just half a box) of the journal, and he will take from the box ten or so copies—each heavy and smooth, looking and feeling so good in bunches like that, like gold bars maybe, only white, white, *white*—and will then close the pantry doors, and will go back up to the bedroom floor. He will then open the first subscription envelope, and will check the name and address of the new subscriber, looking for one of the following: a) a funny-sounding name; b) a name that is two first names; c) an address that indicates that the new subscriber lives somewhere dumb like Alberta; d) the new subscriber is a scientist of some sort (he likes scientists); or e) a name that is also the name of singer assumed dead (e.g., John Lennon of upstate New York). Then he will take from the stack and will open a new copy of the journal—silken! immaculate!—and on the first page, will write a short note to the new subscriber, taking into account both the subscriber's name and his own mood. After careful consideration, and assuming the new subscriber's name is Richard, he will write something like: 1) Hey Richard, where you goin' with that gun in your hand?; or 2) Richard, we're sorry. We were wrong. Please come back. Sometimes he will draw pictures. Some of the pictures he draws: 1) A picture of a chair, in three-quarter view, but with the hindmost leg drawn out of place. Above the drawing he will write: "Richard, Q: What is wrong with this picture?" and then below the picture he will write, "A: Nothing. This picture is perfect." Having amused himself and inscribed the requisite number of copies, he will assemble a stack of white 9x12 envelopes. On each envelope he will apply a self-adhesive 33c stamp, and above it, a $1 stamp. He will then address the envelopes, again taking into account the name and place of residence of each subscriber. Faced with a female subscriber, like "Tracy Olson" say, he will address the envelope to "Sgt. Mjr. Tracy Olson, Jr." Most of the time he creates for the subscribers imaginary nicknames or middle initials, or both, as in the case of Anne Freiermuth, a valued reader and Vassar undergraduate who became, in the interest of entertaining the McSWEENEY's representative, Anne "Where Were You During the" Freiermuth? Brooklyn's own Daniel Fierman became Daniel "Don't" U. Fierman. (This sort of thing, contrary to all logic, has not, hundreds of envelopes later, diminished, for the McSWEENEY's represenatative, in entertainment return.) After addressing the envelope, on the upper left-hand corner of each, he will stamp the McSWEENEY's return-address stamp and below it, on the lower left-hand corner, he will stamp the stamp that says "BOOK RATE." (QUICK ASIDE: McSWEENEY's did not always have a return-address stamp, much less a "BOOK RATE" stamp. For the first hundred or so subscriptions, these indications, the return address and the book rate status, were written by hand, and as fun as this was, it was not, actually, fun. Then came the idea for the stamps. Stamps! Aha! Phone calls were made, and an order was placed down the street, at the stationery shop at the end of 7th Avenue, where 7th Avenue meets that other street, that big one. After two weeks, the representative of McSWEENEY's called and—They are? They're in? I'll be right there!—jogged, almost jogged, practically jogged, down to the stationery store to retrieve the stamps. When he asked the clerk about them the clerk asked if he was the one who called and he said, breathlessly, that he was. The clerk bent down—he had them right there, under the counter! He placed them on the counter and, Sweet Baby Jesus, they were beautiful, perfect—they were like made of a million tiny stars. Anxious to take them home, the McSWEENEY's representative inquired about the inkpad. What about an inkpad? he asked. Inkpad? the clerk said, These are self-inking stamps. You don't need an inkpad! The McSWEENEY's representative was so excited that he temporarily blacked out and dropped the stamps right then, bobbled them and they fell, clacking onto the shiny white floor. He squatted down and—oh, he was practically drunk now—he gathered them and paid for them and then sort of hopped home, something between a jog and a casual walk—and—good God, the stamps were burning a hole in the paper bag. He wanted desperately to try them out, thinking many times of popping into a restaurant or coffeeshop to pick up a free weekly or placemat or napkin or doily or whatever to try them out on. *Stamp stamp stamp!* But he resisted, he resisted long enough to make it home—the last block a blur (he must have sprinted)—and once home and up the stairs to his bedroom, he stamped easily fifty envelopes, all at once, a mad orgy of stamping, the ink—self-inking!—covering liberally, evenly, wonderfully—though only, careful! if stamped while on a flat, flat, sturdy surface (the carpet would not do). The stamps were all that he ever dreamed. See the stamp's handiwork first-hand by sending a check or money order to McSWEENEY's, 394A Ninth Street, Brooklyn, New York 11215. NOTE: MORE INFORMATION ABOUT McSWEENEY'S PRODUCTS APPEARS ON PAGE 190. Those wanting to donate monies over and above the subscription price are encouraged to do so. Donations over $50 will be rewarded with a subscription and a McSWEENEY's-emblazoned T-shirt. Donations over $100 will be met with a kind, handwritten note (or a rambling, drunken note—your choice), the T-shirt, and a lifetime subscription. WE WELCOME UNSOLICITED MANUSCRIPTS, though of course we pay nothing to publish them. SOME GUIDELINES: There are no restrictions on the size or content of submissions, other than that they should all be 2,300 words and about relationships. Any submissions that are not 2,300 words long and about relationships will not be considered, unless they are 2,300 words long and about talking animals. If they are not 2,300 words long and about relationships or talking animals, they should be 670 words and concern problems of race. For the print version, timeliness is much more of a hindrance than a help, though material about impeachment might, considering the events in Washington—whew!—prove very, very funny. For the web component (designed by the peerless Elizabeth Kairys and located at www.mcsweeneys.net), timeliness is tolerated, though in both cases, material possessing beginnings, middles or ends will be read with suspicion. For Issue #3 we are very seriously looking for the following: articles describing in great detail how things are made in factories; short biographies of generals of the Crimean War; and absolutely anything about red pandas—habitat, history, anything. For more in the way of McSweeney's writers' guidelines, visit the website of *Foreign Policy* at www.foreignpolicy.com. DELIVERY OF MANUSCRIPTS: Try not to send submissions via the standard mail. Email is best. Email your submissions, as attachments, executed (ideally) in MS Word, to mcsweeneys@earthlink.net. Printed and mailed submissions are nice, but will never be answered, unless we're publishing them. BY THE WAY: If you have previously sent a submission through the mail and received no response, know that your work was read and loved, but that the person who receives and reads submissions for McSweeney's is incapable of returning them in any sort of reasonable amount of time, if ever. Do not be angry. Do not stop recommending McSweeney's to your friends. Feel free, even, to remind McSweeney's of the existence of your submission. We will have read it, because we always do. Sorry in advance and in retrospect. TO ANSWER YOUR QUESTION: this journal, of which 5,000 copies were made—a 100% boost over last time, aha!—cost $8,529 to print, approximately $1.71 copy. Shipping from Iceland, where we print because we are dumb, was $1,300, bringing the basic bill to about $9,529. Add to that $750, which covered the cost of a McSweeney's representative's trip to Reykjavik for delivery of the discs containing the issue (it fits on five floppies). The trip, though not necessary last time, was recommended in this case, in the interest of keeping everything on schedule. See, the ship that carries McSweeney's from Reykjavik to New York leaves once every two weeks (every other Friday), and Arni Sigurdsson, McSweeney's Oddi Printing Company representative, when informed of the requested schedule, could see no way to accomodate the schedule unless the McSweeney's representative hand-delivered the disc, and waited there, in Reykjavik, for four days, for the proofing process and presscheck, all of which the McSweeney's representative was more than happy to do, given that, in February, it was practically free, and in Iceland there are volcanoes. Of the copies printed, about 600 are spoken for by our growing, teeming horde of subscribers. Of the remaining 4,400 copies, approximately 250 will be given away to deadbeat friends. That leaves 4,150 copies for bookstore distribution. Of those, we see ourselves selling most of them—maybe 3,800—meaning, depending on retailer discounts, a retail gross of about $12,400, after shipping. So, on the newsstand front, we stand to net about $4,500, though as we all know, that will never happen. Again, it looks, on paper, like we will pocket about $10 per subscriber, before paying contributors and staf—oop! DISTRIBUTION: McSweeney's is distributed by the following asute and straight-shooting distributors: Armadillo, Desert Moon, Small Changes, Last Gasp, and, in most of Canada, Doormouse. McSweeney's CHANGES TO AND NOTES ABOUT STYLE: from now on, there will no longer be spaces allotted before and after em dashes. However, we have not changed our stance with regard to the ellipsis. At McSweeney's, we use a space after the ellipsis but not before. Some people suggest these should have spaces fore and aft, and should look like . . . instead of... We say our way is the only sensical way, the ellipsis, when you really think about it (and we wish you would) being attached to its last word, a trailing off from its last word. Come to think of it, there should be a distinction. When it sets off two complete thoughts or sentences even, it should have spaces before and after. If it is simple a trailing off... it should be like so... OTHER NOTES: Heeding to a request from his office, all future references to Sen. Trent Lott (R-Miss.) will simply read "Trent." ALL OTHER TYPOGRAPHICAL AND STYLISTIC IDIOSYNCRASIES, BETWEEN THIS ISSUE AND THE LAST, AND FROM ONE STORY TO THE NEXT, ARE INTENTIONAL AND WERE CREATED TO AMUSE THE STAFF. NOTE: McSweeney's is no longer published in the following languages: German, French, Arabic, Spanish, and Southern. This journal was typset with a small group of fonts that you already have on your computer, using software you already own. ASSISTANCE FROM: Elizabeth Kairys, Dana Goodyear, Juliet Spear. ASSOCIATE EDITING: Todd Pruzan. EDITING/DESIGNING: Dave Eggers.

ISSUE THREE:

COPYRIGHT © 1999 TIMOTHY McSWEENEY'S WINDFALL REPUBLIC. All rights are reserved, unless they are held by the authors in question, in which case those people are welcome to them. ADDRESS: McSweeney's is located at 394A Ninth Street, Brooklyn, NY 11215. FREQUENCY: McSweeney's was conceived as a quarterly but has already fallen, awkwardly, as expected, before only our second schedule-observance hurdle. EVEN SO, SUBSCRIPTIONS ARE AVAILABLE. They cost $31. REASON FOR PRICE CHANGE: This issue of McSweeney's reflects a slight price change. Whereas individual copies of the journal once cost $8, they now cost $10; subscriptions, which at various times were $20, $32 and $28, now go for the $31 mentioned above. There are two reasons why we now have to charge more. Number 1: Many months ago, in New York City, McSweeney's held a grand event. After a month or so of planning, and much negotiating and hand-wringing, the McSweeney's Representative (the M.R.), with the expert help of Mr. Sean Wilsey, secured a venue for a gala that we hoped would bring about 500 guests, and finally allow the city to forget that masked ball from the 40s, or whenever — the one hosted by the small bald man with the toady eyes. The venue we chose, after scouring the city for many weeks, was a Chinatown banquet hall called Jing Fong, big and beautiful, all red and gold and glass. For the use of the hall, inclusive of fully *1,000 pieces of food*, Jing Fong's executive manager, Albert, wanted $2,000. Well, naturally, we were aghast. But then we thought of America, and its economy, and how it's only as good as its weakest, most stingy, most non-participatory, most wallflowerly link, and so called back and said okay. Of course, we immediately passed the costs onto our guests, charging them $5 per for the privilege of attending a night of fun and reading aloud of words, in at least one instance while wearing cavemen costumes. The night came, and indeed, over 500 people showed up, waited in long lines for drinks, and of course talked incessantly while our beleaguered geniuses attempted, doused in a single spotlight, to entertain them via microphone and their carefully prepared entertainments, but alas, well, ahem... anyway, at the end of the night, we had, in cash form, about $2,330. The money, gathered by McSweeney's staff person Diane Vadino and her kind, volunteering friends, was shaped in the form of a large oval wad and was collected and put in the M.R.'s sporty black backpack, which was, a few hours later, along with a notebook containing 100 or so pages of notes pertaining to a book in progress, the cure for all the world's afflictions and plans for a wind-and-solar-powered bomb, left in a cab and never seen again. This is the truth. So. $2,330 gone and what did we feel? Well, we felt exhilaration. Yes, it was kind of thrilling. The money was gone — we called every conceivable police precinct for weeks (and gosh they were nice, with pretty much every operator or desk police person ending the conversation with, "Well, I sure do hope you find it." Isn't that nice, that that happens, in New York City, even under Mr. Rudy?), but it was not to turn up; it was gone. Still, the loss, like losing anything, from friends to uncles to cars, makes us feel closer to our bones, and makes our blood surge, and makes it more clear that we are doing some things in ways we should not do them, and so we felt strangely giddy, we did, that even with a ridiculous amount of money like that gone, we're still here, alive and in resting soundly in bed, and could wake up in the morning, slowly if we wanted to, and have some nice fruit in our underwear, reading about people who have also lost things, people, homes, everything. So come tornado! Come mudslide! Take it all away! Our hearts will burst! You will have to do better than that! Yes. So, the point is that all these months later, in the interest of sharing with you our life-affirming, loss-induced exhilaration, we are passing its cost onto you, in the form of the price change mentioned above. The second reason for the hike concerns helping us cover all the bells and whistles in this and future issues. Perhaps you already saw the gatefolds. Are the gatefolds not nice? The gatefolds are nice; it cannot be denied. Do you like them? Yes? Good. You paid thirty-six cents for them. In addition to the gatefolds, we have added more pages. The last issue was 192 pages. This one is 288. That accounts for approximately forty-five cents extra, apiece. Then the color, which with the gatefolds and extra pages and all brought the price per copy to a completely impractical $2.40 or so per copy. And oh lord that's before shipping. With the transportation, via boat, from Reykjavik, and the shipping to us, or to your distributor, add say .45 per copy. All in all, before the elusive incidentals, the issue cost us (you) about $3.03 to make. When we ship them to you directly — subscriptions, like — it costs about $1.33 in postage. So, about $5 total invested in each issue, before paying anyone a dime. Then of course the distributors take their cut, and… well, you get the idea. So $10. Consider yourself an infantryman in the battle for the 15,000 Dow. OF COURSE, IF YOU WOULD LIKE TO PAY MORE THAN $31 FOR A SUBSCRIPTION: You may do so. Donations over $50 will be rewarded with a subscription and a McSweeney's-emblazoned T-shirt. Donations over $100 will be rewarded with a subscription, a McSweeney's-emblazoned T-shirt, ten trade magazines, including *ChemicalWeek,* and a drawing of someone sleeping. Donations over $200 will be rewarded with a lifetime subscription, the T-shirt, a very-very-rare copy of Issue No. 1, the trade magazines, a pair of socks, the McSweeney's HQ phone number, and the extremely exclusive quarterly McSweeney's Gold Circle Newsletter, which contains material and news available nowhere else, and some cursing. WHEN YOU SUBSCRIBE: Please indicate which issue — No. 2, No. 3, or No. 4 — you would like to begin with. Without this indication from you, the M.R. will be left listening for clues as to your wants. He will listen to the swallows, to the ladybugs, to the wind, but he will hear nothing. Eventually he will guess. And no one wants that. A NOTE ABOUT THE VERACITY OF CERTAIN ARTICLES: There are no tricks in this issue. The articles that appear to be nonfiction — including Mr. Hoff's and Mr. Steinhardt's — are exactly that. We say this because at one point during production we asked our unparalleled copy editor, Chris Gage — who, by the way, got the job after pointing out, in a series of letters, every last error in our first two issues (the letters ran ten or so pages) — what he thought of Paul Collins's piece called "Banvard's Folly." Well, he said, it would be great, he said, if only it were true. Well of course it's true, we said to him and now say to you. Who would make up a story that long, which contains no laughs — only a nearly incredible picture (excuse the pun) of turn-of-the-century American wonder? The answer is no one. Paul Collins does not lie. Paul Collins teaches at a Christian college. Speaking of truth herein, A NOTE ABOUT GARY GREENBERG'S ARTICLE: We at McSweeney's are torn about printing an article that appears, at first blush, to be ghoulishly fascinated with a convicted murderer. Do know: We at McSweeney's are not interested in the glorification of murderers. However, we are running this piece because while we are only passingly interested in Mr. Kaczynski, we are very interested in the article's author, Mr. Greenberg, and his strange journey. NOW, NOT TO MAKE LIGHT, BUT SPEAKING OF LETTERS FROM THE IMBALANCED: Again and again, we are asked why this journal is called Timothy McSweeney's this or Timothy McSweeney's that. Who is Timothy McSweeney? people ask. Is he real? they want to know. Do you know your pants are stained in an unflattering way? they say. The answer is this: Timothy McSweeney very well might be real. You see, McSweeney is a family name of the M.R.'s; his mother, born Adelaide Mary McSweeney, was raised with three sisters and one brother, outside of Boston, Mass. Many years after marrying and moving to the Chicago area, she and her son, the M.R. — no one knows why he was singled out — began to get letters from a man who called himself Timothy McSweeney, who usually wrote from various institutions given to mental welfare, and always Timothy had plans for visiting her and her family at their quiet suburban home. To the best of the M.R.'s knowledge, his mother never responded, and Timothy never came calling. Still, to this day, the M.R. does not know whether or not he actually has an uncle named Timothy. Was this Timothy some kind of family embarrassment, a hare-lip or club-foot, all his life hidden from view? No one can say. No one can say. SUBMISSIONS TO MCSWEENEY'S are encouraged, with the following caveats: a) responses will be slow; b) responses may not happen. This is no reflection on your work. It is a reflection on us, and a poor reflection it is. GUIDELINES: Submissions are accepted via Post Office mail and email, though emailed submissions are more likely to elicit a response. When emailing your submission, please attach it (in any format but Wordperfect) and also — this is new — paste the first 300 words into the email message. That way, we can tell if your submission, like 40–50 per cent of all those we receive, is in the form of funny fake news. Because there are other (very good) outlets for that genre, we will leave it to them to bring your work to the world. Post Office submissions should list the author's phone number, on each and every page. Submissions without a phone number will not be considered; they will be doused in ether and burned for warmth. MARGINS: All margins should be one inch, unless your piece is about animals who do funny things, in which case the margins should be one-half inch on all sides except the bottom, the margin for which should be two inches. SUBJECT MATTER: All submissions should be about things that people are talking about. Before you write, please read magazines and newspapers and watch the nightly news, in order to find out what people are talking about. Then offer *your take* on what everyone is talking about, thus adding another voice to those talking about those things everyone is talking about. Soon enough, of course, people will begin talking about what you have been saying about what they were talking about. It will be great; you will see. LENGTH: All submissions should be turned in at 820 words, but will be edited down to 450. COVER LETTERS: Should be brief and flattering. They should include reference to awards won and schools attended, as we have no other way of judging the quality of your thoughts. NOTES ABOUT AND CHANGES TO STYLE: We refuse to capitalize champagne. Our dictionary, the *American Heritage Dictionary of the English Language,* does not capitalize this word when it is being used to describe the beverage, and thus we will not capitalize this word, unless we are talking about the former province of northeast France, and because we will never talk of this former province of northeast France, we will never capitalize champagne. As for em dashes, we have reversed our position. We will now be using one space fore and one aft. From now on, the term "The Butcher of Baghdad" will read "The Butcher of Belgrade"; "1999" will be alternately "in the wake of Littleton" or "in this age of $5 billion IPOs for start-up ISPs"; "Bretagne" will be "Britney"; and "Briana Scurry's game-winning save" will be "Brandi Chastain's game-winning goal." ALSO: Sports will henceforth be the depositories for all of our hopes, will symbolize everything, and will change the lives of everyone the world over. HEARING A CHILD SAY BOUDOIR: It is strange and intoxicating. THE KIND OF RAISINS A GYM TEACHER SHOULD GIVE HIS STUDENTS AFTER THEY HAVE RUN THE 440: Cinnamon raisins, handed out from his moist palm. POORLY MADE CHAIRS: Should not be made. ARE THE RIVERS THAT FLOW FROM HOT SPRINGS HOT? They are often very warm. DO THEY GIVE OFF STEAM? Yes, and they smell vaguely of sulfur. CAN YOU SHOWER BENEATH THEIR WATERFALLS? Yes. HOW DOES IT FEEL? It feels like you have won the lottery and fallen in love on the same day, on your birthday, on a purple moon made of velour. IS LOVE PERMANENT, LIKE STAINS, AND SOME KINDS OF MAGIC MARKER? Yes, but it changes, in intensity and hue, like toys left in the sun. MARTIN VAN BUREN: He had a certain charm. ANDRE DAWSON: Man, he was something. This journal was designed with borrowed software and typeset with stolen fonts. COPY EDITING: Chris Gage. WEBSITE DESIGN: Elizabeth Kairys. WEBSITE MAINTENANCE: Kevin Shay. GENERAL EDITORIAL ASSISTANCE FOR THIS ISSUE was provided by Carolyn Zick, Jessica Calloway, Aimee Rinehart, and of course Christopher Matthew. FACT CHECKING/ASSISTANT-EDITING: Geoff Van Dyke. STAFF: Diane Vadino. ASSOCIATE EDITOR: Todd Pruzan. EDITOR AT LARGE: Sean Wilsey. [*Rest omitted*]

ISSUE FOUR:

Gurnee, Il, 60031. PLEASE NOTE THIS NEW ADDRESS, WHICH IS GOOD NEWS FOR SUBSCRIBERS OLD AND NEW: We now are working with a subscription service/fulfillment house—thus that Gurnee address (by the way, do you know what is located in Gurnee? Two good things: 1) Great America, a large amusement park full of large amusements; and 2) A huge pyramid replica, with a gold-plated exterior. This is true. It's visible from the highway (Hwy 41), and should not be missed)—which will ensure that your issues are delivered promptly and accurately, and that service on new subscriptions will be speedy and tidy and good. When ordering your subscription, please indicate which issue—No. 4 or 5 (all others are sold out)—you would like to begin with. Without such an indication, we will assume you would like the subscription to begin with Issue No. 5, due sometime in the spring. Should you have questions or problems with your subscription, please notify us at subscriptions@mcsweeneys.net, another new address. SUBMISSIONS GUIDELINES: A good deal of what appears in this journal comes through the mail or internet, unsolicited, from strangers like yourself. Thus, we encourage you to send what-have-you to McSweeney's, and in one of two ways: via letter mail, sent to 394A Ninth Street, Brooklyn, NY, 11215; or via email at submissions@mcsweeneys.net (note yet another new address). When emailing, please indicate in your message's subject header whether your submission is meant for the Web version (where it is more likely to be published, due to the site's high content turnover), the print version (chances are not as good, given the (in)frequency), or, if you do not have a strong preference (or are willing to pretend that you do not), say so, and the odds leap in your favor. IF YOU ARE SENDING POET-RY: please do not. We do not presently publish poetry, as much as we do enjoy it. SUBJECT MATTERS ENCOURAGED FOR SUBMITTERS OF SUBMISSIONS (use of one or more of these subject matters will endear you and your writing to our editors): Caves; balloons; balloons stuck in caves, and unhappy about it; balloons living in caves, and feeling good about it; large trees with people living in them; wind; gold; talking animals who only speak Spanish; men who live in caves; women who live in caves; chairs that are too big; houses that are too big; holes that people fall into; geysers; holes that are deep but are too narrow for people to fall into; volcanoes; things that are round but flat; things that are small but emit loud noises; clouds that appear in bedrooms, over beds, during sleep; waterfoxes, landwhales, and riverkittens; planets covered with yellow water; old men who run very fast; old men with two-by-fours for feet; birds with arms instead of wings; people with very long fingers, the bones of which are too brittle to use; how things are made in factories; how things are made in factories in Africa; how things were made in factories in Africa between 1939 and 1945; giant people who carry small purses; small people who drag from place to place large knapsacks full of pillows; anything at all about the ocean monkeys of the former Upper Volta; anything at all about the Hand People of Franz Josefland; anything about the furry, self-propelling rocks of the Dakotas; anything at all about anyone named Lucy, Isabelle, Paulina, Geoffrey, or Will; anything mentioning the pre-1990 Jonathan Pryce or (tastefully) incorporating former Congressman Fred Grandy; and anything at all about the Swamp Women of Lourdes. LENGTH: Web submissions should be around or under 700 words, unless you want them to be longer, in which case you may write them at the length of your choice. Print submissions cannot be less that one word, and cannot be over 100,000 words, unless there is a compelling reason to have them longer or shorter, in which case you may do as you wish. WHEN EMAILING YOUR SUBMISSION: please paste the piece's first 300 words in the email, and then attach the entire thing, in a universally-readable format, ideally MS Word. Also, and this is VERY VERY IMPORTANT: put your name on your submission. Not just on your email, but in your piece, atop the first page, as in, "Birds Who Have Arms for Wings," by Tracy O'Mara. That is a very helpful thing for us, to have your name on the piece. WHEN SENDING YOUR SUBMISSION VIA REGULAR MAIL: in addition to a printed copy of the piece, please, if possible, enclose a floppy disc bearing the story, as we do not and will not type. PAY-MENT: at present, we offer none. (But we do hope that this policy can soon be abandoned, in favor of another policy, one which involves compensatory fabulousness. Check the website for new developments along these lines.) NOW, SOME EDITORIAL NOTES ABOUT THIS ISSUE: First, those concerning STYLE: We have once again reversed our position with regard to em dashes. We will this issue be using no spaces fore or aft—but we reserve the right to reverse our position again, if position-reversal seems appropriate. Our particular ellipsis usage remains constant. CHANGES TO WORD USAGE: from now on, instead of "knapsack" we will say "rucksack." "Hors d'oeuvres" will be spelled "orderves." Henceforth, we will call Wednesday "Hump Day," because that day lands in the middle of the week yes ha ha, while we will cease use of the word "henceforth." "Ringlets" will again be "profile cyclones," not "head slinkys." We have not stopped thinking that "nosegay" is wholly interchangeable with "corsage," and we are going back to the use of Massachus Etts when referring to that state. As a result of a vote taken at our last retreat, we will no longer be using these words: golem, foosball, miffed, frumpy, concomitant, hectare, table tennis, candelabra, grippe, mountebank, cistern and Tinseltown. For "ring" we will say "chime." For "burn" we will say "badge." IN TERMS OF THEMES, THIS-ISSUE-WISE: Not so fast. Simply because a) In one of the enclosed booklets there is talk of the *cover* art of V. Nabokov's paperbacks; and just because b) Misters Moody and Lethem herein appear with *cover versions* (italics Moody's) of Sherwood Anderson's "The Egg" and Franz Kafka's "The Trial," respectively; and because c) Each story in this box, just about, is discrete and has its own *cover;* and because d) There is a manifesto of sorts about book *cover* design a few pages hence, please do not go leaping ahead, assuming and presuming and thinking smugly that this issue has a theme, a theme that could be summed up in the word: Covers. The assumer of such an assumption would be wrong. Wrong. Wrong because never would we, *us*, who have all these advanced and expensive degrees in publishing and thus should know better, never would we succumb to the temptations of theme issues, not one of which has ever been successful in the history of all of the world, subsuming and diminishing of content—not to mention exhausting of interest—as such endeavors invariably are. But, while we're talking about it all, we would not mind here making a few comments REGARDING COVERS: Now see, as a sort of experiment, all authors of the fourteen discrete booklets within these confines were given the option of providing their own artwork for their booklets' cover. And the first very good thing that happened is that all of them did. Provide artwork for their covers. Almost all, that is—Mr. Murakami was unable to get his act together in time, so we used a picture from our files, completely unrelated to the content of his story, and all the better for it. Otherwise, all authors took up the challenge. Most sent photographs they liked or took themselves or had already taken or had friends or relatives take. Mr. Johnson sent a picture drawn by his son, Matt. Mr. Saunders provided a snapshot he took while in Russia years ago. Ms. Heti awoke early on a Sunday and traveled to the house of a photographer friend in Toronto, and together they found something appropriate. Ms. Cohen researched pictures at her local and helpful public library. All were pleased to have been given the option, and the second very good thing that happened is that every last person provided something perfectly appropriate and instantly appealing. In every case, the choices of the authors made sense, and immediately gelled with and then enhanced their work. And it's no wonder. The author, as creator of the work, knows. He or she knows from what well of creation the work springs, and can go back to that well for the piece's illustrative accompaniment. Does anyone but the author know the way to this well? Probably not. Take even the most unusual of the covers—Mr. Johnson's for instance. Johnson's story is about, among other things, suspicion and subterfuge and conspiracy and quite possibly the end of the world. And what does he give us for that piece's cover? He gives us a pencil drawing done by his young son. Does it make any sense? Well, sort of. The piece has the word "Hellhound" in its title, and the drawing features a sort of hellhound, albeit one with the not-so-scary name of Harold. At first glance, it would seem to be a too-light take on the story, and therefore dissonant and misleading. In the hands of a professional, the cover might have been dominated by pictures of dusty landscapes, guns, drugs, scampy motels, with perhaps the play's title rendered in demented lettering, as was Mr. Johnson's last novel's. But had any of those things been done, would we be more pleased than we are by the son-done cover? No. Does the son-done cover please us? It absolutely does. Do we prefer this cover, brimming with character and back-story as it is, over a cover executed by a designer who is a stranger to the author, and perhaps has not even read the work being illustrated? We do. We are happy, the author is happy, and the editors of this journal are happiest of all, because when the authors do their own covers, we are free to draw pictures of mammals with beaks, and octopi. NOW, ODDLY ENOUGH: this plan, of granting control of the outward presentation of their work to the authors, was in place well before Mr. Maliszewski gave forth his Nabokov tract, which of course deals, in great detail, with the problem of book jacket design. SO: Is it a problem? Yes, it is a problem. One can count the number of authors who have been satisfied with the look of their books on one hand. Perhaps two, if the one hand has less than five fingers. But why in all the world should an author, who has poured simply all of his or her being, not to mention hundreds of thousands of hours, years of one's life, be unhappy with what that book looks like? It is akin to a barber giving a customer a bad haircut. Let us say that a customer walks into the barber shop, wanting his hair cut a certain way: short in the front, long in the back, as is the style today. The barber listens to the desires of the customer, nods his head, but then does this: he ignores the wishes of his customer. Instead, he cuts the hair short in the back, long on the sides, and with a large letter "s" shaved into the top of the head. Why? Because this barber sees the customer's hair as his own vehicle for expression. The barber's behavior is strange, because it's obviously not he, the barber, who has to walk around with the haircut. No. It is the barb-ee, who now has to go forth, into the world, looking silly simply so the barber feels expressive. Yes. Well. The point is, the barb-ee, as bearer of the barber's work, should have full control over the way he looks, and if not full control, a good deal of input, and if not a good deal of input, full control. Applying this lame analogy to books, we ask: why should the author not be satisfied, or gleeful even, with the way his or her book looks, the way it is being presented to a glancing and fickle public? Is it not sort of unconscionable that a publisher would ever allow it—much less bully it into being—otherwise? And yet it is accepted as par for the course by authors, designers, and publishers alike. Always there is contentiousness, unhappy compromise, and lingering bitterness. [By the way, the personal experience of the writer of this tract has been very good, because he asked for and received much control.] [*The rest of this screed has been omitted, because it's just too annoying to reprint here.—Ed.*]

ISSUE FIVE:

 MCSWEENEY'S is a quarterly journal published three times a year and distributed as best we can. If you are a bookstore or newsstand and would like to carry McSweeney's, please look into one of the following fine distributors, most of whom pay us on time: Bernhard DeBoer, Small Changes, Doormouse, Desert Moon, Austin News, Last Gasp, Tower, Armadillo, and no doubt a few others we are forgetting right now and from whom we will be hearing shortly. SUBSCRIPTIONS ARE AVAILABLE. They now cost you, the home reader, $34 for three issues, or $44 for four issues. The price continues to rise as we become more familiar with calculators and spreadsheets. NOTES ABOUT AND CHANGES TO STYLE: We will not use "such as" when "like" sounds better. And there will be no umlauts, unless absolutely necessary. And we have for the third time in as many issues changed our position regarding em dashes and the spaces that might accompany them. Though recently we railed against the notion of spaces before and after, we have come back to this way of thinking/punctuating, and thus you will find, in this issue, spaces on either side of every em dash, fashion be damned. Speaking of style and consistency and inviting damnation: For a few moments, during production of this issue, we were tempted to make all of the stories herein, including Ms. Klemm's for instance, conform to precisely the same set of grammatical rules and stylistic doings. It is, after all, the way things are done — consistency! obedience! logic! we are told, by people with tight shoes. But then we thought, after a nice sandwich and a cool drink — an epiphanic sandwich and cool drink, really — that this conformist way of punctuating would not be a good thing to do at all. Thus we are with this issue instituting a rule we are calling Our Almost Unquestioning Embrace of All Authors' Stylistic Quirks or Whims, As Long As They Be Reasonably Well-Thought-Out Rule. This rule dictates that: we will no longer (not that we ever did so much) be altering any author's style, in really any way at all, to fit ours, or to make it consistent with any other part of the issue. So, you will notice some very distinct-in-some-places differences between approaches to various issues of style and even grammar. You will notice for example that Ms. Elizabeth Klemm, of "Mr. Squishy" fame, chooses to use numerals instead of spelling out her numbers. By observing our OAUEoAASQoWALATBRW-T-O Rule, we resisted our urge to AP-stylize her piece, and so left it as is. Ms. Klemm also prefers not to use a comma after her use of e.g. "Why?" we asked, after our copy editor, Mr. Chris Gage, who works above the restaurant marked by the giant sombrero, asked us. "Well," she said, "I don't ever hear a pause between 'for example' and the rest of one's statement, especially if that 'for example' is couched deeper in a sentence, e.g. 'This sentence is instructive of many things, e.g. redundancy." We agreed with Ms. Klemm here, too, and also allowed her the use of her single-quotes, where full, double-type quotation marks might usually be in order. Why does she prefer this this way, by the way? Is she of British background? She is. (Originally, at least, though she now lives in Chicago.) Another British-type person, Mr. Alastair Reid, was about to be subjected to a standard sort of tweaking before we remembered our new rule, and so left alone his use of "kerb" for curb, even though it looks funny and might, come to think of it, mean something else entirely. NOW THEN: A major innovation/departure first appearing in this issue is one concerning size of type. Many times we have heard complaints from readers lamenting our small type, not just in seldom-read sections like this, but more importantly, when used for the text of the journal's main stories and essays. We have in the past employed a font size of 10.5 pts, with the lines of type laid over a grid of 13.5 pts, representing the leading. But now, we have, after much soul-searching, decided to *up* these numbers, out of fear that we might have, in the past, put off a reader or two, who might have found our previous scheme daunting or annoying or simply less good than it might have otherwise been. So, we have now opted for a type size of 11.2, with a leading of 13.8. Easier to read? By all accounts. We do this sort of thing for you, the home reader, because we feel as if we owe you something, even though you probably would never do the same for us, given the way you were brought up, in all those clean rooms, with all those perfect plants, and never sure from whence your next affection-involving encounter would come. HERE: It is light all day and all night. OTHER NOTES OF NOTE: We would like to announce that with this issue we are plunging headlong into the *World of Normaler Fiction*. Our first foray into this territory, wherein there is narrative and things in general make sense without involving cavemen or ocean monkeys, was probably with Judy Budnitz's "Flush," in our third issue. This story was uncharacteristically "normal" for her, and for us, but in the end, somehow, it just *worked*, and so we ran it, and it was subsequently chosen for the O. Henry collection, which is a nice thing to be included in, and involves, we hear, a monetary award in excess of one million dollars. And so now, with this issue, we are again exploring the world of this kind of world of fiction, with a number of pieces that are friendly to read, and make a good deal of sense, and have beginnings and middles and, for the most part, ends. These stories — "The Days Here," "Soot," "The Observers," and "The Hypnotist's Trailer" — all are so mature and unself-conscious that upon first reading them we barely knew what to do. Were they for us? No, no! But maybe. Could they be? We wondered and wondered. "The Observers" was the most problematic of all, given the odds it stacks against itself. Firstly, it's about a man's state of mind after a breakup. Secondly, it involves the gazing at stars and the thinking about said stars in relationship to one's life. Thirdly, it features or mentions snowflakes and old grade-school crushes. How could such a story succeed? We did not know, especially after checking with / doing some rudimentary calculations from our Short Story Subject Matter Point Addition/Deduction Chart, a small and applicable portion of which is right here, below: [*chart omitted from this edition*]. As you can see, Mr. LaFarge — who also has a funny-sounding name, like he comes from some crazy place like Hungary or Japan — wanders into a number of our subject-matter danger-zones, and yet somehow, despite it all, his story works. We do not know how Mr. LaFarge makes the story work. Do you know? We do not know. AND YET EVEN SO: When we told Mr. LaFarge that we would like to publish the story, we were told this: We were told that *another magazine*, another small nonpaying magazine like ours, this one called *6500*, was *already running the story*. We were taken aback, and then we were beside ourselves, and then we stood there, aback and beside ourselves, enjoying our duality, and then we had a nice tall cleansing glass of orangeade, sharing it with ourself, and thought: Well, if we wanted to publish the story in the first place, then we should just damn go ahead and publish it anyway, because it seems exceedingly unlikely that there are people out there, people who probably have their own very significant real-life problems to deal with, who would care if this story, "The Observers," had been published, a few months prior, in another magazine, especially if this story is full of good things, which it is, and especially if this world is not long for this world, which it is not. Now. HERE: the fjord is called Hvalfjgrdur, and the farm on which this three-room house sits is called Bjarteyjarsandur, and the fog is frequent and the clouds go low, chopping off the tops of the high green ridge across the water. BRIEF PLUGS FOR A FEW OTHER PIECES: RJ Curtis's work, of which we were sent a lot and thus had to choose between many fine things, is as precise and goofy and exhilarating and sad as anything we've seen in a while. She is currently getting an MFA and should be given an arrangement to publish more things, and soon. Similarly, our piece by Jason Ockert, "Mother May I," is doing something very good, is written with fluidity and much music, and is actually part of something larger, which really must be seen to understand fully; and so he also should be given lots of space in other pages, and possibly an award or two. To accompany each award, we are asking that each author be granted a cash payment of between $20,000 and $45,000, depending on the story's length, the present location of the NASDAQ, and the author's telegeneity. SUBMISSIONS POLICY: All submissions are welcomed and encouraged, especially now that we have enough people helping us read to ensure that your work is read in a timely manner (somewhere between one week and three months). So please submit, and be patient, because we look forward to and rely on the work of strangers, new people, to fill our pages, and to make us excited about opening mail. Oh sure, our last issue contained an unusually high percentage of work done by well-known sorts of writers, but this fifth issue represents a return to our more customary mix, graphed below, in the shape of a kind of Death Star. ABOUT THE COVERS FOR THIS ISSUE: There are three different versions. No. 1 features a map on its dustjacket and pictures of Ted Koppel on its inside cover. No. 2 features, on its dustjacket, a man with some sort of horrible facial lesion, and inside, text removed from Susan Minot's piece about Uganda. The dust jacket of No. 3 looks very much like the type-only covers of our first three issues, with the interior cover also looking like this sort of cover, albeit bearing its type backwards, and possibly otherwise altered in a way so clever you will shudder and spit out the milk you were drinking in your family room with your family and with

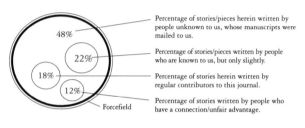

your dolls, your tummy on the shag carpet, your knees bent, ankles hooked together, swaying back and forth to the soulful sounds of the theme song to "Chico and the Man" — such a sad song. OUT HERE: It is getting lighter. There is no traffic on the road below. There is very little traffic on this road winding around this fjord — the "whale fjord" it's called, as this was where whales were slaughtered, when that sort of thing was still done around here — so there isn't much traffic around here, not since they built the tunnel. Time was that the only way from Reykjavik to Akranes and all points north was all the way around this fjord — a

Percentage of stories/pieces herein written by people unknown to us, whose manuscripts were mailed to us.

Percentage of stories/pieces written by people who are known to us, but only slightly.

Percentage of stories herein written by regular contributors to this journal.

Percentage of stories written by people who have a connection/unfair advantage.

48%

22%

18%

12%

Forcefield

stunning if circuitous route. But then came the tunnel, and now people go under the water and straight through. WE ARE NOT TRYING TO ENTICE YOU or FORCE YOU TO BUY MULTIPLE ISSUES: No, we are not at all doing that. Just to prove it to you, we will be making the alternate covers available to anyone who wants one/two/three of them. We do not know exactly how we will do this — details will be on the website (www.mcsweeneys.net) — but somehow we will find a way. For you. HERE: There are small blond children who come over and hide below the windowpane and when you go out to scare them they run away screaming and a little later, one of them bangs her head on the swingset and has to be comforted, the tears wiped from her filthy face man what is that all over her face? Chocolate? It's too red to be chocolate. HERE: The two blond kids have not seen the birds' nest by the door. It's hard to miss the birds' nest by the door. It's about chest-level, and you know what it is? It's a birds' nest, at chest level, by the door. And you know what's in it? Five little hatchlings, who hatched only days before our arrival, and were then just these little disgusting piles of organs covered with a translucent pink membrane. But now, only a week later, there is furry feathery stuff there, eyelids and half-open eyeballs, and their mouths are always open, begging in a frankly unappealing way, with their orange-yellow beaks that used to be whitish, almost clear. HERE: We lifted the little blond people to see inside the nest. We wanted to tell them not to touch the hatchlings but did not know how to say these words in Icelandic, so we said nothing, and just grimaced while they stared into the furry nest, their jaws and eyes agog. AND ABOUT THE TUNNEL: The tunnel is fine. It is very long, and very dark, and it has two lanes and is exciting to drive once, but very boring every time thereafter. But driving around the fjord, under these mountains and those cliffs and that ridge over there, with the birds hovering high and floating round, well, that drive never gets old. It takes much longer, though. OTHER QUESTIONS ANSWERED? Sure. WE WERE TOLD THAT THIS ISSUE WOULD BE BREAKING THE FOURTH DIMENSION. We lied. That will be done with the next issue, on which work is already underway. I AM SHORT OF TIME AND WANT TO SEE IF YOUR MAGAZINE IS WORTH MY VALUABLE MINUTES. WHICH STORY SHOULD I READ FIRST? Ann Cummins's story, "The Hypnotist's Trailer." WHY THAT ONE? We do not know. It is very strange but very direct. It is a powerful thing that will mess with your head. HOW CAN THE WATER IN THE FJORD BE HEADING OUT, TOWARD THE OCEAN, WHEN THE WIND IS HEADING INLAND? We were just wondering the same thing. WHY ARE YOU PEOPLE ALWAYS TALKING ABOUT PRINTING AND PRICES AND NUMBERS AND SCHEDULES? IT IS NOT OF INTEREST TO MANY OF US. We realize this. But we are, right now, interested in it, deeply so. We are fascinated by how easy it all is. We are amazed by how these things are made, how long they take, how much they cost, and are naturally curious to see how it all works from here — how the books — we are talking here of Neal Pollack's book (and, shortly thereafter, Lawrence Krauser's *Lemon*) — are distributed, how they get out there and into people's hands. Can we do it? We do not know. But in general we are wondering if our theory holds true. You see, when everyone is talking about electronic books — is that what they're called? — and about books-on-demand (see Rodney Rothman's experience with those, page 47), and about the future of books and all, we think that the direction we should be going is obvious, and is in some ways the opposite of the way most people are talking about going. Our theory holds that a) People like hardcover books. They like them because they are good to look at, and are permanent, and are decorative, and can be given as gifts, and kept until one dies; b) However, hardcover books are often unaffordable; and so c) People reluctantly want to buy certain books in paperback form; but d) Given how accessible the technology is — not just typesetting technology, but also bookselling technology (for instance, Amazon.com, on which anyone can sell any book), just about anyone can (or should be able to) easily print a book in a hardcover way, and still charge what they're starting to charge for paperbacks — $14! — and thus expect nice sales (see a & b above), while bringing home a much greater net proceed. Does this make sense? In short, we are talking about smaller and leaner operations that use the available resources and speed and flexibility of the market (i.e., the web and other consumer-driven methods), to enable us to make not cheaper and cruder (print-on-demand) books or icky, cold, robotic (electronic) books, but better books, perfect and permanent hardcover books, to do so in an fiscally sound way, and to do so not just for old-time's sake, but because it makes sense and gives us, us people with fingers and eyes, what we want and what we've always wanted: beautiful things, beautiful things in our hands — to be surrounded by little heavy papery beautiful things.